A VICTIM OF CONVENIENCE

Also by John Ballem

Novels
The Devil's Lighter
The Dirty Scenario
The Judas Conspiracy*
* Reissued as *Alberta Alone*
The Moon Pool
Sacrifice Play
The Marigot Run
Oilpatch Empire
Death Spiral
The Barons
Manchineel
Murder as a Fine Art
The Oil Patch Quartet

Poetry
Lovers & Friends

Non-Fiction
The Oil and Gas Lease in Canada

A VICTIM OF CONVENIENCE

John Ballem

A Castle Street Mystery

THE DUNDURN GROUP
TORONTO

Editor: Barry Jowett
Copy-editor: Andrea Waters
Design: Alison Carr
Printer: Transcontinental

Library and Archives Canada Cataloguing in Publication

Ballem, John, date
    A victim of convenience / John Ballem.

ISBN-10: 1-55002-617-8
ISBN-13: 978-1-55002-617-7

I. Title.

PS8553.A45V52 2006   C813'.54   C2006-901334-9

1   2   3   4   5   10   09   08   07   06

Conseil des Arts du Canada   Canada Council for the Arts   Canada   ONTARIO ARTS COUNCIL
CONSEIL DES ARTS DE L'ONTARIO

We acknowledge the support of the **Canada Council for the Arts** and the **Ontario Arts Council** for our publishing program. We also acknowledge the financial support of the **Government of Canada** through the **Book Publishing Industry Development Program** and **The Association for the Export of Canadian Books**, and the **Government of Ontario** through the **Ontario Book Publishers Tax Credit** program and the **Ontario Media Development Corporation**.

Care has been taken to trace the ownership of copyright material used in this book. The author and the publisher welcome any information enabling them to rectify any references or credits in subsequent editions.

J. Kirk Howard, President

Printed and bound in Canada
Printed on recycled paper⊛
www.dundurn.com

Dundurn Press	Gazelle Book Services Limited	Dundurn Press
3 Church Street, Suite 500	White Cross Mills	2250 Military Road
Toronto, Ontario, Canada	High Town, Lancaster, England	Tonawanda, NY
M5E 1M2	LA1 4XS	U.S.A. 14150

For Grace,
who shares my affection for this toddling town.

chapter one

"Another one!" The rookie cop who had been on patrol in the southwest sector gave up the struggle to sound professional and, hand clapped to mouth, bolted away to retch helplessly into the shrubbery.

Chris Crane, the primary in the serial killer case, tactfully looked away. As required by protocol, both he and the young officer remained behind the yellow tape while the forensic unit checked out the scene. In the course of his career, most recently five years as a sergeant in charge of the Forensic Crime Scenes Unit, then as a lead detective in Homicide, he had been at the scene of many murders. Still, he had to swallow hard against the gorge rising in his own throat as he looked at the victim's naked, mutilated body. In life, she must have been beautiful — a knockout. Except for the half-shut eyes, glassy and suffused with blood, her face was unmarked, the same as in the other three killings.

The victim was tanned and fit; Chris visualized those long, lovely legs bounding lithely over a tennis court. She would have been somewhere in her mid-thirties. The deep stab wounds low in her chest were the ones that had killed her, but the killer hadn't been satisfied with that. The nipple had been sliced off her right breast; the blood, now dry, had trickled down first to fill, then overflow, her navel. Worse, far worse, was the dark red blood matting the light brown pubic hair and spreading obscenely across her inner thighs. In a mocking gesture, the killer had clasped her hands together as if in prayer and placed them at rest on her blood-streaked abdomen.

Turning away from the corpse, Chris saw Brenda, looking chagrined, coming back to join him. He motioned her to follow him as he went over to question the witness who had found the body and called 911 on his cell.

The witness, a stockbroker, had been walking his dog in this remote part of the park, as he always did first thing in the morning. His name was James Stanley. Separated from his wife, he lived by himself in a condo on the Old Banff Coach Road and worked at Loyalty Capital, a well-known downtown brokerage firm.

Stanley explained that walking the dog in the park was the last thing he did before leaving for the office. That would account for the shirt and the tie he had loosened for comfort. It was early because he had to be at his desk when the markets opened in Toronto at seven-thirty Calgary time.

"It was Duke." At the mention of his name, the Lab sitting obediently at his master's side wagged his tail, making a swishing noise in the scrub grass. Stanley patted the broad head and continued. "He was off leash, which he's not supposed to be ..." As he said this, the broker paused to look somewhat askance at the detective. Chris gave him an understanding smile and motioned for him to continue.

"That's why we were up here, where almost nobody ever comes. Then Duke started to bark. He doesn't bark all that much. Labs usually don't as a rule. And there was something about the way he was barking. Deep, way down in his throat. More like a growl. I could tell he had found something."

Nodding his thanks, Chris closed his notebook and looked across at the Crime Scenes team. He had worked with both members. In fact, Gwen Staroski had been his protégé. She was intelligent, sure, but it was her powers of observation and her perceptiveness that made her so valuable. Chris smiled to himself as he recalled the Murray murder: Gwen had been the one to recognize the possibility that the blue paper clip, which had seemed so promising a clue, might have been deliberately planted by the suspect. Short, with a broad, plain-featured face and stocky body, she was no looker, but she had this great intuitive sense about people, which Chris had come to rely on. Despite the fact that they were now in different units, he had been able to second her because of the urgent need to solve the case that was holding the city in the grip of terror. Now it seemed she was going to return the favour.

Holding a plastic bag containing white coveralls, latex gloves, and surgical masks, she walked over to Chris. "I guess you still know how to work a crime scene," she teased, mischief glinting briefly in her steady brown eyes, her voice muffled by her mask.

"I'll be good." With the ease of long practice, Chris pulled on the white coveralls while Gwen tied the strings of his mask. "More of TLC's handiwork, damn his black soul," he muttered as he slipped under the tape.

"It certainly looks like it. But ..." The doubt in her voice made Chris glance sharply at her. "There are a couple of things you need to look at," Gwen went on as they stood gazing down at the body, ignoring the electronic flashes as her partner photographed the scene with a digital camera.

"I see what you mean." Chris placed a gloved finger against a suspiciously erect breast and gently jiggled it. "She's had breast implants. Like the last one. Only this time the killer hasn't ripped them out."

The third victim's breasts had also been surgically augmented, and that had driven the killer into a frenzy. Both breasts had been savagely slashed until they lay slack and flat against her chest.

"There's more. I put the hands back the way they were, but look at this." Gwen tugged at the clasped hands, stiffened by rigor mortis.

"The cross is on the wrong hand." Chris frowned as she turned the right hand palm up. "It should be on the left."

"I know. That could be very significant, or not significant at all. The cross looks the same. Traditional. An upright and a cross bar. It's the same length as the others — eight centimetres. Lightly incised with a very sharp, thin blade. Possibly a razor blade."

"What about rape?"

"Violated. But not raped. Like the others. The usual foreign object. Not a bottle, though. Too deep for that. From the look of things, it penetrated her colon. That would have killed her as well. In a matter of hours if she didn't receive surgical attention."

"As our distinguished colleague Steve Mason would say, the creep probably couldn't get it up. It could also be that he didn't want to risk leaving his DNA behind."

"He could have used a condom."

"Not completely safe. If you'll forgive the pun. There's always the risk of semen leaking out on withdrawal. Or one of his pubic hairs might get caught up unnoticed with hers. I remember one case where the guy shaved his pubics for that very reason."

"I know the one you mean." Extracting a rectal thermometer, she held it up. "Rigor mortis is well established. That and her liver temperature tell us she's been dead for eight to ten hours. The night was cool, so it's probably closer to eight. Depending on how long she's been out here."

Pointing down at the purplish path on the left side of the victim's ribcage, Chris said, "That tells us she wasn't killed here. She would have been transported here in a vehicle of some kind."

"We'll spray the top of the hill and check for tire prints. But the grass is real dense, so I don't hold out much hope. Al and Dennis should be here soon, and I'm going to have the scene secured all the way across the field over to the road and down to the base of the hill."

"It's the same story from the top down to here. He would have carried her down, as the bruise under her right knee tells us." Chris mentally chided himself for automatically assuming the killer was male. Still, all the psychological evidence pointed to the killer being a man, and not many women would have the physical strength to carry a body weighing at least fifty-five kilos for a distance of fifty metres down a steep incline. Male or female, the rocky terrain offered no clue.

Gwen and her team would be working the site for another three hours or so. Knowing he could depend on her to fill him in on anything of interest, Chris decided to go back to headquarters and open a file to begin the formal investigation. The first step was to identify the victim. There was no ID, but as Gwen had remarked, "It doesn't take long for people to start looking for someone like her."

The media was waiting in the parking lot across the river. They were held back by four uniformed police officers but were close enough to shout questions at Chris. "TLC strikes again. Right, Detective Crane?" It was more a statement than a question. The killer's chilling pseudonym, one he had conferred on himself, an acronym for "tender loving care," had become public knowledge. It was a cruel, mocking reference to BTK — "bind torture kill" — the infamous signature of Wichita's serial killer who had tortured and strangled ten victims from 1974 to 1991 and who'd escaped detection for years.

Most of the eager faces were familiar to Chris. He had dealt with them before as the serial killer story gathered steam. Tim Mahoney from the *Herald* was there in the front row, standing beside Bill Clarke, the crime reporter for CTV television, and a cameraman recording the scene. Pat, short and rotund, whose last name Chris didn't know but who was from the *Calgary Sun*, was taking pictures with a digital camera; behind him stood Phil Dummett, a freelancer who wrote think pieces that were attracting an increasing amount of attention, and Amanda Fraser, the local stringer for the *Globe and Mail*. The others he didn't know.

As expected, his standard disclaimer that it was too early to divulge any information was greeted with groans of weary resignation. Partly hidden by the open door of the cruiser, Chris methodically finished stowing his gear inside, then eased himself into the driver's seat. He stared straight ahead as he inched forward through the forest of out-thrust microphones and importuning faces.

Morris Pettigrew, senior partner of the corporate law department of the McKinley law firm, glanced uneasily around the boardroom table. The meeting had been called for 8:30 and it was now 8:45. Clearing his throat, he said, "I can't imagine what's keeping Adrienne. She has a thing about punctuality."

"There's no point in starting without her," the general counsel of the client oil company remarked. "She's been in charge of the file since the get-go."

"I'll see if I can track her down." Jeff Ingram got up from his chair. The young lawyer, just four years out of law school and three years at the bar, was working with Adrienne Vinney on the Madison Energy share prospectus.

"Do that." Pettigrew nodded. "While we wait, we'll have some coffee." At his nod a white-jacketed server moved around the table, refilling cups.

The four executives seated with Pettigrew at the polished mahogany table — the president and CEO of Madison, together with the general counsel, the vice-president for exploration, and the chief financial officer — were the picture of corporate success and the rewards that went with it. And those rewards were due for a handsome increase when the new share issue hit the market. Buoyed by the spectacular success of its drilling program on the Lost Horse Block, Madison's shares had climbed steadily in recent months, and the new issue was bound to sell at a premium. Despite this, there was a palpable air of tension in the conference room. The company lawyer nervously tapped a pen against his teeth until a glare from the president made him put it down.

In a few minutes, Ingram, looking puzzled and upset, returned with the news that Adrienne hadn't arrived at the office. Nor had she called in.

"I just don't understand this," Pettigrew muttered. "She knows how important this meeting is." Looking at Ingram, still standing in the doorway, he asked, "Did you try her at home?"

"Her assistant did. Fifteen minutes ago. No answer."

"She could be caught in traffic," Madison's president offered, but without much conviction.

"Not Adrienne." Pettigrew frowned. "That lady plans ahead. Knowing her, I would have expected her to be in her office two hours ago, preparing for this meeting."

"So would I," the general counsel agreed. "Adrienne is conscientious to a fault." Giving Pettigrew a worried look, he said, "I don't like this, Morris."

The senior partner looked at his watch. "I suggest we give her another fifteen minutes. If she doesn't show up by then, Jeff should contact the hospitals, and …" he added after a moment's hesitation, "the police."

Ingram's phone calls to Calgary's three hospitals drew a blank. There was no record of any Adrienne Vinney having been checked in at either Emergency or General Admissions. Nor anyone fitting her description. Doing his best to seem unconcerned, Ingram walked the short distance down the carpeted hall to Adrienne's legal assistant's cubicle. No word from Adrienne.

The blue pages of the telephone directory listed a number for Missing Persons Coordinator under Calgary Police Services. That was the place to start, but as soon as he began to describe Adrienne, he was told to hang on while his call was transferred.

"Homicide." The voice was brisk and business-like.

"I want to report a person who seems to have gone missing."

"Describe the person. But first could I have your name and address, sir."

There was a moment's silence when Ingram finished describing Adrienne in words that he realized could have come from a besotted lover. Then, in a voice softened with professional sympathy, his listener said, "It's possible we might have some information for you, sir. I'm afraid I must ask you to visit the medical examiner's office and view a body. You may be able to identify it."

Ingram only half listened as he wrote down the street address. Adrienne was dead. That, and only that, would explain her failure to show up for the meeting. The detective offered to send a car and driver for him. "That won't be necessary. I can make my own way there. But I have to talk to some people first."

chapter two

So the victim was a lawyer. A partner in the largest law firm in the city. Chris Crane sighed and put the two-page report down on his grey metal desk. That was the sum of everything useful they had learned in the twenty-four hours following the discovery of the body. Homicide, along with the other sections of Major Crimes — Robbery, Sex Crimes, and Child Abuse — was housed on the tenth floor of the police headquarters at 133 6th Avenue SE. Originally the building had been the head office of Dome Petroleum. Subsequently it had been acquired by the city and renamed Andrew Davison in honour of the man who had been a long-serving mayor back in the 1930s and '40s. A bronze plaque commemorated his career in civic politics. It was common for police officers to say they were "heading to Andrew Davison" when they were on their way to headquarters.

Homicide's complement of eight detectives sat at small desks, each partially separated from the others by forty-five-centimetre-high partitions. Three rows of unoccupied desks at the back were reserved for occasions when it was necessary to bring in temporary reinforcements. The only office cubicle belonged to the staff sergeant, whose work was purely administrative. The plan was to promote the interchange of ideas between the detectives. It worked for the most part, but there were times when Chris found himself longing for the small office that had been his when he was the sergeant in charge of the Forensic Crime Scenes Unit. Never more so than when the raucous voice of Steve Mason boomed out from his desk, two over from and one behind Chris's. As it was doing now, dressing down a snitch for not coming up with the name of a dead prostitute.

Mason resented Chris and made no secret of it. He was openly contemptuous of the fact that Chris was a lawyer — "a member of the bar, for Christ's sake!" — who didn't practise law and had no damn business being a policeman. It didn't help that Chris was known to have private means and to enjoy an upscale lifestyle. Gwen had once tried to explain to Mason that Chris loved working with and solving puzzles and mysteries. And what better way to do that than as a detective? The thrill of the chase and the attendant risks and human consequences would make it even more irresistible for someone like Chris Crane.

"That's what made him so brilliant at decoding a crime scene, and why he'll be so good at this," she had told the skeptical Mason shortly after Chris's transfer to Homicide had been announced.

"Aw, don't give me that bullshit! You've got the hots for the guy. That's your problem, Staroski," Mason had replied.

Deep in thought, Chris heard, rather than saw, Gwen opening the bulletproof door of the Homicide section. Over Mason's protests that it was a breach of security, he had arranged for her to have a temporary pass. Smiling, he logged off the Net and a colour photo of his parrot, Nevermore, appeared on the screen saver.

Returning his smile, Gwen could see how Mason could have thought she had the hots for Chris. He was devastatingly attractive in a dark, intense sort of way, lean, blue-jowled despite scrupulously shaving every morning. His eyes, grey and piercing under well-marked eyebrows, were his best feature. Robyn, his ex-wife, frustrated by his single-minded dedication to solving crimes, had given up on him a year ago. That's when he had acquired the parrot. Blanche wouldn't like her thinking like this. But Gwen wouldn't give up what she and Blanche shared for anything. Certainly not for a man, however attractive. She and Blanche were so lucky to have found each other. She felt a momentary inner glow at the thought of the cozy apartment they shared.

These thoughts running through one part of her mind didn't distract Gwen from the business at hand. "Do you think Vinney might have been killed because of something connected with her work?" she asked Chris.

"It's possible," he answered slowly. "I guess anything is possible at this stage. We don't know anything about her personal life, apart from the fact that she was a highly successful lawyer. She was single and lived alone. But we don't know yet whether she had a boyfriend, or boyfriends. I've been sitting here thinking about that cross."

"Wondering about it being on the right hand, and if that means anything?"

Chris's nod turned into a grimace as they heard Mason heave himself to his feet and come over to join them. Another disadvantage to the open seating concept was that it allowed everyone to know what was going on in every file. The serial killer case had by far the highest profile, and Mason couldn't stay out of it. Indeed, he thought that he, not Chris, should have been in charge of the investigation.

There was nothing to be done about Mason, not at the moment anyway, so Chris answered Gwen's question. "It's got to mean something. In some cultures, Arabian mostly, the left hand is considered unclean."

"That's what they wipe their asses with," Mason surprised them by saying.

"Right. The cross being on the left hand in the previous cases could have been an act of exorcism on the part of the killer."

Hitching his belly to hang more comfortably over his belt, Mason said, "Or it could be just the guy getting his rocks off. You ask me, which you don't, this is a pure sex crime. The guy can't get it up, so he takes it out on women. That's how he gets his jollies. The cross is part of that mumbo-jumbo. Fantasy, like Mavis says. For once that profiler bullshit of hers makes some sense. It don't matter where the cross is. All the killer cares about is that it's there."

"You have a point," conceded Chris, pleased that for once he could agree with the burly detective. There wasn't room on his desk to spread the photos out, so he held them in his hand. Flipping through them, he asked Gwen, "Your search of her condo didn't turn up anything untoward?"

"Untoward." Where did the son of a bitch get off using words like that? Mason thought, giving his sagging pants another hitch.

"Except that it's to die for," Gwen sighed. "It's in Eau Claire. It's not a penthouse but the next thing to it.

It's so cool. Everything in shades of grey and silver, low coffee tables of polished stainless steel, Minimalist paintings. Cushions scattered here and there. Floor-to-ceiling windows with a great view of the Bow River. You would love it, Chris."

"You sound like the Home Page in the *Herald*, for Christ's sake!" Mason snorted.

Chris smiled and asked, "No fingerprints, no blood? Nothing useful like that?"

"No blood. Fingerprints, yes. Mostly hers. A few others that we're trying to match. One is bound to be her cleaning woman, who comes in twice a week. The place is immaculate."

"So she wasn't killed there?"

"Couldn't have been. Not with those wounds. The place would have been awash in blood."

"Your report states that she could have been rendered unconscious by a blow to the back of her head. That could have happened in her condo, and she could have been taken somewhere else to be assaulted and killed."

"That could have been the way it went down," Gwen agreed. "But there's nothing to tell us one way or the other."

"That's bullshit!" Mason exploded. "The killer probably grabbed her when she was out for a run. She *was* a runner, we know that. If the creep saw her in shorts, he wouldn't be able to control himself."

"There are shorts and running bras in her closets. We don't know yet if any are missing. The cleaning woman might be able to tell us. Chances are a busy professional woman like Vinney might not do her own laundry," Gwen said

"Has this cleaning lady been located yet?" Chris asked.

"Yes. Her name is Mary Lunn. She claims to have been very fond of her employer. I'm going to question her when we're finished."

"We *are* finished." Chris pulled back his shirt cuff to glance at his watch. "The Chief has called a press conference for a half hour from now. He wants me there."

"Lucky you," said Gwen, grinning.

chapter three

Later that day, alone once more, Chris pondered the possibilities. At this stage, there were three. A sex killing by a serial killer. That's what the evidence pointed to. Except for the cross being on the wrong hand. And the breast implants left untouched. The killer couldn't have missed them. He must have felt them when he was slicing off her nipple. Everything else was consistent with the previous murders. The second possibility was a bitter ex-lover. Adrienne Vinney had been a remarkably attractive woman. The cleaning woman might be able to fill them in on that side of the victim's life. If there was one. In her mid-thirties, a partner in a prestigious law firm, she could have been wrapped up in her career to the exclusion of everything else. Her work as a corporate lawyer was the third possibility, and this was his line of country. Since her identity was already in the public domain, he was free to talk to those who might have known her. Chris picked up the phone.

Tom Forsyth's expression was bemused as he watched Chris fill out the bar chit in the Petroleum Club's lounge. "You're sure as hell not the average policeman, with your membership in the Petroleum Club and—"

"It's very useful for making contacts," Chris interjected to forestall any further discussion of his lifestyle.

"Of which you make very good use." Forsyth took an appreciative sip of his martini. "Is this a purely social occasion, or are you here to swab me down about the delectable, recently deceased Adrienne Vinney?"

His friend's casual, almost light-hearted reference to the gruesome murder surprised Chris, but he made no mention of that as he replied, "A bit of both, actually. It's been a while since we've had a drink together, and I'm sure you would have known the delectable Adrienne, as you call her. You were both in the same line of work."

"*Were.* Funny how the past tense bring things home, isn't it? Well, you're right. She and I *did* work together on a number of corporate files, representing different parties to the transaction. Mergers and acquisitions mostly. We also did a couple of income trust conversions. In a nutshell, she was very bright, worked like hell, and was a pleasure to work with. A couple of her partners at McKinley are good buddies of mine and they tell me she is — was, rather — one of the highest billers in the firm. Right up there with old Pettigrew himself."

"Have you worked on any files with her recently?"

"Not since the Freeholders royalty dispute six months ago. We were on the same side in that one." Forsyth's smile was reminiscent. "We won a million-dollar settlement for our clients. The fair Adrienne showed no mercy. The lady is one tough negotiator."

Chris could see that Tom was growing restive under the questioning, but he persisted, "Can you think of anyone who might have thought she was *too* good a negotiator? Someone who felt she had cheated him out of his rights, and resented her for it?"

"No, I can't. And that's highly unlikely in any case. Her practice is exclusively corporate law: mergers and acquisitions, public share offerings, that sort of thing. No disputes. No adverse interests. Just a matter of satisfying the security commissions and stock exchanges. Difficult, I grant you, and frustrating at times, but not adversarial, if that's where you going."

"I'm not going anywhere in particular. I'm just casting about. And I appreciate your patience. Bear with me while we have another martini."

"This one is on me." Tom handed a chit to a passing server and tilted back in his chair to regard Chris with a quizzical look. "How come this interest in her legal career? I thought she was a victim of our serial killer. I can't see him being interested in what she did for a living. It would be that awesome body of hers that would turn him on."

In point of fact, none of the killer's previous victims had been what you would call ravishing beauties. Young, wholesome, and healthy, yes, but nothing like the Vinney woman. Except maybe for the third one, the one with the breast implants. But even she wasn't in the same class as Adrienne Vinney. No need to mention that, though. "How well did you know Adrienne, Tom?"

"What kind of question is that? I'm a married man!" Tom was making a joke out of it, but there was an undertone of something else — regret, maybe? — in his voice.

"You wish." Chris grinned, keeping it light.

"You're not asking these questions for the fun of it, are you?"

"No. I'm investigating a murder."

"So you are. Well, what do you want to know? There's not much I can tell you."

"Any information on her personal life would be helpful. Boyfriends, girlfriends. That sort of thing."

"You'll have to ask someone else about her friends. But what I can tell you is that men were a distant second to her career. Very distant." Forsyth sighed. "You know Scott Millard, don't you? The criminal lawyer?"

"He's cross-examined me a couple of times on the witness stand. He's very good. Very well prepared. No wonder he gets so many high-profile cases."

"He speaks highly of you, too. He admires the way you analyze situations. Says you make a deadly witness for the prosecution."

"You and Scott are good friends, aren't you?"

"Have been for years. We play squash together twice a week at the Glencoe. He almost always wins. And we're both Benchers of the Law Society."

Tom paused, and Chris prompted, "You were saying?"

"This is so far out I feel silly even mentioning it. Scott and Adrienne had an affair, but she broke it off not long before we worked together on the Freeholder claim. She never mentioned it. She wouldn't. But I heard all about it from Scott. He was devastated. I even managed to beat him a few times at squash. He hated that. He hates to lose."

"That's what makes him a good defence counsel. You say he was devastated?"

"Absolutely. He just couldn't bring himself to believe it was all over. I think he expected to marry her. That's how serious he was."

"Do you know how long their affair lasted?"

"Six or seven months. They weren't living together or anything like that. I can't see Adrienne ever living with anyone. Do you intend to interview Scott?"

"As soon as I can arrange it. It's just a process of elimination."

"I would just as soon that Scott doesn't know I was the one who told you about him and Adrienne."

"He won't. Their relationship must have been known to a number of people. It won't be necessary to identify my source. I'll simply be relying on the well-known 'general knowledge.'"

Calgary's brief rush hour was over by the time the two friends left the club and stood for a moment on the sidewalk outside its 5th Avenue entrance.

"I can see the thrill of the chase in your eyes." Forsyth smiled as they shook hands. "That's why my offer of a partnership in the firm goes begging."

"It's not so much the thrill of the chase, as you put it, as it is finding the correct answer."

As always, Chris took pleasure in walking home along 4th Street, vibrant with its eclectic mix of shops and restaurants, apartments, condos, and medium-rise office buildings. His condo was a penthouse, on the thirty-second floor of The Windsors on the banks of the Elbow River, flowing down from the Rockies to join the Bow at Fort Calgary. The click of the opening door brought a guttural "Hello, Chris" from Nevermore. The words, which Chris had taught him, were getting clearer and more distinct each day. Depositing the mail on the hall table, Chris went over to the parrot's cage, a large affair, more of an indoor aviary than a cage. Nevermore was a Congo African Grey, larger than his cousin, the more common Timneh variety, and had a bright red tail and black beak. The parrot cooed softly as Chris scratched him on the cheek and carried him over to his stand. African Greys were reputed to be the best talkers of the parrot family, and Nevermore, at only fifteen months, showed promise of living up to that reputation. He could say his name and called out, "Hello, Chris here," when the phone rang. From time to time he surprised and delighted his owner by trying out a new word or sound. His most recent accomplishment was "Good boy" in Chris's approving voice. All in all, he was entertaining company.

Looking around his high-ceilinged quarters Chris thought it must be much the same as the way Gwen had described Adrienne Vinney's condo. Post-modern cool, except that the colour contrasts were provided not with cushions, but with paintings, mostly Western Canadian — foothill scenes by Gissing, a spring chinook by Turner, mountain peaks by Glyde, two large paintings of vintage airplanes by Drohan. An equally large oil by Collier of icebergs floating off Banks Island in the Arctic had pride of place over the marble fireplace.

The library, with bookcases to the ceiling, a built-in ladder on rollers to reach the highest shelves, desk and tables in warm walnut, and soft leather armchairs, was in sharp and reassuring contrast to the other rooms.

The condo, like many other aspects of Chris's lifestyle, was wildly out of keeping with his salary as a police officer. It was widely assumed that he had inherited wealth and dabbled in criminal investigation for something to do. Many, like Steve Mason, thought of him as a dilettante. Only his brokers and a few members of the financial community knew the truth: that he'd made himself independently wealthy by shrewd and well-researched investing, exclusively in energy stocks and trusts. He had kept a low profile for a number of years before saying to hell with it. The luxurious condo and the Ferrari 360 Spider convertible parked down below under a dust cover in the stall next to his Dodge Durango were the results of that decision. He was also supporting his ex, Robyn, while she studied law at the university. He was not obligated in any way to do that; it was something he wanted to do.

The morning light spilled in through the floor-to-ceiling windows, looking east over the Elbow. Seated at the granite-topped breakfast table, Chris glanced up at the wall clock over the fridge: 6:36 a.m. The concierge would have delivered the morning papers by now. He always started with the penthouse. Chris took a swallow of coffee, gave Nevermore a piece of toasted English muffin, and pushed back his chair. He subscribed to all four morning papers — the *Sun*, the *Herald*, the *Globe and Mail*, and the *National Post* — and all four were arranged neatly on the carpeted hallway outside his front door.

He poured himself another cup of coffee before steeling himself to look at the papers spread out on a coffee table. The sensational story of the latest gruesome murder took up the entire front page of the *Sun* and the top half of the *Herald*'s, and was the lead story in the *Post*, while being relegated to the bottom half of the front page in the *Globe*. The headlines in the two Calgary papers were identical, both screaming "Killer Strikes Again." The accompanying articles feasted on the prominence of the latest victim and the fact that she had been naked and mutilated when found. Predictably, the police came in for a lot of heat over "the killer in our midst" remaining at large and killing at will.

Chief Johnstone's press conference late yesterday morning had been to try to reassure an angry and frightened public. Johnstone was an able administrator and did a good job of running the Police Service, but he had an unfortunate propensity for the cliché. Chris winced as he read how "no stone would be left unturned" and the investigation was a "full court press." But the clichés couldn't hide the fact that an aroused citizenry was demanding an arrest.

Chris had spotted Phil Dummett at the press conference, standing at the back of the room. Had he written anything about the latest murder? Pushing his empty cup to one side, Chris flipped through the papers. Maybe he was saving up to do a piece for a magazine, *Maclean's* maybe. No, here it was. On the third page of the *Post*'s front section. As usual with Dummett, it was more of an in-depth treatment rather than straight news reporting. It said all the appropriate things about the horror of the crime, emphasizing the achievements of the victim and the brilliant career that had lain before her. Then it took a different tack with a not unsympathetic discussion of the demons and grotesque fantasies that must be driving the killer to commit such terrible deeds. It was almost certain to be picked up and circulated by the news networks, which would be what Dummett was aiming for.

The guy could sure as hell write. As he folded the *Post* and placed it alongside his empty coffee cup, Chris remembered what it was that had been niggling at the back of his mind. Ken Patterson, one of his fellow Homicide detectives, was a friend of Dummett's. He wasn't familiar with all the details, but while Chris was still with FCSU Patterson had used Dummett to plant some information in the press. That information had led to a tip from a neighbour of the victim that eventually resulted in the arrest and conviction of a suspect. The fact that Dummett worked as a freelancer didn't hurt either. He wouldn't have to worry about his responsibility to his employer.

Maybe what had worked before could work again. Chris's lips tightened. For sure nothing else was working for them!

"Mr. Millard is in court," the legal assistant informed Chris. The court wouldn't be in session until ten o'clock, two hours from now. The criminal lawyer must have gone over to the courthouse early to prepare for the trial, checking his notes or conferring with his client. Chris knew as he rang off that this would not be the right time to interview Millard, who would be totally focused on what he had to deal with in court. The case he was engaged in had generated a lot of media attention. The accused, Millard's client, was a city employee, a low-level supervisor in the Planning Department. Reporting for work one morning, he had been called into the manager's office to be summarily fired.

Shaken and white-faced, according to his fellow employees, some of whom had been aware that he was to be dismissed that morning, he had rushed past their desks and cubicles and stormed out of the building. Less than an hour later he'd returned with a Smith & Wesson .38 concealed in his jacket pocket. Marching directly across the floor to the manager's office, he'd shot him twice in the chest as he sat behind his desk. Then he'd shot and killed the female clerk who had filed a complaint of sexual harassment against him. While his co-workers had watched in horrified silence, he'd placed the muzzle of the revolver against his own temple. But his index finger had refused to squeeze the trigger. He'd stood like that for a full minute, a look of disbelief on his face. Then his arm had fallen to his side, the gun pointing harmlessly at the floor.

His only hope lay in being found not guilty by reason of insanity. If the jury bought it, he would receive a more lenient sentence than the mandatory life sentence that would be imposed if he was convicted of murder. For the not-guilty plea to succeed, Millard would have to convince the jury that his client was in such a state of mind that when he shot his victims he was not capable of appreciating that what he did was wrong. Chris mentally shook his head. A tough case to make. Especially since the accused had shot only those two persons who, in his eyes, had wronged him. Chris decided to drop in on the trial toward the end of the morning session.

In the meantime, he would talk to Patterson about his plan to use Dummett to leak some information that might lead TLC into making a fatal error. Chris turned to look back at Patterson, sitting at his desk two rows to the rear. He was on the phone. Chris had worked with the boyish-looking detective on a couple of homicides back when Chris was with FCSU. Patterson's fair-haired and youthful good looks were somewhat diminished by thin lips that curved too far upward when he smiled. It always put Chris in mind of a crescent moon. "It's because Ken's upper lip is so short," he had once told Gwen when she'd remarked on it. Patterson was good to work with. A university graduate himself, he wasn't disconcerted in the least by Chris's law degree and Harvard MBA.

As soon as Patterson finished his phone conversation, Chris went back to talk to him.

"Phil's a good guy. Bright as hell. But" — Patterson looked dubious — "I don't know how he would react to this."

"He's done it before."

"Yeah. But we weren't completely upfront that we were using him. He was a little ticked off when he found out."

"You're still on good terms with him?"

"We're tight. Like I said, he wasn't happy about it, but he knows it was a bit of a feather in his cap as a journalist."

"Being part of this case would be a much bigger and brighter feather. And this time we would be upfront about what we had in mind. Appeal to his public spirit and sense of civic duty."

"I think he'd buy into that. You will be the reliable source, I assume?"

"Yeah. I'll give him something he can't resist. Try to set up a meeting for later this afternoon. Four o'clock. I've got some business over at the courthouse before then."

The white-haired orderly gave Chris a slight nod of recognition as he stood in the marble foyer of the courthouse, looking up at the list of cases and courtrooms scrolling down the TV monitor. *R. v. Harris* was in courtroom 302.

The Crown had elected to first try Harris with the clerk's murder. The trial had attracted a fair number of spectators. Three media types in the front benches had open notebooks on their laps; the remainder appeared to be friends and relatives of the victim and the accused. The dead woman, Chris remembered reading, was black, so the small cluster of black people sitting on the left side would be her family and supporters. A smaller group in the straight-backed benches on the other side of the aisle would be the family of the accused. It was like a church wedding, Chris thought as he took his seat, the bride's party on the left and the groom's on the right. He didn't know the presiding judge, a woman in her mid-fifties, seated on a raised dais under the coat of arms, the scarlet sash of a justice of the Court of Queen's Bench in vivid contrast to her black robe. The accused, a balding, inoffensive-looking man, blinking behind rimless glasses, sat in the prisoner's box, watching intently as his lawyer prepared to cross-examine a witness for the prosecution.

Scott Millard, a look of polite bafflement on his snub-nosed, deceptively guileless face, stood at the lectern, resting both hands on its slanted surface as he surveyed the witness. He was wearing a barrister's court gown of black cotton, or "stuff" as it was called in court circles, with a waistcoat of the same material, a wing collar, and white tabs. He was still young, as barristers go, which explained why, despite his brilliant record of court victories and being a Bencher, he had yet to be appointed Queen's Counsel. That appointment was sure to come with the next New Year's List, thought Chris, entitling Millard to wear silk.

The witness that Millard was gazing upon so benignly was a key one for the prosecution. He was a well-known psychiatrist who had testified in his direct evidence for the Crown that the accused, although distraught, clearly knew that what he had done was wrong. As the silence grew, the psychiatrist stroked his neatly trimmed beard and nervously pursed his lips in and out.

"Tell me, Doctor," Millard began in what sounded like a throw-away question, "how much time did you spend in the company of the accused, Mr. Harris?"

The witness hesitated, looked over at the table where the Crown attorney and his junior sat, and finally mumbled, "One hour."

"One hour! That's it?"

"Yes."

"No further questions." Scott Millard gave the jury a dumbfounded look and, shaking his head, resumed his seat at the counsel table.

A murmur, quickly silenced by a glare from the bench, rippled through the audience. The family of the accused whispered excitedly among themselves.

"Court will resume at two o'clock," the judge announced, gathering up her papers.

The lawyers' locker room in the basement of the courthouse was the best place to intercept Millard. The defence lawyer would have to go there to disrobe, even if that meant, as it often did, just exchanging his gown and waistcoat for a sports jacket. Signs were posted in the basement warning that it was a restricted area with access limited to lawyers and courthouse staff. No problem there. Chris Crane was a member in good standing of the Law Society.

Chris waited just inside the entrance to the large subterranean chamber, crammed with rows of green-painted lockers and echoing with the slam of metal doors and the banter of lawyers as they changed into civilian clothes. He was beginning to wonder if Millard was going to work through the lunch break when the lawyer walked in. He paused when he saw Chris and mouthed, "Me?", pointing to himself. Chris nodded and Millard said he would be with him as soon as he put his gown and briefcase in his locker.

"I realize you are in the middle of a trial and that this might not be a good time," Chris said as Millard, *sans* gown and briefcase, returned. "We could meet later if you like. But," he added, "we're in the early stages of the investigation, and time is crucial right now."

"I appreciate that. The trial is just about over. I'm just calling one witness, and closing arguments won't be until tomorrow. Let's go up to the cafeteria and grab some lunch while we talk."

"Let me guess," Chris said as he and Millard picked up their trays and joined the short queue of diners filing past counters laden with food. "Your witness will be a famous psychiatrist who will have spent considerably more than an hour with the accused."

"Considerably more." Millard laughed, helping himself to a slice of blueberry pie from the pastry counter. "Several days in fact."

"I don't understand the prosecution. Leaving their star witness vulnerable like that."

"It's not entirely their fault. I know the celebrated Dr. Murray. He's an arrogant, opinionated son of a bitch who thinks he's infallible. Besides, the prosecution has consistently dismissed the insanity plea as a non-starter from the get-go. They thought all they had to do was go through the motions," Millard said as they took their seats and started to eat.

"They've probably changed their mind after what you did to Dr. Murray. Or what he did to himself."

"You think so?" Millard gave Chris a keen look and, pleased by what he saw, smiled as he pushed his empty soup bowl to one side.

"I was watching the jury. They didn't like the good doctor. Juries don't appreciate being talked down to."

"I hope you're right. If they buy the insanity defence it will make one hell of a difference for Harris. Instead of spending the rest of his life in prison, he will be sent to a mental hospital for treatment. His case will be reviewed every year and he will be released if the doctors find that he's sane. However, that's not what you're here to talk about."

The criminal lawyer seemed remarkably composed about his former lover's murder. He might have been able to find relief by immersing himself in his work. Professionals could sometimes do that. The good Lord knew trial work was challenging enough to banish all thought of anything else. "I believe you were well acquainted with Adrienne Vinney?" Chris began.

"Well acquainted? That's one way of putting it, I guess. We had an affair. It lasted several months, but that's been over now for the better part of a year. Her call."

"How did you feel about that?"

"How do you think I felt? I loved her. More than I've ever loved anyone in my life. Or ever will again." Millard paused for a sip of coffee. "But I've come to accept that she was right. The relationship — I hate that word — would never have worked in the long run. Not with each of us having separate, totally demanding careers. Not to mention outsize egos." Putting down the cup, he looked Chris in the eye. "I gather she died a horrible death?"

"As you know, there's not much I can tell you about that. But it was pretty grim, all right."

"The thought of her in the hands of a serial killer makes my skin crawl." For the first time the lawyer let his emotion show. "Are you going to catch the guy? That's a stupid question, I know."

"We're doing our best. You can help by telling me if you know of anyone who might have held a grudge against Ms. Vinney. Anyone who might have wanted her dead."

Millard stared at the detective. "I thought we were dealing with a serial killer. A guy like that would only be interested in Adrienne as an object of his perverted fantasies."

"I'm sure you're right. But we can't afford to rule anything out. Not yet. Can you answer my question?"

"Only in the negative. As you probably know by now, Adrienne had a corporate practice. Not the kind where you're likely to make deadly enemies. Not like criminal law, where the people you deal with can turn on you. Usually, it's the police who made the arrest and the Crown prosecutors who are the targets, but we defence lawyers can come in for our share too. A client thinks that you've let him down, didn't do a good job of defending him, and so on. Blames you for his being in jail. It's not the same in the corporate world."

"But the stakes in that world can be very high. And corporate criminals land in jail too."

"That's true. But to answer your question, I don't know of anyone who had a hard-on for Adrienne. Not in that sense, anyway," he added with a bitter smile.

"What about the other sense? Have their been other men since you?"

"How in hell am I supposed to know that?" Millard flared. "I haven't been keeping tabs on her, for Christ's sake! I'm not some kind of stalker."

He doth protest too much, methinks. The Shakespearean line leapt into Chris's mind, but he spread his hands in a placatory gesture. "I have to ask these questions. You know that."

Looking somewhat shamefaced, Millard nodded, and Chris plowed on. "Would you tell me where you were Sunday night? Particularly from, say, nine o'clock on."

"At home. Alone. Working on cross. It was after midnight when I went to bed."

"It couldn't have taken very long to prepare your cross of Dr. Murray. It was admirably succinct."

"It was, wasn't it? As things turned out. But I could have gone into much greater detail if I thought it necessary. Anyway, the cross-examination I was working on had nothing to do with the Harris case. I'm representing the accused in a rape case that's set down for trial the week after next. The defence is that it was consensual sex." He bared his teeth in a ferocious grin that briefly transformed his bland young face. "I'm afraid the complainant is in for a rough ride when she takes the stand. The lady has quite a track record."

"I feel sorry for her already."

"That's an interesting point. I'll remember to ease up on her so I don't get the jury feeling sorry for her. You ever think of practising law?"

"I like what I do." Chris paused to finish off the last of his dessert, then said, "Since you were alone I guess there's no way of corroborating your story."

"It's not a story, Detective. It's the truth. But you're right. I don't have an alibi. I'm sorry about that. I know you people like to eliminate 'persons of interest' as early as possible. But there it is." Stacking his empty plates and dishes on the tray, Millard got up from the table. "Sorry I couldn't be of more help."

"Appreciate your taking the time. Good luck this afternoon."

chapter four

As he often did, Chris took a little detour so he could walk along the Stephen Avenue Mall on his way back to headquarters. Office workers lingered over lunch on outdoor patios or sat on benches basking in the sun, while a band entertained the noonday crowd with twangy country music. A Native Canadian, wearing a chief's headdress, sold dream catchers from a makeshift booth; an amateur comedian drew groans from his audience as his jokes fell flat; and buskers, a modest harvest of coins glinting in the instrument cases open at their feet, strummed guitars and played accordions and violins. As he walked past, Chris checked out at the entrance to Scotia Centre, hoping to see Joan Cunningham. But there was no sign of the disabled panhandler with her mobile platform and pet cockatiel. Every few blocks a street person sorted through the contents of a garbage bin. A late spring sun shone down on the lively scene.

Dummett put down the magazine he had been leafing through when he saw Chris emerge from the elevator and walk across the lobby toward him. His manner was easy and relaxed as he held out his hand and said, "You and I have never met formally, but I guess we know each other."

"We do," replied Chris as they shook hands. The journalist topped Chris's five-foot-eleven by a lanky two or three inches. He smiled when Chris added, "I make a point of reading your material whenever I come across it."

Chris recalled Gwen, back in their Crime Scene days, once remarking that a couple of the girls in the office thought Dummett was hot. Chris could see how that might be. Dark hair, parted in the middle, fell over a high forehead; the face was long with prominent cheekbones and a strong jaw line. An engaging smile lightened what otherwise would have been a severe countenance. Chris found himself warming to the guy.

Picking up a slim leather briefcase, the journalist followed Chris over to the elevators. Chris had decided to hold the meeting on the tenth floor with the idea that being in close proximity to the Homicide section might make Dummett more willing to co-operate.

"Will Ken be joining us?" Dummett asked as he placed his briefcase on the table that, together with four straight-backed chairs, comprised the furnishings of the small interview room.

"I didn't think that was necessary. But I can ask him to join us if you like."

"No. It's just that he was the one who called me. But it's entirely up to you, Detective."

"Chris, please."

"Great. And Phil for me." Once again that easy smile. "Okay, Chris, it's your dime. What can I do for you?"

"I hope it's more what we can do for each other." Chris paused, and continued when Dummett gave an encouraging nod. "As you know, I'm the lead investigator in the serial killer case. I'm sure you're also aware that the investigation is pretty much stymied at the moment."

Again Dummett nodded and waited for Chris to continue.

Clearing his throat, Chris said, "That's where you come in, Phil. It's our hope — my hope, actually — that you might write something that would goad the killer into some kind of a reaction. Make him do something that would provide us with a clue." Chris paused to look at his visitor. "Is this something that you could be comfortable with, Phil?"

Dummett returned the look with a grave stare of his own. "Depends. Is what you want me to write kosher? Authentic. Not something that can come back to discredit me as a journalist?"

"Absolutely. I am your source. I will have to remain anonymous for obvious reasons. But what I will tell you is legitimate. As well as being newsworthy."

"And what is it I have to do in return for this information?"

"Release it to the public."

"Fair enough." Dummett opened his briefcase. "Can I tape it? I guess not," he sighed when Chris shook his head. "Okay. I'm listening."

Chris drew a deep breath. "You will write that you have reliable information that the police do not believe the Vinney killing is the work of the serial killer known as TLC."

Dummett absorbed this in silence for a moment, then murmured, "It's newsworthy all right. Not to mention sensational." Another pause, then a frown. "Why don't the police come right out and say that? ... Of course. You can't make it official. It has to be a rumour. A leak. Stupid me."

"Not stupid. But you understand why it has to be done this way?"

"Completely. And thank you for playing straight with me. I appreciate that."

"How will you get the word out?"

"It'll be on the wire. Which means I've got work to do." Making no effort to hide his excitement, Dummett got to his feet. "This is bound to get under TLC's skin. Either way. If he killed that lawyer, he'll want the credit. If he didn't, he'll be worried about what the police know that he doesn't. I like it!"

"I'm glad. Here is my card with my cellphone number. Could I have yours?"

"Absolutely. Here you are."

At precisely 6:28 the following morning Chris stationed himself behind the front door of the penthouse. He waited for a couple minutes after hearing the soft thud of the papers landing on the doormat to give the concierge time to get back on the elevator, then opened the door and scooped up the newspapers.

The story, with Phil Dummett's byline, was the same in all four papers; only the headlines differed. Variations on the same theme: "Police Search for Second Killer"; "Is There More Than One Killer?"

Dummett had certainly carried out his end of the bargain. Now to see if it stirred up any response from TLC.

There was nothing he could do about that. It would either happen or it wouldn't. Next on the agenda was to interview some of Vinney's colleagues at the law firm.

Patterson was out of the office at a crime scene so there was no chance to talk to him about the meeting with Dummett. But the other detectives — with the exception of Mason, who remained at his desk — crowded around Chris, pummelling him with questions. When the excitement died away and they went back to their desks, he turned to Gwen. "What have you arranged with the McKinley people?"

"We start with Jeff Ingram. He was Vinney's junior. You're to see him at ten-thirty."

"Her junior is a good place to start," Chris said approvingly. "I want you to come with me, Gwen. See how her associates come across."

"Sure. And one of the senior partners, a Mr. Pettigrew, wants to meet with whoever is in charge of the investigation."

"I'll be happy to oblige him. After we've heard what this Jeff Ingram has to say. Meanwhile, you can fill me in on what we know about Mr. Ingram."

"Not an awful lot," Gwen began. "So far ..."

"I understand you worked very closely with Ms. Vinney?" Chris posed it as a question, but it came out as a statement of fact.

"She was my mentor," Jeff Ingram replied in a hollow voice, gazing solemnly at the two detectives. The look on his pudgy, soft-chinned face reflected his sense of loss. Ingram was showing more signs of grief than the others Chris had interviewed, including Scott Millard. But there was something else besides grief. The eyes, heavy lidded and of indeterminate colour, were alert and watchful behind round, metal-rimmed glasses. Probably afraid of saying something that would get him in trouble with the partners. This was borne out by his reaction when Chris asked about the files he and Adrienne had been working on recently.

"I can't answer that. Solicitor-client privilege." The reply was rehearsed, either by himself or on instructions from the firm. Ingram clearly intended to avoid saying anything that might jeopardize his career.

"We have ways of finding out, you know," said Chris with a meaningful glance at Gwen.

"I realize that. It would be better if you found out that way."

Chris shrugged. "I'm sure Mr. Pettigrew will tell us when we see him."

"If Mr. Pettigrew gives the okay, I'll be happy to tell you everything I know about the files." Ingram smiled his relief. "I don't see how that will help your investigation, though."

Chris let that pass. "What about her life outside the office? Can you tell us anything about that? Anyone she was involved with? Anyone who might have had it in for her?"

"I know nothing about that part of her life. Absolutely nothing. We never spoke of anything besides work. There was no need to."

"Adrienne's dance card was always full." Morris Pettigrew's smile was reminiscent, tinged with sadness. "She will be sorely missed, not only for the files she generated but also for her work ethic. She set a wonderful example. For all of us."

"That's what we would like to talk about. Her files." Chris and Gwen were perched rather uncomfortably on the edge of a padded black leather sofa in Pettigrew's spacious office. The portly lawyer remained behind his desk, the size of a drilling platform, its polished surface completely bare except for a computer terminal.

"That's what I hear."

Chris wondered how Pettigrew had heard that, but he let it pass. The legal grapevine at work, undoubtedly. Pettigrew was saying, "I thought we were dealing with a serial killer. The notorious TLC. What a cruel joke those initials are!" The senior partner shook his head. "His, ah, 'activities' have been in the headlines for months. He seems to be leading the police on a merry chase, I must say," he added, a glint of malice in his eyes, deeply set in pouches of flesh. "You'll forgive me, but I can't help feeling that if you had managed to catch the killer, my brilliant partner would be alive."

And billing up a storm, Chris thought sardonically. Aloud, he said, "The evidence does seem to point to a serial killer, but we have to explore every avenue. We would be remiss otherwise."

"I understand. So you want to know about the files she was working on?" Pettigrew swiveled his chair around to face the computer and clicked on the mouse. "There they are. Only five, as you can see. But big. Very big."

Gwen made a note of the names while Chris walked over to the desk and peered at the screen. Not surprisingly, they were all oil companies. This was Calgary, after all. "Can you tell us something about them?" he asked.

"Certainly. Ensign Petroleums is engaged in merger negotiations with another company. The next one, Premium Resources, is fighting off a hostile takeover bid. Madison Energy is about to come out with a new share issue; an oil sands consortium is selling its interest to China's national oil company; and Pegasus Energy is folding natural gas properties into an income trust. As I said, she had a full dance card.

Fortunately, we have adequate bench strength in the department to take over."

"Energy trusts are really dominating the stock market these days."

"And they will continue to do so. It's a way for a company to realize on its assets and make them available for distribution to the unit holders."

"It also means those funds are no longer available to explore for oil and gas."

"True. The industry is maturing. There's no doubt about that." Pettigrew shot Chris a speculative glance, as though somewhat surprised by his comment. Then, as if suddenly remembering something, he smiled. "You're the lawyer, aren't you? I missed the connection at first. I've heard of you."

Still looking at the computer screen, Chris said, "The Madison share issue should be well received by the market. Their shares have been hot ever since the Lost Horse field came on stream."

If Chris hadn't been standing so close to Pettigrew he would have missed the sharp intake of his breath. Without moving his head, he shot a quick downward glance at the seated lawyer. A nerve jumped in Pettigrew's flushed cheek, twisting his lips in an involuntary grimace.

"Something wrong?"

"No, no. I was just thinking that I will have to take on that file myself. We have already lost a couple of days."

It was more than that. Things could change rapidly in the oil patch. Fortunes made and lost overnight. Madison Energy could stand a little close examination. Although it was hard to see what connection it could have to the Vinney woman's murder. Chris mentally congratulated himself that there were no Madison shares in his portfolio. He had thought of buying some when the news of the Lost Horse discovery first broke, but the share price had risen so quickly that he figured the potential for profit had been squeezed out of it already.

A few months later he'd had another chance to invest in Madison. Jack Adams, his main stockbroker, had contacted him, recommending an issue of Madison flow-through shares. With flow-through shares, a company that already had sufficient credits to offset its taxes renounced the tax deductions earned by exploring for oil and gas in favour of the shareholder. Chris could have used the tax credits but was put off by the year's hold on selling the shares. Many companies required the owner of this class of shares to hold them for a certain period of time before they could be sold. A lot of things could happen to an oil company in the space of a year, good or bad. A few weeks later, Chris had been able to acquire flow-through shares in another oil company that did not impose a mandatory hold period.

"This share issue that Madison is making. What can you tell us about it?"

Pettigrew seemed surprised by the question, and something else — uncomfortable? "It's a normal course issue to raise twenty million dollars of new equity to fund the company's ongoing operations. Routine, really. It's received all necessary regulatory approvals."

"So it's a done deal?"

"Yes. For all practical purposes. Twenty million is not what you would call a big deal. Quite modest, in fact. By way of comparison, the Pegasus Energy Trust, which Adrienne was also handling, involves over five hundred million."

He was being steered away from Madison. Why? More to watch Pettigrew's reaction than anything else, Chris asked, "I know about Lost Horse, of course. Everybody in the oil patch does. Does Madison have any other oil and gas production?"

"Not to speak of. A few odds and ends. Minor working interests in some pretty marginal fields. But they've just acquired some Crown acreage up in the Peace River Arch. That's what the twenty million is for. To explore the potential of their Peace River play."

"That's still in the initial stages, I take it. Have they shot seismic over the lands?"

"Not yet. That's next on their agenda. Three-D seismic. They're very bullish on the play. They keep talking about a granite wash, whatever that means. It's beyond a simple lawyer like me."

It might have been beyond Pettigrew, which Chris rather doubted, but it wasn't beyond him. Back in the Devonian geologic age, more than 300 million years ago, huge upthrust blocks of granite were exposed to the surface. They were split, cracked, and fractured by the forces of erosion, and the pieces were washed down the mountainsides by water, hence the name granite wash. Over eons the broken shards were overlaid with other formations and were — what was the word? — lithified into stone; with their cracks and fissures they made excellent reservoir rock to trap petroleum as it migrated to the surface. But all he said was, "That's good to hear. With the revenue generated by their production from Lost Horse, plus twenty million in new money, they won't have to go looking for partners to work up their Peace River play."

"That's right." Pettigrew's response was restrained.

Knowing it was out of line, but wanting to probe further, Chris asked, "Should I pick up some of this new issue?"

"C'mon, Detective. You know perfectly well I can't answer that."

"Sorry. I guess I got carried away. Okay, let me ask you about Ms. Vinney's social life. Outside the office."

"I doubt if she had one. We're all pretty dedicated to

our work in this shop, but none of us could keep up with her. You wouldn't believe the hours she put in." Visibly more at ease, Pettigrew added, "I thought this tragedy was the work of that serial killer. A random act, if you will. I *do* know that one of her extracurricular activities was running. Unlike some of us" — this with a rueful glance down at his own too-generous waistline — "she was very fit. Isn't it likely that her killer saw her when she was out for a run and pounced?"

"Her body was found in Edworthy Park, and she lived in Eau Claire. Not exactly walking distance."

"She could have driven to the park. Maybe she wanted to run there for a change. I'm told it's quite scenic."

"Her Mercedes was still in the underground parkade of her condo building."

"That puts paid to that doesn't it? Was she dressed for running when she was found? Shorts, running shoes, that sort of thing?"

"I'm afraid we can't divulge that information just yet. You understand."

"Of course." Pettigrew shot back the French cuff of his striped shirt to look at his watch. "If that's all, I'm due to meet a client for lunch at the Ranchmen's Club. Running a bit late as it is."

Chris looked at Gwen and nodded. She closed her notebook and they both stood up. Handing the lawyer his card, Chris said, "You can reach me there if anything occurs to you. One more thing," he added. "Would you have a word with Mr. Ingram and tell him it's all right to talk freely to us? At the moment, he's hung up on solicitor-client privilege."

"As he should be. I'll speak to him, but you must realize that solicitor-client confidentiality is a cornerstone of the legal profession. It's not something to be lightly put aside."

"I appreciate that. Just as I want you and Mr. Ingram to appreciate that this is a murder case."

"You can be sure that Pettigrew's instructions to his junior will be very carefully worded," Chris remarked to Gwen as they rode the elevator down to the ground floor.

"They don't have to talk to us if they don't want to," Gwen replied as the doors slid open and they stepped out.

"Nobody does," Chris replied. "Well, you've seen the distinguished Mr. Pettigrew in action. What do you think?"

"He's concerned about something. That's obvious. But it may have nothing to do with the murder."

"You could well be right," Chris agreed gloomily. "For that matter, the fact that the cross is on the right hand instead of the left may not mean anything either. A cross is still a cross, as Steve would have it."

"There's still the matter of the breast implants," Gwen pointed out. "We know TLC hates them. But Vinney's weren't touched."

"The profiler will have a field day with that one. Let's duck into Earl's for a quick lunch. I'm buying."

"I understand that Mr. Pettigrew has talked to you and authorized you to speak freely about the files you handled with Ms. Vinney?" It was mid-afternoon, allowing time for Pettigrew to return from lunch and confer with his junior.

"That's right," Ingram replied guardedly, not meeting Chris's eyes. Chris and Gwen exchanged glances. It was clear that the junior lawyer was on a tight leash. He was nervously eyeing the open notebook Gwen was holding in her left hand.

"You appreciate that the information you can give us is very important?"

"Not really. I can't see any connection between it and Adrienne being killed the way she was."

"We're the best judges of that. It's just a process of eliminating possibilities, getting them out of the way, so to speak. So we can concentrate on more promising leads," said Chris, using a strategy that often helped make witnesses more forthcoming. It wasn't having that effect on Ingram, however. He remained as uptight and tense as before.

"Mr. Pettigrew told us that Ms. Vinney had five major files on the go." Maybe it would help if Ingram thought the senior partner had been open with the police.

"Maybe. I only worked on two of them. She never said anything about the others. She wouldn't."

"Professional discretion, eh?"

"That's right. She was very keen on that. She lectured on legal ethics at the law school."

"Did she? That's pretty impressive." Robyn would be taking that course at some point. Usually ethics wasn't taught until the third year, so she wouldn't have reached it yet. "Which two files were you working on?"

"The Pegasus Energy Trust and the Madison share issue."

"What can you tell us about them?"

"The Pegasus deal is mega!" For the first time Ingram showed some animation. "Five hundred million dollars! We've had to satisfy stock exchanges and security commissions here in Alberta and in Toronto and New York, not to mention the SEC. You wouldn't believe how picky they can be. The SEC sent our application back three times. We're still working on it."

"They've been spooked ever since those corporate scandals blew up on them a few years back."

"Yeah." For a brief moment Ingram looked at Chris like one professional to another, but his guarded look returned when the detective brought up the subject of the Madison share issue.

"Pretty straightforward," he muttered with a half-hearted shrug that didn't quite come off.

"When is it due to come out?"

"By the end of the week, I expect."

"With a Peace River Arch play on top of the Lost Horse discovery, it's bound to be a hot seller."

"Yeah."

"Is there anything you're not telling us about this? Anything we should know?"

"No. Like I say, it's pretty straightforward. Run of the mill. Anyway ..."

"Anyway what?"

"Nothing."

"That's all you're going to tell us?"

"There's nothing to tell."

Chris glared at him, then shot Gwen an exasperated look. There was nothing more he could do at this point in time, and Ingram knew it. It wouldn't only be Pettigrew who had talked to him. McKinley had a criminal law department so it could hold itself out as a full service law firm. Pettigrew would have brought along an experienced criminal lawyer to advise Ingram on how far he was legally required to go in cooperating with the police investigation. Which was precisely nowhere.

"I believe you are withholding something from us." Chris's tone was formal as he and Gwen stood up to leave. "If it turns out that you have been, things will go hard for you."

"I'll take my chances," Ingram replied with a touch of defiance and more confidence than he had shown in their earlier meeting.

"I hate it when that happens," Gwen muttered fiercely when they exited from Bankers Hall onto the Stephen Avenue Mall. "When people clam up on us and refuse to answer questions that could help our investigation."

"I wouldn't have it any other way."

"Your horse is calling you," Gwen said with something close to a giggle as the opening notes of *Valencia* suddenly rang out. Valencia was the name of the chestnut mare that had been Chris's best show jumper, and he had a snippet of the song installed as the ring tone of his cellphone.

He grinned back at Gwen as he answered. "Crane here."

It was Dummett, wanting to know if there had been any response from TLC to his story.

"Not so far as I know," Chris told him. "I've been out all day interviewing people, so there might be something back at the office. If there is, I'll let you know. Anyways, it's early days yet."

But apart from a number of voice mail messages, all that was waiting for Chris on the tenth floor was Madison Energy's annual report. He had asked Jack Adams to send over a copy. He put it to one side to take home.

chapter five

Nevermore was perched on top of his cage when Chris got home. The cage door dangled from one hinge. He ruffled his feathers and cocked his head to stare at his owner, half-defiantly, half-triumphantly, with a bright yellow eye. His belated "Hello, Chris" made Chris smile indulgently.

"So, you finally succeeded!" he congratulated the bird. Nevermore had been entertaining himself for days working with his beak on the nuts and bolts that held the cage together. "All those toys I bought you weren't enough, were they? You want to expand your empire. Well, I can understand that," he added as he carried Nevermore over to his perch.

Nevermore's dismantling of his cage was amusing, not to say impressive. But he couldn't be left loose in the penthouse while it was empty during the day. He could do too much damage. Especially to himself. The penthouse was full of hazards for an inquisitive parrot. And there was Cassie. The parrot and the cleaning lady did not get along. Psittacine birds were notorious for preferring either men or women. Usually, although not always, it was sex linked, with male birds preferring women and vice versa. It was one way of determining the sex of those species of parrot where male and female were identical in appearance. African Greys were known to be more tolerant in this regard than any other parrot species. Nevermore, for instance, positively doted on Angie, the lady from Petcare who looked after him when Chris was out of town. But Cassie brought out the worst in him. It was probably the noise of the vacuum cleaner.

After dinner he would go down to the storage locker where he kept a toolbox and dig out a screwdriver and needle-nose pliers. He would tighten the nuts as much as he could, but that would only slow Nevermore down, not stop him. Maybe there was some kind of non-toxic glue that would cement the nuts in place.

Mixing the one pre-dinner martini he permitted himself, Chris realized the parrot's antics had given him a much-needed break from the Vinney murder. It never hurt to let the brain lie fallow for a spell. Putting a disc by Sonata on the CD player, he settled back with his drink. Music lovers still raved about the concert she had given at the Epcor Centre more than three years ago. Sonata was one of Nevermore's favourites, and he chittered quietly to himself as the music filled the room.

There was a photo of Adrienne along with a brief obituary in the classified pages of the *Herald*. The black-and-white photo did full justice to her beauty, highlighting the to-die-for cheekbones, expressive eyes, and wide, slashing smile. Her life spanned thirty-seven years; her mother was listed as her only living relative. There was no mention of it in the obituary, but inquiries made by the police revealed that her mother suffered from

Alzheimer's and lived in a Halifax nursing home. According to the obituary, Adrienne had died suddenly on Monday, May 26. Now there was a euphemism for you! Funeral arrangements were to be announced. That, Chris knew, would depend on when the medical examiner's office released the body.

Placing the obituary page face up on the coffee table, Chris turned his attention to Madison Energy's annual report. First he read the President's Report, traditionally a summary of the past year's activities with a forecast of things to come. As expected, Madison's CEO was upbeat, hailing the rapid development of the Lost Horse field that had been discovered some eighteen months earlier. Wells in the Alberta Foothills were deep and expensive, but they were also extremely prolific if they encountered oil — some producing more than 2,500 barrels of oil per day. It was an incredible bonanza for a comparatively small company like Madison, and the annual report made the most of it.

Nevermore paused his attack on his favourite toy — a dried coconut shell stuffed with nuts, hanging from the top of his cage — as Chris, briefcase in hand, repeated the words "Goodbye, Chris" four times. The parrot, head cocked to one side, listened intently. It wouldn't be long before he mastered the phrase, which would sound a great deal better than, "Sorry, Nevermore."

Walking north in bright morning sunshine along 4th Street, Chris found his thoughts still occupied by Madison Energy and the Lost Horse discovery. What a thrill it must have been when that wildcat came in! Especially since Madison was still a start-up company just getting underway. He himself participated in the oil patch by owning shares in oil and gas companies, but that was one stage removed from actually getting in there and exploring for the stuff. Maybe someday ...

As the stacked glass cubes of the aggressively modern Municipal Building came into view beyond the leafy screen of the Olympic Plaza poplars these pleasant musings were abruptly displaced by more urgent ones of the serial killings. Putting the Vinney murder aside for the moment, he concentrated on the first three attacks. They were pretty clearly thrill killings, with no apparent motive other than sadistic fantasies. Unlike many multiple killings, the victims were not prostitutes. Maybe the killer was astute enough to realize that the lurid history of streetwalkers being tortured and killed and buried in pig farms or dumped in farmers' fields must have increased police surveillance of their favourite strolls. Or more likely this killer just wanted game that was more challenging, more exciting.

The first victim had been in her mid-twenties, a legal assistant in the law department of an oil company. Seating himself at his desk, Chris first dealt with his phone messages, including two from brokers, then called up her file on the computer. Even making allowances for it being a morgue photo, it was clear that Myra Frazier had been no beauty. But she had been definitely, and amply, female. Her breasts, the right one displaying a dark wound where the nipple should be, were splayed across her chest, and the triangle of pubic hair was dense and dark above fleshy thighs still stained with dried blood. She had been the first of the park murders, her mutilated body having been discovered not far from a pathway in Nose Hill Park.

The killer made no effort to hide the bodies; if anything, he displayed them. At first, Chris had wondered if this indicated a desire on the killer's part to be caught. That was not uncommon among serial killers. Then he concluded that it was probably a reflection of the killer's overweening self-confidence, a gauntlet thrown at the feet of the investigators.

"Awful, isn't it?" Unannounced, Gwen had come over to stand at Chris's side and was looking down at the screen that now showed the second victim, Elizabeth Livens, a sales clerk at Holt Renfrew. She had been mutilated in the same fashion as the Frazier woman. Like the others, her hands were folded piously on her abdomen as if she were at peace. It was obscene. Chris scrolled down and clicked on the name of the third victim, Theresa Thompson. There could be no doubt but that all three were the work of the same sadistic brute. Sickened, he looked away from the screen and glanced up at Gwen.

"I thought you'd be interested in this," she said. "I just heard from a friend of mine at the courthouse that the Harris jury has come back in."

"And?"

"And nothing. The foreperson told the judge that they haven't been able to reach a verdict, and she doesn't think they will be able to."

"What did the judge do?"

"Told them to keep trying."

"Good psychology on her part. Today is Friday, and being sequestered over the weekend should help them concentrate."

"Like knowing you are to be hanged in a fortnight," said Gwen, blithely paraphrasing Samuel Johnson.

"Not exactly," Chris said, grinning in reply. "I go along with most of the crusty old lexicographer's sayings, but I've never bought that one. For my part, I think the prospect of being hanged in a fortnight would make it impossible to concentrate. You really couldn't think of much else."

After a solitary lunch at the Hyatt, Chris was back at his desk, still brooding about the multiple killings. He was convinced that the first three were the work of the same individual, almost certainly acting alone. But the Vinney case? The modus operandi seemed to be the same — the victim had not been killed where the body was found, she had been rendered unconscious before being mutilated, and the mutilation pattern was the same. Except for the untouched breast implants. And the cross. Like the others, it was identical in design to the one used to crucify Christ. Everyone's idea of what a cross looked like. But it was on the wrong hand. Maybe that didn't matter. Maybe what was really bothering him was the victim herself — a high-profile lawyer responsible for important and complex files. Maybe the killer just wanted to up the ante. Or maybe, as Mason kept insisting, he had seen her out jogging and couldn't resist. Chris had switched off the computer and was staring into space, a light frown creasing his forehead, when the telephone rang.

"Forget everything you read in Madison's annual report," Jack Adams said when Chris answered. "They've just come out with a press release as soon as the market closed."

The stock market closed at two o'clock, and it was two-thirty now. Jack hadn't wasted any time in calling him. That must be some press release!

"It's a disaster!" Jack's voice was hushed. "I'll fax the release to you, but the gist of it is that the Lost Horse field has watered out."

"What?" Chris was thunderstruck. Oil fields eventually *did* go to water as they were produced and the reservoir pressure dropped, letting salt water from the ancient inland sea that once covered Alberta flow into the well bore. It was called "coning" in the oil patch, and it normally happened only after years of profitable production as a reservoir was gradually depleted, certainly not after just over a year.

"It's true. It's all in the press release. The carnage when the market opens Monday morning will be appalling. I've got to hang up now, Chris. I've got a bunch of calls to make. Calls I dread making. There will be some very unhappy shareholders out there. One hell of a way to start the weekend."

"Before you go, what happened to the stock today?"

"Nothing unusual. It closed at $18.52, down ten cents for the day. Four thousand shares traded, which is pretty much the normal pattern. But the shit will hit the fan on Monday!"

Would it ever! The carnage awaiting the Madison shareholders when the market opened on Monday would be awful. Horrendous. If anything, the press release Jack faxed over to him was worse than what he had told Chris over the phone. The three wells Madison had drilled and put on production had turned to water almost overnight. In the eighteen months or so since the discovery Madison had drilled two stepout wells. The stepouts were located two miles apart to delineate the extent of the reservoir with the expectation of drilling infill wells to fully exploit the potential of the field. There would be no more wells. Only the cost of abandoning the initial wells to add to the millions of dollars already spent.

Chris read the fax a second time before putting it down on his desk, bemused to find himself treating it gingerly, as if it might explode in his face. He paused for a moment to absorb an almost giddy sense of relief that he was not personally involved in the debacle. It had been so close. But those poor devils who were long on the stock! His copy of the *Herald* was back in the penthouse, but Gwen always brought the paper with her to work. She wasn't at her desk, but the paper was. Chris picked up the paper, pulled out the business section, and turned to the stock quotations. Madison had closed yesterday at $18.62, with a trading volume of 6,982 shares. And Jack had said today's trades were normal.

He had come awfully close to investing in the Madison flow-through shares. They had come out at $10.25 and had climbed steadily up into $18.00 territory. Chris had kept his eye on the stock and more than once regretted the handsome profit he had foregone. He had comforted himself with the fact that the shares had been encumbered with that long hold. Twelve months before they were free to trade; too long to have money tied up with no control over what happened to it. The twelve months must be up by now; it had been sometime last spring that Jack had told him about the upcoming share issue. Could that explain the evasiveness he had encountered at McKinley?

Chris flipped through the annual report, now outdated and rendered meaningless by the Lost Horse disaster. As expected, there were no details of the flow-through shares nor any conditions attached to them. The report contained little other than glowing accounts of Lost Horse. Jack would know when the hold period expired, but there was no point in trying to reach him now. He would be working the phones, spreading the unthinkable news. He would call Jack at home in the evening. That would be a bit of an intrusion into his personal life, but the broker would overlook that. Chris and Jack were not close personal friends, beyond an occasional lunch, but Chris was a preferred client. Besides, the circumstances were extraordinary.

The door of the cage was still in place when Chris arrived home that evening. Nevermore was squatting on the floor, dismantling a collection of wooden blocks and bells braided through a strip of leather. The blocks were chewed until they were mere splinters, and the bells were strewn around the floor. The breeders had told Chris that a destroyed toy is an enjoyed toy. If that was the case, Nevermore certainly enjoyed his toys. Chris chuckled to himself as his avian pet, well satisfied with the day's work, climbed onto his hand.

Chris waited until eight o'clock before calling Jack. By then, the broker would have finished dinner. It was also obvious from his slurred speech that he had finished off more than a few drinks. Chris didn't blame him; he would have put in a soul-searing afternoon.

"Everything about that damn stock is burned into my mind in letters of fire," Jack growled, in answer to Chris's query. "The hold period expired at the close of business last Monday, May 26."

That meant that the shares were free to trade on Tuesday, May 27, which was what Chris wanted to know, but he continued to chat for a few more minutes, commiserating with Jack for having to be the bearer of bad tidings, before ringing off. If the broker wondered about Chris's interest, he didn't mention it. Maybe he figured that Chris had bought some of the shares through another house.

Adrienne Vinney's memorial service was to be held on Monday, June 2, at 1:30 p.m. at a funeral home on Elbow Drive. Folding Saturday's *Herald* and placing it on the breakfast table, Chris decided he would attend.

He would also arrange to have a police photographer with a video camera tape the mourners as they arrived. He had never given much weight to the theory that killers often attended the funeral of their victims, but one never knew. While the parrot supervised from his stand, Chris went about his regular Sunday morning chore of cleaning Nevermore's cage and re-arranging the toys — the breeders had assured him that this would help keep the bird from becoming bored. The familiar routine left him free to think. If someone who was obviously out of place showed up, that could provide a lead worth following. Even if there were two killers, one of them might make an appearance for some twisted purpose of his own. He decided to assign a woman detective who had never been part of the investigation to attend the service.

At four-thirty Sunday afternoon, Chris placed another call to Jack Adams. The broker sounded clear-headed and crisp as he answered.

"I know your phone will be ringing off the hook tomorrow," said Chris, "but I need to know what happens to Madison when the market opens."

"You need to know, Chris? Are you a shareholder? Or" — he paused — "is this Chris Crane the police officer?"

"I am not a shareholder. If I had decided to pick up some Madison shares, I would have done it through you. You're the expert on that company."

"Don't rub it in," Jack groaned.

"Sorry. What do you expect to happen tomorrow?"

"The Exchange will call a halt to trading in the stock to give people time to absorb the news and decide what they're going to do."

"How long do you figure the halt will last?"

"Not more than half an hour, I expect. The news

will have been pretty well disseminated over the weekend in any case."

"Then what happens?"

"Well, the market opens at seven-thirty. If we assume the trading halt lasts for thirty minutes, the bloodletting will begin at eight. It will be a slaughter. It's not as if Madison had any other significant assets to fall back on. Their other producing interests are strictly nickel and dime. Plus a mountain of debt."

"How do I get through to you on the phone?"

Jack paused before replying. "Place your call at eight-fifteen. I'll be on the phone, but Lorna, my assistant, knows your voice and she'll put you through.

"It's terrible, Mr. Crane. Just terrible." Lorna's voice was subdued, almost awestruck. "Jack is expecting your call. Hang on."

"Madison is now a penny stock, Chris. The last trade was at ninety-eight cents. Not even the vultures are buying."

"You don't sound surprised."

"I'm not. Take away Lost Horse and that's what Madison is — a penny stock."

"What about the Peace River Arch play they were hyping?"

"Forget it. There's no way they could finance it. Not after this. It's a disaster. Plain and simple."

"Yeah. I'll let you go now, Jack. Thanks."

Chris was thoughtful as the phone conversation ended. Jack had sounded awfully down. That was understandable in the circumstances. But he was a professional, and Madison was just one stock, one of the many he traded on behalf of his clients. What had befallen the Madison shares should have been all in a day's work to him. Regrettable, of course, but the sort of thing that happened from time to time. Unless. Unless he had become a believer in his own sales pitch.

The trading in Madison shares for Thursday and Friday of last week had been in the normal course. But what about Tuesday, when the hold period had expired? The main branch of the Calgary public library was just a couple of blocks away. It would just take a moment to walk over there and check out the Toronto Stock Exchange listings in the Wednesday and Thursday papers. The quotations in Wednesday's *Herald* for the previous day's trades showed an opening price of $17.80, a high of $18.01, and a close of $17.93. Essentially unchanged. But the volume! 102,000 shares had changed hands. More than ten times the normal volume, with a dollar value in excess of 1.8 million. Wednesday's volume of 12,700 shares was higher than usual, but not by that much. It could be completely innocent, of course — nothing more than shareholders who had used the tax credit taking advantage of their first opportunity to sell and free up some capital.

Back at his desk, Chris placed another call to Jack, using Lorna's good offices to get through to him. There was a perceptible pause on the other end of the line when Chris requested the identity of the sellers in Tuesday's trades.

"That information is confidential, Chris. You know that."

"No big deal, Jack. I just thought it was something you would know." No use in pressing the matter. Not now. Jack had a valid point and knew it. Still, it was interesting that the normally accommodating broker had clammed up. And he was the one who would know. He had been the principal marketer of the flow-throughs, so normally the shares would be lodged in client accounts held in trust by his brokerage house. Anyone wanting to sell the shares would have to do it through him or his firm. Unless the seller held the share certificate in his or her own name. But that was unlikely.

chapter six

There was no coffin. The printed program, with the same photograph of Adrienne as in the obituary on the cover, made it clear that this was a memorial service, not a funeral. The remains were to be returned to Halifax for burial in the family plot. Chris knew the medical examiner was due to release them tomorrow. He and Gwen seated themselves toward the rear of the hall, half filled with mourners. Chris judged them to be almost entirely members of the legal profession. In the front row a woman wearing a dark wool dress that looked too warm for the late spring weather sobbed quietly into a handkerchief. Chris recognized her as Adrienne's legal assistant, whom he had met while having his unsatisfactory interviews with Jeff Ingram. Jeff was seated across the aisle from her, beside Morris Pettigrew on the aisle. The McKinley firm was out in force. There had been an ad in the paper that the firm was closed for the day out of respect for their late esteemed partner.

Tom Forsyth was looking back over his shoulder to catch Chris's eye. They exchanged nods and subdued waves. There was no sign of Scott Millard. The Harris jury was still out and the defence lawyer must have felt compelled to stay within reach of the courthouse. Chris thought that if it were him, he would have come to a different decision. This train of thought led him to remark on how few purely social friends were there. Contemporaries she might have known and socialized with. The price of her fierce dedication to her career.

The organist finished playing the last notes of a Bach fugue, and Morris Pettigrew rose from his seat and proceeded to the lectern. "Adrienne was not a religious person," he began, speaking into the microphone, "but I know it would be a comfort for all of us to join in singing that beloved old hymn, 'Unto the Hills.'"

When the congregation was once more seated, he delivered a short and moving eulogy, dwelling on Adrienne's love for the law and her devotion to it. He concluded by saying that he could only speak about the Adrienne they knew since she had arrived in Calgary a few years ago, and now he would call on Ian Carmichael, a childhood and college friend of hers from Halifax, who had flown out to be with them today.

A tall, strikingly handsome man in his thirties took Pettigrew's place at the lectern. "Adrienne and I grew up together," he began. "I first saw those blond pigtails in grade three, and we were classmates from then on. She was always the class sweetheart, and it wasn't just because of her looks. She was friendly and outgoing, and excelled at sports, particularly track and field. In her last year of high school she was the class president and was voted the most popular student. It was in law school that she really came into her own." Carmichael paused as if to collect himself.

"He's still in love with her," Gwen whispered to Chris.

"Adrienne loved the law," Carmichael continued. "From the very first she was at home in it, intellectually and philosophically. So much so that she was the gold medallist in her graduating year. I know that you, her Calgary friends and associates, are fully aware of her love for the law and her aptitude for it. As in high school, she continued to be immensely popular. In her sophomore year she was elected Monroe Day Queen, and that, let me assure you, is a very big honour at Dalhousie."

As he carried on for a few more minutes with his glowing tributes, Gwen again whispered to Chris, "If that guy is married it's a good thing his wife isn't here to listen to this." Chris nodded, his attention focused on Carmichael's concluding remarks.

"If any one of Adrienne's sterling qualities stood out more than the rest, it was her integrity. I remember one incident in particular. At the end of our graduating year in high school we were writing the provincials — exams set by the government. A friend of hers had provided Adrienne with a copy of the questions from several years back, and she had distributed them to some of her chums, including me, to help us prepare for the finals. When the exam questions were handed out, we were astounded to discover they were identical, word for word, to those in the copy Adrienne had been given. Some of us lesser mortals might have treated it as a gift from the gods, but it was too much for Adrienne's sense of fair play, and she immediately brought it to the attention of the instructor, and the exam was rescheduled with a new set of questions."

So Adrienne was a whistle-blower. Interesting, possibly significant, thought Chris as Carmichael ended his remarks with a graceful little comment about how much Adrienne would be missed, both here in Calgary and back in her home town.

On behalf of Adrienne's friends and associates in the firm, Pettigrew invited everyone to a reception at the Calgary Golf and Country Club, just up the street, and the mourners got to their feet to sing a final hymn. They remained standing when it ended, preparing to leave, until the strains of a bagpipe froze them in place. A kilted piper marched through an open doorway and stood at the front of the hall, marking time while he played a stirring Highland march. Then he did a slow march down the aisle, followed by Pettigrew, Ian Carmichael, and the rest of the mourners.

A small knot of onlookers, including a TV cameraman and reporter, plus some members of the press, stood outside as the crowd filed out into the sunlight. Chris saw the TV camera zooming in on him and Gwen but no questions were shouted at them as they walked to their van. The fact that the police had attended the memorial service for TLC's latest victim would be on the six o'clock news.

The entrance gate to the golf club was at the end of a short cul-de-sac extending west from the intersection of Elbow Drive and 50th Avenue where the funeral home was located. Ken Patterson and another Homicide detective were sitting in an unmarked police cruiser parked with other vehicles on the curb in front of a balconied apartment block. Chris carefully avoided looking at them as he drove past. A security guard standing inside a little watchtower made of dark Rundle stone waved the line of cars through. A driveway curved down to the clubhouse through lush fairways and greens dotted with golfers and golf carts.

Morris Pettigrew had stationed himself at the head of the staircase to form a one-man reception line. He frowned at the sight of Chris, and he hesitated before accepting the detective's proffered hand. "I saw you at the service," he said. The inference that the police had no business being there was clear. "I trust you will remember this is a wake for a dear and valued friend."

"A dear and *murdered* friend," Chris corrected him quietly, and moved on.

The firm had laid on a lavish spread: canapés, sandwiches, and other delicacies were laid out on damask-covered tables; servers circulated with glasses of champagne and wine and took orders from those who preferred something stronger. Champagne flute in hand, Ian Carmichael stood by the concert grand, shaking hands and greeting people in a sort of informal second reception committee. Chris and Gwen declined an offer of champagne from a passing server and joined the line-up waiting to have a word with the visitor from Halifax.

"I'm Detective Chris Crane and this is Constable Staroski," Chris said as their turn came to greet Carmichael. "We're investigating Ms. Vinney's murder. We would appreciate a word with you."

"Of course," Carmichael replied, not missing a beat. Putting down his empty champagne flute, he followed the two detectives over to the floor-length windows overlooking the first tee.

"I'm not sure how I can help, but I am anxious to do whatever I can. I can still hardly bring myself to accept the fact that she is gone."

"It was clear from the way you spoke, sir, that you and the victim were lifelong friends. Your remarks were very touching, if I may say so."

"Thank you. It was a task I could have done without."

"'Scotland the Brave' was a great send-off for her, being from Nova Scotia."

Carmichael brightened momentarily. "You recognized the tune? Good for you! It was her favourite. That's the first thing I did when I arrived here — arrange for a piper. Adrienne was an outstanding piper herself, but nobody out here seems to know that."

"She played the bagpipes?"

"Superbly. She was the pipe major of an all-girl pipe band that travelled all over North America giving concerts. But the people I've talked to out here have never heard of her playing the pipes. I find it hard to believe that she would give them up just like that."

"Maybe she would go up to the mountains to play them."

"You think so? That's a wonderful thought! That's what I will tell myself she did. Thank you."

"I was particularly struck by what you said about her integrity. I got the impression it was at the core of her being? That business of the exams was very revealing, I thought."

"That was classic Adrienne. Miss Integrity. Everything had to be above-board with her. That's just the way she was." Carmichael broke off to gaze out at the dauntingly steep fairway, a fond little smile on his lips. The smile quickly faded as reality came flooding back. Without looking at Chris he said, "I'm sort of curious about why you're asking questions like this. Adrienne was the victim of a serial killer. A case of being in the wrong place at the wrong time, as I understand it. I don't quite see how her personality enters into it."

"Serial murders are not quite as random as people think. The killer enjoys the process of selecting his victim. He will study her habits, often stalking and watching her for days. Some of them kill when the urge comes upon them, of course. But others like to know their victim, however vicariously."

"Jesus! The thought of her being stalked like that makes me ill to my stomach." He turned to face the detective and said, "I have a question of my own. The impression I get from you who only knew her here in Calgary is very different from the Adrienne I knew. She appears to have done nothing but work, no outside interests, no extracurricular activities. Just work."

Not quite accurate. Chris kept the thought to himself as he spotted Scott Millard in conversation with Tom Forsyth. The criminal lawyer must have arrived while he was talking to Carmichael. "We both know how demanding the legal profession can be," he said to the Halifax lawyer. "Especially in a factory like McKinley. She made partner in record time, I'm told. You would have to be pretty single-minded to achieve a goal like that."

Nodding in the direction of a small group of people over by the piano, chatting among themselves and obviously waiting for a chance to speak to Carmichael, Chris said, "I'll let you go now," and handed him his card. As always, it made him feel like an insurance salesman. "But if you can think of anything, anything at all, that might be helpful, give me a call. And I would appreciate a call before you leave, in any case."

With a slight downward motion of his hand he signalled Gwen to remain behind and stay close to Carmichael, then walked over to where Tom Forsyth and Scott Millard stood, conversing easily together. "Jury still out?" he asked Millard.

"Hung," the criminal lawyer replied succinctly. "No chance of reaching a verdict, so the judge discharged them."

"That's a bit of a victory for you, I would say."

Millard shrugged. "I guess it is. Considering what we had to work with. But the Crown will lay charges again."

"But you're in the driver's seat now," Forsyth put in. "The hung jury is bound to shake the Crown's confidence."

"They'll work harder next time," Millard replied.

Forsyth laughed. "Knowing you, you'll probably plea bargain him down to not guilty by reason of insanity, and your client will spend his days at some cushy government-financed retreat, playing golf and doing laps in the swimming pool."

"Harris doesn't play golf." Millard grinned. It was obvious that his client would never do hard time. There was a hint of something different in his voice — what? jealousy, perhaps? — as he went on. "Tom tells me that guy you were talking to was a childhood friend of Adrienne's."

"A bit more than that, I think. C'mon. I'll introduce you."

"Wait till I recharge my drink." Scott signalled a server and ordered a double Scotch on the rocks. He was either celebrating the hung jury or winding down from the stress of the trial. Taking a deep swallow of whisky, he followed Chris over to where Carmichael was in conversation with some of the mourners. When he spotted Chris heading toward him, Ian nodded polite agreement to what someone was saying and shifted his attention to the approaching twosome. Chris performed the introductions, then excused himself.

Seemingly absorbed in selecting a sandwich from the lavish array of goodies spread out on a table, Gwen observed the encounter from a distance. It was over by the time she finished a remarkably delicious egg salad sandwich. Face flushed a dangerous red, Millard exchanged his empty glass for a full one and stalked off to rejoin Tom Forsyth. As she reported to Chris, the tension between the two men was immediate, and almost palpable. "That Millard guy was really wound up. He's a lot smaller than Carmichael and seemed determined to make up for it. From the way he was carrying on, you would think he and Vinney had been getting it on until the day she died."

"That's what he would have wanted. Let's go talk to him."

Glass in hand, an agitated Millard was saying something to Forsyth, spitting out the words. Forsyth flinched, but managed not to blink as he was sprayed with saliva. Both Chris and Gwen heard "... some religious pervert ..." before the criminal lawyer became aware of their presence and abruptly stopped talking.

"Who's a religious pervert, Scott?" inquired Chris mildly. "Were you thinking of Adrienne's murderer?"

"It was just talk. Everybody knows most serial killers have fantasies of playing God. Holding their victims' lives in their hands. That kind of crap." Turning away, Millard struck up a conversation with his counterpart in the McKinley firm who had come over to congratulate him on the hung jury.

Murmuring something about having to leave, Forsyth handed his empty wine glass to a passing server and drifted away.

"Religious pervert. Do you suppose he knows about the cross?" asked Gwen in a voice that was almost a whisper.

"It's entirely possible that he does. A highly successful criminal lawyer like him is bound to have informants."

"But the cross is a holdback. Are you saying he has an informant in the police?"

"It wouldn't surprise me. Not the least bit."

Gwen absorbed this in silence for a few minutes, then said, "He's sure soaking up the booze, too. That pretty little Asian server is beginning to look at him kinda strange as he keeps ordering double Scotches."

"Scott's not at his best today." Millard would bear watching this afternoon. For his own protection. Because of the memorial service there would be a heavy police presence in the area, and they would be only too pleased to charge the defence lawyer with impaired driving. Scott was about to commit another *faux pas*. Placing his empty glass on a nearby table, he took out his cellphone and was about to dial when a shocked maître d' rushed up. Cellphones were taboo on the club premises. Millard looked at her as if he were about to protest, then pocketed the phone with a snarl.

It was time to intervene. "Hey, Scott, how did you get here? Did you drive or come by taxi?"

"Drove." Millard was instantly alert.

"The police are out in force today. It might be better if I gave you a lift home. You okay with that? Gwen and I are about to leave."

"What vehicle are you driving?"

"Not to worry. It's one of our unmarked vans. You know what they look like. Nobody associates them with the police."

As they reached the top of the driveway, where he stopped to let a foursome play through, Chris said in mock reproof, "You shouldn't be breaking training like this. First thing you know your squash partner will be beating you."

"Tom? He won't be my partner for long. He's packing in the law, and he and Madge are moving to a tax shelter in the Caribbean. Barbados, the last I heard. Madge has been down there for a couple of weeks, scouting out a place for them to buy."

"Tom Forsyth packing it in? He's never mentioned it to me. Not that there's any reason why he should. I didn't realize he had that kind of money."

"He never talks about it." Millard sat up in the passenger seat. He seemed to have shaken off the effect of the whisky he had consumed and was obviously relishing the story he was about to tell. "I wouldn't have known about it except that the ranch foreman consulted one of my partners who does civil litigation. He wanted to sue for wrongful dismissal. Just drop me somewhere downtown where I can grab a cab," he said as they turned off Elbow Drive onto 8th Street.

"Wouldn't think of it," Chris, his curiosity fully aroused, told him. "Where do you live?"

"In the northwest. I have a condo near the university. It's completely out of your way."

"No problem." Chris exchanged glances with Gwen in the rear-view mirror. It would give them lots of time to hear what Millard had to say. "What's a ranch foreman who's lost his job got to do with Tom?"

"The ranch in question belonged to Tom's family. Been in it for generations, I gather. Like all these outfits, it had a name — Crooked Tree Ranch, something like that. I can't remember exactly." Crooked Tree? The Taylor ranch was called Bent Tree. It would seem trees didn't grow all that well out in the foothills. The whimsical thought didn't prevent Chris from hearing Millard say, "I gather the ranch wasn't all that successful, but it survived. When Tom's parents passed on, it was left to him and his sister. She and her husband lived on the ranch and managed it. Until" — Millard paused for effect — "it was annexed by the city in their last land grab. That meant it could be subdivided, and a developer paid top dollar for it."

"Jesus!" Chris breathed. "Do you know how big a spread it was?"

"A quarter section. Sixty-four hectares. I looked it up at the Land Titles office."

"No wonder Tom can afford to pack in the law. Do you know when it was sold?"

"Early last year. Sometime in March." He glanced uneasily over at Chris. "You're probably wondering how I know all this. I was curious, that's all. Knowing Tom as well as I do. I've never mentioned it to him. Not even when he told me about his plans."

"Perfectly natural. I would have done the same." Chris changed lanes as a bus in front of him slowed for some passengers waiting at a bus stop. "When you register a transfer at Land Titles you have to declare the value of the property. Right?" Chris turned it into a question, although he already knew the answer. "So they can assess the registration fee."

"It was an agreement of sale, not a transfer. The purchase price was to be paid in two annual instalments. The title would be transferred only when the second instalment was made."

"What was the purchase price?"

"It was 4.8 million. Thirty thousand an acre. Tom's share is 2.4 million, which should allow him to live comfortably, if he's careful."

And doesn't pay too much in the way of taxes, Chris added to himself.

"Turn off here," Scott directed as they drove north on University Drive. "I'm just at the end of the street." A cement truck was pouring concrete for a walk leading up to the entrance and workers were smoothing out topsoil for a lawn. "I just moved in last week," Scott said as he climbed out and Gwen took his seat. "Like nearly everything else in this town, it's still being unpacked.

Appreciate this, Chris," he raised his hand in a half-salute as they drove off.

"Want to run it up the flagpole?" Gwen asked after they had proceeded in silence for several minutes.

Chris laughed. "Been watching old movies again? I know what you're thinking, but it won't fly. Okay, let's review the bidding."

"Now who's been watching old movies? What we have just learned could be the lead we've been looking for."

"All we've learned is that my good friend Tom Forsyth has come into a nice piece of change."

"Yes, 2.4 million to be precise. With the taxman waiting to grab his share. You always say that good police work involves eliminating possibilities. Let's see if we can eliminate your good friend Mr. Tom Forsyth."

"Okay. Here we go. We know he received a large amount of cash sometime last March. He is knowledge-able about these things, what the securities people call a sophisticated investor, so he would know one of the most effective ways to reduce income taxes is to purchase flow-through shares."

"I know there are such things as flow-through shares, but just how do they work?"

"An oil company that is not liable to pay income taxes, because of deductible expenditures or previous tax losses, issues shares and renounces the tax deductions created by its exploration activities to the shareholders, who can then deduct from their taxable income."

"So Forsyth buys some flow-through shares?"

"We don't know that. But it's not an unreasonable assumption. Tom deals with the same stockbroker as I do, a guy by the name of Jack Adams. Jack was very high on the Madison flow-throughs when they first came out, so, as I say, that's not an unreasonable assumption."

"Let's make it. Then what?"

"The plot begins to thicken. Many companies, in fact most of them, require the owners of their flow-through shares to hold on to them for a period of time, often as much as a year." It wasn't necessary to mention that this was something Chris always avoided when purchasing flow-through shares for his own account.

"Which is why we spent so much time at McKinley, asking all those questions about Madison Energy."

"Correct. The hold period on the Madison shares expired just days before that announcement sent them down the toilet."

"So anyone who sold as soon as the shares were free to trade would be one happy camper?"

"To put it mildly. *Very* mildly."

"Someone must have known what was happening before they came out with that press release. Someone in the know."

"Absolutely. Wells have been known to water out in an amazingly short time, but not overnight."

"Vinney would be one of those who would know. Wouldn't she?"

"Almost certainly. She was working on the prospectus for a new share issue. The Lost Horse field going to water is a material fact that would have to be disclosed." Now there was an understatement!

"Ms. Vinney was famous for her integrity."

"As we have just been told." Chris braked to a sudden stop as a black Lexus ran a red light. Fortunately their speed was reduced to little more than a crawl in the busy and congested Kensington district. "Calgary drivers think a yellow light is a signal to step on the gas," he muttered.

Gwen, who had heard this complaint many times in the past, merely smiled. "We also know that Mrs. Forsyth was away in the Caribbean. Did they have any children?"

"One boy. A young teenager. He's in the East, attending a boarding school."

"So your friend Forsyth is free to come and go as he pleases."

"True. You and I have built a nice theoretical case, Gwen. But it's all based on unproven assumptions with not one iota of evidence linking Forsyth to the Vinney killing. Without evidence, there's no case."

"We haven't been looking for it. Evidence, I mean."

"That's true. Not yet anyhow. We can at least find out if he had a motive. I'll pay a little visit to our broker friend in the morning. He's not been all that forthcoming so far, claiming client confidentiality. But I think I know how to make him co-operate. And then there's the matter of transportation. We know Vinney was moved from the actual murder scene to the park. Forsyth usually lunches at the Petroleum Club, at the community table. Why don't you park outside the club tomorrow at noon and take his picture if he shows up? We'll have someone take it around to the car rental outlets to see if he rented a vehicle, most likely an SUV, at the critical time."

Chris fell silent for a moment to concentrate on a difficult lane change so he could head east on 5th Avenue. That accomplished, he continued in an almost musing tone, "Of course, there's another possibility. How about this? Scott was setting us up. Making us think of Tom Forsyth as a potential suspect."

Gwen almost giggled. "What a delightfully evil mind you have! But aren't they the best of friends?"

"They are. But best friends have been known to betray each other. Maybe he knows Tom has an alibi. Or maybe Scott just had too much to drink."

"Well, that we know for sure."

Chris waited until eight o'clock, when the market would have been open for half an hour and the early rush of trading would have subsided somewhat, before taking the LRT to the low-rise building where Acute Capital was located. Jack was the principal partner of the brokerage house and prided himself on running a no-frills operation. The office reflected that approach. Under a high ceiling with exposed beams and rafters, the space was completely open, with no private offices or cubicles, only rows of desks crowded together. *Like the set-up at Major Crimes*, thought Chris. Phones, their muted rings barely audible, rang constantly. Jack's expression as he shook hands with Chris was an uneasy mixture of the welcome due an important client and wariness.

"Jack, I realize you are troubled over this business of client confidentiality, but this is a murder investigation."

"What murder? As if I didn't know."

"You know all right. The lawyer, Adrienne Vinney. Did you know her?"

Was there a flicker of hesitation on Jack's part before he replied? "I know *of* her, of course. She was well known in financial circles, because of the files she handled."

"Let's cut to the chase, Jack. Last Tuesday, 102,000 shares of Madison traded. Ten times the normal volume."

"Not surprising. It happens every time a stock comes out of hold."

"Understandable. Just give me the names of the sellers."

"You know I can't do that, Chris. Client confidentiality is the cornerstone of this business."

"It looks like you're forcing me to get a search warrant, Jack. That means a police squad will take over your office, go through your records, and question your staff."

It was a bluff. The chances of obtaining a warrant from even the most accommodating judge were almost non-existent on the basis of what they knew. It was all surmise, with no evidence. In fact, Chris couldn't see himself swearing the necessary affidavit to support an application for a warrant. Even old Jepson, a Provincial Court judge notoriously biased in favour of the police, wouldn't buy it. "Maybe a warrant is the best way to go, Jack. Then your clients will know you had no choice."

Jack sighed. "I like you better as a client, Chris. But what can I do? Hang on a minute while I go to the back office and look up the trading summary for May 27."

Minutes later, he returned with a one-page printout. "This is a summary of the day's trades," he said, reluctantly handing the printout to Chris.

T.J. Forsyth was the first name on the list. Tom's middle name was Joseph, so there was no doubt about it being him. Tom had been quick off the mark. He had sold a block of 75,000 shares at market, averaging $17.86 per share. The deductions flowing from 75,000 shares would certainly make a big dent in his taxable income. Probably bring him close to the point where the minimum tax kicked in.

The list was surprisingly short; there were only three other sales, two of ten thousand shares each and one of seven thousand. Obviously many shareholders had decided to hold on to their stake in Madison Energy, confident that its value would continue to increase. Poor bastards.

"Appreciate the cooperation, Jack." Chris folded the page and stuffed it in his breast pocket.

"Sure." Jack grimaced wryly as they shook hands.

The noose seemed to be tightening around Tom's neck. But was it really? Everything was capable of an innocent and completely plausible explanation. Engrossed in his thoughts, Chris almost walked past the young woman perched at eye level on her mobile platform outside Scotia Centre until he heard her faint, reproachful, "Hey." It was enough to stop him in his tracks and work his way over to her through the stream of pedestrians heading in the opposite direction. Joan Cunningham appeared on the mall, looking for handouts, at very infrequent intervals, usually months apart. Her strange little body, almost non-existent below her arms, was splayed out on the carpet of her platform, and, as always, she was reading a book. Her face, framed with dark, slightly curly hair, was attractive, and her smile as she welcomed Chris was pleasing. Somehow it made her malformed body seem less grotesque but infinitely more heart-rending.

Immediately after seeing her for the first time Chris had sought out a neurosurgeon friend of his who in turn had put him in touch with a neonatologist, a specialist in neonates — newborn infants. Although inured by years of practice to the horrors that can attend pregnancy, the physician's voice was hushed as she told Chris his friend suffered from *arthrogryposis congenita multiforma*. Chris wrote down the mind-numbing name as she spelled it out for him. "It's very rare," she added. "And almost totally incapacitating. It prevents the fetus from developing normally, especially the lower body. The gastrointestinal tract is usually functional, because it develops first high up in the body, but that's about it. Her legs, for example, would be little more than vestigial appendages." She looked at Chris as she said this, and he nodded confirmation. Below her shoulders, the unfortunate young woman's body dwindled away to almost nothing, making him wonder how it could possibly contain her vital organs. She had later surprised him by informing him that she enjoyed sex. He would take her word for it.

"Hello, Joan. Long time no see." Chris reached out to gently scratch the cockatiel's neck feathers. The little grey parrot, tethered to his owner's platform, was always with her.

"Did you miss me?" Joan asked with an impish glint in her eyes.

"Of course. What have you been up to?" The question was casual, but Chris was genuinely curious about what went on in this strange little person's life. He was pretty sure she really didn't need to beg for handouts on the street; it seemed to be more like a diversion for her.

"Enjoying life," she replied with a touch of defiance, as if he doubted she could. "What about you? When are you guys going to arrest that killer?"

So she knew he was with the police. How had she discovered that? Street talk, most likely. Street people had a way of knowing things. Things that were important to them. Like the police.

"We're doing our best."

"Well, it doesn't seem to be good enough. Him being on the loose makes people like me nervous. But he's in for a surprise if he comes after me."

The cockatiel, growing impatient with the humans paying more attention to themselves than to him, gave Chris's finger a gentle nip and raised his foot. Chris, recognizing this as a sign the bird wanted to be picked up, laughed and held out his half-closed fist.

"He likes you," Joan approved, as her pet, now comfortably perched on Chris's hand, ruffled his feathers and began to preen. "Nicki's good with people, but he usually doesn't want to be picked up like that. Not by strangers."

"He knows I'm a parrot person." Chris slipped a folded five-dollar bill into the coffee can fastened to the front of her apparatus. The can already held a considerable harvest of coins. Joan's attractive face, coupled with that tragically deformed body and her pet bird, was a real attention-getter, and passersby frequently stopped to look. Some dropped loonies and toonies in the can, almost as if paying admission to a sideshow. Chris wondered if that thought ever occurred to her. Chances were it did. According to medical texts he had consulted, victims of *arthrogryposis multiplex congenita*, as the affliction was also called, usually had normal mental capacity. There was nothing wrong with Joan's thought processes.

"I've got to head back to the office," he said, handing Nicki back to her. Now he knew the bird's name, and she knew he was with the police. They were getting to know each other. Maybe she was writing a book. She was always reading, and she could be gathering material with her occasional appearances on the street.

"Hurry up and catch that creep," she called out after him.

He raised a hand in acknowledgment and kept on down the mall. Should he have warned her? It wouldn't have done any good. Anyway, she wasn't the killer's type. Not unless the weirdo took it into his head to see what she looked like naked. Joan had boasted that he would be in for a surprise if he came after her. Jesus. He turned and retraced his steps.

Joan was smiling her thanks to a stout, middle-aged woman who, with a few muttered words, dropped a loonie in the coffee can.

"I want you to promise me something," Chris said as the woman walked away, shaking her head in sympathy. "I don't want you to say another word about the killer. Not one word. You could be making a target of yourself."

"Now that would be exciting!"

"I'm serious, Joan. Listen to me. Word gets around, and if the guy hears you've been talking about him, he could come after you. He's a psychopath. Promise me you will never mention or talk about this subject again."

"I promise. Thank you for caring. Touch me, Chris. Just for a moment. Please."

The tanned skin of her forearm was cool and smooth. It was the first time she had used his name. He gave her arm a gentle squeeze and stood there for a moment as they smiled at each other. A panhandler, sitting propped against a wall on the opposite side of the entrance, stared at them with something close to awe in his bleary eyes.

Both Gwen and Patterson were waiting for him when Chris stepped through the security door on the tenth floor.

"It looks like Phil's story struck a nerve," said Patterson. "We have a note from TLC. Here is a copy. The original is with the lab."

Chris absently nodded approval as he took the copy. "At least we know it's from our boy."

"Yeah. The signature checks out."

It had come as a shock when the serial's signature initials, TLC, appeared on that anonymous weblog. All efforts to trace the source had so far failed. Weblogs were truly anonymous. As soon as it appeared, it was fair game, and the media ran with it. All was not lost, however. Presumably because the blogger wasn't aware of it, the website didn't reveal that the initials "TLC" were arranged vertically within the outline of a computer-generated heart. Like the one on the colour photocopy Chris was looking at. As always, the message above the mocking signature was brief:

oNLy TLC Knows

That message reminds me of something, but I don't know what," mused Gwen.

"I know," Patterson interjected. "There was a radio program that was popular way back when. My grandfather used to talk about it. Sometimes he would come out with a line from it: 'only the Shadow knows.'"

"That's it," Chris agreed. "You still hear it every now and then, even today. Well, it doesn't tell us much we didn't know already. He doesn't take credit for the Vinney murder, but he doesn't deny it either. How was this delivered? Maybe that will tell us something."

"It will tell us something we already know — that TLC is one ingenious son of a bitch," Patterson muttered. "Here's a copy of the envelope it came in."

Chris frowned at the address on the copy of the envelope. The printed letters were in lower case, strung together and pasted on the front of the envelope. It read: "detective mason."

"The street address isn't Steve's," Patterson told him. "It belongs to a neighbour who lives two doors down. The neighbour brought it over and gave it to Steve. The neighbour's fingerprints will be all over it and so will Steve's, but we can eliminate those."

"Clever. Very clever. We have cordoned off the scene?"

"Done. McKay and Peplinksi from Crime Scenes are out there now, checking for footprints, tire marks, and anything else of interest. But we're dealing with paved surfaces, so don't get your hopes up."

"I'll try not to," Chris replied grimly.

"Are you going to let Phil know?"

"I pretty well have to, Ken. I promised. Besides we want to keep him onside."

"Well, at least he reacted," Dummett sighed when Chris told him about the message. "I had hoped for more. And I know you did."

"That's true. But we have the way the note was delivered and the contents of the note itself. That might tell us something after the profiler is done with it."

"How much of this can I use?"

Chris was prepared for the question. There was a delicate balance to be maintained. "How about this? You break the news that the killer has sent a note to the police."

"And what the note says?"

"Not verbatim. But you can say that the note — if it is from the killer — is ambiguous on who killed the Vinney woman. We're going to issue a press release to that effect."

"Give me an hour. That's all I need."

"It'll take longer than that to have the release approved."

There was an unmistakable note of excitement in the journalist's voice as he said, "If our friend sees that I have sort of an inside track he might start paying attention to me. Wouldn't that be something?"

"It'll be something all right. It could also be dangerous. Maybe I shouldn't have involved you in this. Take care, Phil."

"Don't worry. I'm not TLC's type."

chapter seven

The opening bars of *Valencia* broke into Chris's thoughts.

"It's Gwen, Chris. Where are you?"

"Heading north on Fourth. On foot. Right now I'm at Twelfth Ave. What's up?"

The "on foot" brought a fleeting smile to Gwen's lips. Chris liked to say he did some of his best thinking while walking to work. "We have another DOA. In a park. Where else? Stay where you are and I'll pick you up. It'll be easier if you go over to the west side."

Another murder in the park. What did that do to his theories about the Vinney killing? Theories that were only half-formed and flimsy at best. The light changed and he walked across the intersection. Traffic in the northbound lanes was backed up for two blocks as office workers streamed into the downtown, and the sidewalks were clogged with pedestrians heading in the same direction. The morning was bright and inviting, and he had switched off his portable radio so he could think without interruption. But Gwen's news had swept everything else aside. No point in speculating. Not until he had examined what the latest crime scene had to tell.

"Your gear's in the back," Gwen told him as he climbed into the passenger seat.

He nodded. "What do we know?"

"Not one hell of a lot, so far. The body is in Fish Creek Park, just inside the gate. The mounted patrol discovered it on their first patrol of the day."

Fish Creek Park, named after the creek that flowed through it, was very extensive and was most effectively patrolled on horseback. There was also a riding stable in the park so it was a simple matter to board the horses. Four members of the police service, trained in horsemanship, in rotating shifts of two on and two off, had been assigned to patrol the thickly wooded park and its many winding paths.

Which hand would the cross be on this time? Or would there even be one? No point in asking Gwen. The information from the police patrol would have been minimal to avoid any chance of having it leak into the public domain. Travelling against the flow of traffic, they made remarkably good time and in less than twenty minutes Gwen was turning off Anderson Road onto 37th Street paralleling the northern boundary of the Tsuu T'ina Reserve. The road leading to the park was at the bottom of the hill.

A mounted Calgary police officer touched the wide brim of his black Stetson and rode beside them as, toting the crime scene equipment, they walked down to the unpretentious entrance.

"You are hereby deputized a member of the Crime Scene team," pronounced Gwen as they stopped to climb into the white coveralls.

"I am deeply honoured," replied Chris, zipping up his suit.

The harmless little performance would allow Chris immediate access to the body.

A sign said that the park would be closed and locked at 10:00 p.m. and that trespassers would be prosecuted. The gate was a single bar that could be swung into position across the road. It was still closed and locked when the patrol checked it, but a pedestrian lugging a body could simply duck under it. The killer hadn't carried his victim very far; the naked body was displayed — the word leapt into Chris's mind — on the first picnic table, not more than one hundred yards inside the gate. Joan. The position of the body lying there on the table reminded him irresistibly of his disabled friend splayed out on her platform. But this woman was no Joan. Her figure was fully formed, with a complete complement of arms and legs. Chris noted with some surprise that, unlike the other victims, she was in early middle age, the envelope of her flesh beginning to soften and spread. Not at all the type the serial had gone for in the past. Maybe she was just someone who had the fatal misfortune to turn up at a time and place where she could be abducted with impunity.

Whoever she was, she had been mutilated in the same fashion as the others — right nipple sliced off a slack breast, hands clasped on her abdomen, and bloody, violated genitalia. Apart from what was on the body, there was no blood, confirming that she would have been killed somewhere else and transported here. Deliberately trying to keep his thoughts unfocused, Chris continued to gaze down at the body. The air was still and the sound of a police horse mouthing its bit as it cropped grass was oddly comforting. A wave of nostalgia swept through Chris at the sound. It was soon interrupted with the click of Gwen's camera shutter as she began to photograph the scene. Long shots of the victim's torso, then close-ups of the wounds. Out of the corner of his eye, Chris watched her bend over the body as she unclasped the hands and turned them over. Several clicks of the shutter later, she gave him a brief affirmative nod and mouthed, "Left." Unexpectedly, he experienced a sense of relief. They were back on familiar ground. Familiar deadly ground.

The separate slam of car doors announced the arrival of Ken Patterson and the not so welcome Steve Mason, as well as the medical examiner, a balding, bespectacled man in his late fifties. Mason looked worried and uncharacteristically subdued. "We've got to wrap this up, Crane. Pronto. I got a call from Chief Johnstone on the way down here. He's royally pissed off."

Maybe he's running out of platitudes to feed the press, thought Chris unkindly. As if on cue, Mason muttered, "The press is camped outside the park gate, baying like a pack of wolves. You got any leads? Anything at all?"

"We can be pretty sure she wasn't killed here. There's not enough blood. Plus the fact that she's older than the others by quite a bit."

"I can see that, for Christ's sake! You figure that means something?"

"It might. If we assume there are two killers, not one, out there." Expecting a sarcastic retort, Chris paused, then continued when Mason merely nodded. "Killer number one is bound to be a psychopath who likes them young. Not necessarily beautiful, but young. If the other one killed not for the thrills but for a rational, comprehensible motive, and wants us to believe it's all the work of the original serial killer, he wouldn't worry too much about his next victim. So long as she's female and handy. When we find out who she is, we'll know more."

By early afternoon they knew who she was. Maud Simpson had not shown up for work that Thursday morning. It was the first time in the twelve years that she had been employed as a receptionist at the Ranchmen's Club that this had happened. When repeated calls to her home, a walk-up apartment in the Beltline, three blocks east of the club, went unanswered, the police were contacted. Her route to and from work took her past Memorial Park, which, although it had been substantially upgraded in recent years, was still notorious as a hangout for gays, hookers, and drug dealers. That didn't necessarily mean anything, although the habitués of that park were very much of the "mind your own business" school, and the dense clumps of shrubbery lining the pathways offered effective concealment for whatever might be going down. A detective was dispatched to question the regulars, but without much hope of finding anyone who might have witnessed the unfortunate receptionist's abduction. Or would talk about it. If in fact that's where it happened.

The Simpson woman had been abducted from somewhere, but not, it seemed, from her apartment. Its neat contents and furnishings were undisturbed, everything in its place. The only discordant note was a hungry black and white cat, mewing and pacing around its empty dish. A co-worker of the victim volunteered to look after it. It had been six o'clock in the evening and full daylight when Maud Simpson left the club. Four hours before Fish Creek Park closed for the night. God only knew what she had suffered in those hours. Almost certainly she had been picked at random by the killer. A victim of circumstance. On second thought, not so much circumstance as convenience.

The medical examiner would perform an autopsy on her. It had the highest priority, but even so the results wouldn't be known until the following day.

Nevermore, bold parrot eyes glittering with triumph, was perched on top of his cage when Chris let himself into the penthouse. The cage door hung down from one hinge. "You *do* like solving puzzles, don't you?" Chris murmured as he carried the African Grey over to his stand. "Well, I can't blame you. So do I."

There was no choice but to follow the breeder's advice and get a small padlock. It was a nuisance, having to mess around with keys, but there was no other way. Surely Nevermore couldn't jimmy locks. Or could he?

Shaking his head at his unrepentant pet, Chris opened the sliding door and stepped out onto the patio, carefully shutting the screen behind him. A rufous hummingbird hovered over the feeder on a blur of wings. He had been a little tardy in putting out the feeder this year and had been astonished to find a tiny male hummer hovering at the exact spot where that miraculous, constantly replenished flower should be. Chastened, and filled with wonder at how this mite of a bird could fly thousands of kilometres from its winter home in Central America to a column of air not more than six centimetres in diameter, Chris had quickly remedied his oversight.

chapter eight

"City in Grip of Terror," the 110-point headline blared in the blackest of ink over a photo of Maud Simpson's shrouded body being carried on a gurney out of Fish Creek Park. The account of the killer's fifth victim occupied three-quarters of the front page. A photo of a grim-lipped Chief Johnstone appeared on the inside page. He confirmed that the police were receiving messages that might be from the killer but steadfastly refused to release any details of the latest murder, taking refuge in the fact that "the investigation is ongoing." The police were following up a number of promising leads and an arrest was expected in the near future. Chris groaned to himself when he read again that the investigation was a "full court press." The groan became a hiss of indrawn breath as he read the concluding paragraph: "Detective Chris Crane, once the star of our state-of-the-art Forensic Crime Scenes Unit, is the primary, leading a crack team of Homicide detectives." Smooth. Very smooth. By turning the spotlight on him, the Chief was cleverly deflecting the media's attention away from himself and onto Homicide. Their roles would be abruptly reversed if and when the serial was arrested.

Dummett's contribution was splashed across the top of the third page in the *Herald*'s front section under the headline "What Makes A Serial Killer?" After recounting the details of the grisly scene in the park, the article turned into Dumett's trademark, a think piece. In the second paragraph Dummett answered the question posed by the headline with a single word: *power*. To decree life or death. The ultimate power trip. Especially for someone, the article speculated, who otherwise had no power, who might be the product of an abusive childhood, abandoned by his parents, unsuccessful in the workplace, scorned by the opposite sex — a loner with lots of time to weave erotic fantasies. It was stuff that could be culled from any textbook on the subject, but written with a style that made it seem fresh and plausible. While the article did nothing to minimize the unspeakable horror of the murders, there was a disquieting subtext that the killer might be driven by forces over which he had no control.

I know what you're up to, my friend, Chris thought. He carefully folded the newspapers and placed them on the counter beside the neatly stacked breakfast dishes. Nervous that his preoccupied owner might forget him, the parrot croaked, "Treat." It was almost the first word the bird had learned. Chuckling, Chris obliged, then went into the bedroom to finish dressing.

Gwen had come directly to headquarters instead of making her usual brief stop at the Crime Scenes office, so she was already at her desk by the time Chris arrived. They exchanged a few words about the escalating media coverage, then Gwen asked, "You read Dummett's piece?" It wasn't really a question; she knew he would have.

He nodded, and she frowned. "It was almost as if he was making excuses for our bad guy."

"I agree. And I know why."

When Gwen raised a questioning eyebrow, he went on. "I'm almost positive he's deliberately trying to ingratiate himself with the killer. He knows, like we do, that deep down, serial killers crave attention. Publicity. Notoriety. He is practically inviting TLC to get in touch with him. Give him some inside info he could use to create more publicity. To their mutual benefit. Ultimately he's hoping to expose the killer — a journalistic coup to end all coups!"

"What you call career-making!" breathed Gwen.

Once back at his desk, Chris logged onto his computer. The icon on the toolbar told him there was mail. He hit the envelope symbol and the message flashed across the screen:

NO WOMAN IS SAFE FROM ME

"Look at this, Gwen," Chris called out, beckoning the detective to join him.

"So now he's communicating with you directly. He knows you're his real opponent, Chris. He's challenging you."

"Mano-a-mano, eh?" Chris muttered. "He's sure as hell getting bolder. Whoever he is."

"That panache of his could have led him into making

a fatal mistake. It should be possible to trace that e-mail."

"I'll put a team of experts on it. But we'll find it originated with a public server. One of those internet cafés where anyone has access. We'll get Cyber Crimes on it. It could take months and they may never find the sender, but it's worth a try."

"The signature pretty well rules out it being the work of a crank," observed Gwen. "Unless there's been another leak."

"Don't scare me like that, Gwen. The last thing we need is someone playing mind games with us. Our working hypothesis is that it's the killer. Let's hope he keeps it up until he gives himself away."

"The killer, or *killers*? You haven't ruled out the possibility of there being two killers, have you?"

"By no means. Still, the latest case doesn't jibe too well with the copycat theory. Unless of course Vinney's killer struck again for that very reason. To make us believe there is only one serial killer."

"Or unless the copycat has developed a taste for the game. That's been known to happen."

"What a charming thought!" Chris called up the file of another case on the computer. Later that morning he was to meet a Crown prosecutor at the courthouse complex to fine-tune a couple of questions the Crown wanted to use in cross-examination. The case was an old one that had taken two years to get to trial and had nothing to do with the serial killings. It was almost a relief to think, however briefly, about something other than the serial and his victims.

Unexpectedly, Joan and her cockatiel were stationed at their usual spot outside the mall entrance to Scotia Centre. Weeks could go by with no sign of her, but here she was, twice in only a few days. Was it the chance of seeing her that had led him to return so often to headquarters via the mall, as he was doing now, on his way back from the courthouse, rather than the more direct route along 6th? Chris saw that she had spotted him and raised his hand in greeting as he drew nearer. The cockatiel shifted from foot to foot in a little dance and whistled.

"He's glad to see you," smiled Joan.

"And I'm glad to see *you*. I didn't expect to see you again so soon."

Joan propped her arm up on the platform and Chris held her wrist in a gentle grip. "Is the pressure getting to you, Chris? The press has really been howling for blood."

"We can't let it distract us. Although there are times when it's hard not to." Chris held out his free hand for the bird to climb onto. "What's the word on the street?"

"A lot of them don't even know what's going on. Their brains are so fogged with drugs they can't think about anything except how they're going to get the next fix. The rest find it kinda exciting. Gives them something to talk about. It doesn't exactly break their hearts to see the police going around in circles."

"And what does Joan think?"

"I think about his victims, and what they are going through. Being tortured before they're killed. The papers don't tell you much, but they *are* tortured, aren't they, Chris?"

"Yes. They are." Placing the bird back on the platform, he started to reach into his pants pocket.

"Don't, Chris." She covered the coffee can with her hand. "I don't want your money. I would come here more often," she said after a pause, "if I thought it meant seeing you."

"I'll keep an eye out for you. And you take care. Remember what I said."

"Can't catch him, can you, cop?" The voice came from what looked to be a bundle of rags. Chris peered down at the unkempt figure squatting on the concrete pavement. At first he appeared to have no legs, but Chris saw they were drawn up beneath him and hidden by his tattered coat. Matted grey hair fell over his face to intermingle with a scraggly beard. He didn't look up, but kept a rheumy gaze fixed on the soiled cap in front of him. No coins decorated the inside of its grimy crown. Passersby would write him off as beyond all hope, not worthy of their charity.

"Not yet." Chris bent down to drop a toonie in the upturned cap, seeing as he did so the faded crest above its peak. The insignia of some club, probably golf. "It's very frustrating. Do you know anything that could help us?"

"He is vain. He will kill again. You will not catch him until he wants you to."

"What if I were to tell you he kills for financial gain? That these killings are not random, but are motive-driven?"

"Not correct. These are thrill ..." The voice that had been clear and distinct trailed off into a mumble. Chris caught the word *narcissism* as it surfaced from the unintelligible stream, but the rest was an incoherent babble. He tried to prompt the derelict with a few more questions, but gave up as he realized the man had retreated into his own world. Wherever and whatever that was.

chapter nine

"I think it's time for a return visit to McKinley's."
Chris stopped by Gwen's desk. "We know considerably
more now than we did before. This time we'll tape the
interviews."

Gwen nodded and took a tape recorder from
the top drawer of her desk. She possessed a photo-
graphic memory and, once back in the office, could
transcribe a verbatim report of what had transpired.
This time, however, Chris wanted the lawyers' voices
on the record. ·

Ingram had to be called out of a meeting, but his expression betrayed no resentment as he ushered them into a
small, windowless conference room. He apologized for
the cramped quarters, saying that all the other conference rooms were booked.

Chris began by recording the details of the interview — date, time, and identity of the witness — then took Adrienne's junior back to the circumstances of the ill-fated Madison share prospectus. Jeff readily confirmed Adrienne's sterling reputation for integrity and was more forthcoming than previously about what had really happened. "It's all pretty much in the public domain, anyway," he said.

Chris nodded encouragingly, although privately he thought that it wasn't all that straightforward. If there had been a cover-up, however brief, those involved could be liable in civil damages. It soon became apparent, however, that Ingram was choosing his words with considerable care. There had been increasing concern over the performance of the Lost Horse field, but the intrusion of the salt water had been so sudden, so unexpected, that, not surprisingly, the oil company executives argued they needed more time and more information to properly evaluate the situation. He conceded that Adrienne had been very concerned and felt that they should go public right away.

"As early as Monday, the twenty-sixth, the day her body was found?"

"Yes. She made her position very clear. We met with the Madison people and Mr. McKinley all Sunday to discuss what should be done."

"How long did this meeting last?"

"Until five in the afternoon."

"And?"

"She was still insisting that we notify the stock exchange in the morning before the market opened." Ingram shifted in his chair. "I can see where this is leading, but can I ask why? Aren't the police satisfied that she was the victim of our serial killer?"

"As I told you before, we have to eliminate every possibility. For that reason, I have to ask about your relationship with Ms. Vinney. Specifically, were you two intimate? Sexually intimate?"

"Are you serious? Yes, I guess you are," Ingram said when Chris continued to stare impassively at him. "Our relationship was professional. Strictly. She was my boss, and I had the greatest respect and admiration for her. Working with her was a great privilege and opportunity for me. It was a wonderful learning experience."

"She was a very attractive woman." Chris stared unblinkingly at the lawyer.

"And you're a bit of a hunk yourself," Gwen added with a smile, although the pudgy-faced Ingram was anything but.

"All those nights working together," Chris murmured.

"'Working' is the word. That's what we did. Work." Ingram shot them an exasperated look. "That's the truth. Whether you believe me or not."

"We believe you. And you've been very helpful. Thank you."

Chris extended his hand and, after some hesitation, Ingram took it. Gwen switched off the tape recorder with an audible click.

A female legal assistant waited for them in the hallway to inform them that Mr. Pettigrew would like to see them.

"Are you making any progress?" demanded the head of the firm's corporate department from the depths of an outsize armchair. The detectives were seated on the adjoining sofa, behind a glass-topped coffee table. He frowned but made no objection when Gwen placed the recorder on the table. "But first let me offer you some coffee."

"That would be very welcome," Chris replied with a small sigh. "Gwen and I have been on the go since early this morning. The criminal element in this town manages to keep us very busy."

"I'm sure it does." Pettigrew paused with the coffee cup at his lips. "But my concern is with your investigation into my partner's horrible death. Unimaginably horrible."

"Of course." Chris took a careful sip of the coffee. It was almost too hot to drink, but he welcomed the caffeine jolt. "All I can tell you is that we have dedicated every available resource to it. Our investigation is still in the early stages."

Morris Pettigrew was unimpressed. "I've heard that unless a murder is solved within the first forty-eight hours, the chances of it ever being solved are substantially reduced."

"That's often the case, I agree. If you're dealing with what one might call random killings, where the only motive is the gratification of some psychological depravity. It's otherwise when there is a rational, purpose-driven motive; where the killer has a reason, personal or financial, to eliminate a specific victim. Cases of that sort take longer to unravel."

"Are you telling me that Adrienne was not the victim of this unknown person who seemingly kills for the thrill of it?"

"No, I'm not, sir. Ms. Vinney being the victim of a serial killer remains the most likely outcome. One we are pursuing vigorously."

"So I gathered from the interview your chief gave to the press." There was a glint of humour in Pettigrew's pouched eyes. "If I'm not mistaken, he went so far as to refer to a full court press."

"Yes. I read that as well. However, when the victim

is as high-profile as Ms. Vinney, one has to investigate other possibilities."

"I know nothing of her personal life. Insofar as her professional life is concerned, I can think of nothing that would make anyone want to kill her."

"She was very much involved in the Madison deal and the Lost Horse disaster."

"As I told you previously, that was one of her major files."

"The one she was working on at the time of her death."

"Yes."

"I understand she was concerned about timely disclosure?"

"Is that what young Ingram told you? Well, it's true. She did express some concern, but we all realized that time was required to determine the real extent of the problem. A similar thing happened in the Ladyfern field in B.C. but it continues to produce, albeit at a reduced rate."

"I know something about Ladyfern. It turned out to be not quite as bad as was thought at first. According to Mr. Ingram, however, Ms. Vinney was insisting on immediate disclosure. Before the market opened."

"That was her view. It was not mine."

"Did you plan to override her?"

The suggestion seemed to startle Pettigrew. "It was *her* file, Detective."

"So it was her call?"

"Yes."

"The Madison executives must have been pretty unhappy?"

"Of course. But their concern was for the company. Lost Horse was its principal, and for all practical purposes its only, asset."

"The shares they owned would be hammered, and

their share options would be worthless."

"As individuals they would suffer severe financial setbacks. No question about that. But I can only repeat what I observed, which was that they were devastated by what it would do to the company. They were the ones who had created Madison Energy, brought it into being, and celebrated its discovery of the Lost Horse field."

"A devastating blow. As you say, sir." Chris placed his empty cup to one side and prepared to stand up. "You and Mr. Ingram have been very helpful. I trust we may talk to you again if the need arises?"

"You can talk to me, certainly. Although I can't think why. But you'll have to reach Ingram at his new address. He's leaving us and going with another firm. Torrance, Forsyth."

"Because of the Madison affair?"

"Good Lord, no. Can't you think of anything else, man? They have offered him a partnership in the firm. I understand they first approached him some months ago. In time he would have become a partner here, but under our policy it would be another two years before he could be considered for partnership. I think it's a mistake on his part, but" — he shrugged — "these young hotshots are an impatient lot."

"I think we better have another chat with 'young Ingram' as Pettigrew calls him," said Chris as he and Gwen waited for the elevator on the forty-fifth floor. Once inside, he pressed the button for Jeff's floor, seven levels below.

"Mr. Ingram is with clients," the receptionist informed them. "But I will let him know you are here."

"We'll wait." Although far less grand than the one on the forty-fifth floor, the reception area was impressive enough. The decor was Western: a large oil of a cattle drive dominated one wall; a mountain scene hung on another. Chris sauntered over to the floor-length windows to gaze out at the cityscape. The closely grouped office towers glistened in the bright sunlight. He turned as a door leading from the office space opened and Jeff Ingram entered.

"We won't keep you long," Chris assured him, before the lawyer could say anything. "Is there some place where we can talk in private?"

"This way." Ingram led them through a doorway on the opposite side of the reception area and into a small conference room, windowless like the one where they had met earlier that morning.

"I understand congratulations are in order." Chris smiled amiably up at the lawyer, who had remained standing as if to cut the meeting as short as possible.

"So Pettigrew told you, did he?" Ingram slowly subsided into a chair.

"Tom Forsyth is a friend of mine. He's a good guy."

Ingram acknowledged this with a slight inclination of his head.

"Was he the one who invited you to join the firm?"

"What's that got to do with anything? As it happens, he was. We've known each other for some time."

"You must play squash," Chris smiled.

"I do. Tom and I belong to the same club."

"I expect you probably mentioned the Madison situation to him?" Chris's tone was casual, but his eyes remained fixed on Ingram. The lawyer's eyes narrowed and his lips tightened as he glared silently back at his interrogator.

"You did, didn't you? It would be a perfectly natural thing to do. One law partner to another." In fact it would be completely unethical, but Ingram's reaction convinced Chris that Ingram *had* talked about it with Forsyth. Hoping to impress his new mentor.

"You told Forsyth about Adrienne refusing to sign off on the Madison prospectus, didn't you, Jeff?"

Ingram's lips tightened even more and he continued to glare silently back at Chris.

"You wouldn't want to start off your new career with being charged with obstructing justice, would you, Jeff? I don't think your new partners would be too happy about that."

"Are you serious? About charging me with obstructing justice?"

"Absolutely," Chris replied. It was a bluff, but Ingram didn't seem to know that. His area of practice was far removed from criminal law.

"Okay. I did say something to Tom about Adrienne and the Madison file. But it was just lawyer talk."

"Sure. And as part of that lawyer talk you would have told him that Adrienne wanted to go public with Lost Horse watering out? The truth, Jeff."

"I mentioned it. Yeah. I told Tom I thought she was right. They were going to have a big meeting about it on Sunday. But I knew she wouldn't change her mind."

"When did you and Tom have this conversation?"

"On a Saturday. We played squash in the afternoon and had a drink after."

"Saturday, May 24?"

"Yeah. The same weekend Adrienne was killed." Ingram looked as if he wanted to say something more, but held back with an obvious effort.

"You should have told us this before," Chris admonished him mildly to signal that the interview was over.

"Why on earth should I have?" protested Ingram. "It wasn't relevant then, and it isn't relevant now." He paused, then asked in a more subdued tone, "Are you going to tell Tom about this?"

"Not at this stage. And you're right. It's probably not relevant. But it's the sort of thing we need to know. I take it we can assume that you won't say anything to Tom yourself?"

"Good Lord, no!" Ingram shuddered.

"There, as the logicians would say, is our nexus," remarked Chris as he and Gwen walked east along the mall.

"Now we know for certain that Forsyth knew Vinney was going to blow the whistle," Gwen agreed.

"We also know that he wasn't the only one who knew. And he wasn't the only one who would suffer ruinous losses when news about the field became public. Those executives stood to lose more than Tom. Far more. Maybe we should take a closer look at them. So far we've ignored them as possible suspects. But they had the same motive as Tom did. No." Chris shook his head while they waited for the pedestrian light to change. "That's a non-starter. They're insiders and are required to file insider reports on any dealings with company stock. Apart from anything else, they could go to prison for using insider information if they sold any of their shares."

"Too bad," said Gwen as the light changed. "I was beginning to like the idea of corporate tycoons committing murder by moonlight."

"They're not tycoons. Not any longer. Excuse me for a moment." Chris left her side and went over to talk to Joan. Bemusedly, Gwen watched him as he chatted animatedly with the extraordinary creature and petted her little grey bird.

"You got a thing for her?" she asked when Chris

rejoined her and they resumed their progress along the mall.

Chris laughed. "No, I don't have a *thing* for her, as you put it. But I like her, and I admire the way she copes with the world she is forced to live in."

"She has a pretty face."

"You have a visitor," the tenth-floor receptionist told Chris as soon as he and Gwen stepped off the elevator. They had used the rear entrance of the building instead of the main entrance.

"Who is it?"

"His name is Phillip Dummett. He's a journalist. Says he knows you."

"That's right. Where is he?"

"Downstairs. In the public reception area. I'm not authorized to let him come up here." Chris nodded, and she asked, "Should I tell them to let him come up?"

"Yes. Is there an interview room I can use?"

"Number three."

"What gives, Phil?" Chris waved the journalist into a chair across the table from him.

"This gives," replied Dummett, unsnapping his briefcase with barely suppressed glee. "I'm now on TLC's mailing list," he added handing Chris a stamped envelope.

Chris accepted it gingerly, holding it between thumb and forefinger. "Is this the original? What about fingerprints? Have you had it tested?"

Dummett shrugged. "It's the original. There's no way our friend would leave any prints on it. Take a look inside."

The top of the envelope was neatly slit open.

Chris reached in the breast pocket of his jacket and took out a pair of latex gloves. Slipping them on, he extracted a single sheet of paper that precisely fitted the envelope. Like the other missives from the serial, the message was terse and used letters cut from a newspaper:

DREAMs ɴoᴛ ᴅEᴍ0ɴs
TLC

There was no outline of a heart around the initials. That could mean two things: either TLC only used the heart when communicating with the police or the message was a hoax. Maybe Dummett had mailed it to himself. That was unlikely. A journalist on the cusp of international fame wouldn't run a risk like that.

"The word *dream* is extra large. It looks like it was part of an advertisement," Chris observed.

"That's the way I read it too. It's from an ad for dream homes."

"It should be possible to trace where it's from."

"I already have. It's from the New Homes section of last Saturday's edition of the *Herald*."

"It seems he didn't much care for the idea he was possessed by demons."

"That's right. He wants us to believe that he enjoys what he does. That selecting a victim, stalking her, imagining what he's going to do to her, is a sport that gives him pleasure. Not something driven by demons. That's what nearly all these serial killers talk about after they've been arrested — the excitement of the chase, stalking the victim and planning how best to catch them. Ted Bundy talked about that a lot."

TLC doesn't seem to go in for the stalking bit; he seems to be more of an opportunist, thought Chris. But he let it pass. Instead, he remarked, "Bundy talked about a lot of things. A lot of them contradictory."

"He sure did. But he was always consistent about one thing: the thrill of hunting on and around university campuses — it was always a university. That's where he found the young, beautiful, long-haired women he liked."

"Liked to kill," Chris amended. "But you're right, they can't seem to stop talking about themselves. Dennis Rader — BTK — desperately tried to impress the cops. He thought they were his buddies, and he was crushed when they finally terminated the interviews. When he allocuted to his guilty plea at trial they couldn't shut him up. He went on and on about the things he had done and how he had justified them to himself. Some relatives of the victims refused to stay in the courtroom; he was enjoying himself too much."

"We're on the same wavelength, Chris. Look at Berkowitz, holding court in prison for his biographers. These monsters need to be recognized. To be famous. Most importantly, to justify what they've done. That's why I got this letter. TLC had to set the record straight. That he's driven by dreams, not demons."

"That was quite an article you wrote. You seem to know a lot about what makes these psychopaths tick."

"I've read the literature. I think I know how to get under this guy's skin."

"It sure looks that way. Are you prepared to continue with this?" Seeing Dummett hesitate, Chris went on, "You don't have to, you know. And there is always the element of danger in dealing with psychopaths."

"That's not what bothers me. I just don't want to do anything that will damage my reputation as a journalist. So far, I don't think it will."

"Nor do I. Assisting the police in their investigation of a serial killer can hardly damage one's reputation. It's up to you, of course. But this," he tapped the letter, "this is helpful."

"I know. Okay. But," Dummett added with that sudden, engaging grin, "I expect to be there when this goes down?"

"That depends." Chris opened a drawer in the table and took out a box of latex gloves. "The next time you get mail from our guy, use these."

Not long after Chris had accompanied Dummett down to the lobby, a constable phoned in to report that a clerk at the Budget car rental on 6th Avenue had recognized Tom Forsyth from Gwen's photos and confirmed that he had rented a silver Honda SUV late in the afternoon of Saturday, May 24. "We didn't need his photo. They picked it out all right, but the suspect used his driver's licence and Visa. Apparently he wanted a grey one, but silver was all they had left. I guess he didn't want to be too conspicuous." Chris grunted an affirmative, and the detective went on to report that the vehicle had been turned in on Tuesday, May 27, and had been rented out twice since then. At the moment it was in Banff and was due to be returned sometime tomorrow.

"Are you going to ask the Mounties to impound it?" Gwen asked when Chris told her about the SUV being in Banff. "Once they've traced it."

"Yes. I want it transported down here on a flatbed to the police garage. And I want it given a thorough inspection as soon as it arrives. Chances are it will be pretty well sterilized. The rental people will have cleaned it inside and out between trips, not to mention what Forsyth might have done before he turned it in. Oh, one more thing, Gwen."

"Yes?"

"Contact Budget and make sure the people in Banff are provided with a replacement vehicle."

The two police officers assigned to tracking down purchases of plastic sheets hadn't met with the same success. Both a Canadian Tire and a Rona outlet reported a modest run on plastic sheets that Sunday. Something to do with the late spring weather inspiring householders to spruce things up. None of the clerks or cashiers were able to identify Forsyth, which was hardly surprising in view of the volume of sales. Quite a few of the purchases were paid for by credit cards, but none were Forsyth's.

"Keep on it," Chris told them.

Everything seemed to be on hold until morning. That meant he could attend the dinner party at Marie and Doug Church's home in Mount Royal with a clear conscience. Doug was a merchant banker who had made his fortune arranging financing and IPOs for start-up oil companies. Mason liked to sneer at what he called "Crane's high-society friends," but Chris was very much at home in those circles. It was, in fact, what he had been born into, his family having been prominent members of society for generations in Westmount, Montreal. Doug, like a number of Chris's civilian friends, had assumed that he had been demoted when he went from being a sergeant in charge of the Forensic Crime Scenes Unit to being a detective. Doug had been the only one who knew Chris well enough to ask him about it, and had smiled with relief when Chris told him the ranks were equivalent.

chapter ten

Society in Calgary, high or otherwise, was a very eclectic mix, reflected Chris, taking the first sip of his martini in the opulent living room of the Church residence. True, there was a smattering of Old Calgary — descendants of ranching families and pioneer oilmen — but the majority were professionals who had come west to make their fortunes and had made it big. The economic engines of that success were the oil patch, the technology that had grown up around it, and the financial and legal services that promoted and facilitated those activities. That mix was pretty well represented at tonight's gathering, Chris observed as he surveyed the assembled guests. He knew them all, except for one attractive woman about his own age. She seemed to be alone. Had Marie succumbed, like some of his other hostesses, to the temptation to match him with "someone suitable"?

His suspicion was confirmed when Marie took him by the arm and gaily announced that he had to meet her good friend Sarah.

The amused and coolly reserved look on Sarah Struthers-Milvain's charming face told Chris that she was well aware of what their hostess was up to. Her hand was pleasantly cool, and the large diamond on the third finger of her right hand and her hyphenated name told their own story. Chris remembered her ex as a colourful and entertaining oilman from the U.S. who three or four years ago had sold his company to an income trust and retired with a new trophy wife to a tax haven in the Caribbean. Chris had met Jim Milvain a couple of times at oil patch receptions but had never had occasion to meet his first wife. Sarah was poised and articulate. Chris congratulated himself on having such an agreeable companion for the evening.

The Taylors were the last to arrive. Standing in the entrance at the top of a short flight of stairs, Cameron Taylor, the patriarch of the ranching family, doffed his white Stetson and apologized for being so late, saying that the road in from Longview had been blocked by an overturned cattle liner.

"They needed some help to round them up," added his wife. Phyllis Taylor was a tall, handsome woman. Chris knew she was originally from a small town in Ontario, but she had thrown herself into the ranching lifestyle with wholehearted enthusiasm and could hold her own with any cowboy.

"They couldn't have asked for more expert help than the Taylors," Marie Church laughed, kissing Phyllis on both cheeks. "Alberta's pre-eminent ranching family!"

Watching Taylor carefully place his trademark hat on a closet shelf, Chris reflected that many would think it an affectation, but he knew it was a genuine part of the rancher's persona. A past president of the Calgary Stampede, he was one of its biggest boosters, as well as being a third-generation rancher and running some 2,200 head of Hereford cattle on the Bent Tree ranch in the foothills. Both he and his wife were in their early sixties; they were accompanied by their son, Cameron Jr. — always called Cam to avoid confusion with his father — and Melanie, their daughter-in-law.

It had been some months since Chris had last seen the Taylors, and he was struck anew by the resemblance between father and son. Both were of medium height, with powerful, stocky builds and rather snub facial features. Their similarities ran deeper than the physical resemblance. Cam was every bit as dedicated to the ranching way of life as was his father.

"Hi, neighbour!" Cameron Taylor greeted Sarah warmly, taking both her hands in his. Still smiling, he shook hands with Chris, who waited for him to make his usual joke about the ongoing range war between the police and criminals. He always said that the good guys were winning, although he never said who the good guys were. But the recent epidemic of killings didn't lend itself to harmless banter.

"So you're neighbours," said Chris when the Taylors had moved on to mingle with the other guests.

"Country neighbours." Sarah smiled. "My place is twenty kilometres south of Bent Tree."

"Somehow I can't picture you running a ranch."

"I don't. But I do live on an acreage near Longview. My daughter, Linda, is horse crazy, so we moved out there where she can keep her horses. We both love it. Do you ride, Detective Crane?"

"Don't call me that! Please. My name is Chris. I can ride, although I haven't for some years." This wasn't the time to mention his horse show career. He wondered if he was about to be invited to go riding with her, but they were swept up in a swirl of party conversation before she could say anything more.

"Let's go outside! It's too nice to stay indoors," someone exclaimed, and Chris and Sarah joined the exodus of guests through the open sliding doors.

"They've done a wonderful job with this place," she murmured.

"Superb," Chris agreed inhaling the cool summer air. "Spectacular, in fact."

Indeed, the Churches' Mount Royal home *was* spectacular. It commanded an unobstructed view of the downtown skyline, and its spacious grounds covered two residential lots. After tearing down the original house and constructing a huge, ultra-modern mansion, complete with indoor swimming pool, in its place, they'd purchased the adjoining property and built a tennis court where the house had once stood.

"It must be wonderful to live here!" Glancing to one side, Chris saw the speaker was Melanie Taylor. No hyphenated name for her. Not in that family. Melanie was short, with a figure just beginning to verge on chunky and tightly waved dark hair. Because of his friendship with Cam, Chris was an occasional dinner guest at the Taylor ranch and knew she was originally from Toronto. She and Cam had met while both were attending the University of Toronto. A city girl like her could easily grow weary of life on the remote ranch and long to be back at the centre of things. Especially for someone who, according to Tom Forsyth, had been a real hottie before meeting and marrying Cam.

Cam was saying something about the magnificent view of the Rockies from their ranch, but Chris, distracted by the sudden intrusion of Tom into his thoughts, scarcely heard him. When he tuned back in, Melanie was suggesting that the four of them find a table on the terrace and sit together for the buffet dinner.

After they had taken a few bites of the first course, a baby shrimp salad, Chris asked Cam about how things were at the ranch. A few years ago when mad cow disease was ravaging the cattle industry, he would never have raised the subject. But now the panic created by a single case of *bovine spongiform encephalopathy* — the jaw-breaking scientific name of the disease reminding Chris of Joan and her disability — had subsided, and international borders were once again open to Canadian beef.

The rancher's response was enthusiastic and upbeat. A steady stream of cattle trucks were once more heading south to the American market. The Western Canadian herds that had been so severely culled as a result of the trade embargos were being restored to former levels, which created a tremendous demand for top breeding bulls. Last fall's sale — Bent Tree's seventy-fourth annual bull sale, as Cam pointed out proudly — had seen record prices. This year's sale promised to do even better.

"That makes it the seventy-fifth!" Sarah marvelled.

"Seventy-five consecutive years with no interruption. Good times and bad times."

"That calls for a celebration!"

"Plans are well underway. It's going to be one major blowout!"

"Speaking of parties," Melanie asked Sarah, "are you going to the ATP fundraiser next week?"

"I'll be there."

"Then why don't you come with us? We can call for you if you like." She paused and glanced uncertainly at Chris. "Unless, of course ..."

"I'd like that," Sarah replied smoothly into the awkward silence. "I'll call you tomorrow to arrange things."

For the rest of the meal conversation flowed along familiar channels. The ideal weather of spring and early summer was touched upon with the reassuring qualifier that there had been enough moisture to ensure a good crop, the upcoming Stampede was noted, and the latest example of Ottawa's lack of interest in western concerns was briefly and dismissively mentioned. Finally, inevitably, the subject of the serial killer was raised.

"This person obviously has a thing for public parks," said Sarah putting her fork down and looking at Chris. "Shouldn't that give you a clue as to his identity? I would think a profiler could do something with that."

"I'm sure it's been factored in." His reply was deliberately noncommittal, and his tone made it clear that he didn't intend to discuss the case. Everyone at the party would know he was involved in the investigation, and anything he said would be seized on and repeated. The killer's choice of parks as venues for disposing of the bodies had not only been factored in, it was both a vital clue and a frustrating complication in the profiler's analysis. Dr. Mavis Ross, the consultant psychiatrist on retainer to the police, was more at home doing geographic profiling, working out the radius, often very small, of a killer's operations from his home base. So far the profiler had tentatively concluded that the killer was male, physically strong — no surprises there! — sexually inadequate with a hatred of women, sadistic, and an exhibitionist. The last characteristic she inferred from the way he displayed the bodies of his victims, rather than trying to hide them. She agreed that the crosses being on different hands was significant and could indicate that two killers were at work. The existence of the crosses was a holdback by the police, and the fact that they were always present tended to contradict the possibility of there being two killers. But the copycat, if indeed there was one, could have learned of it somehow. Scott Millard, for example, almost certainly knew ...

Chris's reverie was brief, but still long enough to be noticed. He came out of it to find Sarah looking at him with amused cool grey eyes. "Sorry," he apologized. "I was thinking about something there for a minute."

"Parks, maybe?"

He was saved from having to reply when some friends came up to talk to Sarah. Diners were leaving their tables and joining together in groups as servers began to remove dishes and table cloths. Chris and his three companions remained together, chatting with the other guests. They were listening to a local member of the legislature expounding on the need to conserve the province's vital water resources when Cameron Taylor came up to tap his son on the shoulder. "We have a long drive ahead of us, and tomorrow we move the B herd to summer pasture."

"And I have an even longer drive," said Sarah, joining the increasing trickle of guests bidding goodnight to the hosts.

"I'll see you to your car." Chris fell in beside her.

When they stepped out from the front entrance they found the Taylors admiring the Ferrari, parked as usual in the driveway at Doug Church's insistence. They were familiar with the car from Chris's occasional visits to their ranch.

"She's beautiful, Chris," Cam called back over his shoulder as he and his family continued walking up the driveway. "But you know something? I wouldn't trade my champion cutting horse for her."

"Now there's a real ranching dynasty!" exclaimed Chris. "Four generations!"

"It's about to come to an end." Sarah replied.

"Oh? How come?"

"Melanie can't have children. She was born without a uterus. There's nothing that can be done."

"Yet Cam still married her. Must have been true love."

"She didn't tell him until after they were married. He puts a pretty good face on it, but his parents were livid."

"I can imagine."

"Cam is right. She *is* gorgeous." Sarah gently touched the gleaming hood of the sports car. "So this is what they call Ferrari red."

She probably also thought it was an unlikely vehicle for a police detective to be driving but didn't mention it. Class, thought Chris.

"*Your* wheels aren't exactly shabby!" he chuckled as they approached the high-end Mercedes sedan and she dug the keys out of her purse. The rumour was that she had received a $10-million divorce settlement.

She pressed a button on her key chain and there was a click as the doors unlocked. Turning, she held out her hand. They looked at each other in the light of a street lamp, both with the hint of a smile and a look of wariness in their eyes.

"I enjoyed the evening," she said.

"So did I. Very much."

"Goodnight, then."

"Goodnight."

chapter eleven

"The police garage just called. The SUV Forsyth rented that weekend has arrived." Chris stood up and beckoned to Gwen. "Let's go see if it's got anything to tell us." he added.

"The fact that it's been driven by other parties since Forsyth turned it in isn't going to help," Chris muttered as the two of them exited from the rear of the building and walked over to the side lot where the police vehicles were parked. "Unless we come up with something that can be linked directly to the victim. I'll drive," he said as the door locks of the cruiser clicked open.

"A nice blood sample or a blond hair that matches Ms. Vinney's DNA would be very helpful right about now." Gwen adjusted the safety harness on the passenger's side. "Thanks to your knowing about flow-through shares, hold periods, and things like that, we've got a very convincing motive. But ..."

"I know. No hard evidence," Chris finished the sentence. "And the chances are against finding anything incriminating in the vehicle. If my scenario is correct, Vinney would have been rendered unconscious, transported somewhere to be killed, mutilated, and then deposited in Edworthy Park."

"So that's one, maybe two trips in the vehicle. Lots of opportunity for something to be left behind."

"Not if our killer was careful. As someone like Forsyth would be. Anyway, we'll know soon enough," said Chris as they pulled into the police garage.

The Honda, its silver finish caked with mud, held centre stage. Its doors and tailgate stood open and two Crime Scenes investigators were examining the interior.

"Anything?" asked Chris as a plainclothes constable backed out of the door on the passenger side and stood up, pressing his hands against his lower back.

"Lots. If you're interested in candy bar wrappings, empty Coke cans, half-eaten cheeseburgers, and soiled paper serviettes. There were three young kids in the family and they sure left their mark. Apparently the mother wanted to clean up the mess, but the Mounties wouldn't let her touch anything."

"They did the right thing."

"I know. But it sure doesn't help. Contaminates the scene something fierce. Don't look promising anyway."

A canvas-covered metal frame big enough to fit over the vehicle stood off to one side. It was used to block out the light when luminol was sprayed over a surface to detect traces of blood.

"The luminol didn't come up with anything?"

The constable shook his head. "Not a trace. You want to have a look?"

"I'll wait and see what, if anything, Gwen finds."

Magnifying glass in hand, Gwen was bent over the

passenger side of the front seat. "Nothing here. I'll try the rear compartment," she said as she straightened up.

"All we need is a single hair, or a stray fibre," Chris said softly as he stood beside her, peering into the jumble of portable camp stools, backpacks, and skateboards.

"You've photographed everything?" Gwen asked the constable holding the camera.

"Everything. It's all tagged and identified," he told her.

"Then let's remove this stuff and see what we have."

"Surgical," Gwen pronounced after fifteen minutes of prying and probing. "If this vehicle was used to transport a body, it was wrapped in something completely leak proof."

"No surprises there. Thanks to TV everyone knows what we do and what we can come up with."

The two of them remained on the scene for another half-hour, watching, for the most part, as the Crime Scenes constables continued their search of the Honda. There were fingerprints, both clear and smudged, on the steering wheel, glove compartment, door handles, and virtually every surface that could hold a print. Many were small and could only have been made by a child. The family who had rented the vehicle had provided their fingerprints on the understanding that they would be destroyed after they had served their purpose.

"Call me if you turn up anything," Chris said as he and Gwen walked over to their van.

"Don't hold your breath," one of the constables grunted from under the Honda.

"Crane here." God, he sounded like Nevermore!

His smile was replaced with a frown when he heard Tom Forsyth's terse, "We need to talk, Chris."

Chris was equally terse. "Where and when?"

"This afternoon. Four-thirty. The O.N. bar." There was a click as Forsyth rang off.

Tom Forsyth was sitting at a table that was partly screened by a fretwork partition of dark wood, but afforded a good view of the entrance. It was too early for the cocktail hour and the popular bar was less than a third full.

"What will you have to drink?" was his only greeting.

"Whatever you're having."

"Two glasses of red wine, please," the corporate lawyer said to the server who had appeared at the table as soon as Chris arrived.

"You wanted to talk," said Chris after the two men had stared silently for several minutes at the untouched wine.

"I should sue you bastards," Forsyth gritted.

"Dangerous. Think of Oscar Wilde and the Marquis of Queensberry."

"Very funny." Forsyth was not amused. "Two of your colleagues showed up at the office this morning, flashed their badges around, barged into a meeting I was having with an important client, hauled me back to my office, and proceeded to interrogate me about Adrienne's murder."

Chris struggled to remain expressionless as he cringed inwardly. "What were their names?" As if he couldn't guess!

"Some buffoon called Mason. He did all the talking, and I never did catch the other guy's name. That son of a bitch Mason tried to bully me into confessing to her murder! You can imagine how that fiasco went over at the firm!"

Chris took a calming sip of wine. "Detective Mason is not noted for his tact."

"Tact! That bastard is a disgrace! A menace who shouldn't be allowed out of his cage! And then there's you." When Chris took another sip of wine and made no reply, Forsyth went on, "Forcing Jack Adams to disclose information about my stock transactions. Threatening him with a warrant if he didn't." Forsyth inhaled deeply, as if to control his pent-up anger. "For your information, it has always been my intention to sell the Madison shares the moment they were free to trade. I was counting the days until Tuesday, May 27. I had already taken advantage of the income tax deduction and I had other plans for the cash."

And if Adrienne Vinney had still been alive, there wouldn't have been any cash, Chris silently reminded himself. Now Forsyth was saying, "That kind of information is confidential, for Christ's sake! If I decide to sue, you'll be one of the defendants."

"Nothing is confidential in a murder investigation." Chris paused at the sight of a young, petite Asian woman standing in the entrance. Giving a little wave, she began to walk toward their table." Who's that?"

"My alibi." Forsyth stood up and held out his hand. She took it with a demure little smile, settled onto a chair with a graceful twirl of her skirt, and deposited her outsize handbag on the floor beside her.

"This is my friend, Chris." Forsyth introduced Crane, who had resumed his seat across from her. "Chris, meet Mai Lin." Chris was rewarded with a tantalizing glimpse of cleavage and an entrancing smile as she acknowledged the introduction with a deep bow.

"Well, gentlemen," she began in a voice that had an unexpected edge. "What did you have in mind? A threesome? That would be very nice, but it costs extra."

"Not exactly." Forsyth gave a little cough. "Chris is a detective."

"I'm outta here!" Mai Lin scooped up her bag and jumped to her feet.

"He's not Vice. Relax." Forsyth grabbed her by the elbow. "Tell her, Crane."

"He's right. I'm not with Sex Crimes. I'm investigating a homicide, and if this is about what I think it is, you have nothing to fear."

"He's not interested in what you do for a living. Isn't that right, Chris?"

"That's right."

Chris met her eyes as she gave him a long, searching look. It seemed to satisfy her, for she sat down, her back rigid and skirt folded primly across her knees. "All you need to do is to answer a few questions," Forsyth told her. "And don't worry about your fee. I'll take care of it. Now I want you to tell Chris where you were the night of May 25. That was the Sunday before last."

Mai Lin paused for a moment before saying, "I was here, in this hotel, with you."

"Are you sure?" queried Chris. "I noticed you seemed to hesitate for a moment."

"I'm sure. I was just trying to sort out the date."

"I can see where that might be a problem in your calling."

The almond eyes flashed at him, but her expression eased when she saw he was being matter-of-fact, not sarcastic. "I remember because he" — a finger indicated Forsyth — "hired me for the whole night. That doesn't happen very often. Fifteen hundred dollars."

"How much of that night did you spend together?"

"All of it. We had a room service supper in his room."

"When did you leave?"

"Just after seven in the morning. He wanted to

order breakfast, but I wasn't hungry."

"Satisfied?" Forsyth leaned back in his chair and regarded Chris with a slight smile.

Chris quirked an eyebrow. "Seems pretty conclusive."

"Is there anything else?" the escort asked Forsyth.

"No, Mai Lin. That does it. You've been very helpful. I'll put you in a taxi."

"Well, you can call off the dogs now," said Forsyth when he returned.

"Yeah. It would seem that way."

"Cops!" Tom shot him an exasperated look. "Okay. I'll be getting my Visa statement any day now. It will show a charge for this hotel on that night, and also fifteen hundred dollars payable to Tanya's Fitness Spa. How do you like that for a name? I'll show it to you. Chris, can you just tell that bastard Mason that I have an unbreakable alibi without going into details? I'm not particularly proud of that little escapade, but Madge was out of town, and," he added with a touch of defiance, "I felt like celebrating the fact that I would be able to sell my Madison shares on Tuesday."

"I'll talk to Detective Mason. You won't be suing him or anyone else, though."

"Oh?"

"Let me remind you again of poor Oscar Wilde and his 'Ballad of Reading Gaol.' You wouldn't want your little escapade to become public knowledge, would you, Tom? Somehow, I don't think Madge would approve."

Forsyth laughed. "That lawsuit business was just so much talk on my part. But that Mason character would get anyone's back up. Can I give you a lift?"

"No thanks. It's a nice evening for a stroll."

"Suit yourself. No hard feelings?" Forsyth held out his hand.

"None." They shook hands, and Forsyth headed for the elevators that would take him down to the parkade.

"That son of a bitch!"

Chris was actually fuming! Not his style at all. "Could you by any chance be referring to the good Detective Mason?" asked Gwen with a sly grin. It was after six, but she was still there checking some notes she had typed.

"How did you guess?" Chris, his good humour restored, smiled back at her. "Can you believe what he did? Marched into Forsyth's law office, yanked him out of a client meeting, and practically accused him of being the serial killer! Tried to make him confess. With no evidence. He must have heard us talking about Forsyth and figured he'd grab all the glory for himself. Just the sort of tactic that endears the police to the public!"

"Steve is from the old school. He spent years as a beat officer on the street. I find it helps to keep that in mind. Besides, he does have his good points."

"He *does*?"

Gwen laughed. "Not many I grant you. But he *is* loyal to his friends. You remember Constable Ralston? Gordon Ralston."

"The guy who in the dead of winter used to transport drunks in his cruiser outside the city limits and leave them in a snowbank to freeze to death. What the street people call a starlight tour. He was discharged from the force in disgrace. When was it? About four years ago?"

"That's him. The brass disowned him, and so did a lot of his fellow officers. But there were those who felt he had received a raw deal. Made a scapegoat. Especially Mason. They're long-time buddies; they were probationary constables together and graduated from the same recruit training course. I know Steve helped Ralston find a job with a security company, and I've seen them having a meal together at Wendy's."

"I'm sure they have a lot in common. But to be fair, Mason has never been guilty of anything like what Ralston did. He's known to have roughed up suspects in his day, but …" Chris dismissed the subject with a shrug.

"Your drink with Mr. Forsyth didn't last very long," Gwen observed, ending the thoughtful silence. "How did it go?"

"Interesting. Very interesting. Here it is. From the top."

"Boys will be boys." Gwen's smile had a trace of complacency when Chris finished. "But there goes a likely suspect. Now what?"

"Exactly."

"I keep thinking about Ingram. It's clear he idolized her."

"Natural enough under the circumstances. But where's the motive? He flatly denied there was anything going on between them. I've got to say I believed him. "

"So did I. But that's not necessarily the end of the story. Indulge me for a moment, Chris. Ingram works very closely with Vinney. They put in long hours together. Night and day. Adrienne Vinney is an extremely attractive woman, and at the very top of her profession. It's not difficult to imagine him falling head over heels in love with her. Let's say, late some night they're working together, and she does or says something that he takes as a come-on. He puts a move on her and gets rebuffed. Worse, she does it in a way that humiliates him, makes it clear that the very thought appalls her. He broods; if he can't have her, nobody can. You know, that kind of stuff."

"It happens," agreed Chris. "We've both seen it. But how about this? Adrienne, being the kind of person she is, lets him down easy. She wouldn't want to alienate him and risk losing him as her valuable junior, so she rejects his advances in a way that doesn't humiliate him but lets him think that, under different circumstances, there's still a chance. So, one night when they're together, away from the office, he tries it again, only this time there's no doubt that she wants no part of it, or him. He can't handle the rejection and hits her, knocking her out. Realizing the consequences of what he's done, he knows he can't let her live, and decides to make it look like the work of our serial killer."

"But how would he know how to do that?"

"Not a problem. At least not an insurmountable one. Lawyers talk. Particularly the younger ones. They meet for drinks after work, they socialize at bar association functions, hockey games, you name it. Some Crown prosecutors would be familiar with the details of the serial killings. How the victims were mutilated, and so on. There's always the temptation to impress your peers." Chris paused. "It's plausible, I guess. At least it's more plausible than the thought of those two getting it on together."

Chris stretched, and looked around the work area. At this hour half the desks were unoccupied. "I guess Ken has left for the day."

"He's out somewhere in the northeast interviewing the ex-husband in that child murder case. Where the girl was drowned in the bathtub. The mother's been charged."

"Ken's the right guy to be interviewing family members in cases like that. He's got the sympathetic touch. He's a great cop. A great partner to work with."

"Let's step outside for a moment, Chris."

Mystified, he followed her through the door into the little reception area.

"I didn't want to say anything in there, but I'd be careful about calling him 'partner' if I were you."

"What the hell is that supposed to mean?"

"You don't know, do you?"

"Know what?"

"Patterson is gay."

"That's crazy! He has a girlfriend. I saw him with her at the annual barbecue in May. He introduced her to me." Chris paused to recalled the occasion. Patterson's date had not been what he would have expected. Glasses perched on a sharp, pointed nose, hair pulled back in a bun, devoid of makeup, she didn't seem like his type. Not at all. "I can't remember her name offhand."

"Irene Gelinas, and she's his friend, not his girlfriend. She works at McKinley. She's a lesbian who's well known in the gay community. She plays the field. Her relationships never last more than a month, and she never has a live-in lover. She and Ken are very close. Very. A mutually supportive arrangement."

"Are you sure about this?"

"I'm sure. Believe me."

"I sort of wish you hadn't told me."

"I wouldn't have, except I thought you had to know. People might take it the wrong way when you talk about your partner."

"Point taken. So the lady works at the same firm as Vinney did?"

"It's a big firm. I'm not sure what it is she does there, but she's not a lawyer."

"You know, I've never suspected this about Ken. Not for a minute. And I've never heard so much as a whisper about it around the office from anyone."

"He doesn't advertise it. Why should he? It's not as if it affects the way he does his job."

"Amen to that. Okay. Information received and subject dropped. 10-4."

Chris fell silent for a moment, then expelled his breath in a small exasperated sigh. "I have only one bone — if you'll forgive the pun — to pick with the gay community, and that's the way they have co-opted two very useful words — *gay* and *queer* — from the English language and made them impossible to use in any other context."

"You're serious, aren't you?"

"Perfectly."

Chris gave a slight shake of his head, as if to clear it of the troublesome thought. Pushing the door open, he said, "Back to our serial."

Once inside, Gwen started to say something, then clamped her lips shut as she saw his frown of concentration. When she saw his brow beginning to clear, she said softly, "You're having one of your 'Crane moments,' aren't you?"

"I guess I am. Now to see where it takes us."

chapter twelve

Mai Lin's professional smile faltered and she took an uncertain step backward.

"It's all right. Don't worry." Chris took her by the arm and gently pulled her into the hotel room.

"I thought you weren't Vice?"

"I'm not. That's not why you are here."

"Oh? You know the rates?"

"That's not why you're here either. I just want to talk."

That brought a raised eyebrow as the escort seated herself, not letting go of the leather carryall on the floor beside her. "Talk costs money, too."

"Later. Right now, I want to hear about that all-nighter you had with Tom Forsyth."

Mai Lin shrugged. "What's to tell? We drank some wine, ate supper, and had sex."

"You stayed all night?"

"That's what I was paid for."

"That's not an answer. Were you there all night?"

"Yes. What's this all about? Am I in some kind of trouble?"

"Not if you answer my questions. And tell the truth."

"Are you sure you're a cop? You don't look like one."

"I am." Chris flipped open his wallet to show her his badge and identification.

"This guy Tom must be in big trouble."

"Not necessarily. We're just looking into a few things."

"Sure." She shot him a skeptical look, which changed to alarm as she asked, "Will I be called on to testify? On the stand? I can't do that. No way."

"It's unlikely. But I can't promise you won't. I *can* promise you immunity if you do have to testify. If you testify willingly and truthfully."

"And if I don't?"

"You will be subpoenaed and examined under oath. The maximum penalty for perjury is fourteen years. But we're getting ahead of ourselves. You said you didn't feel like having breakfast in the morning. Just tell me what you remember."

"Not one hell of lot. I seem to have slept most of the time."

"How often did you have sex? Can you remember?"

"Just the once. After supper. He didn't seem all that interested, if you want the truth. It was all kind of weird. Why would a guy pay for a whole night and not take advantage of it?"

"Why indeed? Let's talk about what you felt like when you woke up."

"I felt like crap, to be honest. The john," she went on, instinctively de-personalizing the client, "had a hell of a time waking me. My head felt like it would split in two.

All I wanted to do was to get back home to my apartment and sleep. I didn't work for two days after that."

"So your all-nighter didn't turn out to be such a great deal, after all?" Chris smiled companionably at her.

"That's right. Like I said, it was kind of weird."

"Have you ever felt like that before?"

"Never. Not once in my whole life." She shook her head. "And I hope to God I never do again."

"Is it possible the john could have gone out for a few hours without you knowing it?"

Another lifted eyebrow. "I dunno. Yeah, I guess so. I was really out of it. I offered to give him back some of his money but he didn't want it."

"Did it ever occur to you that you could have been drugged?"

"You mean like the date rape drug? Yeah, I thought about it. But what was the point? He had already paid to have as much as sex as he wanted. I thought he might have tried some sick perversion on me, but there was no sign of that. I checked myself out, all over. Then I figured I must have had the flu."

"So it's fair to say he could have left you sleeping in bed and gone out without you knowing?"

"The hotel could have burned to the ground without me knowing it."

"Fair enough." Chris fished in his pants pocket. "It's two-sixty an hour, right?" He had given much thought to whether he should pay for her time, but it was standard practice for police informants to be paid, and it wouldn't contaminate her evidence if and when she testified under oath. He winced at the thought of the field day defence counsel would have if they ever found out.

"I don't like to take it, but I'll get shit from the agency if I don't." Mai Lin looked at her watch as she took the money. "There's still time to do something, if you like."

For an unexpected moment, he was tempted. But he would be on the stand and subject to counsel's probing questions.

"Thanks, but I'll take a rain check."

The cage was empty. Jesus! Chris shuddered at the thought of the havoc the parrot could have wreaked. Nothing seemed to be disturbed in the living room, nor was there any sign of Nevermore.

"Nevermore, where are you?"

As if in answer, there came a loud, clanging crash from the kitchen. Telling himself there was nothing there that couldn't be replaced, Chris hurried across the living room.

"Hello, Chris." The guttural greeting brought him up short, and he stood in the archway, unable to resist a chuckle as he took in the scene. Nevermore was perched on the overhead metal rack designed to hold the cooking pots and pans. Most of the hooks were empty, the pots and saucepans piled in a heap on the cooking island below.

"Well, that must have been fun!" Still chuckling, and vastly relieved that Nevermore had concentrated his mischief on the cooking utensils, which made such a satisfactory din, Chris smiled up at his unrepentant pet. He would put the pots through the dishwasher before hanging them back on their hooks. Standing on tiptoe, he reached his hand up for Nevermore to climb onto. He refused to have the bird's wings clipped, which was fine so long as he was around to supervise when Nevermore was out of the cage. But now that he could escape at will ... Chris patted the little package in his pocket. On his way to the hotel he had stopped at a hardware store and purchased a padlock, the smallest size they had, but wide enough so that Nevermore couldn't pull it through the bars into the cage.

"Congratulations, my clever friend, you solved that puzzle very neatly," he said as he put the parrot back in its cage.

Head cocked to one side, Nevermore watched intently as Chris rehung the door and fastened the padlock over the sliding bar that held the door closed.

Nevermore had solved *his* puzzle, and he, Chris Crane, had made considerable progress toward solving his. Not that he particularly cared for the way the answer seemed to be shaping up. But finding answers was what he did. They both deserved a little reward. Chris gave Nevermore three green grapes, put on their favourite Sonata disc, and poured himself a glass of Chambertin.

Nevermore had another little surprise for Chris before he left in the morning. Telephone receiver in his left hand, right hand poised over the dial, Chris paused as he heard the unmistakable sound of numbers being punched in. Another addition to Nevermore's rapidly expanding repertoire.

"Fooled you this time," he told the parrot as he pressed the single key on the speed dial that connected with Gwen at the FCSU office, where she usually went to begin her day. When she answered, he told her he was just leaving for Andrew Davison and asked her to meet him there.

"So our prime suspect is back in play!" Gwen's eyes shone with excitement when Chris finished telling her about his meeting with Mai Lin. "An inspired bit of detective work on your part, if I may say so."

"You may. And thanks. Actually, it was Mason's bull in the china shop tactics that precipitated it. Convinced him it was time to produce his alibi. The alibi he had so cleverly manufactured."

Which, thought Gwen, *explains why you've been so cool about that clown barging into Forsyth's law office, instead of dressing him down the way he deserved. Or filing a complaint. But then you're not the kind to file complaints.*

Chris was still talking. "It was Mai Lin saying she didn't feel like breakfast that got me thinking. And Tom paying for Mai Lin's services with a credit card instead of using cash also struck me as suspicious. He's no dummy, and he would know there's always a possibility of being traced through credit card records. In this case, however, he would want the charge to show up on his statement to further substantiate his alibi. And I once knew a guy who used to doctor his wife's wine with ground-up sleeping pills. She would go to bed right after dinner and he would slip out to carry on his affair with her best friend."

Intrigued, Gwen asked, "What happened?"

"She went to see a doctor, who asked her if she was aware that someone was trying to poison her."

"And?"

"Divorce. A very expensive divorce. And the end of a beautiful friendship."

"I must say you know the most interesting people!"

"Don't I, though?"

"Where do we go from here?"

Much to Gwen's relief, when Chris replied his voice was matter-of-fact, detached. His professional instincts were not to be overruled by the fact that the suspect was a personal friend. "There are several leads that need to be followed up. If Forsyth is our boy, he had to work within a very compressed time frame from Saturday afternoon, when he first learned that Vinney was going to blow the whistle, to sometime Sunday night. Let's think about what he had to accomplish in that time. Remember, it's still hypothetical."

"Yeah. Of course," replied Gwen. "Okay, first, how would he have laid his hands on the drug?"

"I think we can assume it was a street drug. Most likely rohypnol from the way she described what it did to her. Mixed with wine it would be virtually tasteless. And it's readily available on the street."

"Would our boy know that? He practises corporate law, not criminal."

"All he has to do is read the papers. They're full of drug wars and drug busts. Mostly in the northeast. It wouldn't take him long to make a buy up there. I'll talk to the drug squad. They'll know just who to question. They'll need that photo you took along with some others of men in his age group. Maybe we can get a useable ID."

"I'll look after it. What about the hotel? If he snuck out on the escort, some of the staff must have seen him."

"Not necessarily. He could have taken an elevator down to the lower floor where the shops are and gone out the side door. It's locked at night, but it can be opened from the inside."

"The parkade? He would need transportation."

"I'll inquire. But you can bet he'd be too smart for that. There's a free city parking lot less than a block away from the hotel. And we know he rented an SUV that weekend. Both he and Marge, his wife, have cars, so why would he do that?"

"And we think he may have found out how the real killer mutilated his victims from Scott Millard, his good friend and squash partner?"

"Who in turn could have been told about it by an

informant. So far, it's rank surmise, but the pieces do seem to fit."

"Chris?"

"I know what you're thinking — shouldn't we bring Forsyth in?"

"Well, shouldn't we?"

Chris shook his head. "There's no direct evidence to connect him with the crime. All we have so far is a set of highly suspicious circumstances. Highly suspicious, but still capable of being explained away."

"He could be a danger to the public if he's left on the loose. Think of that poor, innocent woman, the one you call a victim of convenience. He might be the one who killed her as well. And there could be others if he's developed a taste for killing. That can happen."

"I know. But I don't think that's why the Simpson woman was killed. If Forsyth killed her, it would be to convince us that Adrienne Vinney was another victim of our serial killer. If so, it was a rational act, not a thrill killing."

"If murder can ever be rational," Gwen amended.

"And don't forget," Chris reminded her, "the cross was on the right hand in the Simpson case. Right being left in this case. If it was Forsyth who killed Adrienne Vinney, I don't see him making a career out of it. He would have nothing to gain."

"He could have found out about the hand the same way he found out about the other mutilations. Professional gossip. But you know the guy. You know how he thinks, and I don't."

"What are you saying, Gwen? That I should recuse myself from the case?"

"Of course I'm not, Chris. The way you've investigated this case has been a model of police work. It's just that I worry about him being out there."

"We're on the same page, Gwen. As usual." Chris choked slightly as he heard himself. He had just committed a cliché worthy of the Chief himself. With an apologetic shrug, he continued, "I'm going to arrange to have Forsyth put under surveillance. Starting this afternoon."

"Thank God!" Gwen breathed. "That makes me feel better. Much better."

She started to get up then sat down again as she saw the receptionist approaching with a plastic bag.

"This came in this morning's mail." The receptionist handed Chris the bag. The envelope inside it was addressed to him with the individual letters clipped from a newspaper. Reaching into a drawer he pulled on latex gloves and waited while Gwen went back to her desk for hers.

Slitting the envelope open with a paperknife, he took out the single sheet of paper, holding it by the top left-hand corner. Like the address, the terse message was in newsprint, a random mixture of capitals and lower case:

g**I**ᵥE ᵤP crane?

The heart-shaped signature attested to its authenticity.

How had he gotten hold of "crane"? It was in lower case. Of course. Last week a window cleaner had been trapped on the fifth floor of the Sun Life Plaza and a mobile crane had been used to rescue him. Both local papers had run the story.

The question mark was written in blue ink. Question marks weren't all that easy to find in a newspaper.

"Make copies for us, and send the original to Forensics," he instructed Gwen. "I'll call Mavis."

"She'll be here in half an hour," he said when Gwen came back with the photocopies. "And we both know Mavis likes to form her own opinion and doesn't appreciate being told what to look for. Let's take a pee break while we wait."

"It'll be interesting to hear what she has to say about the note Dummett claims to have received," Gwen remarked. Chris had discussed the freelancer's visit with both her and the profiler and shown a copy of the communication to both. He had not mentioned it to anyone else. Not even Patterson.

"Let's talk first about the communications directed to the police. Either generally, or now more specifically to you." Mavis Ross looked at Chris. "In my opinion these are the genuine article. I believe them to be from TLC. For one thing, the letters and words are all from the *Sun*."

Chris nodded, half-mesmerized as always by the luminous hazel eyes that regarded the world and its foibles with such calm appraisal. Those eyes had widened in mild interest when Chris, in one of their earlier sessions on a previous case, had informed her she was named after a bird — a European song thrush. "What do the letters being from the *Sun* tell us?" he asked.

"Its readership, generally speaking, is different from the other papers."

"More blue-collar?" Gwen put in.

"That's true. To a certain extent. It also appeals to a younger audience, and those who follow sports. Spectator sports primarily."

"That could be helpful." Chris was well aware that demographics often played a vital role in solving a crime.

"It could," she agreed, then cautioned, "But lots of people who don't fall into any of those categories read the *Sun*. Or the sender could have used it for the reason that he or she isn't a regular reader."

"Okay. You said all the messages are from the same person. TLC. What do they tell us about him or her?"

"Most importantly that this person doesn't want to be caught. When serials start communicating with the police it often means they want to be found out. Sometimes it's because they want to stop; sometimes it's because they crave the publicity that an arrest would bring. The notoriety that to them is the same as fame. Not TLC, however. He's narcissistic, like most serials. Maybe even more so. My guess is he will continue with his campaign. That's what this is," she said, tapping the photocopy with her index finger. "A campaign. Killer versus the police. He's selected you, Chris, as his real opponent. The Chief always mentions you in his press conferences as the detective heading up the crack Homicide team investigating the crimes."

"Does that mean Chris is in danger?" demanded an alarmed Gwen.

"No. I'm pretty sure not. This killer is fixated on women. It's clear he hates them. Look at what he does to them. He now regards Chris as his opponent in a game of his own making. I find myself referring to the killer as 'he,' but that's just for convenience. It could also be a woman."

"Do you really think so?" Chris shook his head. "The vibes I'm getting tell me we're dealing with a man. And very few women have the sheer physical strength to do what this guy does."

As he said this, Chris realized that the profiler, with her large, muscular build, was one woman who was quite capable of doing exactly that.

An amused half-smile told him that Mavis had read his thoughts. She had a disconcerting way of doing that from time to time. Her smile was replaced with faint frown lines as she studied the communications spread out on the table. "There's no question in my mind that our killer is waging war with the police. And as I said, it's pretty clear that he has selected Chris as representing the police. But I'm beginning to suspect that you may have been his designated target right from the start."

"Steve Mason won't like that," breathed Gwen. "He was all puffed up when that letter was sent to him with his neighbour's address on it. He went around saying that TLC realized that he was the real threat. The one most likely to track him down."

Before he made a sardonic remark about Mason's inimitable investigative style, Chris checked himself. It wasn't necessary for Mavis to know about Forsyth's effort to establish an alibi.

"Anything more to be gleaned from TLC's missives, Mavis?"

"He will kill again. And again. We don't know what got him started. But he's addicted to it now. The power over life and death. It's what serial killers get off on. Some of these psychopaths keep score. Compare their numbers with those racked up by their famous counterparts — Dahmer, Gacy, Bundy, our own Clifford Olson and Paul Bernardo. Our boy still has a way to go to catch up to most of them. Maybe not Bernardo, but he made up for it in other ways."

"Phil Dummett talked about the power syndrome as well. But I think it was more of a general comment on his part. Something he picked up from his reading. He hasn't had the advantage of seeing the other letters you believe to be authentic. But what about the letter Dummett allegedly received? Do you think it's genuine?"

"Who's to know? It's a toss-up either way. It doesn't have the drawing of a heart and the newsprint is from the *Herald*, not the *Sun*. On the other hand, it's completely logical that TLC would seek out somebody like this journalist. He would see him as a way to get his message out to the public. And of course this freelancer would realize it was a once-in-a-lifetime opportunity. A mutually beneficial arrangement."

"Mavis's profile of the serial doesn't exactly fit Forsyth, does it?" asked Gwen.

"Not at all," Chris agreed, returning to the interview room after escorting Mavis to the elevator. "The most interesting part is what she said about this being a game. That doesn't fit Forsyth. Not at all. I can't see him as a serial killer. I'm pretty well convinced he killed Adrienne Vinney, but what we need is a piece of evidence to link him to that crime. If only the guys had come up with something from the SUV."

"Like the feather of a meadowlark?" asked Gwen innocently.

"We wish!" laughed Chris. Back in his days with the FCSU, it had been his recognition of a feather lodged inside the grille of a Nissan as that of a meadowlark that had led to the arrest and eventual conviction of a murderer. The western meadowlark, whose range was fast contracting as its habitat disappeared with the advance of urban sprawl, was a bird of the open grasslands and country roadside ditches. The presence of its feather had contradicted the murderer's claim that he'd never been near the scene of the crime.

"There's no way we can get authorization for an arrest with what we have so far," said Chris as he and Gwen remained sitting around the table.

"Everything fits. But it's all circumstantial."

"Convincing, but circumstantial. All right, let's go through it one more time. After all, most murder trials are based on circumstantial evidence."

He had barely begun when there was a knock on the door and the receptionist, at his nod, ushered in two uniformed police. Both wore big smiles.

"We may have struck out on the plastic, but we got a hit on the tape," said the senior constable, a blonde in her late thirties, her cheeks flushed with excitement. "We got a positive ID of the suspect purchasing two rolls of duct tape from the proprietor of a little convenience store tucked under the Crowchild Trail overpass."

"Beautiful!" Chris and Gwen sighed in unison.

"Congratulations," Chris added. "This proprietor is willing to testify?"

"He is. It's a positive ID, and he will be a very credible witness. Here's his name and address." Still smiling, the two constables left.

"Now what use do you suppose a murderer could have for two rolls of duct tape?" Gwen couldn't repress a gleeful grin.

"'Let me count the ways.'" Momentarily elated by this telling piece of evidence, Chris almost chortled as he quoted the famous line from the poem by Elizabeth Barrett Browning, ticking off each point on his fingers. "First you keep her from calling for help by taping her mouth. Then you render her immobile by taping her hands and feet. And then you use it to seal whatever you're wrapping her body in to keep it from leaking blood."

"Now what?"

"Now I apply pressure to Mr. Scott Millard and see if he can add anything to the case against Forsyth."

"I already told you I have nothing more to say on that subject!" The criminal lawyer glared across his desk, strewn with court documents, at Chris.

"So you did," agreed Chris. "But things have moved on since then, and it looks as though you will find yourself being served with a subpoena. Which of course means you will have to tell what you know in open court."

"I know what it means, for Christ's sake!" Millard inhaled a deep breath and exhaled slowly. "You wouldn't be talking about this unless you plan to arrest Tom. Right?"

"The case against him is looking pretty compelling. More and more as we look into it."

"Yeah. I know all about the police and their tunnel vision once they've got a suspect in their sights."

"It's not like that. I'm a little puzzled, Scott. I would have thought that if Forsyth was the one who killed Adrienne and did those things to her, you would be the first to want him brought to justice."

"That's right. I would. But there's a big if. Isn't there?"

"Not as big as you might think. Well," Chris got to his feet. "I guess we'll have to see what the subpoena brings out."

"Sit down! Look, here's what I know. And what I could have mentioned to Tom."

"*Could* have?"

"Okay. *Did* tell him. I told him about her nipple being cut off, and about something being jammed up her … you know what."

Holding his breath, knowing he couldn't lead him, Chris looked at the lawyer, willing him to continue.

"I also told him about the perverted son of a bitch carving a cross on her hand and folding her hands as if she was praying. Like she was some kind of religious sacrifice, for Christ's sake!"

"Hence your 'religious pervert' comment at the Country Club. Did you happen to mention which hand?"

Millard paused, as if trying to remember. "No. I didn't. I didn't know myself." Another pause. "I take it from the way you look that it could be important?"

"It is. This is what you will testify to, if called upon?"

"I will."

"What happened?" Gwen came forward to meet Chris as he arrived back at Homicide.

"Forsyth knew. Now we go see the chief prosecutor and brief him on what we have. He's certain to authorize an arrest." The knowledge that they would be arresting someone who had once been a good friend was a sobering thought, but Chris couldn't deny the thrill of finally fitting the last piece of the puzzle in place.

"We'll take Mason along with us as well. If anything will throw Forsyth off, that should. You never know, maybe he'll be steamed enough to let something slip. Keep an eye on his reaction."

chapter thirteen

Tom Forsyth's almost handsome face was taut with outrage, disbelief, and something else. Something Chris couldn't quite place. Not yet. Aware that the first few minutes following an arrest, when a suspect was at his most vulnerable and liable to betray himself, were crucial, Chris stood back to watch his now former friend's reaction.

Forsyth's lips moved in a soundless curse as Mason intoned the formal words charging him with the murder of Adrienne Vinney. Ignoring Mason, who was hand-cuffing him, roughly jerking his hands behind his back, and advising him of his rights, Forsyth glared at Chris.

"You'll pay for this! All of you," he snarled. "What the hell's going on, Chris? Are you out of your fucking mind? You know I've got an alibi!"

"It won't wash, Tom. Mai Lin isn't an alibi. Her evidence will be part of the case against you."

"Well" — Forsyth tried to shrug, but the handcuffs made him wince — "if you're going to keep on with this nonsense, I better have a lawyer."

"You can call one from the station."

Two uniforms cleared a path for the little procession through a cluster of lawyers, clerical staff, and awestruck clients lining the carpeted hallway. "I'll get Scott Millard," one of the partners called out.

"Don't." Forsyth barked over his shoulder. "He's the one they should be arresting."

"Nice try, Tom. But it won't work," Chris murmured in his ear.

"I want Dave Myrden," Forsyth said as they crowded into an elevator.

"Good choice." Myrden was Calgary's leading criminal lawyer, with an impressive string of acquittals to his credit.

Myrden's office promised to get word through to him at the courthouse, but it would be after five in the afternoon before the busy counsel would be able to join them. Forsyth refused to say another word, beyond accepting a cup of coffee, until his counsel showed up. Until then he was left alone in an interview room, monitored by a junior detective through a window of one-way glass.

The three detectives went down to the cafeteria, almost deserted at this hour, while they waited for Myrden. The Homicide section would be bursting with excitement over the arrest, and Chris wanted to keep his little team focused.

"The cross," said Gwen, screwing up her face at the stale coffee. "It was on the left hand in every case except for Vinney."

"That shit about the crosses on different hands don't mean a damn thing," Mason grumbled. "All that matters is that they're there."

"If they hadn't been on different hands, we might never have spotted the Vinney murder as the work of a copycat. There would have been no reason to look for a motive to kill her, and we would have been left with no motive other than the fantasies of a psychopath," Gwen retorted.

"What you're saying then, Steve, is that so long as the cross is there, it's got to be the work of our serial. You're saying the hands don't matter." Chris pushed his mug of coffee, untasted, to one side.

"Who knows?" The Homicide detective shrugged. "We got a righteous collar. It'll take the heat off the Chief."

If Mason was right, that would mean Forsyth was TLC — the psychopath who had killed five women. That wouldn't fly. No way. It could be in character for him to kill in order to protect his windfall fortune, but Tom was no psychopath.

"I saw Gordon Ralston yesterday," Gwen was saying to Mason, breaking the silence that had fallen over the trio. "He was the commissionaire in the concourse at Bankers Hall. Guarding the art in the sculpture court, I guess."

"Waste of a good cop," Mason growled. Before he could say anything more, a policewoman came into the cafeteria to tell them Mr. Myrden had arrived and was conferring with his client.

"I have instructed Mr. Forsyth to say nothing," Dave Myrden announced as Chris and Gwen entered the room. To Chris's surprise, Mason elected not to join them, saying that Chris was better equipped to deal with a "brother shyster," adding with a sneer that he would take over when they came up dry.

"Do you confirm that my client is under arrest?" The defence attorney, in his mid-forties, cultivated a certain offbeat flamboyance. His thick head of brown hair, darkened with gel, had been brushed so that it stood straight up from his scalp in a bristly pompadour. His shirts were always white, as was the folded handkerchief poking out of the pocket of his Western-cut jacket. The grey striped pants were the same as the ones he wore in court. A pair of gleaming calf-length boots completed the outfit.

"He is. On a count of murder in the first degree."

"On what grounds?"

"Since your client has elected to remain silent I see no reason to disclose our case."

"I am entitled to know the grounds which led you to arrest Mr. Forsyth."

"A powerful motive, a botched attempt to establish an alibi, and opportunity."

"Physical evidence? Anything that would connect my client to the crime?"

"We have a witness who will testify that your client purchased two rolls of duct tape just hours before Adrienne Vinney was murdered."

"Is that a fact?" Myrden rolled his eyes heavenward. "And just how is that supposed to tie my client to the crime?"

"It's difficult to think of an innocent use for all that duct tape."

"Really? I can think of any number of purely innocent uses without even trying."

"More will be forthcoming. His office and residence are being searched as we speak."

"That's it? That's what you have?" The gleam in Myrden's eyes matched the shine of his boots. "I will be applying for bail ASAP. Do you intend to oppose it?"

"I certainly do. Your client is accused of murder in the first degree and is a definite flight risk. It is known that he intended to leave this country and move to a tax haven in the Caribbean. His wife is even now in Barbados looking to purchase a place for them to live."

"Maybe I'll drop the bail application and simply apply to have the charges dismissed for want of evidence." Myrden pushed his chair back and got to his feet. Typically, he had made no notes.

"I have a request." The words grated as they came out of the prisoner's mouth.

"Yes?"

"I must talk with my wife in Barbados, and my son in Toronto. They can't find out about this fiasco without hearing it from me first. They took my wallet from me, but you can get it and charge the calls to my Visa."

"I'll make the arrangements." Chris felt his gut tighten. Jesus. He knew Madge and had met their teenaged son a couple of times. What if he was wrong, and Tom was completely innocent!

So often police work ended in human tragedy. Not for the criminal, who, in most cases at least, had brought about his own downfall, but for his family and friends. Never more so than now. As he sometimes did in moments like this, Chris thought of Dorothy Underwood. That was one instance where he had made a difference. A positive difference.

FCSU had been called in to assist the fraud squad with some forensic accounting in an investigation of a scam involving a non-existent resort development in the Ontario lake district. Mrs. Underwood, an elderly widow, had been one of the victims and had brought suit to recover her substantial loss. The lawsuit had merit and would have succeeded, but her lawyer had persuaded her to accept a token settlement, nowhere near what her claim was worth. In the course of the investigation it was learned that he had been blackmailed into doing this by a threat to reveal a previous professional transgression on his part. Disbarred, he had committed automotive suicide, leaving a bankrupt estate and depriving the widow of any way of recouping her loss.

Chris would never forget the look of slowly dawning hope on that kind face, softened with age, as he told her about the Law Society, the legal profession's governing body, and its assurance fund. The fund was designed to compensate people who had been defrauded by one of its members. He had given her the name of Darlene Pitts, a lawyer who occasionally represented claimants like her pro bono.

The fund had compensated her, enabling her, as she told Chris with tears of gratitude, "to live in comfort and independence. The way Howard would have wanted me to."

The two had become friends and stayed in touch. From time to time Dorothy, as Chris had been told to call her, would phone, or he would visit her modest home on Memorial Drive. A home she had almost been forced to sell. He always brought along a bottle of sherry and they would enjoy a companionable glass or two. She worried in her gentle way when he transferred to Homicide. Just like his mother would have.

It had been a couple months since they last talked. Dorothy had probably been reluctant to bother him while he was pursuing the serial killer. But he would like to talk to her. He would give her a call. But not tonight.

chapter fourteen

Another body. This time in Bragg Creek Provincial Park. Damn. TLC was still one step ahead. He must have suspected that by now the city parks would be under surveillance, so he had moved the action to Bragg Creek, an upscale hamlet of some five hundred souls forty kilometres west of Calgary. It was Mountie turf, but the crime was so obviously connected to the rash of Calgary killings that the Calgary police had been called in. Mason and Gwen had just arrived at the crime scene.

Red and blue light pulsing on the van's dash, Chris sped along Highway 22, oblivious to the magnificent backdrop of the Rocky Mountains off to his right. The highway cut through the western end of the Tsuu T'ina Reserve, and he reduced speed as he went past the entrance to Redwood Meadows, a golf course owned and operated by the Tsuu T'ina Nation. The provincial park was just past the turnoff to the Bragg Creek shopping centre with its art galleries, craft shops, and restaurants. Open countryside gave way to towering pines as Chris followed the winding road through the forest to the park entrance. The entrance was sealed off with crime tape and guarded by two uniformed Mounties. One of them directed Chris to pull in next to a cruiser with the RCMP's inspired logo — a cantering horse and rider from the Musical Ride — painted on its rear fenders.

In the open area just past the gate two RCMP constables circulated among the small crowd of visitors, taking down names and addresses and getting negative responses and shakes of the head when they asked if anyone had seen anything out of the ordinary that morning. Those who were waiting to be questioned were staring at one of the small wooden huts that housed the toilets provided by the Park Service. The police were grouped around its far side. Spotting Chris, Gwen broke away from the other officers and hurried across the gravelled parking lot to meet him.

"Prepare yourself," she warned. "It's gross."

The doors of the two stalls on the near side of the hut were marked "Men," which meant the crime scene must be the women's toilets. Mason didn't so much as nod when Chris joined the group. The RCMP corporal in charge of the detail introduced himself and stepped aside so Chris could see into the hut. The naked, bloodied body of a young woman sat on the toilet. Chris's mouth tightened as he saw the familiar stigmata — the vicious stab wounds on her breast, the bloody pulp where her right nipple had been sliced off, rivulets of dried blood running down the torso and collecting in the ridges of muscles on her taut abdomen. The lady's abs were impressive, which might explain why she remained upright. Because of her position it was impossible to tell if a foreign object had been inserted into her vagina, but her thighs were bloody.

"Do we know who she is?" Chris's voice was tight as he took in the scene. The toilet was just that — a chemical toilet in the small, smelly compartment. Gwen was to tell him later that the floor area measured only seventy-six by seventy-six centimetres, no wash basin, no towels. Only a sign requesting users to please put the top down to reduce odours.

"Not yet," replied Gwen. The dank interior of the toilet was illuminated with electronic flashes as she fired off two exposures in quick succession. Lowering the camera, she said, "That will do it."

"Who found her?"

"A tourist," the RCMP corporal replied. "She went to use the facility just after nine-thirty. She had the bad luck to be the first one to open the door."

"I'd like to talk to her."

"Not possible. She's either in the Foothills hospital or on her way there. She fainted and the paramedics couldn't bring her around. They think she may have suffered a stroke. Not her first one, I gather. I got her name and particulars from her daughter, who has gone off with her in the ambulance."

While he listened to the Mountie, Chris continued to study the corpse. Her well-muscled arms hung down at her sides, the palms of her hands facing inward. Without prompting, Gwen followed as he took a few steps to one side.

"There is a cross, I assume?" he asked, looking into the distance.

"There is." Gwen paused. "On her left hand. It's our boy."

"And not Tom Forsyth," murmured Chris.

Gravel crunched under his shoes as he headed back to the hut. The medical examiner, a woman this time, had arrived and was squatting with her hands on her knees before the victim, her substantial bulk fully occupying the confined space.

"Not much doubt how she died," she remarked over her shoulder, directing her comment at Chris. He didn't know her, but she obviously knew who he was.

"Not much," he agreed. "Time of death?"

Still squatting, she checked the watch almost hidden in the folds of flesh on her wrist, "It's now seven minutes past eleven." Leaning forward, she took the victim's head in her hands and slowly rotated it from side to side. "The current temperature is 22 degrees Celsius. Rigor mortis well established. She was killed around one this morning."

"She was young and obviously very fit," Chris observed. "She couldn't have been all that easy to subdue. Yet there are no indications of struggle on her part."

"She was knocked unconscious with a single blow to the back of the head. After that the guy could do as he wanted with her."

After examining the victim for a few more minutes, the M.E. announced, "I'm done here. I'm releasing the body. I'll need to know her name when you find out who she is. For my records." Hands on ample hips, she gave the police officers a sweeping glance that held a trace of sympathy. "You're not having much luck nailing this TLC, are you?" she asked, then waddled on thick legs across the park to her vehicle.

As soon as she left, Chris stepped back inside the toilet and turned the woman's left hand over. Just as Gwen had said, a fine tracery of blood outlined the simple cross excised into the flesh of her palm.

Chris detached the dashboard light and put it back in the glove compartment. He kept well within the posted speed limit on the drive back to the city, while his mind climbed back on the all too familiar treadmill. The cross being on Vinney's wrong hand was what had led him to look for a logical motive, not just a psychopath, behind that crime. According to Scott Millard, who had no reason to lie, Forsyth didn't know which hand the cross was on. Chris instinctively tightened his grasp on the steering wheel as a cattle liner blew past, horn blaring.

One thing was certain, Tom Forsyth hadn't killed the latest victim. Locked up in jail, this time he had an unshakeable alibi. Myrden would seize on that when he argued his motion to dismiss. There wasn't anything that could be done about that, but now there was a fresh murder to investigate. An essential first step was to establish the identity of the victim. Switching on the mobile with a practised sideways movement of his chin, he called Missing Persons and asked for the names of anyone who had been reported missing late last night or sometime this morning. When he was told there was a list of eight, he contacted the Homicide section and had one of the detectives begin making inquiries.

Detective Balfour put his hand over the mouthpiece to report, "Nothing yet," when Chris walked in. Nodding, Chris sat down at his desk and switched on the computer. The icon on the toolbar told him he had mail. He clicked on the envelope icon and a brief e-mail appeared on his screen:

more your style crane?

The e-mail was from a Hotmail account. About as anonymous as you could get. Cyber Crimes could trace it back to the internet café where it originated but not to the individual work station. Chris printed a copy of the e-mail and stared unseeingly down at the page. There was no need to re-read it. But what could it tell him?

In life, the young woman on the toilet seat would have been a looker. More so than the other victims, except for the smashing Adrienne Vinney, who had been drop-dead gorgeous. Grimacing at the "drop-dead" bit, Chris pondered the implications. It reinforced his conviction that Vinney wasn't among TLC's victims. If she had been, the message wouldn't ring true.

The messages from TLC — once again, it was necessary to proceed from the assumption they were from the killer — were meant for him personally. Not surprisingly. Anyone who followed the news would know that he was the lead investigator. Although less likely, it might also be someone who had a score to settle with him. Someone who had been convicted because of the evidence he had provided when he was still with Crime Scenes. God knew there were enough of those. Swinton! Harry Swinton. The name jumped out at him. Never would he forget the murderous hatred seething out from the prisoner's box as he testified about the palm print on the bottom of the window frame.

Except for that, the robbery had been perfectly staged. No fingerprints, no footprints, no DNA. Surgically clean. But the thief had overlooked the print left behind when he strained to open a balky window to exit the premises. Swinton realized Chris's evidence would convict him, and he muttered, "I'll get you for this, Crane!" as Chris left the witness stand and walked past the prisoner's box on his way out of the courtroom. Swinton had been sentenced to five years in prison, so he would be out by now. Five years

— probably reduced to four for good behaviour — in the slammer could cool a guy out. Or they could fuel his rage. Chris decided to run a check on Swinton and see if anyone knew what he had been up to since his release. The reference to the physical appearance of the victims reinforced the probability that the e-mail had in fact come from the killer. Still, their photos had been in the papers. And, as Mavis had remarked about the earlier messages, there was nothing in their content that was not in the public domain. Except for the signature.

The profiler would have to see the e-mail right away. Maybe it would give her a better idea of who was sending the taunting messages. He was pretty sure she would conclude they were from TLC, but he needed to hear it from her.

"We got a hit." Detective Balfour pushed back his chair and walked the few steps over to Chris's desk. "The victim's name is Ann Marin. Her roommate reported her missing around midnight. I just talked to the roommate, and the description is a perfect match."

"We need to talk to this roommate. What's her name, and where is she?"

Balfour looked down at a small notepad. "Sylvia Dubrinski. That's her name. She works in the production accounting department at Shell. I had to call three times before I got through to her. She was phoning around, trying to track down the roommate. I told her we would want to interview her."

"Right. We'll need a photo of the victim to show her. For a positive identification. Let me see how Staroski is making out."

It wasn't just the photo that Chris wanted. The witness was a woman, and he wanted Gwen and her insights with him when he interviewed her. He called her on her cell, and she told him she was on the way back and was already at the intersection of Highway 8 and Sarcee Trail. She would be there in ten minutes or so.

Production accounting was on the twenty-sixth floor of the Shell building, and the manager of the department, a suitably grave expression on his face, was waiting for them as Chris and Gwen stepped off the elevator. He conducted them to a small workroom, introduced them to Sylvia Dubrinski, pointed out the coffee and ice water on a table against the wall, and withdrew, closing the door behind him.

In her mid-thirties, Dubrinski was of average height, comfortably overweight, and composed. She nodded when Gwen showed her the digital photo. It was a head shot, there being no need to distress her by showing her the gruesome indignities that had been done to her friend's body. In a firm, quiet voice she told them that Ann had been a trainer at the Fitness Now Health Club on Bowness Road, a few blocks away from the apartment they shared. She had gone for a run, as she always did, at ten o'clock last night. "When she hadn't returned by eleven-thirty, I called Missing Persons."

"Isn't that a bit unusual?" Chris interrupted her. "People usually wait until some time has elapsed before reporting someone missing."

"You didn't know Ann Marin," Dubrinski retorted. "She always did things a certain way. Her own way. She went for a run every night. Without fail. She started out at ten, was back at ten-thirty for a shower, and in bed by eleven. She had to be at work in the gym by six. That's when a lot of jocks want to have their workout. When she hadn't returned by eleven-thirty, I knew something was wrong. That's when I reported her missing."

"She was very attractive." Chris picked up the photo. "She must have been very popular."

"Men were always putting the make on her, if that's what you mean." Dubrinski made a small moue of distaste. "But she wasn't interested."

"Oh?"

"And I don't mean she was a lesbian, either." This with a quick glance at Gwen. "She wasn't. She was in love with herself. Period."

"A narcissist," Chris said.

"That's what she was. To the max."

"If you will forgive me for saying this, you don't appear to be very upset by her death."

"She was the roommate from hell. If you want the truth. She answered an ad I placed in the personals three months ago. I needed help with the rent. I help support my widowed mother," she elaborated in answer to Chris's puzzled look. He nodded, and she continued. "Right from the get-go she criticized everything I did, the food I ate, my friends, my lack of exercise. My clothes. Everything. You should have seen the tasteless crap she wanted me to eat. It made me want to puke just looking at it. I told her she had to leave by the end of the next week."

"I see. What about friends, relatives?"

"None that I knew of. She never mentioned any, and I never saw her with anyone. The only calls she ever got were from the gym where she worked."

"We would like to do a search of your apartment, if it's all right with you?"

"I don't mind, but I want to be there when you do."

"Of course. Could we do it now, do you suppose?"

"Sure. I'll just tell the supervisor."

"Detective Staroski and I walked over from the police station, so we'll have to go back and get some transportation. Can we pick you up out front?"

"That won't be necessary. I'll meet you at the apartment."

"Quite an earful," murmured Chris as the two of them walked south on 3rd Street.

"She likes you. That's why she opened up like that."

"I think it was more like venting her frustration at the 'roommate from hell.'"

"I see we're taking the long way home," Gwen chuckled as they crossed 7th Avenue and continued south.

"The mall is more interesting, and it's only a couple of blocks out of the way."

"And we just might run into your girlfriend."

Chris merely smiled.

"There she is. You're in luck." Gwen nudged Chris as they made their way along the crowded Stephen Avenue Mall. "She really does have a beautiful smile." She jumped back as a speeding bicycle courier cut in front of her. "You'd think we could do something about that," she complained, watching the courier darting in and out of the pedestrian traffic, leaving indignant stares and muttered imprecations in his wake.

"There's a $75 fine for riding bicycles on the mall, but the courier companies just write it off as a business expense. You okay?" asked Chris when he saw Gwen rubbing her left shoulder.

"Yeah. It's just a nervous reflex. I could feel the wind as he went past. Anyway, and as I was saying, she does have a lovely smile."

"Would you like to meet her?"

"No. It's you she wants to see. You go ahead. I'll wait for you."

"I think I'm jealous," Joan laughed as she raised her right forearm for Chris to hold, and the cockatiel lifted its foot, inviting Chris to pick him up.

It was too good to miss. Gwen turned off the flash on the compact digital camera she always had with her and surreptitiously snapped off a shot. Passersby slowed to stare at the little tableau. To them it was a curiosity, but Gwen was genuinely touched. His friendship with this cruelly deformed person was just another facet of the complex man whom she would always think of as her mentor.

"I worry about you, Chris. It must be terrible for you. All these killings."

"And no arrests," Chris added grimly. "That's what's so frustrating, Joan." The coffee can taped to the front of her platform was almost three-quarters full. She had to be the street's most successful panhandler. People reacted to her, sometimes with genuine sympathy, sometimes with a "but for the grace of God" shudder or atavistic, superstitious fear. "There was another one last night," he told her.

"I know. A fitness instructor."

"Have you heard anything more?"

"No. Only that she was sitting on the john. The creep's getting weirder by the minute."

"Yeah. I've got to go." Chris lowered his hand to let the bird climb back onto his perch. "You take care, Joan."

"I'm not his type," she laughed, unknowingly repeating what Phil Dummett had said.

Halfway down the block, squatting a few feet out from a storefront, was a pile of dirty blankets. An upturned ball cap in front of the unlovely heap was the only indication that a human being lurked somewhere within. The afternoon was warm. Even hot. Maybe the blankets kept out heat as well as cold. More likely, they kept out the world.

The untidy heap stirred when Chris dropped a loonie in the cap, clinking against the two coins already there. A pair of red-rimmed eyes stared up at them from beneath a tangle of dirty brown hair. "Thanks. You want to know something about the crippled girl, cop?"

"What's there to know?"

"She never keeps the loot people give her. Gives it all to the Sally Ann. Go figure."

"Fascinating. Did you know?" asked Gwen as they moved on.

"No, I didn't. I sometimes suspected that she didn't need the money. Thought she might have been researching a book. Or maybe it was a diversion for her."

"A neat little mystery for you to solve."

"I'm not sure I want to solve it."

As expected, Ann Marin's apartment produced nothing in the way of clues. It did, however, highlight the gulf between the lifestyles of the two women who lived there. It was almost as though a line had been drawn down the middle. The victim's bedroom was spartan, monastic in its stripped-down simplicity. One narrow bed, no pictures or photographs, a chest of drawers with a brush and comb precisely aligned on the otherwise bare top. The clothes closet, however, was a different story. Gwen gave a low whistle of appreciation at the sight of its contents, neatly arranged on hangers. Sports and athletic attire — shorts and sleeveless shirts — took up one end, with running shoes in racks on the floor below. Just like the way things had been arranged in Adrienne Vinney's clothes closet. The remaining three-quarters of the space was given over to everyday wear. Except that there was little that was everyday or ordinary about the dresses. Reaching in, Gwen turned a black number so it faced out. The décolletage was deep, almost down to the navel.

"I guess it was a case of look but don't touch with our Ann." Gwen let the dress swing back into place.

In contrast, and in keeping with her personality, Sylvia Dubrinski's room had a rumpled, lived-in appearance. Family photos adorned the dresser, together with scattered pieces of costume jewellery — earrings and a matched set of pearl necklace and bracelet. Nowhere was the difference between the two women more starkly evident than in the bathroom. It was equipped with two basins. The counter on Ann Marin's side was bare and gleaming, everything tucked away in drawers or neatly arranged on the glass shelves of the cabinet. On Sylvia's side, the counter was lightly dusted with spilled face powder and littered with lipsticks and jars of skin cream. A toothbrush was upended in a smudged water glass.

"Thank you for your courtesy in letting us examine your apartment," Chris said as the three of them stood in the living room.

"You're welcome." Sylvia shrugged. "You didn't find anything, though, did you?"

"Her dresses were interesting," Gwen said. "Not what we expected, if you know what I mean."

"I know what you mean. She liked to tease."

"I find it hard to believe she didn't have any men friends," Chris frowned. "Yet you say she never went out on dates."

"Never. Not once in the time she was here."

"And you have no idea of any family she might have?"

"None. It was like she appeared out of nowhere."

"You didn't ask for references?" Gwen was mildly incredulous.

"She paid the first month's rent in advance. That was good enough for me."

"We'll be releasing her belongings soon," Chris told her. "Have you thought of what you're going to do with them?"

"The Goodwill people, I guess. Her dresses wouldn't be of much use to you or me, would they?" she replied with a sly smirk at Gwen.

"What puzzles me," mused Chris, ignoring her dig at his colleague, "is that she went for runs late at night even though there is a serial killer on the loose. That doesn't make any sense."

"Ann figured she could take care of herself. She was an expert in martial arts. I think she half hoped to meet up with him."

"You never told us you rode, Chris." Over the phone, Cameron Taylor's voice held a note of mild reproof. "You never mentioned it. Not once."

"I'm afraid riding is very much in my past. There was a time when it was a big part of my life. But I didn't keep it up when I moved out here."

"A mistake on your part, my friend. But one that's easily corrected. Sarah suggested you might like to join our little group on our regular Sunday morning meets. A bunch of us ride out for a couple of hours then have a tailgate lunch. This coming Sunday it's here at Bent Tree. I've got a mare that would be perfect for you. She has beautiful manners and never puts a foot wrong. We start out at nine in the morning. Very civilized hour."

"It sounds great, Cameron. But you know what I'm dealing with these days. I really can't justify taking the time off."

"It's the most productive thing you could do, my boy. Different perspective, change of pace. A person can get too close to a problem. Lose the big picture. Besides, it's only a Sunday morning. You can go back to those evil crimes in the afternoon."

It was tempting. Very. Out here people knew him as a police detective, not as a well-known horse show rider. Famous in certain circles. He had always enjoyed riding and being around horses. Cameron Taylor was right. It had been a mistake to let it drop. He felt an undeniable frisson of excitement at the thought that it was Sarah who was behind the invitation. That night at the Churches' party he had told her that he used to ride. The lady would cut a dashing figure on horseback. And it would only be for a few hours.

"Cameron, I'll be there if I possibly can. Unless something comes up."

"Understood. We'll look forward to seeing you at eight o'clock. Give you some time to meet the mare and get fitted out with tack. All you need to bring is yourself."

Chris was still trying to come to grips with what he had just agreed to do when his phone rang again.

"What? Who's there?" The caller's voice was suspicious. Tense.

"It's just my parrot. Who is this?"

The person on the other end took a moment to digest this before saying, "It's Phil Dummett. Are you alone?" Another brief pause, then a chuckle, "Apart from the bird I mean."

"I am. Do I take it you have heard from our mutual friend?"

"Not yet. But I expect to very soon."

"Oh?"

"I've written a piece about him. It'll be on the op-ed page of Saturday's *Herald*. I've titled it 'The Anatomy of a Serial Killer,' so he'll be sure to find out about it. He's bound to react."

"What approach did you take? Sympathetic? That he shouldn't be blamed for the crimes he's committed? That it's not really his fault?"

"C'mon. You know me better than that. I've taken the analytical point of view, that he probably had an unfortunate, possibly abusive childhood, trouble at school, a feeling of social insecurity, of never being able to fit in with his peers, and no luck with women. The sort of background that could turn a vulnerable person into a sociopath. Make him want to prove that he's smarter than the rest of society."

"That sure as hell won't endear you to him. I thought you were going to take the sympathetic approach. Pretend to be on his side."

"I am in a way. The overall tone of the piece is that because of his background he may not be able to control what he does. But what I'm really hoping for is that he will feel he has to deny that he came from an impoverished family and that he feels socially inferior. If he falls for it, and I think he just might, we're bound to learn more about him."

Dummett could be on to something. Like every serial, TLC had an outsize ego, and wouldn't appreciate being cast as an underprivileged loner. "Keep me informed," said Chris as he hung up.

The Bragg Creek homicide was featured on the late-night national television news along with the usual reports from the world's trouble spots. It was followed by the local news, which devoted a full three minutes to a description of the bizarre circumstances, along with clips of the crime scene and the removal of the body. So many people had been present in the park when the unfortunate visitor opened the door of the toilet that it was impossible to keep a lid on the lurid details. Except for the cross.

Turning off the television, Chris unexpectedly yawned. He pressed a wall switch and the living room drapes whirred closed, cutting off the lights of the city. Recognizing the signal to go to sleep, Nevermore ruffled his feathers and muttered a drowsy, "Good night, Chris." At first, Chris had followed the expert's advice and draped a blanket around the parrot's cage at night, but the bird quickly vented his displeasure by ripping great tears in it. Closing the drapes and turning off the lights worked just fine.

"Goodnight, Nevermore. See you in the morning."

"To die sitting on the john!" The club's program director seemed more intrigued by the manner of Ann Marin's death than upset by it. "How she would have hated being found like that!"

"She didn't die on the toilet, if that's any comfort," Chris, annoyed by the director's attitude, informed him. "She was killed somewhere else before being put there."

Sensing Chris's disapproval, the director asked, "How can I help?"

"Whatever you can tell us about her, and her background, would be useful."

"I'll tell you what I know, but it's not one hell of a lot. Ann kept pretty much to herself, apart from her classes. She was a good trainer. Strict but competent."

"How did she get along with your clients?"

"With the men, very well. Not so well with the women. She could be very demanding. Impatient. I assigned her to the most advanced classes, and that worked out okay."

"How long has she worked here?"

"Three months, give or take a few days. I'll get you the exact dates from our employee records, but three months is close enough."

"What about before that? Where she was from, where she worked. That sort of thing."

"She came from Vancouver. She worked at a health club there. The same franchise as this one. They recommended her, told us she was good at her job, bit of a loner, popular with some clients, not with others. Pretty much the same as things turned out here."

"We're anxious to get in touch with any family she may have. Do you have anything on file?"

"We don't. Vancouver may. I can find out for you right away."

"That will be very helpful. But before we do that, a couple more things. As you said, she seems to have been a bit of a loner. But was there anyone here, staff or clients, that she was close to?"

"There *was* one guy. An accountant. Goes in for long-distance running. Marathons. Always took her class. They got along. I had the feeling they thought they were superior to everyone else around here. They were much the same age."

"You'll let us have his name and address?"

"His name is Lindsay MacDonald and he works at DeLong Furness in Bow Valley Square. I'm not suggesting anything here, Detective. You asked if there was anyone she seemed close to, and that's him. At least closer than she was with anyone else."

"According to her roommate, she was an expert in the martial arts?"

The director smiled slightly and shook his head. "Not so. She was outstanding when it came to gym work and running, but the martial arts were not her forte. Not at all. I don't know why. But she never practised it. I can see where she might let people believe she was an expert, though. People would expect it of her." He paused, then said, "I know where you're going with this, Detective. That she should have been able to defend herself against the killer. There's no doubt she could have put up some very effective resistance, but not like a real martial arts adept." Another pause. "She was another victim of the serial killer, wasn't she?"

"That's the way it looks. But we have to keep an open mind."

chapter fifteen

Scooping up the newspapers from the hallway, Chris carried them back inside the penthouse and over to the breakfast table. Before he could sort them, however, there came a plaintive squawk from the parrot's cage. Chris grinned and went into the living room, where he unlocked the cage and carried Nevermore and his perch to join him at breakfast.

"You'll have to wait for your toast," he told the parrot as he picked up the front section of the *Herald*. Dummett's piece was on A-24, the editorial page. Under its eye-catching title, it was prominently positioned dead centre on the page. Its contents were as the journalist had summarized in his phone call.

"TLC is *not* going to like this," Chris muttered to himself as he rapidly scanned the article. Which, of course, was what Dummett intended. There was also a subtle suggestion that maybe the killer was himself a victim — a victim of character defects and low self-esteem that drove him to commit these heinous acts. That would drive TLC right up the wall — to be depicted as a victim instead of the all-powerful master of life and death. If Dummett wanted to provoke a reaction from the serial, he was sure going about it the right way! But what form would that reaction take? The freelancer might end up with a lot more than he bargained for. He who would sup with the devil ... That wasn't right. How did it go? He must have a long spoon that must eat with the devil. That was it. Shakespeare.

It was only when he was stacking the dishes and cutlery in the dishwasher that Chris began to think about tomorrow and his date to go riding out at Bent Tree. And to see Sarah. It was time to dig out his long-neglected gear. Halfway to the front door, he paused and looked back at the parrot sitting innocently on his perch. It would only take a few minutes to retrieve his stuff from storage. Still. He put Nevermore back in his cage, promising he wouldn't be long.

The breeches still fit. Not surprising — he hadn't let himself put on any weight since coming to Calgary — but gratifying all the same. The knee-length riding boots were as blackly gleaming as when he had stored them in cloth bags for the trip west. Cameron was right, it had been a mistake not to keep up his riding. True, he had been totally engrossed in the challenges of his investigative work, but that was no excuse. Nor was it the real reason.

Breeches draped over one arm, Chris closed and locked the door of his underground storage space, picked up the boots, and walked across the bare concrete floor to the elevator. On the way up to the penthouse he wondered if boots and breeches might not be a bit much for the Bent Tree meet. Maybe he should wear jeans instead. He would call Sarah and ask her advice. It had been her idea to have the Taylors invite him to join their little riding circle. And it was a perfectly plausible reason for talking to her.

A bright and youthful voice answered the phone. That would be the daughter, Linda. How Nevermore would love her voice! Chris smiled across the room at the parrot, once more on his perch. When Sarah came on, she sounded every bit as warm and exciting as he remembered.

"English tack will be completely appropriate," she assured him. "That's what Linda and I and some of the others will be wearing. The Taylors, of course, ride Western, but it doesn't matter. The mare we've picked out for you goes very nicely under English saddle and snaffle bit."

"Great. Then I'll come booted and spurred. But please keep in mind that it's been some years since I've been on the back of a horse."

Sarah's laugh, light and musical, rang delightfully in Chris's ear. "Remember what they say about bicycles. You'll be just fine. Misty is a pleasure to ride. She's an Anglo-Arab, by the way. You'll love her."

That was reassuring. Very. Now Sarah was saying how much she looked forward to seeing him in the morning. He wished there was some reason to prolong the conversation, but inspiration eluded him. Maybe he was kidding himself, but he thought he could sense the same feeling on her part. He would see her tomorrow in any event he consoled himself as they rang off.

That was tomorrow. For the rest of today he would concentrate on the serial killer. He had struck five times, six if you included the Vinney murder, but Chris thought that wasn't his work. Five or six, it didn't matter. With that many killings there should be something — some clue — that would point to a possible suspect. Could there be more than one killer at work? Altogether apart from the Vinney case. There had been a change in the choice of victims. The latest, Ann Marin, the fitness trainer, was a real head turner. Yesterday, Chris had watched the autopsy being performed under the bright, bleak lights of the medical examiner's office. Watched that toned body lying naked on the table while the pathologist sliced and probed. She had been raped, if that was what you would call it — a foreign object of some sort had been inserted into her vagina, cruelly tearing it. A large lump at the base of her skull showed how she had been rendered unconscious and helpless. How had someone like Ann Marin allowed that to happen? According to her boss at the gym she was no expert in the martial arts, although she held herself out as one. She must have believed her own hype, which explained why she'd insisted on going for her nightly run.

That cold, don't-touch-me face was unmarked. Except for the broken blood vessels in the whites of her eyes. Unequivocal evidence of death by strangulation. Chris had thought of her as a looker, and *that* she certainly had been. Apparently a tease as well. After an hour or so of fruitless and frustrating ratiocination, Chris, realizing he was just going back and forth over the same familiar ground, sighed, and got up from his chair.

Nevermore, who had remained quiet while his master cogitated, stirred with a ruffling of feathers and uttered a hopeful, "Treat."

"You know it's Saturday, don't you?" Stretching, Chris grinned, his good humour restored. Going to the kitchen, he cut off a slice of banana and carried it back to the parrot, bemused as always by the almost reverential care with which Nevermore took the delicacy in that formidable black beak.

chapter sixteen

The Ferrari burbled throatily as Chris waited for the light to change. The driver of a rusted-out Ford pickup in the next lane gave him a thumbs-up and leaned out the window to ask with a broad grin, "Wanna trade?"

"I wouldn't want to cheat you!" Chris laughed and pulled away as the light turned green, revelling in the Ferrari's acceleration as he took it through the gears. This early on a Sunday morning the southbound traffic on MacLeod Trail was light, the lanes almost deserted. A few kilometres after MacLeod Trail had morphed into Highway 2, he took the De Winton turnoff and headed west toward the mountains. A roadside sign pointing the way to the Calgary Polo Club, and others advertising riding stables, told him he was in horse country. The land stretching for miles in every direction was flat and green. Incredibly green. A few farmhouses, some of them more like mansions, were set well back from the road. As he had on previous occasions while driving out to visit the Taylors, Chris found himself thinking that this wouldn't be a bad way to live. But not for him. He needed the mental stimulus of solving crimes. At the moment, and discounting the copycat murder, the score card read: TLC, 5; Crane, 0.

The hell of it was there was nothing he could do to advance the investigation. There were no clues to follow up, no avenues to explore. At this stage everything depended on getting a break — a tip from a member of the public, the killer making a mistake. Creating a link to another website, for example. A few years ago that had led to the discovery and shutting down of a website that was undermining morale in the police department. It was too much to expect TLC to make a mistake like that, but he did keep sending messages, and *that* could turn out to be a fatal mistake on his part. As he grew bolder, he might tip his hand. Maybe the stuff Dummett was writing would get under his skin. But from what he knew about TLC — hell, he didn't *know* anything! From what he *guessed* about TLC, the serial would only reveal what he wanted to, when he wanted to.

His brooding didn't prevent Chris from noticing the change in the terrain as he continued to drive west. Farms gave way to ranches, and wooded hills and valleys replaced the flat prairie as the eastern slope of the Rockies took shape in the distance. Grazing cattle and nodding oilwell pumpjacks dotted the hillsides. He had read somewhere that there were more than forty thousand of them pumping away in the province. Just east of the historic oil town of Turner Valley, Chris turned left onto a narrow two-lane road leading south to Bent Tree.

The entrance to the ranch was spectacular. A white fence that seemed endless led up to the arched gateway, flanked by a larger-than-life steel sculpture of a tree with broken branches and a twisted trunk. The five-barred gate stood open. Easing the Ferrari over the cattle guard — metal pipes spaced a few inches apart over a shallow ditch — Chris recalled jumping five-barred gates like that with the Westmount Hunt. It was also a standard jump in horse shows. The long driveway curved up a gentle incline, crossing over a bridge that spanned a small lake where ducks and geese swam among the lily pads. The ranch house, an imposing two-storey residence of cedar siding and dark Rundle stone with a wide veranda, stood on a terrace above the lake. Some years earlier, before the mad cow panic wreaked such havoc in the Canadian cattle industry, Cameron Taylor had converted the old ranch house into quarters for the staff and built the new one where it could command a view of the mountains and look down on the little lake, one of his pet projects. Like the farmhouses Chris had passed, the house was large, almost like a small lodge. More than 6,200 square feet, Cameron had told Chris while giving him a tour. The people who lived on the land out here obviously had a thing about space, indoors and out. Spacious or not, Chris doubted that Melanie enjoyed living there cooped up with her in-laws. The barns, stables, and other outbuildings were to the rear of the house and set well back from it.

The yard outside the corral swarmed with activity — riders, most in Western attire but some in breeches or jodhpurs, backed their horses out of trailers or saddled those already on the ground. Everything came to a halt when Chris drove in. A teenaged rider gave him a wide grin and a thumbs-up. The red Ferrari was an exotic bird among the pickups and horse trailers, a couple of them splattered with mud. Blitzkreig, the German shepherd guard dog, was nowhere to be seen. He would be locked up somewhere.

Sarah, smashing in riding clothes, handed the haltershank of her horse to a young girl who could only be her daughter and came over to greet him.

"I'll introduce you to Misty," she said after they had shaken hands and exchanged long, questioning looks that seemed to take up where the first one left off. Had there been a slight catch in her voice? Chris dared to hope as he followed her.

"I've been admiring your horse, Sarah. From his size and looks he's got to be a Hanoverian?"

"He is. His name is Mango."

"Which means the first letter of his sire's name began with M. As required by the Hanoverian stud book," he added when she raised an eyebrow.

"Right. Mango also happens to be my favourite fruit. Did you ever own a Hanoverian?"

"No. But I've ridden several. They're great show horses. Do you show him?"

"No. Linda's the show rider in this family."

His first sight of Misty was reassuring. Her name suited her: she was a whitish grey. Smallish, not more than fifteen hands, three inches — metric just didn't seem to cut it when it came to horses — showing more Arab than thoroughbred. Tethered to a corral railing, she was chomping quietly on the snaffle.

"Well, what do you think of her?" Cameron asked as he came up behind them.

"I think she looks just right. I'm really looking forward to the morning."

"Now that we know you ride, we'll make you part of the pack." The rancher gave Chris a quizzical look. "I still think it's funny you never mentioned it before."

"Press of business, I guess." Chris tried to shrug it off, but it sounded lame even to his own ears.

"Nobody asked him," said Sarah, coming to his

defence. "Let's have you meet the others."

"Some I know already. From the other times I've been out here." Chris replied as he shook their hands. Without counting, he figured they numbered fifteen, give or take one or two.

"And this is my Linda!" Sarah's hand rested lightly on her daughter's shoulder.

The youngster's smile was friendly and composed. Her features were a replica of her mother's — the same crisp English cameo profile — but she had inherited a slightly olive tinge to her skin from her father.

"Mount up, everybody," Phyllis Taylor called out, ducking her head as she rode a bay quarterhorse out of the stable doorway.

Lengthening her stirrup, Sarah sprang lithely onto the back of her seventeen-hand Hanoverian and watched approvingly while Chris tightened Misty's girth, hopped once on his right foot, and swung himself on board.

The first part of the ride was across an open field, where a herd of Herefords grazed. The cattle paid them little attention; a few raised white faces to look, then went back to cropping the short grass. The resident donkey, pastured with the cattle to drive marauding coyotes away, remained on the alert as the riders went by. The danger was over by now but coyotes could exact a heavy toll in calving season. Cam Taylor, mounted on a colourful pinto — more accurately a skewbald, Chris mentally corrected himself, since it was chestnut and white, not black and white like a true pinto — rode beside them for a while, then trotted ahead to open the gate into the next field.

"Melanie hasn't joined us," Chris observed.

"She never does," Sarah replied. "She claims she's allergic to horses."

The northwest corner of the next field had been fenced off for a well site. The horse's head of the pumpjack, painted a bright orange, moved slowly up and down, pumping oil into an adjoining storage tank, dull silver in the sunlight. Seeing the wells, people often assumed that the ranchers on whose land they were located must be rolling in money. But, as Chris had learned in law school, as far back as 1887 the federal government began to reserve all mines and minerals from the land grants it issued to the settlers. Only those few landowners whose title predated 1887 owned the oil and gas rights. In 1930 the feds had transferred the reserved minerals within its borders to the province of Alberta. All the majority of the landowners received was a modest rental for the few acres of surface required for the wellsite and access roadway.

"You were right about the bicycle bit," Chris said to Sarah, riding companionably beside him. "It feels great."

"Ready for a canter?"

"After you."

When Sarah put the Hanoverian into a smooth canter, Misty pricked up her ears, but didn't break stride and kept on at a brisk walking pace. The little mare had manners, just as Sarah had promised. Chris touched his heel to her right flank and she immediately began to canter on the left lead. Everyone was cantering now, and they swept across the field in a loose line abreast.

The woods began on the other side of the next gate. A trail wide enough to accommodate three horses riding side by side had been cut through the mixed stand of pine and aspen.

"There are jumps up ahead," warned Sarah. "Quite low, actually. But you can ride around them. That's what most people do."

"Does Misty jump?"

"She can handle these jumps."

"We'll see how it goes."

The jumps were natural looking. Inviting. The first one consisted of three thick logs laid on top of each other. Chris watched Linda and Sarah clear it effortlessly, but decided to follow the Western riders trotting around it. The next one was irresistible: a snake fence with an opening for non-jumpers, stretching across a small clearing. It was low, three and a half feet, but high enough to make a horse pay attention. Sarah flew over it, looking back at Chris as she landed. Instinctively, without the need for conscious thought, he increased the pressure of his legs and pointed Misty at the fence, leaning forward as she took off.

"Bravo!" Sarah applauded.

"It feels wonderful!" Exhilarated, Chris patted the mare's neck.

The rest of the ride was sheer delight, making Chris realize how much he enjoyed the sport of riding and everything that went with it. And it didn't hurt that Sarah was openly impressed with his jumping style. They took the last fence — a log over a ditch — together.

"I'll pay for this when I get out of bed in the morning, but it's been great," he said as they let the horses walk home on a loose rein to cool out.

"You two looked pretty good out there!" Dismounting, Linda unsnapped her riding helmet and pulled it off, shaking loose her soft, almost honey blond hair, the same shade as her mother's.

"You looked pretty good yourself!" Chris countered, relieved to find himself steady on his feet after the long ride.

"Linda and I leave for Pennsylvania the day after tomorrow," Sarah announced, slipping off Mango's saddle. "She's registered for a show jumping course at the Harrisburg Riding Academy. Don't pout," she scolded him playfully. "It's only for three weeks."

Chris acknowledged the thrust with a smile and said, "Harrisburg is a great school. I wonder if Jeff Godfrey is still there?"

"He's the chief instructor," a wide-eyed Linda replied. "Do you know him?"

"Used to. We competed on the same show circuits. I've been in quite a few jump-offs with him."

"Awesome!"

Sarah was clearly intrigued, but let it pass.

A buffet lunch was served on the terrace above the lake. Cameron Taylor was chatting animatedly with Chris and Sarah when his voice trailed off and a look of weary resignation settled over his weatherbeaten face. Knowing what he was likely to see, Chris took a quick glance over his shoulder. Melanie, wearing a summery print dress, was coming down the steps from the veranda. Chris stood up and put on a welcoming smile as she approached. Whatever Melanie might think of the other "horsey" guests, it was clear she both liked and admired Sarah. And there was much to admire, thought Chris — Sarah's blond beauty, her style, her personal independence. How Melanie must envy that!

As the alfresco lunch drew to a close with coffee and fresh berries for dessert, Sarah surprised Chris by asking if he would like to see her place. After hesitating for a moment, he accepted. First, he would call the dispatcher on his cell to check for any messages. If there were any new developments, he would beg off. Dispatch told him nobody had been trying to reach him.

Sarah's two-horse trailer was no longer there. The Mercedes was parked where it had been. She explained that Mac, who looked after her place, had driven over to collect the horses.

The hills were higher and the valleys deeper as they drove south, toward Longview. An oil service rig, a scaled-down version of a drilling rig, stood out on top of the highest hill against an achingly blue sky.

So this is what $10 million gets you, thought Chris as he followed the Mercedes up the driveway. Sarah's house had been lovingly and thoughtfully designed to fit into its surroundings. One storey, not overly large, with an attached garage, gabled roof of grey tile, and exterior of cedar siding and the soft brownish tones of Revelstoke stone, it blended perfectly with the foothills landscape. It was charming, but Chris couldn't help thinking it was a bit rustic for someone like Sarah. A large, handsome dog greeted them with a happily wagging tail as she unlocked the front door and they stepped inside.

"A Bernese Mountain Dog," Chris breathed, holding out his hand for the animal to sniff. "Beautiful!" The tail wagged even harder, so he patted the massive head, black with white and rich red patches. "I really miss having a dog, but living in a condo, I have to make do with a parrot."

"I've heard about that bird. I gather he's quite a character."

"He's entertaining, all right. You'll have to meet him."

"That I look forward to. Her name is Primrose, by the way," she said, giving the dog an affectionate pat. "Prim, for short."

If the exterior of Sarah's house was rustic, there was nothing rustic about the interior. Large abstract paintings hung on the walls, the furniture was severely modern, chrome and leather, occasional tables topped with granite or glass. Like his own place, only more so.

"Very nice," said Chris, walking across the living room tile floor to gaze out at the mountains, closer and more sharply defined than at Bent Tree. "You pay your respects to the rural setting on the outside, and do your own thing on the inside."

"They're really both my thing. In a way. Do you like it?"

"I do. Very much. It's inspired."

"Would you like something to drink?" They were alone, Linda having excused herself to start packing.

"I'll pass, thanks." Watching Linda walk down the hallway, Chris remarked, "The school year must be over?"

"It is for her. Last week. She goes to Strathcona. Tell me, how did you enjoy Misty?"

"She's a sweetheart. I had a great time. Thank you for arranging it, by the way."

"You're welcome. I'm curious, Chris. Watching you ride, it's obvious you're in the expert class. And you've competed with Jeff Godfrey. That means the A circuit. Did you ride professionally?"

"Strictly amateur."

"Why did you give it up?" asked Sarah in that cool, direct way she sometimes had. "Did you have a fall?"

"I didn't. My girlfriend did."

"Bad?"

"As bad as it gets. She became a quadriplegic."

"My God. How did it happen?"

Chris paused. This was not something he talked about. Not since he had moved out west. Not even with Robyn. But Sarah was a horse person. Which Robyn definitely was not. Sarah would understand. And for some reason it felt right to tell her about it.

"We were trying out a new horse. A chestnut gelding I thought would be a good hunter prospect for her. He was going great guns, really moving on at his fences, until ... until the stone wall." He glanced at her, and she nodded. The stone wall, a solid obstacle made of wood painted to look like stone, was a required jump in every working hunter class. "He refused and sent Cynthia flying over his head. She landed on the other side with a broken neck. She was what they call a high quad. C1, the first vertebra, the one just below her skull, was fractured."

"So she was totally paralyzed?"

"Totally. She had a power chair, so she could move around, but that was it."

"How does a quadriplegic drive those things? I've always wondered. Knobs, I suppose."

"A high quad like Cynthia can't use knobs. They can't move their arms. It's all done by head control. Sip and puff. You sip on a tube to stop or back up, and puff to go ahead. In Europe it's called suck and blow, which I've always thought to be a more accurate description, but I guess that's not politically correct on this side of the Atlantic."

"You're very well informed on the subject. You kept on seeing this Cynthia?"

"All the time. Took her on outings. Walks. Sometimes to parties. Her family didn't like me doing that. They blamed me for what happened to her."

"That's not fair!"

"Maybe not. But that's how they felt. I kept thinking I should have tried the horse out myself first."

"That wouldn't have changed anything. You're a strong rider, and the horse would have jumped the wall for you. But there would be no way of knowing how he would go for her. We both know how horses will take advantage of a rider whenever they get the chance."

She was right. He had long ago come to acknowledge to himself that what had happened to Cynthia was an accident. One of the things that could happen with horses to anyone at any time. You were taking a chance every time you put a foot in the stirrup. Still, it was comforting to hear it from someone knowledgeable like Sarah.

"Do you still keep in touch with Cynthia?"

"She's dead. Suicide."

"Shocking. But not surprising. A young girl, beautiful … I'm sure she was beautiful?"

"She was. Blond and beautiful. She looked quite a bit like you, as a matter of fact."

"Oh?" Briefly at a loss, Sarah recovered to say, "Thank you." She was hesitant about pressing him further on the subject that was obviously still so painful for him, but she wanted to pursue the story to the end. Why? she asked herself. To get it out in the open and put it behind them was the not altogether unexpected answer.

"How did she manage the suicide bit?" she asked. "Being as disabled as she was. I understand that they usually need help from someone."

"She did it on her own. Her family had a summer place on a lake in the Laurentians. Cynthia always loved it, even more so after her accident. I think she felt a certain sense of freedom there. Her parents had some of the pathways paved, and she could travel around the property by herself. One afternoon she went out on their private dock and kept on going. As always, she was buckled into her safety harness."

Sarah wisely decided there was nothing she could say. It was awful beyond words. She let a few minutes go by, then got to her feet and held out her hand to Chris. "C'mon. I'll show you around."

The dog went with them as they walked over to the field where Mango and Linda's thoroughbred had been turned loose with two other horses. The rail fence was stained a reddish brown.

"That horse of your daughter's has conformation to burn. Short coupled, sloping withers, and clean legs. He's got it all."

"He does, doesn't he? We haven't had him that long. Young as she is, Linda was outgrowing the Pony Club shows and wanted to move up to the junior ranks. So I bought Royal Lancer for her. His stable name is Lance. Linda has already won one junior hunter class and placed in a working hunter class with him. Incidentally, would you like to ride while we're away?"

"Would I! But—"

"I know," she interrupted. "You're under incredible pressure. But if you ever have a few free hours, why don't you drive out and go for a ride? I know you would enjoy Mango. Mac will be here, and he'll fix you up."

Gazing at the rolling foothills and the wide open spaces stretching all the way to the horizon, Chris replied, "Riding a horse like that over country like this — how could I possibly resist?"

"Good. Now I'll show you the stable and introduce you to Mac."

Mac was standing in the aisle between the box stalls, saddlesoaping the tack Linda had used that morning. Somewhere in his mid-fifties, he had a lined face, under the wide brim of a cowboy hat that once had been white, sporting a two-day stubble.

"Folks up at the ranch were saying you look real good on the back of a horse," he said when Sarah introduced the two men.

"That's good to hear. I *have* been on a horse before. I had a great time."

There were six stalls in the stable, two of them bedded down with straw. Those would be for Mango and Linda's Lance. They left the wrangler cleaning the saddle and strolled back to the house along a path bordered with freshly planted annuals.

"That's a Northern Harrier." Chris stopped to listen. "Their cry is distinctive. It's so faint and weak it doesn't sound at all the way a hawk should."

"There he is." Sarah pointed up at the hawk dramatically outlined against the immaculate blue of the sky. "He's got a gopher. Now watch the performance. They nest on the ground and his mate will fly up to meet him. Here she comes."

A second hawk took to the air and climbed with rapidly beating wings until she was just below the male. Rolling onto her back, she caught the gopher as he dropped it and dove back to earth to feed the clamouring nestlings. With another of his feeble calls, the male hawk flew over to an adjoining field to resume his low level hunt for unwary gophers.

"Now, that's what you call a division of labour!"

"Do you feel like something to drink now? I have a nice Chardonnay on ice," Sarah asked as they walked into her designer kitchen, all stainless steel and polished stone countertops.

"Perfect. That's Nevermore's latest trick," he said with a proud smile as she opened the fridge and took out a bottle of wine. "The sound of a fridge door opening and closing. He came out with it yesterday."

As soon as they were seated with their wine in the living room, the dog plunked all her ninety pounds squarely on Chris's booted foot.

"Prim likes you." Sarah smiled approvingly. "She's my early warning system."

Buoyed by the promise of Sarah's words, Chris began the long, scenic drive back to Calgary. The Ferrari's top was down and the cool late afternoon air riffled through his hair. The CD player was stacked with some of the music he liked to listen to while driving: Sonata's violin version of *Habanera*, Placido singing *Valencia*, and lively Spanish airs by Granados and Rodrigo. He turned up the volume to counteract the rushing wind.

Waiting for a chance to turn onto the main highway and join the traffic flowing north to the city, Chris realized with a start of surprise that almost an entire day had passed without him thinking about the case of the serial killer. That just proved what an intoxicating, memorable day it had been. The joy of riding that well-schooled mare, and knowing that horses were once again back in his world. He should never have forsaken them and everything that came with them — the thrills, the spills. Yes, spills. He had had a few spectacular tumbles over jumps in the field and show rings, but that was part of the game. Cynthia. She would want this for him.

The message light was flashing when Chris arrived home, but he didn't need it to know there had been phone calls. Nevermore was doing his imitation of a phone ringing.

One of the messages was from Doug Church. Chris had already made a courtesy call to thank Doug and his wife for the party, and now he would tell them about his day at Bent Tree. The other message was from Dorothy Underwood. She apologized for bothering him when he was so busy with the awful things that were happening, but she thought it might be all right to call since it was Sunday. Smiling, he dialled her number.

Cutting her apologies short, he assured her that she wasn't interfering with anything. In fact, he had spent the day horseback riding in the country.

"That sounds delightful. I've never had anything to do with horses myself, but I'm sure it must be very relaxing."

Relaxing wasn't the word Chris would have chosen for a sport that could involve jump-offs over five- and six-foot jumps, but he murmured, "It was most enjoyable."

"I'm so glad. I've been reading what Phil wrote about that dreadful killer! You deserve to have some pleasure, having to deal with creatures like that."

"Phil? It sounds as if you know him?"

"Oh, I do. Since he was a little boy. His mother, Ethel, is my best friend. We play bridge every Tuesday afternoon up at the Edgemont Club. With two other old friends. Always the same foursome. I haven't driven since Howard passed away, and Ethel always calls for me and drives me to the club. So kind. Ethel and her son are very close. She's awfully proud of him."

"I'm sure she is. Well, Dorothy, as you say I'm very tied up, but I do want to see you. I was thinking of you not long ago. I'll come round for a visit the first time I get a chance."

"Wonderful!"

chapter seventeen

"Well, well, what have we been up to this weekend?" demanded Gwen, watching Chris walking to his desk.

"Just a little stiff, that's all. It'll soon pass."

"I hope she was worth it." Gwen chuckled wickedly.

"I'll never tell." Chris settled into his chair and unfolded the copy of the *Herald* he had brought with him. The letter was headed "When" and signed by Michael Lambert, who was not further identified except as being from Calgary. But Chris knew who he was. Lambert was a professor at the Faculty of Law who taught criminal law. The *Herald* had devoted two full columns to his letter, which began by listing the six murders, thereby implying that the Vinney case was also the work of the serial killer. "Wrong. Dead wrong." Chris had muttered to himself as he read the paper with the morning's first cup of coffee, but it fuelled his own lingering uncertainty about Forsyth's guilt.

After a dramatic opening — "A killer walks among us" — the letter went on to express surprise, not to say astonishment, that the police, despite all the scientific resources at their disposal, had been unable to track down the sadistic monster who could seemingly kill at will, taunting the police all the while. Lambert did acknowledge that there had been an arrest in the case, but made the point that even if the charges stood up in court, which it was clear he doubted, it still left the other killings unsolved and TLC at large. He concluded by asking when the taxpaying citizens could expect their police force to put an end to the deadly rampage.

What did he know about Lambert? Not much. Their only contact had been some months ago as fellow members of a panel on criminal law at a Law Society seminar. Lambert was about his own age, intelligent and articulate. Self-confident, verging on cockiness. Already balding, he had an irritating habit of flicking his finger at his neatly trimmed moustache. How had he come to know about the communications? Maybe it was just an educated guess on his part. But it wouldn't have been all that difficult for him in any case. As a professor of criminal law it would be logical for him to cultivate the detectives who investigated crimes. It would enrich his lectures and raise his profile with his students and colleagues.

His letter to the editor was another piece of self-promotion. But it also put him on the radar screen. If it were possible, Chris would have liked to bring the professor downtown for a full-scale interrogation. But there was no way that could be justified. Not yet. Meanwhile, he would have to make do with what was available.

Beginning with the first letter, the one addressed to Mason's neighbour, Chris compared the communications received from the killer (or, as he was careful to remind himself, presumably from the killer) with

Lambert's letter to the editor. He didn't expect to find any stylistic or linguistic similarity, but maybe there would be something, some nuance, that would indicate they were sent by the same person. There wasn't. At least nothing he could spot. It was obvious that both the sender of the messages and Lambert entertained a high opinion of themselves, but that he already knew. Maybe the profiler could come up with something that he had missed. He would have Mavis take a look at them.

He would also have one of the Homicide detectives make some discreet inquiries. See if they could find out where Lambert might have been at the time of the murders. Almost certainly it would turn out to be a red herring, but in this business one couldn't afford to overlook any possibility.

"Your buddy, Forsyth, nearly got bail." Peter Blair sounded incredulous, and more than a little alarmed.

"What?" Chris held the receiver away from his ear and stared at it. "He's charged with first-degree murder, for Christ's sake! Premeditated murder."

"I know." The Crown prosecutor sighed. "It's almost unheard of for bail to be granted in a murder case, but it does happen. It damn near happened here. To begin with, we drew Justice Gourley."

"Jesus." Gourley was notorious for making things difficult for the Crown. So much so that on a couple of occasions he had been asked to recuse himself but had refused, and his refusal had been upheld by the Court of Appeal.

"Exactly. And, let's face it, the case against Forsyth is circumstantial. No eyewitness, no smoking gun. He's a highly respected member of the legal profession. The only thing that made Gourley think twice was the fact that Forsyth and his wife had been looking to buy a place in the Caribbean. I argued that made him a flight risk. It was a near thing, I can tell you."

"I didn't realize Myrden was going to make a bail application. He told me he was going to apply to have the charge dismissed."

"He is. He's just taking a different tack. He informed the court that he intended to ask for a preliminary inquiry."

Preliminary inquiries were no longer mandatory, but they could be requested by either the defence or the Crown. At the hearing, the Crown was obliged to disclose its case, but there was no risk to the defence. They weren't required to show their hand. Myrden would concentrate on attacking the Crown's case and the lack of hard evidence connecting his client to the crime.

"You'll be our lead witness at the inquiry, Chris. You and two rolls of duct tape. And an allegedly drugged escort, of course."

"I know. Circumstantial. But don't forget the motive, Pete. A very compelling motive."

"Motive. Your trademark. What is it you always say, Chris, find the motive and you find the perpetrator?"

"It works for me. Anyway, nothing has changed. Right from the get-go Myrden said he was going to have the charge dismissed."

"It'll be up to you to see that doesn't happen, Chris."

"Thanks. Thanks a bunch."

Chris was still frowning at the phone when the staff sergeant came out of his cubicle and informed him that the mayor had called a high-level conference and he was to attend. The meeting was to start at two o'clock in the mayor's office.

"The reason for this meeting," the mayor, Loretta Cyrcz, a large, dark-haired woman in her mid-forties, began, "is obvious. We have a vicious killer running loose in our community. The citizens" — *She means voters,* Chris thought to himself — "are asking why we can't seem to bring this monster to justice. I ask myself the same question. The killer's rampage has been going on for how long now?"

"Seven months, two weeks, and five days." Chris supplied the answer.

"Thank you," said the mayor, with a slight, ironic lift of a penciled eyebrow. "I see it's weighing on your mind as well."

"Of course," Chris muttered, earning an irritated look from Her Worship.

"Apart from your commendable command of the timeline," the mayor continued, "can we dare to hope that an arrest is imminent?"

"There *has* been one arrest," Chief Johnstone offered. Careful as always, Chris noted, not to call her by name. On occasion the mayor made political capital of her Ukrainian surname, laughingly introducing herself as "Loretta Eyechart." In English it was easily pronounced "search," but Johnstone never trusted himself with it.

"*One* arrest. For a murder that I understand does not form part of our serial killer's campaign. Isn't that correct?"

The Chief deflected the question to Chris with a motion of his hand.

"That's correct."

"The man you arrested, a well-known lawyer, has been charged with the murder of a fellow lawyer, Adrienne Vinney. I had the pleasure of meeting her once.

At some oil company reception. A remarkably attractive, intelligent woman."

"We believe we have the right person in custody in that case."

"What you in the police call a righteous arrest?"

"Some do."

"But not you, Detective. Very well. Can we safely assume that *her* murder was *not* the work of the serial killer?"

"We believe it was a copycat murder."

"The killer, the real serial killer, has been operating in our midst for, as you pointed out, Detective Crane, more than seven months. Surely, in all that time, he must have left some clues behind. What about DNA? The victim puts up a struggle, scratches her attacker, and ends up with his DNA under her fingernails. That sort of thing." The mayor sighed. "Maybe I've been watching too much television. I guess things aren't that simple in real life."

"Unfortunately, Ms. Cyrcz, they're not. The only DNA at the crime scenes has been that of the victims. And so far as we can tell the victims' bodies show no sign of a struggle. It's hard to be sure about that because they were mutilated so severely, but that's how it looks. The medical examiner is of the same opinion."

"So where are we?"

"At this stage our best hope is that a member of the public will see something and phone it in, or the killer will make a mistake."

The chairman of the police commission stirred in his chair and spoke for the first time. "So what you're saying, Detective Crane, is that the police are reduced to relying on blind luck to solve this case?"

"Not quite, sir. Our investigation is ongoing. And there's always a chance the killer will give himself away."

"According to a press release, the reason for which I must say escapes me, the killer has been taunting the police. Sending them notes and e-mails."

"That's correct sir. We think it's him. Or her. Although it could also be someone playing games with us. On the plus side, when a serial killer starts sending messages to the police it often leads to their downfall. Deliberately or not, the messages sometimes contain clues that give the killer away."

chapter eighteen

"Do you know what that asshole, Lambert, is doing?"

"I have no idea, Steve, but I'm sure you're about to tell me."

"He's checking out the crime scenes. Starting with the one in Nose Hill Park. He's over in Bowness right now. Taking photos and talking into a tape recorder."

"Is he alone?"

"Yeah."

"He's probably doing research for a paper in some law journal. Anyway, there's nothing illegal in what he's doing. All the crime scenes have been released and the public has access."

Chris walked over to Gwen's desk and told her what Mason had reported about Lambert visiting the crime scenes. "What do you make of that?" he asked in conclusion.

"Well, I agree with you that he's probably writing a paper on the case. You know what they say about university professors: publish or perish."

"God knows Lambert is ambitious. He's always putting himself forward, giving talks to groups — Rotary, Chamber of Commerce, the Canadian Bar Association, you name it. That letter to the *Herald* was part of the pattern."

"If he *is* writing a paper he'll come down hard on the police."

"Unless we make an arrest before it's published." Chris paused. "There *could* be another explanation, though."

"I know what you're thinking. That Lambert is our killer. That the whole thing is an ego trip on his part."

"Pretty farfetched, huh?"

"Not necessarily. You've met the guy, Chris. Do you think he's capable of pulling something like this? Committing murder just to prove how clever he is?"

"He's an egotistical son of a bitch. No question about that. I've made a few preliminary inquiries. He's single. Lives alone. So he's free to come and go as he pleases. Highly regarded as a teacher."

"So, what do we do?"

"Let's find out how the professor is spending his summer holidays."

"Like the man himself said, we made his day." Gwen shook her head in bemusement as she and Chris exited Murray Fraser Hall, the building that housed the Faculty of Law. "He's something else!"

"Isn't he just? He could hardly contain his glee at

being interviewed by the police. It'll be a highlight of his lectures in the fall semester."

"Interesting the way he refused to account for his whereabouts on the nights the murders were committed."

"That was quite an act he put on. The right of the citizen to maintain his privacy, etcetera. He was right, of course. Without a subpoena, we couldn't force him to answer. He toyed with us, Gwen," Chris said as he drove out of the campus, almost deserted now that the academic year was over.

"Toying with you can be a dangerous game. Where are we with the professor, Chris? Do we eliminate him as a suspect?"

"Not yet. And not quite. We'll run a few more checks on the learned Professor Lambert before we turn him loose. He didn't do or say anything to incriminate himself, but he didn't clear himself, either."

"The Stampede signs are beginning to spring up everywhere," Gwen observed as they entered the downtown area.

"It's when they start setting up the viewing stands along the route of the parade that I realize the Stampede is really upon us."

"It's on your desk," a detective looked up from his computer to say. This time the message was in words cut from a newspaper and taped to a sheet of plain white paper:

YoɒR iGNorInG Me crane NO ‖iKE

"It's been checked for fingerprints and DNA. Nada," said the detective, who had followed him over to his desk.

Chris nodded and told him to fax the message and the envelope it came in to the profiler. Maybe Mavis could make something out of the ungrammatical English. Probably not. But one thing was obvious. The killer was getting restless. Bored.

As expected, Dummett's article inspired a flurry of indignant letters to the editor. "How could anyone find excuses for a monster like this?" was the almost universal theme. One writer took a more thoughtful approach, agreeing that a fatal combination of factors — social and psychological — could make a human being fall into such evil depths of depravity. "That being said," the writer concluded in the final paragraph, "the time for understanding and treatment is when, and only when, this individual is safely behind bars."

After checking to make sure that all the letters were on that one page, Chris separated it from the rest of the paper and put it to one side. The letters would be analyzed in detail later. Mavis Ross was probably poring over them already.

chapter nineteen

Ranches in southern Alberta were in for another rash of cattle mutilations. Chris paused in the act of knotting his tie when the newscaster mentioned the well-known rancher, Cameron Taylor, a past president of the Stampede, whose prize bull, Bent Tree's Apollo IV, had been shot and mutilated. The attack, similar to those suffered by other ranches in the area in previous years, had been discovered early that morning when a ranch hand went out to check on the valuable animal in the field where he was pastured.

As soon as he arrived in his office Chris placed a call to the RCMP detachment in Turner Valley. He didn't know anyone there, but when he identified himself, he was put through to the corporal in charge.

"One of our officers is out there now," Corporal Kanciar told Chris. "But if it's like all the others, she won't come up with anything useful. It was a headshot. We'll recover the bullet, but it won't be traceable. None of the people out here register their weapons."

"The Taylors are good friends of mine. I'd like to help. I know it's not in my jurisdiction, but would you mind if I and a member of my team took a look at the scene?"

"No problem. I'll let Constable Lonechild know you're coming, and have her secure the scene until you arrive."

"Constable Lonechild." Gwen pronounced the name slowly, savouring it, as they drew up to the little group standing around a RCMP cruiser. "Female and First Nations. Two quotas in one. Good for them! Totally awesome!" she breathed as the Mountie came forward to greet them. Tall, her slim waist and wide shoulders set off by the khaki tunic and Sam Browne belt, she had the coal black eyes and light saffron skin of her race.

The other members of the little group hung back while the police officers introduced themselves. The Mountie knew that the two city detectives were working what she called the "outdoor privy case." She also had been informed that Chris was a good friend of the Taylor family, which explained why they were taking an interest in the case of the mutilated bull.

"Thank you for coming, Chris," said Phyllis Taylor as they shook hands. "With your help we may catch these perverts who prey on helpless animals."

"A bad business," agreed Chris.

Her husband waved a hand to acknowledge the new arrivals but remained by the gate, the German shepherd rigid at his side. Blitzkrieg wore a studded collar but no leash. His ears pricked forward, his golden brown eyes stared unblinkingly at the two detectives, but not a muscle moved in his statue-like pose. During his past social visits Chris had not had any contact with the guard dog, apart from seeing him at a distance patrolling the borders of the ranch. The dog was kennelled outside and was never in the house. A young man in faded jeans and plaid shirt was the third member of the little trio. He would be the ranch hand who had discovered the dead bull. With a slight shake of his head Cameron indicated that Chris should keep his distance.

The two detectives quickly slipped into their prophylactic clothing and lifted the crime scene equipment out of the van. The dog gave a warning growl deep in his throat and looked up at his master as the detectives, wearing masks, white coveralls, and latex gloves, walked toward the gate. Cameron said something and they moved off to one side.

The bull pasture was more of a corral than a pasture; the walls were high and constructed of thick planks some thirty centimetres apart. The heavy gate was fastened with a latch, but not locked.

"We'll dust for prints," said Chris as Gwen photographed the latch. "Although I doubt we'll find anything useful. Too much traffic."

The grass inside the fence was thick and cropped short. Scrunching down, Gwen sprayed the ground and photographed wherever there was the slightest indentation that might yield a footprint, leaving an identification marker at each spot.

"Thank God for cowboy boots and their high heels," she muttered.

"Which all the men out here wear. Women too," Chris corrected himself. Phyllis Taylor was wearing cowboy boots. Gleaming black with a floral design etched in white. Unzipping the canvas bag he was carrying over his shoulder, he took out swabs and test tubes.

The Hereford bull was lying on its right side; the broad white blaze down the front of its head was matted in blood still oozing from the bullet hole in the forehead. More blood stained the left side of the massive head where its ear had been severed. Waving off the buzzing flies, Chris confirmed that only the ears had been removed. A strangely restrained mutilation that was identical to the previous cases. The general public had not been informed about the precise nature of the mutilations, but the information had been included in the bulletins circulated to other police forces in the area.

"The guy has a thing for ears," he muttered, slapping at a fly that persisted in landing on his cheek.

"Which is kind of weird, when you think about it," Gwen replied as she placed markers on the ground to identify the photos she was about to take. "You would expect something more exotic, like the testicles."

"They took the ears with them." Despite the bright sunlight Gwen was using the Nikon's flash as she snapped off a series of rapid fire shots.

"Trophies. That could be helpful. Trophies have been the downfall of many criminals. There's no better evidence than a collection of souvenirs taken from the victims."

"As in Dahmer."

"The most celebrated example of all. It was the body parts in his fridge that finally did him in." Chris waved at the Mountie, who had stayed behind while they examined the ground, signalling her to join them, then bent down to collect blood samples. The blood would almost certainly prove to be from the bull, but it still had to be checked.

They had an audience when they walked back out: a small crowd of neighbouring ranchers, plus several members of the press, conspicuous with their tape recorders and cameras. The spectators were held back by crime scene tape. Corporal Kanciar had sent reinforcements, two constables who had stationed themselves at either end of the tape.

Blitzkrieg was being led away, pacing obediently at the side of the hired hand.

"What brings you here, Detective Crane?" one of the reporters called out. "A bit of a comedown for you, isn't it? Has TLC taken to killing livestock?"

"We don't think so." Chris smiled good-naturedly and walked over to talk to the journalists. "We're here to help the RCMP in their investigation. The killing and mutilation of ranch animals is a serious problem that has been going on far too long. The Mounties are determined to bring the criminals to justice. That's why we're here." He went to on to talk about the outbreaks of this type of random vandalism that had occurred in recent years, and that it had to be stopped. Gratified that he had given them something to file, they accepted with good grace his "You know I can't comment on that" answer to the inevitable question about the serial killer investigation.

While chatting with the reporters Chris cast a seemingly casual eye over the onlookers. He recognized the majority of them as participants in last Sunday's outing, both riders and non-riders. Some smiled and gave discreet little waves, clearly intrigued by seeing him in his role as a police detective.

There were no objections when Chris asked for consent samples from those who had been in the pasture legitimately to look at the carcass. They were to stand on specially treated pads to leave an impression of their footwear, then have photos taken of the soles of their boots, provide DNA samples, and be fingerprinted. The grass in the bull's paddock was dense and cropped short, so it hadn't yielded much in the way of footprints. Still, there was a procedure to be followed.

"It's just to see if the vandal or vandals may have left any trace of themselves," he assured them. "In order to do this, we need to eliminate any traces you might have left." In answer to a question from Cam, he promised that the data would be destroyed and no records of it kept when it had served its purpose.

"Phyllis was there, too." Cameron Taylor beckoned to his wife, and she ducked under the crime tape to join them. Seeing that there was nothing for them to sit on, one of the neighbours offered his cane with the folding seat he used while watching outdoor equestrian events. One by one they perched on it, holding up their legs so Gwen could photograph the soles of their boots. Then she swabbed their mouths for DNA and Chris fingerprinted them. Out of the corner of his eye he saw Melanie stop and stare at the spectacle. She was fitted out for jogging — white shorts, athletic bra showing through her thin white shirt, and running shoes. Wiping the perspiration from her face with the towel draped around her neck, she shook her head in wonder and skirted around the rear of the crowd, arms held chest high in a passable version of a power walk. *Probably can't understand all this fuss over a dead bull*, thought Chris.

Saying, "We're done here," he told the Mounties they could take down the tape. He would remain on the scene for a while, mingling with the onlookers on the off chance he might learn something useful. They were more than mere onlookers. They were here to show support for the Taylors and solidarity against the unknown vandals. He nodded sympathetically when a rancher, one who had ridden alongside him for a spell on Sunday, growled, "I hate to see a good animal wasted like that." This was met with murmurs of agreement.

"You guys come up with any clues?" another rancher demanded, pushing a stained white Stetson up from an overheated face.

"Nothing that leaps out at you," responded Chris. "We'll know better when the lab has a look at what we've collected."

"I simply cannot understand why the police just can't seem to find out who is doing this. It happens every year and nobody is ever arrested." The speaker was a middle-aged woman, lean as a fence post, with a lined, leathery face under her wide-brimmed hat.

"Give the detectives a chance, Jean," remonstrated the man, almost certainly her husband, standing next to her. "They've just been brought into the picture. Maybe they'll come up with something with all that fancy forensic stuff." Turning to Chris, he held out his hand. "If you're as good a detective as you are a horseman, Crane, this bastard will be behind bars in no time."

"We'll sure do our best." Tugging a bale of straw down from a stack, Chris stepped up on it and looked out at the crowd. Counting the Taylors and the ranch hand, there were thirty-eight of them.

"Whether you realize it or not," he began, "you who live and ranch in the area represent the best hope of bringing the perpetrator or perpetrators of these cruel and senseless attacks to justice. You who are familiar with everything that goes on around here are the most likely to spot anything out of the ordinary. We ask you to remain vigilant, be on the lookout for anything that strikes you as being different. It doesn't have to be suspicious, just different. If you see anything like that, please contact the RCMP in Turner Valley immediately. You can speak to Constable Lonechild or the corporal in charge of the detachment. If they're not there, talk to any officer who is. They will pass whatever you tell them on to us in Calgary."

While Chris was speaking, Gwen videotaped his audience as unobtrusively as possible.

"It don't seem right," a rancher, the same one who had deplored the waste of a good animal, protested. "Spying on your neighbours like that, reporting them to the police. That's like what they do in communist countries."

"I hear what you're saying, sir." Chris, who had been about to step down, lifted his foot back up onto the straw bale. "We're not asking you to become police informers. Or anything remotely like that. What we're asking is very specific and temporary. It will be over and done with just as soon as the culprit is apprehended, and your livestock is once more safe from attack."

"He's right, Ben," someone said, and there was a general murmur of assent.

"What will happen to this damn pervert when you catch him?" called out a rancher in the rear row.

"Thanks for the vote of confidence. We'll try to deserve it." Chris's smile turned grim. "He will go to jail. Section 444 of the Criminal Code provides that anyone who wilfully kills, maims, or injures cattle is guilty of an indictable offence and liable to imprisonment for a term of up to five years."

"Are you saying that the Criminal Code deals specifically with cattle?" asked the rancher.

"It does. Shows just how vulnerable cattle can be to vandalism. Turned out to graze in open fields, they make easy targets."

"Well, Chris." Phyllis was waiting for him as he jumped down from the hay bale. "Your reputation may not have preceded you, but it certainly has caught up to you. Walter Murray made a few telephone calls to some horsey friends back East, and now everybody knows about your illustrious career as a show jumper. People find it fascinating that a well-known detective is also a famous horseman."

"I'll do my best not to disappoint them. I must say, however, that Melanie didn't seem all that impressed. She looked at us as if we had gone mad when we were doing our thing with the boots. Speaking of Melanie, I had no idea she was a fitness buff."

"It's a very recent thing with her. She says it's a way to pass the time out here in the sticks, but I have a feeling it's more than that. Maybe it's just wishful thinking on our part, but she seems to have a more positive attitude lately. She misses Sarah. They've become very good friends." She paused, then added with a roguish little smile. "She's not the only one who misses Sarah, is she, Chris?"

"I'm sure we all will rejoice to have her back," he replied with mock gravity.

"There's a good chance that the person we're looking for is in this bunch." Chris lightly tapped the computer screen.

"As in the funeral syndrome?" Gwen asked. "It worked in the Vinney case."

"But that wasn't much of a test. As a friend of the victim it was natural for Tom Forsyth to attend."

"Some friend!"

Chris acknowledged her point with a rueful smile, then turned to the profiler. "What about it, Mavis? Can you spot a likely cattle mutilator in that merry little band?"

"That would be asking too much, " she said without taking her extraordinary eyes off the screen. "That's a remarkably homogeneous collection of people. They all have the same look. Outdoorsy. Weatherbeaten. Not only Caucasian, but Anglo-Saxon. Celtic. Very attractive in their own way. You can tell they're ranchers."

"See anyone else of particular interest?"

"They all look worried. Not surprising. I'm looking for a young person, or more likely persons — it's a young person's sort of crime. Almost mischievous, in an evil way. But these people aren't young. At least not that young. Zero in on that guy, off to one side. The one with the plaid shirt. Bring up his face. There—"

Before she could say anything more, a detective gave a cursory knock on the door of the interview room and stuck his head in to announce in a slightly awestruck tone that there was an RCMP constable with some files for Detective Crane.

"Bring her in," said Chris, grinning. No need to guess who it was.

"Here is the physical evidence." Constable Lonechild put a cardboard box down on Chris's desk. "It's not much. Most of the stuff — photos, interviews, and so on — is in the computer. The corporal has given you the access code, I believe."

"That's right. We'll be getting to it shortly." Chris introduced her to Mavis Ross, then pointed to the close-up of the man Mavis had picked out. "Do you recognize him?"

"It's Mr. McRae. Angus McRae. He owns the Lazy Z."

There was a silence for a moment as they stared at the unlovely visage filling the screen. Unkempt black eyebrows scowled over squinty eyes framed in a web of wrinkles, the bridge of the nose had been flattened in some past encounter, and the cheeks and chin were covered with dark stubble.

"Has McRae lost any livestock to the vandals?" Chris asked the Mountie.

"A bull. Three years ago, I think. Yes, it was three years ago."

"A valuable animal?"

"I don't know. It was old, I remember that."

"Is McRae popular with his fellow ranchers? Well respected?" This from the profiler.

"I can't answer that. I do know that the Lazy Z is pretty rundown. Cattle keep escaping and running around the countryside. That doesn't sit too well with the other ranchers. Once, two years ago, one of his bulls broke out and got into another rancher's field and bred some of his prize cows. There was a big stink about that."

"I can imagine," Chris murmured, briefly entertained by the scene her account had conjured up. "All right, Mavis, tell us what you find so fascinating about the worthy Mr. McRae."

The profiler shot a questioning glace at the uniformed Mountie, then, when Chris nodded, said, "He's the only one who doesn't look worried. He looks angry, mad at something. I know," she went on, overriding Gwen's interjection. "Anger is an appropriate emotion for a rancher under these circumstances. It's what one would expect. But there's something more in his expression. He's puzzled. And upset. I'm not saying he's the one," she added after a pause. "I'm just saying he's the most likely candidate in the group. The perpetrator could be someone completely different. Someone who wasn't there."

"Nonetheless, it's worth following up." Chris swivelled in his seat to look at Lonechild. "Was McRae ever questioned about his whereabouts when the attacks occurred?"

"No. There was no reason to. He wasn't a suspect. We didn't *have* a suspect."

"Do I take it then that none of the local people were asked to account for themselves?"

"That's right. We figured it had to be townies. No rancher would treat animals like that."

"I see. Okay, I'm going to suggest to Corporal Kanciar that McRae be questioned as to where he was and what he was doing last night. He can't very well claim not to remember. Some of the others should be questioned as well, so he doesn't think he's being singled out."

An hour later, Chris pushed his chair back. "Well, Gwen, we've been through every piece of evidence in the RCMP files. What have we learned?"

"I would say we have learned that most, if not all, of the earlier incidents — if that's what we're going to call them — were carried out by the same perpetrator. And it looks like it's just one person."

"Based on?"

"Footprints, mainly. If the Mounties didn't do a full-scale crime scene investigation, they at least took photographs. The scene was pretty contaminated, but there were some fairly distinct impressions around the head. That would be where our guy squatted down to do the cutting. Very neat and surgical according to the reports."

"Apollo's wounds didn't look all that surgical. Let's have a close-up of them." When the photos appeared on the screen, Chris muttered, "I sure wouldn't call that surgical. More of a hack job, I would say."

"Especially where the right ear was. You can see where there were several abortive cuts before it was finally severed."

"Maybe that's why McRae looked upset. Amateurs horning in on his act."

Just before they were about to call it a day, Corporal Kanciar called in to report that McRae had an alibi. "I paid a call to the Lazy Z just after supper," he told them.

"Both he and his wife stated that after doing the chores, they watched TV until ten, then went to bed and slept until the alarm went off at six."

"Do you believe her? He looks like the sort of guy a wife would be scared of."

"She's pretty scary herself. They're both drinkers, and rumour has it that they knock each other around from time to time. But she's never filed a complaint, and they're isolated as hell out there on the ranch." Kanciar paused. "Yeah, I believe her. I think her evidence would stand up in court."

Apart from the cattle mutilations, there had been no complaints recorded at the Turner Valley detachment that could be connected in any way with animal abuse. The Calgary police files were more rewarding. Over the past five years, there had been twelve complaints of cruelty to animals. Nearly all the complaints had been made by neighbours and involved teenagers. All had been investigated. Two had been found to be groundless. Some others had been resolved with stern warnings from the police. Three had led to charges being laid, and one, the most heinous, had resulted in jail time for the offender. He was convicted of cruelty of animals, specifically the torture and killing of cats, and sentenced to six months imprisonment to be served in the Calgary Young Offenders Centre. Since he was seventeen at the time his identity was protected under the Youth Criminal Justice Act. That had been four years ago, which would make him twenty-one. No longer a teenager.

Which could pose a problem, Chris cautioned himself. Male teenagers changed as they matured and the rush of hormones levelled off; teenage gangs broke up and the members went their separate ways. Still, the torture of the unfortunate cats had been so extreme, so fiendish, that cruelty must be deeply embedded in the perpetrator's genes. The animals had been disembowelled and the toms castrated. The investigating officer had been one Constable Hibbell. Chris didn't know him, but that was easily fixed.

"Sure, I remember the case." Henry Hibbell, two years retired from the police service, motioned Chris to take one of the lawn chairs. He had been cultivating the tiny patch of garden in his backyard when Chris arrived. "The little bastard was kinda unforgettable, know what I mean? Bright as hell and with a fuck-you attitude. But at the same time, kind of likeable, know what I mean?"

"Tell me about him. Starting with his name."

"Mark Leonard. His father is the CEO of some oil company. Lives in Mount Royal." Hibbell gave a reminiscent shake of his head. "Leonard would never look you right in the eye. Always turned his face sideways. I took hold of his head once and made him look straight at me. I'll never forget the hate in his eyes when I did that. It took me a while to figure out why."

"And what was the reason?"

"His ears. They were different. One was big and really stuck out and the other one was small and kind of twisted in on itself. Know what I mean? They didn't look too bad if you didn't see them both at the same time."

"Jesus!"

"Struck a nerve, have I?"

"You have for sure. It may be coincidence, but listen to this."

"It fits! By God, it fits!" Hibbell breathed after Chris had filled him in on the cattle killings. "It's just the kind of thing the little prick would do. You're going to keep me in the loop on this, Crane?"

"You got it. Does Leonard live with his family?"

"He did back then. His family tried to do the right thing. Visited him at the centre, sent him to a shrink when he got out. But he was too much for them. He moved out, or was kicked out. I don't know which." He paused as his wife, gently waved grey hair framing her pleasant face, brought them coffee and date squares.

"Do you know if he still lives in Calgary?"

"Yeah, I know. He does. I see you look surprised, Crane. But I've kind of kept my eye on Mark Leonard. Can't seem to get him out of my mind. He's a stone killer. I'm almost positive he'll graduate to killing people. If he hasn't already. He's got a mean streak a mile wide."

"What does he do for a living?"

"Deals drugs. He's a distributor, not one of the top guys."

"I suppose you just might know where he lives?"

"In the Beltline. In an apartment in the 600 block. I'll write out the address for you when you leave."

"Does he live alone?"

"Yeah. Except for the snake."

"He keeps snakes?"

"One snake. A real monster. Never seen it myself, but that's what the beat constable tells me. Mark Leonard is one creepy guy."

"Those squares are absolutely delicious." Chris told Mrs. Hibbell when she came out with a fresh pot of coffee.

"If the snake is that big it must be a boa constrictor," Chris remarked when the kitchen screen door closed behind Hibbell's wife.

"Bigger. Much bigger. The other people in the building say it's some kind of python. They don't like it one bit. They've complained to the landlord, but he refuses to do anything. Maybe Leonard is his supplier."

"A snake like that could require live food."

"Yeah. Leonard's neighbours don't like that either. Every week or so he brings chickens home to feed the brute. Quite open about it, apparently. He's not so open about the cats and small dogs he traps and smuggles into his apartment."

"Creepy. Like you said. I need to talk to the officer who patrols the area."

"Bob Lavoy. He works out of District 1, and he's pretty tight with some of the people who live in the area. He keeps me up to speed on Leonard." The retired police officer paused to stir his coffee. "I've got his DNA," he added with an attempt at offhandedness that didn't quite come off.

"You do?"

"I know what you're thinking. Young offenders charged with minor crimes can't be compelled to give a DNA sample. But Leonard was a smoker. Still is, probably. I fixed him up with a package of Players Light. There's a couple of butts in my safe. They could never be used as evidence against him, but ..."

"But they could tell us whether or not he was connected to a crime."

Chris, with the cigarette butts in an envelope on the seat beside him, drove out of the Killarney district and headed downtown on 17th Avenue. The only problem was that there had been no DNA collected at the past crime scenes and the perpetrator hadn't left any behind in the Taylor case. But the ears!

chapter twenty

All thoughts of ears and bulls were driven from Chris's mind when his mobile reported the discovery of another body. Cursing, he put the cherry light on the dash and gunned the Durango. He would proceed directly to the crime scene without checking in with headquarters.

The Devonian Gardens! How in the hell had they missed that? It was a park, albeit an indoor one. Right in the centre of the downtown core, on the fourth floor of TD Square. Chris berated himself for not having placed it under surveillance, but he had just never thought of it as a park in the conventional sense. But as a public park it met all the criteria for the serial's signature. How had the killer managed to stash his victim there?

Three police cruisers, lights flashing, were parked outside TD Square when Chris arrived. Propping a police card up on the dash, he jumped out of the SUV, showed his badge to a uniform, and rushed inside.

A crowd had gathered around the elevator on the Plus-15 level by the time Chris arrived. The glass elevator that served the gardens had been sealed off and would be examined later for clues. Chris spoke briefly to the two uniforms behind the crime tape and, besieged on all sides by the outthrust microphones and cameras of the media, rode the escalators up to the fourth floor.

The loud splashing of fountains was the only sound as he walked into the conservatory, for that's what it was, with its glassed-in roof and lush tropical foliage. He couldn't really be blamed for not thinking of it as a park, he told himself, as he followed a constable along the brick pathways where couples and small groups of visitors whispered among themselves or stood frozen in awed silence.

"It's him all right." Gwen was waiting for him on a little footbridge spanning a pool where large, colourful carp swam.

"Left hand?"

She nodded and fell in beside him as they approached an archway painted white and decorated with plastic flowers, leading into an open space designed for wedding celebrations.

"One of the gardeners found her," Patterson, looking as clean-cut and preppie as ever, informed Chris. "He thought it was a bundle of rags, then he saw what was inside."

"We already have the gardener's fingerprints," Gwen assured Chris before he could say anything.

The slim, tanned body of a young woman with a shaved pubic area lay on a bed of rough dark brown cloth amid the flowers and shrubs at the foot of a grove of cedars. She had been mutilated and violated in the same manner as the others. Apart from the severed nipple, her firm breasts, which had no need of implants, were untouched. From the absence of blood it was clear that she also had been killed someplace else. Like TLC's other victims, the toxicology report would show no drugs in her system. Unlike some serials, he didn't keep his victims drugged and helpless for days to be tortured and raped at will. With TLC it was snatch, torture, and kill. Followed by the daring and dramatic display of the mutilated body. There were times when Chris wondered if the display wasn't the climax of the experience for TLC. If so, this one must have given him a real thrill.

"How in God's name did he get her up here?" As he spoke, Chris gazed around at the open expanse of the Devonian Gardens. "This place is busy all day and it's closed at night."

"We figure we have the answer to that," replied Patterson. "One of the security guards saw a couple get off the elevator not long before closing last night. Arabs. He had a beard and one of the headdresses they wear. She was in a wheelchair and covered head to toe in a … what do they call it?"

"Burka."

"That's it. The guard is over there. You can talk to him when you're ready. He didn't see much more than that. He says those people don't like to be stared at. He remembers the man's beard was white."

"Anyone see them leave?"

"The same guard did. She was still in the wheelchair."

"Or *something* was. Easy enough to arrange. Prop up the burka somehow. A stick would do it." Chris fingered the cloth with his gloved hand. "This isn't a burka. It's just a blanket that's been used to cover her. I take it we don't know who she is yet?"

"Not yet."

"Let's start with the tanning salons."

"Your hunch about the tanning salons paid off." Gwen's smile was mischievous as she emphasized *hunch*.

Going along with her little game, Chris replied, "That was no hunch, but pure deductive reasoning. Who was she?"

"Marion Klasky. She was a regular at the Monterey Tanning Studio on Seventeenth Avenue. She was employed as a physiotherapist at the Talisman Centre for Wellness on MacLeod Trail. They're faxing us her file, but we already know she was twenty-eight years old, single, and lived in an apartment on Thirteenth Avenue and Seventh Street."

"The Beltline."

"Right. It's also not far from where she works. When she didn't show up this morning, they tried to reach her, but all they got was her answering machine."

"What time did she get off work yesterday?"

"Three o'clock. They open at six. A lot of their clientele are oil company executives and office workers who want to get an early start on their day."

"Like Ann Marin, the fitness instructor." Chris paused when his phone rang. He listened intently, then said, "We're on our way" and hung up.

"We have a hit on the wheelchair," he told Gwen. "Let's go."

Lightning flashed and thunder crashed as they exited the rear of the building and hurried over to where the police vehicles were parked. Gwen flinched and grabbed Chris's arm.

"You'd think I'd be used to that," she apologized. "But it gets me every time."

Raising his left arm to check his wristwatch, Chris chuckled. "Right on time. Five o'clock in the afternoon. In July. In Calgary. What do you expect?"

Forks of lightning lit up the sky and thunder rumbled and rolled as they joined the rush-hour traffic. "When you think about it," said Chris, easing the unmarked van to a stop as a traffic light turned yellow, "this case *should* provide us with some useful clues. Which is something we haven't had so far. This time our boy had to work out in the open. He had to risk discovery in order to pull off the Devonian caper."

"The Devonian caper. I like that," Gwen interjected. "It would make a great title for a book."

"I gues it would at that. Getting back to the subject at hand, the killer had to acquire a wheelchair, as well as a disguise. To do that, he would have to expose himself to other people. Not like the previous cases, where he could operate completely on his own."

The ease and speed with which the wheelchair had been tracked down seemed to bear out what Chris was saying. There were only a few retail outlets in the city that carried them, and it hadn't taken long to locate the likely source of the chair.

"Our killer must be well-heeled," Gwen remarked thoughtfully as they pulled into a parking spot in front of a small, independent drugstore in a nondescript strip mall. "Wheelchairs cost a bundle."

The unlit cherry light on the dash of an otherwise unmarked white Ford sedan showed that Homicide was on the scene. Ford seemed to be the police flavour of the year. Fleet discounts no doubt. Inside the store, Mason was questioning a balding, middle-aged man who seemed to be the proprietor.

"There's your answer." Chris nodded at two rows of wheelchairs lined up in a corner of the store under a sign reading "Pre-Owned Wheelchairs."

"A sense of humour, no less," he murmured in an aside to Gwen as they joined Mason and the owner by the cash register.

"They sold a chair to an Arab last week," Mason announced. "For $250."

"Sure beats the price of new one," the owner informed them complacently, sounding, thought Chris, just like a used-car salesman. His hopes that the man could provide them with a solid lead to the killer were soon dashed. The purchaser's face had been hidden behind a beard and sunglasses. "Yes, the beard was white." His head was covered with "one of them scarves," and he was wearing some kind of a cloak that reached down to his ankles. Fingerprints? He was wearing gloves. The proprietor figured that had something to do with his religion. Credit card receipt? He had paid cash.

There was no point in asking why the man's appearance hadn't aroused some curiosity. They were in an ethnic quadrant of the city.

"I think it's great you're doing this," said Gwen when the proprietor explained that he didn't make any profit on the used chairs and that he regarded it as an act of social responsibility on his part. "But doesn't Alberta Health Care cover the cost of wheelchairs for those who need them?"

"Yeah, but there's plenty what fall through the cracks. Immigrants, people who are in the country illegally, don't know about Health Care, don't trust the system. It's a different world up—" he stopped talking as a loud thunderclap rattled the windows and a drumfire of rain began to pelt down.

"I know. It's a good thing you're doing. And we appreciate your help," said Chris.

Heavy raindrops, almost hail, bounced off the pavement as he and Gwen dashed across the sidewalk to their van.

"We're getting close, Gwen," said Chris above the clack of the windshield wipers. "This is the first time anybody has actually *seen* the monster."

"But *what* did they see?"

That question kept recurring as Chris, after a solitary dinner in a nearby restaurant, sat in his study, mentally reviewing the file. True, the killer had exposed himself with the Devonian caper — a label that to Chris would always be inextricably attached to that file — but he had been damned clever about it. Still, he *had* left some potential leads. The beard was almost certainly false, although a canvass of the costume and novelty shops had so far drawn a blank. The brown cloth in which the victim's body had been wrapped was being examined by experts on a priority basis, but was unlikely to produce anything that could be linked to the killer.

Frustrated, his thoughts veered off to the cattle mutilations. Could there be a possible connection? Unlikely, although both displayed the same twisted cruelty. The psychopath who took human life so sadistically wouldn't be content with killing mere animals.

Why, Chris asked himself, had he gotten involved in the affair of the dead bulls? There was no doubt that the combined resources of the FCSU and Calgary Homicide greatly improved the chances of solving the vandalism spree, which had distressed some very fine people. And the Taylors, the latest victims, were good friends. Sarah. Was it because of her? Wanting to impress her? Whatever the reason, having involved himself in the case, he would damn well crack it.

Before he could begin to plan how to go about achieving this desirable outcome, he was startled by the sudden ringing of the phone on the end table next to his armchair. It caught Nevermore, half-asleep on his perch, unawares, and he failed to call out his usual greeting.

"No parrot this time?"

"He's asleep."

"You know who this is?"

"I do. What's up?"

"It's too nice a night to stay inside. You should go for a walk. I'll be at the corner of Thirteenth Ave. and Fourth. I'm driving a Pontiac Solstice."

Putting a drowsy and unprotesting Nevermore back in his cage, Chris took the elevator down to the ground floor, exchanged a word with the concierge, and let himself out into the night. Dummett was right, it was a gorgeous evening: the rain had stopped, and the air was invitingly cool and refreshing. A gibbous moon hung suspended in a starry sky over the downtown skyline.

Despite the warmth of the evening, the top was up on the sporty little two-seater. Dummett waited until Chris had buckled himself in before handing him a large brown envelope. "The letter's inside," he said as they drove west on 13th. "And I haven't touched it except with gloves."

"Good for you," smiled Chris, pulling on his own gloves. Dummett switched on the interior light.

The plain white envelope was postmarked Calgary, the same as the others. That didn't tell them anything they didn't already know, except it confirmed — if, Chris reminded himself, *if* it was genuine — that the serial was still operating within the city.

you got it wrong kid i like doing them

Everything was in lower case, with no punctuation.

"He knows what you look like."

"So it would seem. My byline is getting to be pretty well known. It wouldn't be hard to track me down."

"That doesn't bother you?"

"It goes with the territory. Besides" — Dummett gave Chris a sideways look as he switched off the light — "it'll be worth it when I'm there to see you do the takedown, and I get first crack at writing it up."

"That's assuming there will be a takedown and assuming that you've been of some material help to the investigation."

"I already have. Look, the guy calls me kid," Dummett expostulated. "I'll be thirty on my next birthday, for God's sake!"

"That could be helpful, I agree."

"And the way he dismisses that stuff I wrote about a deprived childhood and parental abuse."

"He would deny that anyway, even if it were true."

"Maybe. But there's the way he just dismisses it out of hand. Like it's not worth arguing about."

"Interesting. I'll keep this. Have some tests run. Not that I expect them to tell us anything."

"Sure. Keep it. I made a copy for myself."

"Where will I let you off?"

"Fourth and Elbow will be fine."

chapter twenty-one

After a restless night of fitful sleep, Chris decided to walk to work. It was early, and maybe inspiration would strike on the way. When he stepped off the elevator, the concierge slid out from behind his desk and hastened to open the imposing front door.

"Looks like there's something going on over there, Mr. Crane," he said, pointing to the cruiser parked at the curb beside the grassy riverbank. "It just arrived a few minutes ago."

"I'll check it out." The police vehicle, another Ford, was unoccupied and its lights were dark. Whatever it was, responding to it hadn't been classified as an emergency. Not yet anyway.

The empty wheelchair stood on the pedestrian path on the north side of the Elbow River. A constable, hatless (another sign things were cool), was talking to a young man dressed in running clothes. A cellphone was fastened to the elastic waist of his shorts. The police officer turned as if to intercept Chris, then raised his hand in an informal salute when he saw the badge. "We don't know what we're dealing with yet, Detective. This gentleman came across the wheelchair and called 911. He thinks it might be a case of suicide."

Chris peered over the riverbank. "I can see why he would think that." At this point, it dropped sharply away, and it would be easy enough for a disabled person to crawl over to the edge and fall in.

Taking latex gloves from his breast pocket, Chris squatted on his heels to examine the chair. While far from new, it looked to be in good repair.

"I called it in, Detective Crane. The fire department rescue squad is on the way."

"Good. Have you or this gentleman touched the chair, or handled it in any way?"

The policeman, looking slightly nonplused, shook his head and looked at the jogger, who did the same.

"Excellent. I'll have it bagged and taken to the lab. And," he told the officer, "I want this treated as a crime scene. I'll send for backup."

Flashing lights and the low growl of a powerful motor signalled the arrival of the rescue squad. Chris went to meet the three men clambering down from the truck and asked them to stay clear of the area around the chair.

"You figure it for a suicide?" the firefighter in charge asked. "Somebody gets tired of life in a wheelchair and decides to end it?"

"That's one scenario. There could be another explanation."

The firefighter told the other two members of his squad that they would start by walking along the riverbank. At this point the fast-flowing river was narrow enough that they should be able to spot a body from there.

There was the tearing sound of Velcro as Chris lifted the seat cushion. "That won't be necessary," he said, staring down at the envelope taped to the leather seat. "This is no suicide." In newsprint letters, the plain white envelope was addressed, "deTecTive crane."

"Are you going to open it? It's addressed to you."

Chris shot a look, half exasperated, half amused, at the young constable. "Not yet. We'll let the lab have a look at it first."

The serial might be taking more risks, but not with his latest communication. No fingerprints, no DNA. The letters making up the message were all from the *Sun*. The "crane," no doubt, would be from the killer's stockpile of the window washer story.

Like its predecessors, the message was terse:

Having fun? I am Stay tuned

Once again, the question mark had been done by hand, in blue ink.

"He's not finished." Chris handed the photocopy to Gwen, sitting across the desk from him.

"So he thinks it's fun? The bastard! What he does to these—" Gwen's reply was cut off by the sudden shrill of the phone. Reaching for it, Chris checked the time on his Rolex. Eleven on the dot.

"This is Corporal Kanciar. There's been a fatal accident at the Bent Tree ranch. I thought you should know."

"What happened? Who's been killed?"

"Mrs. Taylor. Mrs. Taylor, Junior," he added before Chris could ask.

"How?"

"It's bad, Chris. You know that guard dog of theirs?"

"Blitzkrieg. *He* killed her?"

"Ripped her throat out. Lonechild is out there now. And I'm on my way."

"So am I."

Corporal Kanciar came forward to greet Chris, who was following a hired hand along the footpath to the stricken little group gathered around the body lying face up on the ground. "Ripped" was the word. Melanie's throat had disappeared into a raw gaping wound. Streams of bright red blood flowed down both sides of her neck, soaking the grass underneath. She had been knocked off the path by the force of the attack. There was no doubt that the terrible wound had killed her, but she would have bled out in any event.

"A dreadful business." The medical examiner, a family physician from Turner Valley, straightened up from his inspection of the corpse. "There's no doubt as to how she met her end. It's okay to move her."

"Just a moment," Chris interceded as two paramedics moved forward with a gurney. "I'd like a moment to check things out."

"There was no need to set up a crime scene," the RCMP corporal said, as if in response to some implied criticism on Chris's part. "This isn't a crime. It's just an unfortunate accident."

"Maybe. No doubt that it was the dog?"

"None." Kanciar nodded at Lonechild. "Tell him, Constable."

"The animal's muzzle was covered in blood, and his teeth were stained with it. His chest fur was matted with blood."

"You keep saying 'was,' Constable. Where is the dog? I'd like to see him."

"He's dead."

"I shot him." Cameron Taylor weathered face was pale and grim.

"Understandable," Chris replied, looking at each member of the family in turn. He wouldn't have let them crowd around like this, but it was too late now. "You have my deepest sympathy."

The three of them nodded acknowledgement. Cam Taylor's eyes were moist, filled with tears that threatened to spill down his cheeks. Phyllis, patrician as always, had a look of fastidious horror. Her husband was muttering the same barely audible words over and over. "That son of a bitch! May he rot in hell!"

"What son of a bitch, Cameron?" asked Chris, unfastening his field kit as he spoke.

"The son of a bitch who killed that bull of ours. If it hadn't been for that, none of this would have happened."

Chris knew what he meant. It was because of that incident that the guard dog had been turned loose to patrol the ranch. But why had he attacked? He was a trained guard dog. Maybe it was because she was running. That could do it. Or the smell of her sweat. Maybe she was menstruating. No, that was sharks. Could Melanie menstruate? Not without a uterus.

While these thoughts ran through his head, Chris took a sample of Melanie's blood and popped it into a glass tube.

"Is that really necessary, Chris?" asked Phyllis with a moue of distaste.

"Force of habit," replied Chris, contriving to look somewhat sheepish. "Now I'd like to look at the dog."

"Constable Lonechild will show you where he is," said Kanciar. "I'll take statements from these people. It won't take long," he was assuring them as Chris followed the Mountie back along the path. Their route took them some distance away from the main stable yard where a small crowd of neighbours and media representatives had assembled. They were being held in check by a Mountie in the scarlet full dress uniform of the force. He must have been pulled off some ceremonial function.

The dog had been shot once in the back of the head. "The bullet passed through his head and buried itself in the ground." Lonechild pointed to a neat hole in the hard-packed earth.

"Good. I'll retrieve it in a moment." There were no powder burns on Blitzkrieg's head. Taylor, who had been devoted to the animal, would have stood some distance away when he shot him. Probably ordered the dog to sit and stay. Most likely he would have used a rifle. There wasn't a casing lying around, but that didn't mean anything. Cameron would have picked it up.

As Lonechild had described, the German shepherd's muzzle was covered with blood, and its chest was streaked with it. Chris took a DNA sample of the blood from its open mouth.

"Not much doubt about where it came from, is there?" asked Lonechild as Chris, using needle-nose pliers from his kit, extracted the spent bullet from the ground.

"True. But I believe in collecting every bit of evidence there is."

The Mountie nodded thoughtfully, absorbing what he said.

"Once more unto the breach, dear friends," Chris murmured, squaring his shoulders as they headed toward the waiting media scrum.

"Shakespeare. *King Henry V*. The king rallies the troops before the battle of Harfleur." Lonechild smiled. "I majored in English Lit at university."

Before Chris could frame an appropriate response, their eyes were assailed with a barrage of electronic flashes. He gave her a collegial grin as they were engulfed by the media. The reporters' excitement abated somewhat when he assured them that his being there did not mean there was a connection with the serial killings.

"What we are dealing with is a tragic accident, not a crime," he told them. "The Mounties are investigating it, and the corporal in charge will be along shortly to answer your questions."

"Okay, Crane, then tell us about the body in the Devonian Gardens. What about the wheelchair? And the word is the killer left a note."

Chris gestured with his hands to quell the clamour. "Okay. I'll give you a statement. Yes, a wheelchair has been recovered. We believe it to be directly connected with the body that was found in the Gardens. And there *was* a note, but you will understand that I cannot reveal its contents." Turning, he pointed up the path. "I see Corporal Kanciar is coming to join us, and I now turn you over to him. He's all yours."

The media scrum reluctantly turned their attention to the Mountie, and Chris went over to join Phyllis, now standing a little bit apart from the other two members of her family.

"Has Sarah been told?" he asked.

She turned to stare at him. Starting to speak, she choked and swallowed several times. "Sorry. My mouth is dry. No, she hasn't been. There hasn't been time. But she *has* to know. Will you call her, Chris? Please. I've got her Harrisburg phone numbers." Extracting a business card from her wallet, she showed Chris the numbers written on the back. "This one is her hotel, and that one is the stable. Go in the house and call from there."

Inside the Taylor home, paintings of aggressively Western scenes — cattle grazing in fields, mountain peaks under a Chinook arch, cowboys cooking around a campfire — adorned the walls. Framed black-and-white photographs of Cameron's grandparents stared sternly down from the fireplace mantel.

A housemaid, casual in jeans and T-shirt, showed him into Cameron's study-cum-office.

"A terrible thing," she said in hushed tones.

"Awful," agreed Chris.

"She was a very nice lady," the maid declared as she left him.

Mildly surprised at this remark, Chris sat down and began to dial. He tried the stable first, and the woman who answered told him that Sarah was at one of the outdoor rings watching her daughter ride.

"Would you get her for me? And make sure it's someplace where we can speak privately?"

"That's awful," Sarah whispered. "To be killed like that. And just as she was beginning to enjoy her life."

"Phyllis said much the same thing. How Melanie seemed to have a more positive attitude."

"She did. She seemed to have arrived at a decision and was determined to turn her life around and make a go of things there. She was happier, and beginning to reach out to other people. That fitness kick of hers was part of that new approach." Sarah sighed. "How's that for irony?"

"It's ironic, all right. Being attacked by a dog that's part of your family."

"Blitzkreig was not exactly part of the family," she replied after a thoughtful pause. "There was something wrong with him back in the spring. I wonder if that could have had anything to do with what happened."

"What do you mean?"

"He was sick for quite a spell. Really sick. Needed to stay in a veterinary clinic to be treated. I remember Cameron being a little upset because it was right at the height of the calving season."

"I thought that's what donkeys are for. What was wrong with him? Do you know?"

"According to Cameron it was some kind of canine virus." Again Sarah paused. "You don't suppose it could have affected his brain? Made him crazed enough to attack Melanie?"

"It's possible I suppose. I must say, I've never heard of anything like that. I bet Cameron is thinking along those lines right now. Wondering if he should have had the dog put down instead of having him treated by a vet."

"It all seems to go back to that bull being killed. Are you anywhere close to finding out who's responsible for the cattle killings?"

"Not really. I've identified one possible suspect. He fits the profile, but there's no evidence against him. McRae was on the list for a spell, but he's pretty well alibied out." Chris sighed ruefully. "I'm batting zero for one hundred at the moment. This business, and a serial who keeps on killing and laughing at me."

"Well, if it makes you feel any better, there's someone who thinks you're wonderful."

"Oh? Who might that be?"

"Linda. She was impressed with you before, but now that she's been on this course, it's become a case of hero worship. Her instructors talk about you. How good you were. They can't understand why you gave up show jumping to become a policeman."

"The way things have been going recently, maybe I should have stuck with the horses." Brightening, Chris asked, "How's she making out on her course? Acing it, I bet."

"She's loving it. Everything about it. She's discovered dressage. Says it makes a horse respond better between jumps."

"It does. It will also open up some new challenges for her in the horse show world. Are you going to tell her about this?"

"Not yet. Not until she finishes the course and we're on our way home. God, Chris, this is so awful! I still can't believe it happened. Tell Phyllis how sorry I am, and that I'll call her."

As soon as Chris drove into the police parking lot he was accosted by a fuming Steve Mason. "What the hell are you playing at, Crane? Sucking up to your fancy high-society friends when we've got a serial killer on our hands."

There was enough truth in Mason's charge to make Chris flinch. He was uncharacteristically defensive as he replied, "You know as well as I do, Steve, that you can't spend all your time on one case. You have to wait on new developments, new leads."

"Your ass is out a mile on this one, Crane. You're the killer's pet. He's playing games with you. And he's winning. Johnstone is really feeling the heat, and he don't like it. Not one little bit."

"The entire section's ass is on the line too, Steve. We should all be working together on this."

A somewhat contrite Mason conceded, "I guess you're right. But, goddammit, Chris, you know better.

You shouldn't be spending all your time chasing some punk who's killing cows. Not when we've got a mass murderer on the loose."

"What this punk did led to a woman being killed. Maybe not directly, but certainly indirectly."

"Yeah, I heard about that. She a friend of yours?"

"I knew her."

"It's not in our jurisdiction."

"I know that. Think of it as a case of co-operation between two law enforcement agencies. The Chief is big on that."

"You know how the game is played, don't you, Crane? Anyway, it's late. I'm going to have a beer with Gord at the Cuff. He's over there. Waiting for me."

Mason pointed to where a middle-aged man wearing a black short-sleeved T-shirt stood beside a tan sedan three rows over. Physically, Ralston was an imposing figure. Taller than his friend Mason, he looked to be in much better condition: his shoulders and chest were broad, and his waist, while thick, was in proportion to the rest of him. At this distance Chris couldn't make out the details of his facial features, but he recalled Ralston as having a badly flattened nose. According to police lore it was a souvenir of a long-ago scuffle with a car thief. Other versions had it the result of an off-duty barroom brawl. His car was one of the Japanese makes, but Chris couldn't tell which one. So they still let Ralston use the parking lot. Conveniently located at the corner of 6th Avenue and 3rd Street East, two blocks east of headquarters, it was run by the Police Association for the exclusive use of members. Technically, Ralston was not entitled to park there, but obviously no one was inclined to make an issue of it.

"Gordon Ralston? He's going to the Cuff?" The Cuff 'Em Bar catered to off-duty police and was their favourite watering hole. Mason's imposing beer belly bore eloquent testimony to his faithful attendance.

"Sure. Why the hell not? He gets along with the guys. They know he got a raw deal. He didn't deserve to be kicked off the force like that."

As he walked the short distance to the Andrew Davison building, Chris admitted to himself that there was something in what Mason had said about his getting so involved in the cattle case. But, damn it, he wasn't neglecting the serial killer investigation. They had followed up every lead, investigated the background of the victims, and it was never out of his mind. Besides, it looked like the cattle mutilation case had led to Melanie Taylor being killed. Indirectly, granted, but it was the first link in the fatal chain of events that resulted in her gruesome death. It was because of Apollo being shot and mutilated that Blitzkreig had been turned loose on his own to patrol the ranch. Anyway, if there was a conflict, the best way to resolve it was to track down the vandal or vandals who was playing hell with the ranchers' livestock and get that out of the way. And he knew where to start.

chapter twenty-two

The sensational death of a member of a prominent ranching family rated a headline in the *Sun*, a front page below-the-fold story in the *Herald*, and page three in the *Globe and Mail*. The *Globe* also ran a think piece — an interview with a canine behaviourial expert. The expert, one Greg Harding from Calgary, was quoted as saying that normally the German shepherd, while having the makings of an ideal guard dog, did not have the same level of aggression as had been bred into the pit bull. But the level of aggression could vary between individual animals, and the training of guard dogs necessarily encouraged aggression. German shepherds are a more agile and athletic breed than pit bulls, with their stocky build, and attacks by them are more likely to be lethal. The pit bull typically attacks the victim's legs and lower body, overpowering him with brute force. The shepherd will go for the throat, as was the case here. The expert concluded by observing that he found the name of the dog to be significant. The word *blitzkreig* was synonymous with aggression, and it could be inferred that aggression was a quality the owners must have wanted.

Chris clipped the item, folded it, and put it in his jacket pocket. Lost in thought, he was about to leave when he was stopped by a reproachful, "Treat?"

"Sorry about that, Nevermore," he muttered, and went back to the kitchen to prepare the parrot's breakfast treat of buttered toast.

"Sure, we've heard the horror stories about this guy and his pet snake," Lucille Mitchell, the Humane Society officer, motherly and comfortably into middle age, said. "But there's nothing we can do about it."

"You could inspect the premises," Chris suggested.

"Not without the owner's consent, we can't."

"What about a warrant?"

"A *warrant*? Dream on. We'd never get one."

"Don't be too sure of that," Chris told her, indicating the police officer sitting beside him. "Constable Lavoy patrols the Beltline and is prepared to swear that he has reasonable grounds to believe that Leonard is kidnapping small dogs and feeding them live to this python of his."

"That's right," Lavoy confirmed. "Nobody has ever seen him bring a dog home, but the people next door hear barking and whining from time to time. It never lasts long."

"Disgusting, I agree. But that won't get us a warrant. I don't think the Society has *ever* gotten a warrant. Or even applied for one."

"Maybe so. But Judge Olberg is a dog fancier. Dog fanatic might be more accurate. He breeds English bulldogs. Great dogs. I've seen a couple of them. He's a provincial court judge, but he's also an accredited dog show judge. The thought of dogs being fed to a snake will send him right up the wall. Besides, the cruel and inhumane treatment of an animal is an offence under the Criminal Code. And feeding a live dog to a python is sure as hell cruel and inhumane treatment of an animal! We'll get our warrant."

"Open the door, Mr. Leonard. This is the police."

"The fuck you are. What's going on?"

"It's the police. We have a warrant to search the premises."

"Shit."

"Do it." Chris took a step back and pointed at the lock.

"I don't like this. Not one damn bit," the building superintendent complained as he reluctantly selected a key from a metal loop.

"Get on with it, man!" Chris fumed. Leonard could be disposing of evidence or escaping through another exit.

"Okay. Okay." There was a click as the bolt shot back, and the superintendent scuttled off down the hallway to the elevator.

One hand on the Glock, Chris flung the door wide open and charged in, followed by two uniforms and the woman from the Humane Society, with Gwen in the rear. "Quick, the bathroom!" Chris ran toward the sound of a toilet being flushed.

"Freeze!" he barked the crisp one-word command, so beloved of TV cop shows. Cliché or not, it seemed to spring naturally to his lips.

The slim, jean-clad figure seemed not to hear and continued pouring the contents of a plastic bag into the toilet bowl. One of the constables brushed past Chris and grabbed him by the neck, tearing the bag from his grasp. Another bag, still sealed shut, lay on the tiled floor.

"Well, well. What do we have here? This looks surprisingly like cocaine, wouldn't you say, Gwen?" Holding up the warrant, Chris said, "This gives us the authority to search the premises."

Leonard made no reply but stared back at Chris with a look of contemptuous hatred glittering in his narrow eyes. Hibbell had been right about his ears. The one on the right side was conspicuously larger than normal and stuck straight out, while the one on the left was small and curled in on itself. A cauliflower ear, like a boxer's. Chris heard Gwen make a small choking sound in her throat.

"Dealing drugs." The constable holding an unresisting Leonard hissed in his ear. "We got you, my friend."

Chris wasn't so sure about that. The warrant the outraged judge had signed referred to cruel and inhumane treatment of animals, not trafficking in drugs. The evidence about finding the cocaine might never make it to court. Time to worry about that later.

"In here," the Humane Society officer called from down the hall in an awed voice.

"Hold him, but no cuffs." Chris instructed the constable who nodded and tightened his grip on his young prisoner.

"Jesus!" Chris stood in the doorway and stared. He knew that pythons were giant constricting snakes, but that hadn't prepared him for the sheer *presence* of the creature. Forked tongue flicking from its triangular head, it lay coiled on a simulated stone ledge. Chris had paid a quick visit to the library and consulted a textbook, *Living Snakes of the World* by Mehrtens, and knew that the bold pattern of yellow and black identified it as a Burmese python, the species commonly found in zoos and, incredibly enough, in private collections as well. One of the accounts Chris had read told of a Colorado couple who returned home to find the lifeless body of their fourteen-year-old son wrapped in the coils of their pet python, which was allowed to roam free around the house. Adult specimens could attain a length of six metres and weigh close to one hundred kilos. Leonard's pet looked to be about four and a half metres and in glowing good health.

Its raised head and flicking tongue showed that the snake was aware of the humans crowding into the room and staring through the glass front of its enclosure. As they watched, it uncoiled its length and slowly lowered itself down onto the floor. Whatever cruelties Leonard may have inflicted on other members of the animal kingdom, he had spared no expense in the care and feeding of his pet snake. The room, originally meant to serve as second bedroom or study, had been converted into quarters for the reptile. Molded of sand-coloured gunite, it was a realistic duplication of what could have been the python's natural habitat, complete with a pool for the semi-aquatic snake to bathe in. Heat lamps of varying intensity were recessed into the ceiling.

"Rangoon. Very appropriate," Chris murmured appreciatively, looking at the engraved nameplate on the rear wall of the enclosure.

"The capital of Burma. Perfect for a Burmese python," Gwen agreed. "But haven't they changed the name of that country?"

"Officially, it's now Myanmar, meaning 'the golden land,' but to most of the Western world it's still Burma."

"Come look at this." The struggle to maintain a professional calm showed on Lucille Mitchell's face. Turning around, she led them down a hallway to the kitchen.

"He must really love that snake," Gwen marvelled. One corner of the kitchen had been partitioned off with plywood panels. "The whole apartment is geared around it ..." She broke off as a muted whimper came from behind the partition.

Crooning softly, Lucille knelt in front of a portable kennel, identical to those used by airlines to transport pet dogs. Undoing the catch, she reached in and brought out a bundle of white and grey fur. It was a dog, one of the miniature breeds favoured by city dwellers. Most likely a Shih Tzu or some combination thereof, thought Chris as Lucille cradled the tiny animal to her ample bosom and undid the narrow leather strap that held its mouth shut. The little dog, tail wagging furiously, immediately began to lick its rescuer's neck.

"Poor little thing," she crooned. "You're safe now. Peppi. Is your name Peppi? Of course it is," she added as the dog wiggled excitedly in her arms. "Your mistress is going to be so happy to have you back. She misses you so much."

"You know the dog?" Chris framed it as a question, although the answer was obvious.

"I know who he is. Don't I, Peppi?" More happy wiggles. "He belongs to the Bancrofts, who live in Lakeview. He went missing from their fenced backyard three days ago. He couldn't have gotten out, so somebody must have taken him. Mrs. Bancroft called the Society the day after he went missing."

"You've had a narrow escape, haven't you, fella?" Chris patted the little dog's head, receiving frantic licks from Peppi's tongue in return.

"Okay, let's have Leonard in here," he ordered.

"You're in trouble, Mr. Leonard. Big trouble," he informed the sullen young man when he stood before him. "Feeding a live dog to a snake is a criminal offence under Section 445 of the Criminal Code. The court will not treat it lightly."

"You can't prove I did that."

"Oh, I think we can." What was Gwen looking at? She was staring at the electric stove as if it held some vital clue. "What are we going to find when we do an autopsy on Rangoon?"

"You crazy, man? You can't do that!"

It was a bluff on Chris's part, but Leonard couldn't know that. Not for sure. "I want a lawyer," he announced with the air of one who has trumped his opponent's ace. "I'm going to call my dad. He'll get me the best."

"Go ahead and make the call. We'll be in the snake room."

"Lawyer or no lawyer," one of the uniforms said, "we got him on possession of drugs. There's enough cocaine so we can charge him with possession for the purpose of trafficking."

"Right," Chris agreed absently. What the constable said was probably true, despite the limited scope of the warrant, but that wasn't the point. The woman from the Humane Society was peering in at the snake now moving restlessly around the floor with raised head and flicking tongue. She was looking for traces of dog, but that wasn't the point either.

"My lawyer ..." Leonard paused for effect in the doorway. Gwen was doing it again. Deliberately averting her gaze. For sure the mean-faced, squinty-eyed Leonard was no pleasure to look upon, but even so. A look of what could only be relief washed over that unlovely visage, quickly replaced by its habitual air of scornful hostility as the suspect continued, "Millard, Mr. Scott Millard, will be here as soon as he finishes in court. His assistant has instructed me to say nothing."

"That won't be until late this afternoon. In the meantime we'll continue to execute our warrant." Why had Leonard looked so relieved a minute ago? True, he had obtained legal counsel, but that wouldn't account for it. It was much more immediate than that. He had been looking up, over their heads. The nameplate. High on the rear wall, it was the only thing not *faux naturel* in the enclosure. It fitted seamlessly against the wall, with no cracks or lines around it.

"We'll need to search the snake ..." Chris hesitated, seeking the right word. The set-up was too elaborate to be called a cage. "Habitat," he said finally. Out of the corner of his eye he caught the look of dismay on Leonard's face. Recovering, the suspect smirked, "Rangoon won't like that."

"Oh, I think our friends at the zoo can take care of that little problem."

Four members of the zoo staff arrived within the hour. The three men wore green keeper's uniforms, and the fourth, a woman in her early thirties with straight, cropped hair, and whose name was Katherine, wore a dark leather jacket and a grey woollen skirt. "What is it you want us to do?" she asked Chris after the brief introductions were over.

"I need the snake out of there so we can examine the cage. It shouldn't take long."

"He's prime," the youngest of the keepers muttered, nodding at Leonard. "Good on you, man."

Leonard nodded grim acknowledgment.

One of the keepers entered the enclosure through the side door, moving quietly and carrying a white canvas bag in his right hand. In one deft motion he laid it over the snake's head and grabbed its neck, just behind the jaw. Katherine and the other keepers followed him in and took hold of the writhing body as the monster serpent struggled with its captors. Wrapping their arms around its muscular length, they slowly backed it out of the cage. Holding the neck with one hand, the keeper shook the canvas bag open and guided the snake's head into it. Welcoming the darkness and sensing that the bag offered safety, the python slithered all the way into it, helped along by its handlers.

"It's all yours," Katherine told Chris as she tied the top of the capacious and now bulging bag.

There were no screws or bolts attaching the nameplate to the wall, and closer inspection confirmed the absence of any sill or open space, however narrow, around it. But the plate had to be attached to the wall in some fashion. Chris gripped it on the sides with both hands and pulled. After some initial resistance it came away. Magnets. Two of them were embedded in the wall, matching the metal plates on the back of the nameplate. Behind the wall was a small wooden door, like a medicine cabinet. Chris couldn't see any sign of a lock. The giant snake was a more effective deterrent than any lock. A tug, and the door opened.

The ears, dry and shrivelled, were arranged in pairs on a strip of blue velvet. The velvet was mounted on a piece of plywood, making it easy for Chris to pull it out of the hidden recess. Feeling somewhat like a headwaiter offering a delicacy for a patron's approval, Chris confronted Leonard with it. Leonard stared stonily ahead, lips clamped shut.

"You don't have to say anything, Mr. Leonard. The evidence speaks for itself. But you could save time by showing us where the new ones are."

As expected, Leonard remained mute, but Chris caught a fleeting glint in his eyes. Almost gleeful.

"Then I guess we'll have to take the place apart until we find them. We'll start with the kitchen, Gwen."

"Hang on a sec. I've found something." Kneeling in a corner of the cage, Gwen held up a pair of tweezers gripping a minute quantity of something dry and brown. "If this isn't dogshit, I'll eat it."

Momentarily taken aback by her emphatic outburst, Chris replied, "I'm sure that won't be necessary. Bag it and the lab can check it out. The cage has turned out to be a regular goldmine," he went on. "Do you think it has anything more to tell us?" Both Gwen and Lucille shook their heads, and he went out into the hall to tell the zoo people they could put the python back. That proved to be an easy task. As soon as the bag was opened, Rangoon glided eagerly into his home.

"What about him?" asked the young keeper, the one who had admired the snake. "Who's going to look after him?"

"Good question." Chris looked at Katherine, who by now he had learned was the supervisor of the African Pavilion, which housed the snakes the zoo had on display. "Would the zoo like to have him?"

When she looked doubtful, the young keeper chimed in, "C'mon, Kathy. He's sweet. We'll never get a better specimen."

"Maybe I'm getting ahead of myself," said Chris. "Will he be okay for a day or so?"

"Sure. He's hungry, but another couple of days won't matter. If necessary, they can go for weeks without eating."

"That's okay then. This gentleman" — indicating Leonard, who had become visibly agitated but remained silent while the fate of his pet was discussed — "will be released on bail in the morning. The problem will arise if and when he's convicted and sent to jail."

"We'll take over in that case. He'll be well looked after, although he won't be living as high on the hog. He'll have to make do with freshly killed chickens instead of live food. It may take a while to wean him, but he'll go for it when he gets hungry enough."

Anxious to get on with the search, Chris fervently thanked the zoo staff for their help. "Absolutely vital. We would have been completely stymied without you."

While they prepared to leave, he formally arrested Leonard, reading him his rights, and detailed one of the constables to escort him to the Remand Centre. "I'll get in touch with Mr. Millard's office and let them know where he can find you," he told the prisoner, who shrugged and said nothing.

"Right. Now let's find those ears. The fresh ones. Gwen, you and Lucille start with the kitchen and the bathroom. Constable Peplinski and I will do the living room and the hallway and closets. Then we'll backtrack over the other team's territory if we don't come up with anything on the first pass."

When an hour's intensive search proved fruitless, they pressured the reluctant building supervisor to show them where Leonard's car was parked and to unlock his storage space. A rifle in its carrying case lay in plain view on a shelf on the rear wall of the storage room. Leonard obviously relied on his pet to keep his secret secure, thought Chris as he unfastened the case and examined the rifle. A .270 Winchester, it was the same calibre as the bullets that had been recovered from the bulls killed in prior attacks. It was almost certain that those bullets would be a match for the rifle. But it wasn't the weapon that had killed the Taylor bull. Nor was there any trace of freshly harvested ears in either the storage compartment or the car.

Chris felt a sense of disappointment that he admitted to himself was more than professional — he had been hoping to announce to the Taylors that the "cattle bandit's" reign was finally over. But they already had conclusive proof that Leonard was the villain. Still, thought Chris as he slammed shut the trunk of Leonard's Honda, it would have been the final touch to be able to tell Cameron Taylor that the man who had indirectly caused his daughter-in-law's death had been arrested. Sooner or later, they would find where the little prick had hidden Apollo's ears.

"Mind telling me what was going on with you back there?" Chris asked Gwen when they were alone in the cruiser heading back downtown.

"Those ears. Leonard's ears. I knew they would be different, and that they were what had led you to connect him with the cattle killings. I thought I was prepared mentally. Until I *saw* him. My stepfather had ears like that. Exactly like that. My stepfather was not a nice man."

chapter twenty-three

"Now that you've finished that cattle bullshit and arrested a suspect, maybe you'll pay some attention to our file. A little matter of a serial killer running wild in our city. If you remember." Mason's temper was not improved by having had to wait for Chris for the better part of an hour. He was stretching things when he called it "our file," but Chris let it pass.

"Unfortunately, I don't think that 'cattle bullshit,' as you so aptly call it, is over. Not quite, and not yet. What's that? Another billet-doux from our friendly killer?" Chris eyed the single sheet of paper in the detective's meaty hand.

"Yeah." Mason gave the photocopy to him. "Our boy has taken a real fancy to you."

In what now seemed to be the killer's preferred format, the message was in newspaper print and the question mark was handwritten:

LiKe BEing FAmoUS crane? SO dO I

Intent on the killer's words, Chris at first only half-heard Mason's description of how the message had been delivered. "It was tucked behind the windshield wiper of one of our patrol cars, for Christ's sake! In an envelope with my name on it."

"Where was the cruiser when this happened?" demanded Chris.

"Parked on a street in Forest Lawn, responding to a domestic disturbance complaint. And," Mason went on, "the complaint checked out. It was genuine. The serial must have seen the cruiser and jumped at the chance."

"More likely, he would have followed it and waited till the officers were inside. How many responded to the call?"

"Just one. He didn't see anything. He was too busy dealing with the situation. The husband was a mean drunk." Mason gave the photocopied message a contemptuous look. "He knows you're sucking up to that reporter."

"I'm not sucking up to him. I'm using him. He could be a source. Maybe a way to flush our killer out in the open."

Mason snorted. "More likely you're *his* source," he said and turned away.

Of course Dummett was using him as a source. That's the way these things worked. The police dealt with outside sources all the time, and there was always a quid pro quo. Something in it for both parties — a decision to drop charges, money paid to the snitch, revenge on the part of the source. In this case it was a chance at the inside track. Chris's musings were interrupted by the sight of Gwen letting herself in, the door automatically closing behind her. Chris waved her over, but she was heading for him anyway.

"There's another message from TLC," he told her. "But first, what's your news?"

"Are you ready for this?" asked Gwen with an air of suppressed excitement. "Mr. Joseph Leonard, Mark Leonard's father, is here to see you."

Chris tilted back in his chair for a moment, then said, "I'll go down and meet him." Handing her the copy of the TLC communication, he said, "Have a look at this while I'm gone."

The man standing in the first floor foyer was short, like his son, and, except for an incipient paunch, slender. His ears, although inclined to stick out, were normal. Was he now programmed to go through the rest of his life studying people's ears? Chris wondered.

"I'm Detective Crane. You wanted to see me?" It didn't seem appropriate to offer to shake hands.

"I understand you're in charge of the case against my son, Mark?"

"Correct. Give me a moment to find someplace where we can talk."

When they were seated in an interview room on the second floor, Chris said, "I'm sure you're aware, Mr. Leonard, that there is very little I can say to you." He sat at one end of the table, rather than directly across, so as not to be in an adversarial position vis-à-vis Leonard. "Your son has been charged and the evidence against him will come out in court in due time. I understand he's now out on bail, which you posted."

"That's right, but that's not why I'm here." Leaning forward in his chair, Leonard gripped the edge of the desk with both hands and stared earnestly at Chris. "I know my son is troubled and has done some unacceptable things in the past."

That understatement brought a lifted eyebrow from Chris, then he nodded sympathetically as Leonard mentioned how he and his wife had tried to help Mark — taken him to psychiatrists, therapy sessions, behavioural consultants. "You name it, we've done it. But that's not why I'm here," he went on. "My son had nothing to do with that cattle mutilation at the Taylor ranch. Nothing."

"It fits the pattern," Chris retorted. Why did he feel a stirring of disquiet?

"I don't know about that. What I do know is that Mark couldn't have done it. He was with his mother and me. In Toronto," he added, when he saw Chris's skeptical look. "You don't have to take our word for it. Let me show you." Reaching into his breast pocket, he spread ticket stubs and a hotel receipt out on the desk.

"There are only two airline stubs," Chris pointed out. "That doesn't prove anything."

"I know. Mark had the other one. He's probably thrown it away. But that's not important. What *is* important, is this." He turned the hotel receipt around so Chris could read it. "Look. Two rooms. Four nights. We checked out early in the morning to catch a flight back to Calgary. The same day they found the dead bull on the Taylor ranch. Mark was right there with us when we checked out of The Four Seasons hotel. And look at this." His finger traced several items in the account. "We took a lot of our meals in the hotel. Always in the Studio Café on the mezzanine floor. The servers were friendly and we got to know some of them. Especially one. A woman. Marge. She remembered us because of the trouble they took to find some non-alcoholic wine for my wife, who doesn't touch alcohol. This Marge was the one who served the three of us on our last night. Late. We had been to see a play, *What The Doctor Knew*. She will confirm that Mark was with us if you show her his photo."

"Interesting. And I assure you it will be followed up. But I must tell you that the evidence against your son in the earlier incidents is compelling. Conclusive, actually. So I'm not sure I know why you're telling me this."

"It's because of the Taylors. I want them to know it wasn't my son who killed that bull and caused the terrible thing that happened to them. I've met Cameron a couple of times, although I can't claim to really know him. But I have a tremendous respect for the man and his family and what they represent. Pioneers. I've been told you're a good friend of theirs. I want you to tell Cameron Taylor that Mark had nothing to do with the tragedy that has befallen them."

"Why don't you tell Mr. Taylor yourself?"

"I tried. But I can't get through to him. All I get is voice mail, and he doesn't return my calls. You *will* tell him, won't you?"

"As I said, we will be looking into your story. If it checks out, I will convey the information to Mr. Taylor."

"That's all I ask. Thank you, sir."

It would be a simple matter to check Leonard's alibi. All he had to do was fax the photo taken at the time of the little bastard's arrest to the Toronto police and have them contact the hotel. Picking up the phone to set this in motion, Chris knew that the alibi would stand up. It was too transparent not to. So, where to go from here?

Blitzkreig. He was a trained guard dog, but did that explain the bloodchilling ferocity of the attack that had killed Melanie? Maybe she had startled him, stumbled upon him unexpectedly. But Melanie was part of the household. However, as Sarah had said on the phone, Blitzkreig was not what you would call a family pet. And there was no doubt that he had killed Melanie. He would talk to the experts — the members of the K-9 squad.

Gwen waited until he had finished his phone call before handing the copy of TLC's note back to him.

"That fame business is interesting. Do you suppose he's ready to give himself up? Let the world know what he's done?"

Chris shook his head. "That's not the way I read it. It's more like he intends to pull off something even more sensational—" Suddenly he broke off. Jesus! Sarah had called him last night, concerned that maybe she should return home to see if she could help the Taylors in some way. She had talked to Phyllis earlier, who had told her there was no need. There wasn't going to be a funeral for Melanie. They would hold a memorial service, but that would be weeks away.

"Phyllis is right," he had assured her, vastly relieved. "There's absolutely no reason for you to come back here. Linda needs you more than anyone here. Except maybe me," he'd added, earning one of her delightful laughs. He had been prepared to insist that she stay away; thankfully, that hadn't been necessary. As far as the outside world knew — with the likely exception of Phyllis Taylor — he and Sarah were just casual friends. But if TLC ever found out!

Repressing a shudder, Chris smiled apologetically. "Sorry, I had a bit of a flashback there."

"We all have those from time to time. Speaking of flashbacks, they want me over at Crime Scenes. Want my input on something. I won't be long."

"Take your time, and give them my regards."

chapter twenty-four

"**I**t's sure as hell not characteristic of the breed," said the sergeant in charge of the four-officer K-9 squad, frowning.

"He *was* trained to be a guard dog," Chris pointed out.

"I know. I've given this case a lot of thought. A guard dog is trained to warn off intruders by a display of aggression. Normally they won't attack unless given a direct command or threatened by the intruder. If they do attack, it's to disarm or disable the target, not kill."

"Yet here we have a situation where the dog clearly meant to kill. He went for the throat, which you say is not what they would normally do. And the victim was known to the dog. Not on familiar terms, but known. How do you account for that scenario?"

"Training. He would have to be trained to kill. On command."

"Could the dog's owner train him to do that?"

"The owner not being a professional dog trainer?"

"Let's assume that's the case."

"Unlikely. Very unlikely. I guess someone could get hold of a training manual and try a do-it-yourself course. But the end result is almost certain to be a ruined, dangerous animal that would have to be put down, or one badly mauled or dead owner."

"And in the hands of a qualified, professional trainer?"

"No problem. An animal like this Blitzkreig is already conditioned to be aggressive and to obey commands. It wouldn't be hard to turn him into a killer."

"Where would one find a trainer who could do that?"

The sergeant grimaced. "There's an outfit just west of Airdrie, K-9 Kennels — how do you like that for a name? They specialize in training guard dogs; they probably trained the dog we're talking about. We have reason to suspect they will take the training a step further if the price is right."

"Who would want an animal like that?"

"You'd be surprised. It's an ego trip for some of these bastards — bikers, gang members, wannabe toughs. They think owning a dog like that gives them status."

"Tell me more about this K-9 Kennels."

"It pisses me off every time I hear that name." The canine cop exhaled audibly. "Anyway it's not what you would call a kennel, where you would board your dog or buy a pup. It's a training school, and I've got to admit they do a good job. Very professional. But from time to time we hear rumours that they also run an undercover operation where they turn dogs into lethal weapons. We don't know where this is done, or even *if* it is done. All we hear are rumours."

"You've never looked into this?"

The sergeant shrugged. "No reason to. Besides, it's not in our jurisdiction." The sergeant's eyes quickened with interest. "You figure you're on to something, Crane?"

"I hope not. I really hope not. But I've got to check it out. Show me where the, er, kennel is located."

Unthinkable. That Melanie's death could have been murder. Murder by dog. Unthinkable or not, his line of work required him to follow the evidence wherever it might lead. He would soon find out whether the evidentiary trail that seemed to be opening up in this case would lead anywhere. Chris wasn't a member of the Ranchmen's Club, but his principal broker was. He'd give Jack Adams a call, tell him it was time they had lunch together, and mention how fond he was of the toasted lobster sandwiches the club was famous for.

It was Parade Day, the official kickoff for the ten days of Stampede, and the venerable Ranchmen's Club was alive with Stampede spirit. Everyone, including Chris and his host, wore Western attire, and a five-piece band, hired for the occasion, twanged out Western tunes. Drinks in hand, "cowboys" and "cowgirls" milled around the receptionist's desk inside the main entrance. Peering over the crush of white hats, and the odd black one, Chris spotted Maud Simpson's replacement, a woman somewhere in her mid-thirties, strands of blond hair escaping from under her Stetson.

"I'm impressed you were able to get a reservation on such short notice." Chris moved aside to make way for some new arrivals.

"I have lunch here two or three times a week, so they squeezed us in."

Someone in the crowd touched Chris on the elbow. Turning, he saw it was one of the ranchers he had met at the Bent Tree — the one who'd said he would soon catch the cattle mutilator if he was as good a detective as he was a rider. As they shook hands Chris asked him if he had watched the parade.

"Watched? I *rode* in it. Same as always. So did the Taylors. All three of them. There's been a Taylor in the parade ever since anyone can remember, and they weren't about to break with that tradition. No way. They decided not to attend this affair, though."

Before he could reply to this, Jack motioned that they should go upstairs to the dining room for lunch.

Chris put down his half-finished Virgin Caesar and followed him up the impressive staircase.

"Delicious. As always," Chris said as they ate. Halfway through the meal, he took a swallow of Chardonnay and said, "Excuse me for a minute, Jack, I've got to pay a visit."

The men's washroom was midway down a long hall, lined with framed photos of past presidents of the club. It was only a hunch on Chris's part, but someone of Cameron Taylor's stature in the ranching community was almost bound to have served as president at some time or other. There were a hundred or more photos, beginning with what looked like a daguerreotype of the first president, dated 1891, high up on the south wall. His hunch was right. Taylor had been president back in 2000–2001. His photo was on the opposite wall. That was a few years ago, but he still looked very much like his colour photo. And, by God, there was a photo of his father! That Cameron Taylor had been president in 1964–65. The family resemblance was strong. Almost uncanny. Talk about a dynasty! Pretending to admire the display, Chris waited while two couples, chatting animatedly, walked past on their way to the dining room, then took the miniature digital camera from his pocket and snapped off three exposures of the present-day Cameron Taylor. Mission accomplished. Now for the next step. A step that should tell the tale, one way or another.

Airdrie was outside his jurisdiction, and protocol normally would demand that he bring the "horsemen" — the media's favourite nickname for the RCMP — into the picture. But that would mean exposing Taylor as a suspect in the hideous murder of his daughter-in-law. Inevitably, word would get around the ranching community of which he was such a prominent member. And it wouldn't matter if he turned out to be completely innocent. There would always be that lingering taint. Chris needed a backup, someone to witness what went down. The presence of an officer in uniform was bound to attract the attention of the dog trainer, make him more inclined to cooperate. But, as always, the Stampede was straining the resources of the police. For one thing, the surveillance of the parks had been reduced to the occasional drive-by. Gwen was lending a hand to Crime Scenes on a break-and-enter case, trying to find a match for a partial footprint that she had managed to lift from the carpet. But her reaction and advice as things developed at the training kennel would be invaluable. The B&E could wait.

The entrance was suitably impressive, if deliberately menacing. Life-sized metal cutouts of two German shepherds, with jaws agape and teeth bared, surmounted brick gateposts. The gate itself was a metal grille, finished in matte black. It was necessary to get out of the car to activate the call button set into one of the gate posts.

There was a click followed by a metallic-sounding voice asking who was there and what they wanted.

"Detectives Crane and Staroski of the Calgary Police Service. We just want to ask you a few questions."

"Shit!" Then silence. Chris was about to press the button once again when the gate began to swing open. A narrow, gravelled road traversed empty sunbaked fields behind high steel mesh fences topped with barbed wire, then dipped down into a hollow where dog runs extended out from three low concrete-block buildings. All of the runs were empty, and an eerie silence greeted the two detectives when Chris switched off the engine. He and Gwen exchanged glances, then watched a heavyset man step out from behind one of the kennels and walk toward them. He was dressed rough in patched jeans and a soiled shirt stained with dark patches under the armpits.

"Good afternoon, sir." Chris got out of the car and showed his badge. Gwen came around the rear to stand beside him. "You are the owner of this establishment?"

"What if I am?" Up close, he was even less prepossessing. Stubble darkened florid, veined cheeks; a tuft of grey hair sprouted from his chin. Under unkempt brows, his eyes glared belligerently.

"Could we have your name, sir?"

"Jim. Jim Mercer." The words were spat out.

"Thank you, Mr. Mercer." Chris looked around the yard and remarked almost conversationally, "It's very quiet. No barking."

"They bark when they're told to. What in hell do you think you are doing on my property?"

"Looking for some help with an inquiry we're conducting."

A scornful grunt was the only response to this low-key approach.

"All we're asking is for you to look at a photograph and tell us if you recognize the gentleman."

Mercer shook his head and handed the photo back without looking at it.

"You can do better than that. Take another look."

"Our relationship with our clients is confidential." The phrase was obviously rehearsed and trotted out with gusto. It was also bullshit, and Chris was pretty sure Mercer would know that. Chris could always fall back on the threat of obstruction of justice charges, subpoenas, and perjury, but first he would try a softer, gentler approach.

"You know, Mr. Mercer, we're in the same business, you and I. Security. Trying to make the world a safer place for the ordinary citizen. We're on the same side, Jim."

The dog trainer stared at Chris for a long moment, then held out his hand for the photograph. "Yeah, I recognize him."

"What was your connection with him?"

"He brought his dog here for training."

"Who else was with him?"

"Nobody."

"When was this?"

"A few months ago." Mercer paused as if to refresh his memory. "March."

"What kind of training did he want? Blitzkreig ... that was the dog, right?" Chris paused, noted that Mercer was becoming increasingly alarmed, and continued, "He was already trained as a guard dog. By you, I believe?"

"Yeah. This was kind of like an advanced course. Post-graduate, know what I mean?"

Briefly diverted by this turn of phrase, Chris said, "A post-graduate course in killing. Right? Okay," he added when the kennel owner remained silent, "you don't have to answer that. I can tell from your expression that's what you were doing. I hope you were well paid, Jim. Let's take a look at your records."

"I don't keep no records for things like that."

"Listen to me, Jim. You're in trouble and you know it. I can get a warrant and search this place, but things will go better for you if I don't have to. A lot better."

"What do you want?" This with a surly, resigned shrug.

"To see how and where you conducted this postgraduate course." Chris looked around the scrupulously clean yards and still silent kennels. "For starters, how do you keep things so quiet?"

"Muzzles."

"Round the clock?"

"No. A couple of hours in the afternoon. Like now. So they learn."

"What about staff? You can't run this place all by yourself."

"I have a helper."

"I want to meet him."

"It's not a him. It's a her. She's looking at us." Gwen pointed to a window near the front of the second building, where the slender outline of a young woman could be seen peering out.

"I'll talk to her later. Right now I want to see the kil— training ground."

The ATV was hidden behind a screen of evergreens. Mercer lifted off its concealing shroud of branches and piled them neatly to one side. A barely discernible track wound through the trees. "We don't come this way very often," Mercer volunteered as they jolted over a patch of rough ground ribbed with spreading tree roots. "No call to."

A wooden shack, so dilapidated it looked abandoned, stood in the middle of a small clearing. Some large rocks were scattered around its base, looking as if they had once formed part of its foundation. Mercer turned one over, picked up a key, and unlocked the door. Unexpectedly, the interior was neat and orderly. A narrow aisle separated a table, two kitchen chairs, and two padlocked closets from the caged enclosure on the other side. The set-up was clearly designed to handle one animal at a time. Not surprising.

"What do you use for a target?" asked Chris. "A dummy?"

"That wouldn't work." Mercer looked insulted. "Janet, the girl you saw." Taking a key down from behind the ledge running along the top of the wall, Mercer opened the door of the closet nearest the door. A suit of padded, protective clothing hung from a hook below a helmet that had once been a goalie's mask. Padded gloves lay on a shelf. Despite its makeshift appearance, the costume was irresistibly reminiscent of a medieval suit of armour.

"I see the throat has been specially reinforced," observed Chris, fingering the neck of the tunic. "That would be what Blitzkreig would be taught to aim for."

"Only on command."

"And what would that command be? Something like 'kill'?"

Staring down at the concrete floor, the beleaguered dog trainer asked, "What's in it for me if I tell you?"

"As I'm sure you already know, you could be facing a very impressive array of charges. Some serious enough to involve jail time. If you confirm what we already know and close down this part of your operation, things will go a lot better for you. But you *will* have to testify in court. Now, Blitzkreig was trained to kill. That's correct?"

Looking as if a weight had been lifted off his shoulders, Mercer nodded almost eagerly.

"What was the command? It must have been more than a simple 'kill.' That's too dangerous. It could be triggered accidentally."

"You have to send him on with your left hand. Like this." Mercer's arm moved in a wide downward sweeping arc. "It has to be the left."

Like TLC with his damn crosses. Shaking off the thought, Chris drove home the final point. "Mr. Taylor knew the command?"

"Yeah. He did."

chapter twenty-five

"It's always a pleasure to see you, Chris, but somehow I have the feeling this is not a social call?"

"I wish it were, Cameron."

The maid, holding a silver tray with a Thermos and two cups, hesitated in the entrance. In keeping with the Stampede, she was dressed Western. The silk bandana she wore around her neck was black. Taylor waved her away and she retreated.

"I paid a visit to the K-9 Kennels, Cameron."

"So?"

"The owner identified you from your photo. He also confirmed that you paid to have Blitzkreig trained to attack and kill. By ripping out the throat. The same way Melanie was killed. You murdered her, Cameron. Where are you going?"

"To the bathroom. I'm about to piss my pants. I'll be right back."

Held back by his respect and regard for the older man, Chris hesitated to interfere as Taylor left the room and headed down the hall. He waited for the sound of a door closing, and, when it didn't come, eased the Glock from its holster and went out into the hall. Cameron's study was at the end of the carpeted hallway and down two steps. Chris cursed himself as he heard the unmistakable click of a rifle bolt being rammed home. Standing with his back to the window that looked west to the mountains, the rancher held a rifle at a forty-five-degree angle across his chest. There was something indifferent, almost casual, in the way he was holding it.

"Don't do it, Cameron! Put the rifle down. Now!" Chris took a step forward. Two more and he would be close enough to rush Taylor.

"Stay where you are Chris! Don't move!" Now the rifle barrel pressed against Taylor's chin. He closed his eyes and murmured, "Sorry about this," as if apologizing for some minor social *faux pas*. Then the room reverberated with the sharp crack of the Remington. Blood and grey brain matter splattered the broken panes of the shattered window. Thrown backward by the blast, Taylor fell against a bookcase and slowly crumpled to the floor, blood streaming down the front of his cowboy shirt, obliterating the printed image of a bucking horse.

Ears ringing from the blast, Chris knelt beside the body and went through the motions of feeling for a pulse, knowing it was hopeless.

It was Constable Lonechild who answered his call. Corporal Kanciar was off-duty, having worked the night shift. Holding up a hand to warn off the shocked maid, Chris told Lonechild to contact the corporal and get out here herself on the double. Signing off, he strode across the room to the maid who looked as if she was about to collapse in a faint.

Taking her by the shoulders, he said, "He's gone, Lucy. There's nothing we can do for him. The police are on their way. That's it. Good," he added as she took her hand away from her mouth, and choked back a sob. Wiping the tears from her brimming eyes with a tissue he asked, "Where are Mrs. Taylor and Mister Cam?" He couldn't let them walk in unprepared on this scene.

Bending down, he heard her whisper, "Mrs. Taylor is in town meeting Melanie's brother. That's all the family she had. He was in Australia."

"And Cam. Is he with her? It's important, Lucy."

"No." Shaking her head, she drew a shuddering breath. "Mr. Taylor told him to ride across the river to check on the herd in the south pasture."

The Sheep River meandered through the southern part of Bent Tree. Even on horseback, it wouldn't take long to get there and back.

"Listen to me, Lucy. We can't touch anything until the police arrive. I want you to go back up to your room and wait. I'll go outside and intercept Cam."

The two Mounties arrived first. In separate cars, switching off their flashing lights as they entered the ranch property. Kanciar hadn't taken the time to put on his uniform and was only a few minutes behind Lonechild.

"The M.E.'s on his way," he said as they stood looking down at the grisly scene. "We'll dust the rifle for prints, but it's pretty clear what happened." Turning to Chris, he asked, "You say he just got up and excused himself to go to the can?"

"That's right. The bathroom is just down the hall, and when I didn't hear him close the door, I went out to find out what he was up to."

"What made you do that?"

"I don't know exactly. Maybe the way he looked. I just don't know."

"And you saw the whole thing go down?"

Chris nodded and said in a wondering tone, "He even apologized before he pulled the trigger."

"Noblesse oblige," murmured Lonechild.

The corporal gave his subordinate a long-suffering look, then asked as he saw Chris turning to leave, "Where are you going?"

"Back outside," Chris replied. "Cam could show up anytime, and I've got to prepare him for this."

The medical examiner, the same flushed, overweight woman who had attended the Bragg Creek murder scene, was the next to arrive.

"Who's the DOA this time?" she asked, lifting her medical bag down from the front seat of the pickup.

"It's Cameron Taylor, Senior. He shot himself." He added, "I saw it," when she stared at him in disbelief.

"That poor family. First their daughter-in-law, and now this." Shaking her head, she followed Lonechild, who had come out to take her into the house.

Chris braced himself as he saw the horse and rider coming toward him at the full gallop. Cam would have seen the police vehicles and realized something was wrong.

"What is it, Chris? What the hell is going on?" he cried as he vaulted out of the saddle, letting the reins fall to the ground.

"It's bad, Cam. Very bad. Your father shot himself." As he spoke, Chris studied his friend's expression. What he saw was shock and disbelief without the wary flicker of guilt he was half-expecting. "I'll take you inside. It's a crime scene, so you won't be able to touch anything."

"Crime scene. What crime?"

"It's routine, Cam. The police have to check out every sudden death." And this sure as hell was sudden. Chris's lips tightened at the grim thought. Taking his friend by the elbow, he glanced sideways at the quarter horse. Blowing gently, it was standing stock-still. A champion trail horse, it had been trained to remain in place whenever the reins were dropped.

"Why? In God's name, why?" Cam demanded, staring at the crumpled, blood-soaked body of his father.

Chris didn't attempt to answer. Instead, he said, "They haven't finished yet. Let's find a place for you to sit down."

"Mother! Does she know?"

"Not yet."

"I've got to call her! She has to know what happened before she hears it on the news."

"Okay. But don't go into details. Just tell her there's been a serious accident. I'm going to get you a drink."

On his way to the kitchen where he knew the liquor was kept, Chris beckoned Lonechild, "I have the feeling you know your way around horses, Constable."

"I grew up with them. On the reserve. And I spent two years with the Musical Ride."

For the first time that awful afternoon, Chris allowed himself a small smile. "Cam's horse is out front. Could you take care of him? His name is Pistol, but he's cool." No need to tell her what to do.

Dropping two ice cubes into the stiff drink of Scotch, Chris knew what *he* had to do. The Taylors were close and valued friends, but Melanie had died an unspeakable death, her trachea torn, the carotid artery and jugular vein severed. Worse, she would have been still conscious while her throat was being ripped out by those ravening teeth. As patriarch of the Taylor family,

Cameron had tried to preserve its future but had only succeeded in blowing it apart.

"Mother's on her way," Cam said, taking the drink Chris handed him.

"Good. I see the M.E. is leaving, so I better go back in there."

"I'll need a statement from you, of course," said Corporal Kanciar when Chris stood beside him, looking down at the body.

"Of course."

"There'll be an inquest, but" — the Mountie gave Chris another questioning look — "it'll be pretty straightforward."

"Not as straightforward as you might think. There's this kennel just west of Airdrie ..."

Chris turned off MacLeod Trail onto Mission Road instead of continuing downtown. Sarah had to know, and he would make the call from the penthouse. He tried the hotel first, and Sarah answered. Classes would be over for the day.

"Is Linda there with you?" Chris asked as soon as they had exchanged hellos.

"No. She's in her room, taking a shower. Why do you ask? What's happened, Chris?"

"It's heavy. I didn't want her to be there when I told you. Okay, here it is. Cameron Taylor shot himself. He's dead. He killed Melanie."

"I thought Bl— What are you saying, Chris?"

"The dog killed her, all right. When everyone thought he was in a veterinary clinic being treated for a viral infection, he was in a training school being taught to kill on command. To kill the way Melanie was killed. Her murder was premeditated," he went on when the only sound at the other end was Sarah drawing a shocked breath. "It was Cameron who shot the bull and cut off his ears to make it appear the cattle mutilator was back in action. That was to justify turning Blitzkreig loose. But Cameron still had to give the command for him to attack Melanie. "

Finding her voice, Sarah whispered, "We both know how important Cameron thought his family's role as pioneers of the West was, and how much it meant to him. And how he must have hated that Melanie couldn't have children and there would be no heirs to carry on the tradition. But to do this!"

"He must have thought it was the only way out. He could see Cam was deeply in love with Melanie."

"I know. And the awful part is that Melanie was determined to adjust to their way of life. She was actually starting to enjoy herself."

"So I gather. That would only make it worse from Cameron's point of view — no hope of divorce and then Cam marrying someone who could have children. In his obsession, eliminating Melanie would be the only solution."

"It was just Cameron, wasn't it, Chris? Phyllis and Cam weren't involved?"

"I've asked myself that question more than once. And the answer is no, they were not. It was Cameron, and Cameron alone, who took Blitzkreig to the K-9 Kennels to be trained to kill. That's the way the Mounties are treating it, and that's what I believe."

chapter twenty-six

"You son of a bitch! You call yourself a friend!"

"Take it easy, Cam. I did what I had to do. Your dad killed your—"

"Bastard!" A vicious right cross, with all the power of the rancher's compact muscular body behind it, slammed into Chris's unprotected jaw. The force of the unexpected blow knocked him to the ground. Stunned, he lay there, helplessly peering up into a vaporous grey mist. Dimly, he heard the sound of a truck door slamming, followed by a diesel engine starting up. Groaning, he rolled over and propped himself up on his knees. As his head stopped spinning, he managed to stand up and totter unsteadily the short distance over to the Durango.

This sure as hell was not what he had expected when Cam had called and asked to meet on this desolate stretch of road south of the city limits. "That way we can talk without being overheard by anybody," Cam had said.

With careful fingers, Chris tenderly touched his jaw. It ached like hell, but he could move it, so hopefully it wasn't broken. Holding on to a door handle he spat out blood. But no teeth. Thank God. His vision cleared and his eyes snapped into focus. Opening the door, he climbed into the driver's seat and sat behind the wheel, thinking. That had been a sucker punch. Not worthy of the man he had thought Cam to be. Sure, Cam would have been beside himself with grief over the last couple of days as the unspeakable thing his father had done became public. But to throw a sucker punch!

A challenge for a fair fight, okay. But not this. At least Cam had used his fist, not a baseball bat. Holding his aching jaw with one hand, Chris turned the ignition key. He should check himself into emergency and have his jaw X-rayed. But that would make it official and lead to an internal investigation. He would go home and check out the damage in the mirror, then brazen it out at the office.

"Those doors are a bitch, aren't they?" Patterson's tone was light, but his expression was questioning. "A guy can't help running into them."

Forcing himself not to finger his aching jaw, Chris replied, "This was no door. It was a sucker punch."

"Some punch." The detective stared at Chris. The bruise had yet to blossom into its full glory, but it was conspicuous enough to have raised eyebrows and excited whispering as Chris walked to his desk.

"Assaulting a police officer means jail time," Patterson observed, almost offhandedly.

"I'm not going to lay charges. It was personal."

"It wouldn't, by chance, have anything to do with your rancher friend killing his daughter-in-law because she couldn't have children, would it?"

"Drop it, Ken. I said it was personal."

"Okay, okay. But you better hope the boys and girls at Internal don't get wind of it."

Justified or not, Chris was irritated by Patterson's probing, and decided to do a little of his own. It took him a moment to remember the name, then he asked, "How's your friend, Ms. Gelinas? Still seeing her?"

"Of course."

"She's over at the McKinley firm, isn't she?"

"That's right. You're the man of the hour with them. Arresting Adrienne Vinney's killer. She was awfully well liked. Irene really admired her."

"What does Irene do there? Legal assistant?"

"No. She's in charge of their supply department. Computers, stationery, you name it. She's thinking about a career change, though."

"Oh?"

"Would you believe an instructor in the martial arts?"

Although he didn't say so, Chris had no difficulty believing it. From what he remembered of that formidable lady she could easily fill that role.

"There's one outfit that's been after her for months to join their staff. I think she's going to make the move before too long."

"She must be the genuine article, then?"

"She's no Ann Marin, if that's what you're thinking. If TLC ever took Irene on, he'd be in for one hell of a surprise. I think she sometimes wishes he would."

Before Chris could follow up on this, Mason, hot and perspiring from the noonday sun, stopped on his way to his desk and stared gleefully down at Chris's swollen jaw. "What the hell happened to you? Her husband catch you in the act?"

"I ran into a door."

"Sure, and pigs can fly." Mason took off his black

cowboy hat and wiped drops of sweat from his forehead with the palm of his hand. Looking over at Patterson, he said, "Now that the Mounties have solved that big cattle case of his, maybe Crane will pay some attention to *our* case. You know, the guy who gets off by killing and cutting up women."

Beyond compressed lips, Chris made no reply.

Clearing her throat as she joined the impromptu gathering, Gwen said, "Speaking of our serial, the lab found a brown fibre caught in a wheel of the chair. It matches fibres from the towel Klasky was wrapped in. Of course, that doesn't tell us anything we didn't know already. I know," she went on before Chris could say anything, "evidence is still evidence."

"Exactly. Every piece counts. As I've been known to say from time to time." Chris acknowledged her little sally with a smile. It made Patterson grin too. What a pleasure these two were to work with! He would see they stayed together as a team. He could have wished Gwen hadn't told him about Patterson being gay. It certainly didn't seem to interfere with his work as a Homicide detective. There could be a risk of blackmail, but today that wasn't a real factor. People would just shrug it off. But maybe Chief Johnstone wouldn't be so understanding. And Gwen was a lesbian. Funny, but somehow that didn't seem to signify. For one thing, she wasn't in the closet.

While Chris hadn't said anything in reply, Mason's heavy-handed sarcasm had hit a nerve. It was true he had allowed himself to be diverted from the case of the serial killer by involving himself in the mutilated cattle affair to help out his rancher friends and, let's face it, to impress Sarah. Well, he had solved that case all right. Mark Leonard was arrested and charged. First-rate deductive detective work there. But that same detective work had led to Cameron Taylor killing himself. A fate the rancher, with his grandiose obsession with family traditions, unquestionably deserved. But — a stab of pain shot through Chris's jaw — it had put an end to his friendship with the Taylor family. A friendship that meant a great deal to him.

"It hurts, doesn't it, Chris?" Gwen lingered for a moment after the other two drifted away. "And I don't mean just your jaw. I think I know who did this to you. It was that rancher's son. Wasn't it?"

"Yeah." Chris paused, then added defensively, "He took me by surprise."

"He would have had to," Gwen comforted him.

Still smarting from what Mason had said about allowing himself to be diverted from the serial killer investigation, Chris picked up the threads: What manner of man were they dealing with? And was it necessarily a man? A woman, a strong woman, was physically capable of doing what had been done to the victims. There was no trace of semen at any of the scenes. In fact there was no trace of anything, except for the body of the victim. A fibre had been found in the Devonian Gardens case, but that had only confirmed that the wheelchair was the one that had been used to transport the physiotherapist's body. The third victim of the pre-Vinney era had enhanced her natural attributes with breast implants. The killer had been enraged when he'd discovered this, slicing the offending breasts open and tearing out the sacs. Vinney had had breast implants also, but her killer hadn't touched them. That and the cross being on the "wrong" hand were what had suggested her murder was the work of a copycat.

Forsyth. Chris hadn't seen him since his arrest. Patterson had conducted the interrogations, which, attended by Myrden, had gone precisely nowhere. It had been Chris's suggestion that Patterson should be the one to interrogate Forsyth. Partly, he now admitted to himself, because he was reluctant to deal with the man who had once been a good and close friend. Maybe that had been a mistake. Knowing he was the one who had put him behind bars, Tom would bitterly resent him. There just might be a way to put that resentment to good use.

Since he had been charged, he could not be compelled to undergo further interrogatation, or "interviewing," as the police euphemistically called it. Myrden would certainly advise against it. But Tom always did have a high opinion of himself and his own cleverness.

chapter twenty-seven

Later that afternoon, a frustrated Chris Crane switched off the computer and stretched to ease the muscles of his back. He winced as the movement sent pain throbbing through his jaw. The case was going nowhere. He needed to think, to let his thoughts flow free. He would take Mango for a long ride in the foothills.

"Hello Angie. Pretty Angie." That was Nevermore's greeting when Chris let himself into the penthouse. Calling out the name of the Petcare girl was his way of reprimanding Chris for not having paid enough attention to him in the last few days.

Hoping to make amends, Chris carried him into the bedroom and talked to him while he changed into riding clothes. Before leaving, he gave some grapes to the parrot, who croaked a forgiving, "Goodbye Chris."

Three exhilarating and deeply enjoyable hours later, Chris turned off 4th Street onto Elbow Drive. The Solstice, convertible top in place, was parked next to the entrance to The Windsors' underground parking. Its lights flicked on and off, and Dummett stuck his arm out the window to wave him down. Obediently, Chris parked the Ferrari on the opposite side of the street.

"Pretty fancy car, pretty fancy duds," Dummett murmured as Chris settled into the passenger seat.

"Been waiting long?"

"Not too long. You were leaving as I turned the corner and I saw you were dressed for horseback riding, so I gave you a couple of hours and then came back."

How did he know I was going riding? wondered Chris. Then he remembered he had left the Ferrari on the street while he ran back into the condo to tell the concierge about a package he was expecting.

"Did you have a good ride?" asked Dummett, handing him a folded piece of paper. "Don't worry about gloves. It's a copy."

"It was great, thank you. Just great. Where's the original?"

"I'm hanging on to it. For backup, in case I need it. I keep thinking about that stringer for the *New York Times* who fabricated that sensational story about two congressmen being part of a ring that sold arms to Iran. He'll never work again. That's not going to happen to me!"

Chris nodded absently, his attention focused on the letter. It read:

forget the BUllShIt KiD All I want is to fool the FuCKing cops

Even though it was only a copy, it was easy to see that three of the words — *kid, fucking,* and *bullshit* — were constructs, made up from individual letters.

"How did you get this?"

"In the mail. Same as before. And, yes, I have the envelope. It doesn't tell us anything new. But the message does. It would seem our boy doesn't care much for the police."

"That's pretty clear. It could also be a ploy to throw us off the track."

"There is always that. Anyway, I thought you should know."

"Of course I should. This is helpful. What you're doing is valuable, Phil, and I want you to keep it up."

"Valuable enough that I get in on the takedown?" Dummett spoke lightly, but his expression was anxious.

"You're getting there. But that's not something I can control. You know that." Chris reached for the door handle.

Dummett put out a hand to detain him. "There'll be another one of my articles in tomorrow's *Herald.* One that will really rattle the bars of his cage. In it I say that it's clear TLC is challenging the police — daring them to catch him — but that in the end the police will win. Serial killers always get caught."

"That'll push his buttons all right. But that could prod him into action again."

"Which is precisely what we want."

"Not if it means another victim."

"There'll be another victim regardless, Chris. He's not going to stop. Not yet."

"Yeah, I'm afraid you're right." Chris pushed the door open and swung his legs out.

"Nice boots. I always thought it would be neat to ride a horse. Be in control of a powerful animal like that. But I never had the chance."

"It's never too late," replied Chris.

Towelling himself dry after his shower, Chris continued to think about the note Dummett had shown him. Assuming for the sake of argument that it was genuine — and he was becoming more persuaded that the notes sent to Dummett *were* genuine — it was easy to see that a serial would get a perverse thrill out of exchanging barbs with a member of the media. It was clear that the killer saw himself as waging a campaign against the police. Not playing a game with Detective Chris Crane, but attacking the entire police force. Someone who had a deep-seated hatred for the police. Talk about a field of candidates! Chris smiled ruefully to himself as he placed the towel back on the rack. The number of those who had reason to hate the police was legion.

Gordon Ralston, Mason's buddy. Chris had occasionally thought about the ex-cop as a possible suspect, but only in passing. God knew Ralston had reason to feel aggrieved, whether justified or not. By all accounts, he had been a good cop, apart from a heavy-handed way of dealing with troublemakers. He certainly had the physical strength to handle victims the way TLC did, and he was old enough to think of someone like Dummett as a kid.

Chris frowned at himself in the mirror as he combed his dark brown hair. There was nothing against Ralston except the fact that he had been discharged in disgrace from the police force. Conjecture. Pure conjecture. With no physical evidence. In fact, there was no physical evidence against anyone. Even the evidence against Tom Forsyth was circumstantial. Compelling, but still circumstantial.

chapter twenty-eight

Chris's eyes narrowed as he read. Dummett had mentioned him by name. In the third paragraph of the article he referred to Homicide Detective Crane, formerly head of the FCSU, describing him as a "crack detective with the scalps of many wrongdoers hanging from his belt." Christ! By now, thanks to the Chief, Chris was accustomed to seeing his name in print, but that didn't mean he had to like it. For one thing it wouldn't help him do his job as a detective; burrowing away in anonymity was the way to solve cases. But he understood why the freelancer had done it — it would add an element of human interest and drama to the story.

Not that the article needed any spicing up. After listing the murders attributed to TLC — at least he didn't say "credited to" — Dummett had gone on to state that in the end the police with all their resources — databanks, forensic tests and techniques, and "plain, old-fashioned police work" — would inevitably bring him or them to justice. Elaborating on the possibility of there being more than one killer, he mentioned the notorious duos of Bernardo and Homolka, and Douglas Clark and Carol Bundy. After clarifying that Carol was no relation to the "other Bundy," he devoted a paragraph to their sordid crimes, which included executing their victims with a bullet to the head in the middle of an unspeakable sex act.

Raising the possibility that TLC wasn't acting alone was a brilliant stroke, sure to enrage the serial. Chris found himself briefly thinking of that intriguing duo Ken Patterson and Irene Gelinas, a qualified martial arts expert. Shrugging off the idea, he went on reading. The confident prediction that the police ultimately and inevitably would win was also calculated to get under the killer's skin, as Dummett would say. The article was bound to be picked up and widely distributed by some news service. That had happened with Dummett's previous effort, which had been taken on by Reynolds International News. While Dummett might be well on his way to journalistic fame and fortune, Chris couldn't say the same about himself as a detective. So far the public would know him only as the detective who couldn't arrest the deadliest killer to ever prowl the streets and parks of the city. What was the name of that old movie? *The Gang That Couldn't Shoot Straight*. Something like that.

Speaking of arrests, he was due to match wits with Tom Forsyth later that morning.

"All right, counsellor," said Dave Myrden when all the requisite formalities had been complied with, Forsyth agreeing that he was appearing voluntarily and that he knew the interview was being taped. Myrden calling Chris "counsellor" was a ploy on the defence lawyer's part, an implied criticism that an accredited member of the Law Society was wasting his talents by playing detective when he could be practising law, as well as a recognition of Chris as a colleague. "It's your show, but I have advised my client to say nothing. He has nothing to gain." His voice rose at the end of the sentence, turning it into a question.

"What I've got to gain is to convince these assholes that I had nothing to do with Adrienne's murder," Forsyth, furious at having to wear the demeaning faded blue prison garb, interjected, overriding his counsel, as Chris had hoped he would.

"Let the record show that I have advised my client to remain silent." The defence lawyer scowled and shrugged almost imperceptibly. It was obvious he and his client had had words about the advisability of agreeing to this interrogation.

"If we're wrong, the charges will be dropped. You can count on that. We're not in the business of convicting innocent men. But the evidence against you is pretty persuasive, as I'm sure your counsel has told you."

"I have told him no such thing."

"If you say so." Chris looked across the Formica-topped table at the prisoner. "As I'm sure you know, Tom, I've managed to scrape together a fair amount of money myself one way or the other. So I know how you must have felt when you realized that much of the wealth you had earned from the sale of the ranch was going to be wiped out. Not just reduced, but wiped out. Gone. And you don't have another ranch to sell. No second chance for you. And all because of one person. Adrienne Vinney, who had no stake in the matter herself, but was determined to blow the whistle before all the evidence was in. Eliminate her, and your fortune was safe."

"I still would have had a fortune."

"Ah, yes. But not what you would really call a fortune. Nothing like you would have had if you were able to sell all those Madison flow-through shares. And you did sell them, Tom. You were able to sell all of them before the shit hit the fan and they were de-listed. You must have felt pretty good about that. I know I would have."

A smirk flitted briefly across Forsyth's face as he said, "So, the serial killer, the guy you pricks don't seem able to catch, did me a favour. If I knew who he was, I'd thank him."

"It wasn't the serial killer, Tom. His signature was missing. You know, the cross."

"What do you mean, the cross? It *was* there! I—"

"You put it there, Tom? Of course you did. But you put it on the wrong hand."

"That's enough! This farce is over! Not another word, Tom." Face tight with anger, the defence lawyer jumped to his feet.

"What do you bet Myrden tells Forsyth to find himself another lawyer?" Patterson, who had watched the proceedings through the one-way window, was almost gloating.

"It doesn't matter now. It's too late. I knew he couldn't stand the idea that his clever planning wasn't perfect."

"It doesn't amount to a full confession, though," Patterson cautioned. "Damaging as hell, but he didn't come right out and say he did it."

"I'll take it," said a vastly relieved Chris, grinning. No matter what happened in court, he now knew beyond all doubt that he had arrested the right person. What Mason would call a righteous arrest. It was Forsyth, not TLC, who had murdered Adrienne Vinney.

chapter twenty-nine

"**S**hit!" Chris's professionally impassive look had given way to a mask of grief as he peered past the medical examiner at Joan Cunningham's tragic body lying crumpled on the ground.

"I'm so sorry, Chris." Gwen touched his elbow. It was the first time in their long working relationship she had physically touched him. It was also the first time she had heard him say "shit." "I know how much you liked her."

"That's what brought her to this." The three Homicide detectives and one FCSU constable were standing a few metres back to let the medical examiner complete his examination.

"Joan would have hated to be seen like this," murmured Gwen.

This elicited a sad smile from Chris. "I remember she once told me that she enjoyed sex. So *somebody* must have seen her naked like this while she was alive. At least, I hope so."

He turned his head to look at Patterson, who was making gagging noises in his throat. "You okay, Ken?"

"I'm okay," Patterson replied, swallowing hard. "I thought I had seen just about everything. But this …" Clearing his throat, he repeated, "I'm okay."

"I guess there's no doubt TLC did this?" asked Gwen. "He didn't mutilate her the way he usually does."

"Maybe he figured the god of genetics had already done that for him." It was true the usual stigmata of the serial weren't present. Joan's flat, almost non-existent breasts were intact, the tiny half-moon nipples untouched, and no blood seeped between the twisted, rudimentary appendages that were her legs. Her club feet were turned inwards, and her short, unjointed arms were raised skyward as if in supplication to some malevolent deity.

Most significant of all, she hadn't been killed with a deep knife thrust to the heart as had the others. Instead, her head had been almost completely severed in a series of ragged knife cuts.

"Her face was so pretty, maybe he wanted to separate it from her body," suggested Gwen.

"I guess we can safely say VSA — vital signs absent," the medical examiner pronounced with dry irony. "She's all yours."

"Time of death?" asked Chris.

"Sometime early this morning." The M.E., tall, black hair ringing his shining bald scalp like a monk's tonsure, gazed up at the immaculate blue Alberta sky. "Rigor is well-established despite the heat. It's ten past eleven. Let's say three a.m., plus or minus a half-hour."

"What about the way her neck is cut?" asked Chris. "It doesn't look like what you would call surgical to me."

"It's not. Strictly a hack job without the right equipment. The guy must have gotten tired and given up. It's not all that easy to decapitate a person. He did manage to cut through the strap and skalenus muscles — the ones that support your head — and slice through the larynx and sever the carotid artery." The physician closed his bag with a click and walked away with a final doleful shake of his head.

At the mention of "strap" and "skalenus," Chris's neck was gripped in a brief, painful spasm. He had torn those same muscles in a spectacular spill over a triple-bar jump at the Toronto Royal Winter Fair. It had taken three months and a dozen acupuncture sessions before the stiffness in his neck went away.

As soon as the medical examiner turned over the crime scene, Gwen and the detective from FCSU moved in. The detective looked up as Chris, masked and gowned, slipped under the tape and joined them, then went back to photographing the victim. Later he would videotape the scene. Patterson, the colour gradually returning to his cheeks, remained behind the tape.

"Well, the location is right." Chris lifted his eyes from the tragically misshapen body and the almost severed head and gazed out on a panorama of green. The park, only recently opened to the public and as yet unnamed, waiting for a sponsor to come forward, was the last one to be searched since the discovery of Joan's abandoned mobile platform. It was located just west of the city and commanded a sweeping view of the Rockies. "I hope the son of a bitch was properly frustrated when he couldn't put his signature where he wanted."

Joan's birth defect had so deformed her left hand — the fingers clenched and folded into her palm — that the killer had been forced to carve his signature cross into her right hand, where the fingers were not so contracted.

That gave Chris a fleeting sense of bitter satisfaction, until he recalled those same fingers holding his wrist in their affectionate grasp. The cross was the only wound the monster had inflicted, apart from slicing her throat so savagely. The lack of blood from the severed carotid artery showed that she had bled out somewhere else and that the park was the secondary crime scene.

"Oh my God. Look at this! It's her bird," Gwen exclaimed as she carefully lifted Joan's head, supporting it with both hands. The cockatiel's lifeless body was underneath, its neck snapped.

"She called him Nicki," Chris muttered. It was the final horror.

Chris armed himself with a stiff drink of Glenlivet, switched on the TV, and prepared to watch the late local news.

Joan's murder was the lead item. It was described as the latest in the wave of killings that was holding the city in the grip of terror. There was no overt criticism of the police. No need, Chris reflected bitterly. The string of unsolved murders spoke for itself. The newscaster was filling in some of Joan's background, the details of which Chris had learned for the first time that afternoon. Her full name was Joan Cunningham. She lived alone in a one-bedroom apartment in Inglewood. The apartment building was four storeys high and was equipped with an elevator. She was probably best known for her occasional appearances as a panhandler, almost always on the mall, accompanied by her pet parrot, which had been killed along with her. According to those who lived in the same low-rise building, she appeared to be comfortably off. She went shopping regularly, bringing home adequate supplies of foodstuffs, and her clothing was, according to one neighbour, high-end stuff. It was rumoured that she donated the proceeds of her panhandling to the Salvation Army, although this could not be confirmed as yet. There was talk that she had been working on a book. Apart from that, there was no apparent reason why the killer had chosen her for his next victim. She was radically different from the profile of his previous victims. Assuming, of course, that her demise was the work of the serial killer.

It was when the newscast began to zero in on the details of her death that things got a little sticky. "The victim was …" Trying not to squint, the anchor leaned forward to peer at the teleprompter. "… born with …" A deep breath. "… anthrogryposis congenita." He omitted the third word, and Chris couldn't blame him. That hurdle safely past, the newscaster continued with greater assurance to say that it was a debilitating disorder that prevents the fetus from developing normally and results in the unfortunate victim being born severely crippled. "Joan Cunningham was virtually decapitated, but her body was not mutilated in the same fashion as the other victims," he intoned with professional objectivity before moving on to the next item.

Adding a measured ounce of whisky to his drink, Chris went out on the terrace to watch the nightly display of fireworks from the Stampede grounds. As rockets exploded with booming percussions and showers of starry lights, he thought back on the newscast. It had concentrated on the horror of the vicious murder and had refrained from criticizing the police, but that would come. The columnists, especially Jim Letts, would pounce, and editorial writers would wonder why Calgary's finest couldn't bring the killer to justice. Chief Johnstone kept pointing out that Chris was in charge of the investigation, and he had been singled out by name as the primary in an overview piece on the killings that ran in the City & Region section of the *Herald*. And then of course, there was Dummett, goading TLC by predicting that he would soon be caught.

Surprisingly, there had been no more letters to the editor from Lambert. Maybe being interviewed by the police as a "person of interest" had cooled him out, although one would think it was more likely to have provided him with additional ammunition. Now with Joan's murder, the egotistical law professor surely wouldn't be able to resist the opportunity to renew his attack on the police. The prospect made Chris wince. Lambert's stuff was bound to be more telling, more damaging, than anything the other critics could come up with. Dummett could probably match him in the writing department, but Dummett was constrained by his own personal agenda to lure TLC out into the open. There was no doubt the professor knew how to wield a pen. His astonishment at the ineptness of the police was all the more effective for being understated, and his academic background lent credence to what he had to say. Joan's murder, so grotesque and appalling, was almost certain to bring on another stinging attack from him. It would also provide a sensational chapter for the book Lambert likely had in mind.

On second thought, a letter from him could turn out to be useful. Lambert had been mockingly uncooperative when he and Gwen interviewed him that time at the law school and had flatly refused to come up with an alibi. He obviously relished the role of being a suspect. That intellectual arrogance of his might lead him into coming out with something incriminating.

The news anchor had said that so far there was no explanation of why Joan had been killed. The media might not know why, but he sure as hell did. *He* was the reason. It was his friendship that had led to her death.

That and that alone would account for TLC choosing her as a victim. She certainly didn't fit the pattern of his other victims. While he recoiled from the sick certainty of this, his detective instincts seized on the fact that the only contact he had ever had with Joan Cunningham was on the mall. Which meant that the serial must have witnessed at least one and probably more of their encounters. He could have learned of it some other way, of course, but the likelihood was that he had seen them talking to each other. Unfortunately, that did precisely nothing to narrow the field of possible suspects. The Stephen Avenue Mall was the main artery of pedestrian traffic in the downtown area and was crowded with thousands of people every day.

The newscaster had commented on the fact that she hadn't been carved up in the same way as the other victims. Chris was convinced that the serial must have been so shaken by her malformed body that he had been psychologically incapable of doing anything more and had left her torso untouched. But Joan's lifeless form would be under the knife right now. Her autopsy had been prioritized and the impersonal lights of the morgue would be glaring down on her pitiful body as she lay sprawled on a cold steel table.

chapter thirty

"There's a Doctor Chisholm here to see you," the officer behind the desk on the main floor told Chris over the intercom. "He says he's from the medical examiner's office."

"I know him. Send him up."

While he waited for the doctor, Chris wondered what could have led the overworked pathologist to come all the way downtown from Bowness, where the medical examiner's office was located. As soon as he had word from the tenth-floor receptionist that his visitor had arrived, he went out to greet him. He found the doctor, a rotund little man, perched uneasily on the plastic chair in the tiny waiting room. Wearing an identification tag around his neck and clutching a black medical bag in his lap, he was staring bemusedly at the brightly coloured children's toys scattered around the room. The only other occupant was a sullen, scraggly-bearded young man.

"What's with the toys?" Chisholm asked as he followed Chris a short distance to a room marked "Interview."

"Child Abuse. They're on this floor too. They're another section of Major Crimes." Chris unlocked the door of the interview room and waved the doctor in. Chris had dealt with him on a couple of homicides while he was with the FCSU, and he recalled that Chisholm took a keen interest in the criminal investigative process. Putting his bag down on the table, the pathologist punched in a code to unlock it and carefully lifted out a small plastic evidence bag.

"I'll ask you to sign a receipt for this. Preserve the chain of evidence, you know." The pathologist lingered lovingly over the technical words.

Chris hastily scrawled his signature on the form, pulled on the latex gloves Chisholm handed him, and sat back with an anticipatory gleam in his eyes. "Is that what I think it is?" he whispered as he saw what his visitor had brought.

It was a small triangular piece of plastic, less than two centimetres in length, a deep dark red in colour. It could only be part of a car's tail, or brake, light.

"Where did this come from?" asked Chris, gazing reverently down at the fragment.

"From the vic herself!" Chisholm's use of "vic" made Chris reflect that the good doctor had been watching too many cop shows on television. Some of the younger police officers were beginning to pick up on "vic" and "perp" as well. This stray thought somewhere in the far reaches of Chris's brain didn't prevent him from listening with avid attention to what the pathologist was saying. "I found it when I inserted my finger into the top of her small intestine. The gastrointestinal tract is almost always complete and functional in cases of anthrogryposis congenita multiforma," Chisholm pronounced the name of the disability with relish. "It develops early and high up in the fetus." Chris, who knew this from his research, nodded, and the physician continued with a complacent, self-satisfied air, "Many pathologists don't pay proper attention to the intestines and concentrate on the stomach contents. Once they have analyzed those, they think they're finished. But in my clinic we always check the intestines. I've made it part of the clinic's protocol."

Chris had heard the ebullient doctor call the examiner's office a clinic in the past, and then, as now, thought it must be a clinic for the dead. But Chisholm could call it paradise if he liked, for it had come up with this promising clue. The first tangible clue to surface during the entire investigation. It was Joan who had provided it. How brave and resourceful she had been! Somehow the serial must have smashed the light, maybe backed into a pole or a wall, and Joan, realizing she was going to be killed and knowing there would be an autopsy, had managed to swallow the broken piece. She was probably lying on the ground at the time and sucked it up.

"If you found it in the small intestine, she must have ingested it some time before she was killed?"

"Four hours. That's how long it would take to end up there."

Jesus! She had been kept alive all that time while the sadistic brute did whatever he wanted with her. As he had with Maud Simpson, the Ranchmen's Club receptionist. Chris would always think of her as a victim of convenience, who happened to be in the wrong place at the wrong time and had the misfortune to be spotted by the killer when he was out hunting. Maybe it had been the same with his other victims.

But Joan was no victim of convenience. She had been a target deliberately selected because of her perceived friendship with him. The ache in his jaw, which had been gradually subsiding, suddenly flared up. But he had to put that aside and concentrate on the clue she had given him, and use it to track down her killer. While these thoughts ran through his mind, Chris held the plastic fragment up for closer inspection. A raised ridge ran along the bottom, and above it the lettering "T2" was easily discernible.

"That shape after the two looks like it could be a part of a D," Chris muttered. "But the Hit and Run Unit will be able to tell us for sure. That and a whole lot more."

Ron Donlevy, the Hit and Run detective, folded the magnifying glass into its case and handed the plastic fragment back to Chris. "What you're dealing with is an older model Toyota Corolla. Manufactured sometime between 1997 and 2000. That plus the fact that it's from the tail light is all I can tell you."

"That's a good start."

"Where do you want to go from here, Chris? You said it was top secret. My ears only."

"That's the way I want it to be. I'm banking on the killer not knowing what's happened. Oh" — he raised a hand to forestall Donlevy's objection — "he'll know that he broke a tail light, but the chances are he won't know that Jo— the victim swallowed that piece of plastic."

"That must have been some woman!"

"She was." Chris's expression was bleak. "The perpetrator could still be driving around with a broken tail light, or he could have taken it somewhere to be fixed. He would need a police damage sticker for that, wouldn't he?"

The Hit and Run detective gave a dubious nod. "Technically, yes. But for something like a tail light, some garages wouldn't worry too much about that. But he *should* have a sticker. No doubt about that."

"If we start making inquiries we run the risk of alerting our guy. But I need to start somewhere, Ron. Would you get a list of Toyota owners in the Calgary area from the motor vehicles branch? Make that southern Alberta. Coming from Hit and Run, it won't raise questions."

"Sure, I can do that. It will be one hell of a long list, though."

"That's okay. Let me know when you have it, and I'll pick it up."

"I'll get on it." Donlevy's chair scraped on the tile floor of the restaurant. "Thanks for the coffee and doughnut."

Arriving back at headquarters, Chris was immediately aware of the buzz of excitement percolating through the Homicide section. He soon learned the excitement was caused by Steve Mason's success in solving an Asian gang killing.

Mason had been interrogating two subjects, both members of the same gang — first one, then the other — for hours, and had somehow managed to persuade one of them to implicate his partner as the one who had done the stabbing. Solidarity among gang members was legendary, and it was almost unheard-of for one to turn on another.

"How in the hell did you do it?" demanded Patterson.

"Yeah," another of the detectives clustered around Mason's desk chimed in. "They don't talk. Period. They swear some kind of an oath."

"I told him something more powerful than any oath," replied a beaming Mason. "I told him the other guy said his mother was a whore."

"That don't seem all that terrible. That gang runs prostitutes along with drugs."

"But the point is, Cheung knew it was true. He knew his mother had been a prostitute when she was younger. She did it to put food on the table after her husband, Cheung's father, was killed in a drive-by shooting. Cheung knew she had done it for him and he worshipped her. Beat the crap out of some of his classmates at school when they gave him a hard time about it."

"How the devil did you know that?" Patterson was impressed. "That sort of stuff is buried deep in the Asian community."

Mason hesitated, then replied with a show of defiance, "Gord told me. How Cheung felt about his mother. Gord figured it would push his buttons. And he was right!"

The assembled Homicide detectives exchanged glances; a couple of them nodded knowingly. "Old Starlight sure knew his ethnics," muttered one.

Cheeks flaming a dangerous red, Mason heaved himself to his feet. "Don't call him that! Ralston was a good cop. A damn sight better than some I know!" Glaring, he slowly lowered himself back down into his chair.

A detective who had previously remained silent looked as though he was about to dispute the point, but Patterson forestalled him by sincerely congratulating Mason on his successful collar.

"You're right, you know." Another detective leaned over Mason as the little group broke up. "Gord *was* a good cop, and he sure didn't deserve to get shafted the way he did. Give him my best when you see him."

Chris, who had remained on the fringe of the group and had taken no part in the discussion, returned to his desk, where the coloured photo of Nevermore glowed out at him. Minutes later, he had a call on his cellphone.

"We have a hit," Ron Donlevy announced. "A Toyota sedan, Alberta licence plate PUR 714, is parked on the south side of 17th Avenue in the 500 block. It has a broken tail light and no sticker. Parking Control just called it in."

"Do you have the name of the owner?"

"We're running that now. I'll call you back in five."

Chris compulsively checked his wristwatch as the five minutes turned into twenty, and snatched up his cell as soon as he heard the first note of the ring tone.

"The owner of the Toyota is one Grant Sylvester, who resides at 621 13th Avenue South West."

"That's one block east of the Ranchmen's Club. Interesting."

"I know what you're thinking. The address is a mix of rental apartments and condominiums. What they call an apartment-condo."

"Let's pay Mr. Sylvester a visit. It's 5:45. He should be home by now."

"Yeah. If nothing else, he's already committed an offence by driving around without a sticker."

"That'll be a good opening. Let's see how it goes from there. And, Ron, run a check on David Lambert. He's a professor up at the law school. See what make of vehicle he drives."

"What's it about?" Sylvester's voice echoed hollowly in the intercom.

"It's the police. We have a few questions we need to ask you, Mr. Sylvester. Let us in, please."

Standing in the narrow, confined entry, Chris and Donlevy watched the elevator door open and a man, forty-ish, casually dressed in blue jeans and T-shirt, walk across the foyer to stand on the other side of the glass door. "Let me see your badges," he mouthed through the glass, and reluctantly opened the door when the detectives obliged.

"We can talk here. What's the problem?" Sylvester looked more puzzled than concerned.

"You have been reported for having a damaged vehicle without a sticker," Donlevy informed him.

"You're here about *that*?" Sylvester's eyebrows shot up in genuine astonishment. "It's only a tail light, for Christ's sake!"

"It's an offence under the Traffic Safety Act. How did it happen, sir?"

"I was stopped at a stop sign when the guy behind me bumped into me. I'm sure it was deliberate. But I didn't stay around to find out. I know that's how some of these bandits work. They rob you when you get out to inspect the damage. I looked in the rear-view mirror and saw it was an SUV with a bumper guard. Perfect for that little game. And it wasn't in the best part of town, either."

"Where was that, sir?" Donlevy was making notes.

The two detectives exchanged glances when he mentioned a street in the east end. It was a known stroll, although by no means one of the main ones. It was also deserted in the evening except for sex trade workers and drug dealers. The residents tended to stay indoors at night.

"When did this happen?" asked Chris.

"The night before last." Sylvester looked at Chris as though it had just dawned on him. "What did you say your name was?"

"Crane. Detective Chris Crane."

"Now I get it. You're the detective investigating the serial murders. You've been in the papers a lot. That crippled woman who was killed. That's why you're here. You think I had something to do with that? Jesus Christ!" Sylvester looked increasingly alarmed as he spoke. "I'm no killer, man!"

"If that's right, there is no need for you to be concerned, sir. We're just here to follow up a lead. It's a process of eliminating possible suspects."

"Well, I *am* concerned. Damn concerned! There have been too fucking many cases where the police arrest some poor bastard just so they can say they solved the case."

"All you have to do is to account for your actions Thursday night and early Friday morning. So far you've told us you were driving along Forbes Street when you got bumped from behind. What time was that?"

"Just after nine."

"You didn't get out of your car. Very wise. What did you do after that?"

"Well, I didn't stay around there, I can tell you."

When the two detectives continued to stare at him in silence, he shrugged. "You know what I was up to."

"We're not concerned about that," Chris assured him. "Just tell us what you did."

"I drove over to the stroll on 3rd and cruised around for a bit before ... before I connected."

"Can you describe the person you connected with?" Donlevy had spent three years with Sex Crimes before transferring to Hit and Run.

"She wasn't all that young. Thirty, maybe. But she looked, you know, kind of experienced and broad-minded. Know what I mean? She had great legs." A reminiscent smile played across Sylvester's face.

"Long red hair?"

"Yeah! That's why I picked her."

"It's a wig."

"What? It couldn't be! It didn't come off ..."

"It's pretty firmly secured," Donlevy replied dryly. "That's Rebecca. She should be on her corner across from the Westin by now. Why don't we go and hear what she has to tell us?"

"It's cool, Becky."

"If you say so, Ron." The prostitute's wary look relaxed. "I thought you weren't in Sex Crimes anymore?"

"I'm not. And that's not what this is about. All we need to know is whether you recognize this gentleman." He stepped back so she could see Sylvester sitting in the passenger seat. "Like I told you, it's cool," he said when she shot him a suspicious look. "There's no heat, for you or him, so long as you tell us the truth."

"Yeah. I seen him."

"When?"

"Thursday night. He picked me up just before ten. We went back to his pad. It was real nice."

"How long were you with him?"

"Till after midnight. He's a big spender, and my rates get very competitive after the first hour."

"Thanks, Becky. Take care of yourself."

"I will. See you soon, lover boy," she said to the unsmiling Sylvester.

Seeing they were leaving without arresting her friend, a veteran hooker called out from across the street, "Hi ya, Ron. How're ya doin'?"

"Just great, Venus. Good to see you again." Grinning, Donlevy climbed behind the wheel.

"Satisfied?" asked Sylvester, staring straight ahead.

"It went a long way to clearing you," said Chris from the rear seat. "But we still have to impound your vehicle."

"What the hell for?"

"Routine. We could get a warrant if you object. But maybe you should bear in mind you've already committed two offences you could be charged with."

"Are you guys going to charge me?" Sylvester swung around in his seat to look at Chris.

"We could. But you've been cooperative so far, and if you continue to cooperate, I guess we can overlook a few things."

"Help yourself."

"I figure our boy is in the clear," Donlevy remarked after they had posted a uniform to guard Sylvester's Toyota until it could be towed to the police garage and were on their way back downtown.

"So do I. I can't see him tearing back out and committing a murder after spending two hours with your friend Rebecca. Besides, the timeline doesn't fit. According to the medical examiner, the victim was killed around 3:00 a.m. and she was abducted hours before that. I'm just going by the book by having his car checked out. Covering my ass, I guess."

Donlevy nodded sympathetic understanding, then said, "I've got a message," as the screen on the dash lit up. "You can scratch Lambert too," he said, as they read the information on the screen. "He drives a Mercedes E 500, black, four-door sedan."

"Kind of high-end for a college professor," grumbled a disappointed Chris.

Donlevy gave a hoot of laughter. "That from a cop who drives a Ferrari!"

"Touché." Chris grinned.

Most of the desks were still occupied when Chris returned to the tenth floor after Donlevy dropped him off. Some of the officers were on the night shift while others, like Mason, had stayed behind to fill out reports.

"Well, we can eliminate Professor Lambert," Chris

announced. "Reasons to follow," he added with a wink at Gwen.

"I could have told you to forget Lambert," crowed Mason. "He's too busy fucking your ex to be running around killing women."

"You bastard!" Patterson snarled, breaking the appalled silence.

"It's true, goddammit. They've been getting it on for months. They say the husband is always the last to know. Looks like ex-husbands are too."

Chris sat frozen rigid in his chair, staring straight ahead, telling himself it was all right. Robyn was an attractive woman with a healthy sex drive. It was inevitable she would hook up with somebody. He just hoped Lambert wouldn't break her heart. But Robyn knew how to look after herself. That explained why there had been no letters to the editor from Lambert after the first one. Robyn would have shut him down. Chris booted his computer and began to type out a report of his interview with Sylvester.

As the initial shock gradually wore off, Chris asked himself how Mason had come across this juicy piece of gossip. Mason was famous for the sources he had culti- vated in the course of his long career, but the university was definitely not his turf. But Mason was aware that Lambert, however briefly, had been a person of interest. He could have decided to a little investigating on his own and come across the story. There was bound to be talk about the affair on campus. Maybe he had enlisted the help of his buddy, Gordon Ralston, who had plenty of time on his hands. However he had learned about it, how he must have gloated while he waited for the most humiliating opportunity to come out with it!

chapter thirty-one

"I've made three copies." Patterson handed a single sheet of paper to both of them as they joined him around the table. Chris nodded. The original single sheet of paper had been sent to the lab to be checked for fingerprints and any other clues it might provide. Chris knew it was a bootless inquiry, but it had to be done. Protocol. The police continued to receive letters and e-mails purporting to be from the serial, but most were clearly the work of cranks and were easily dismissed. But this was the real thing. It had TLC's signature and was directed at Chris. As usual, the words and letters were newsprint. Most telling was the manner of delivery. It was ingenious, as always with TLC.

The note had been discovered by a postal service carrier when he collected mail from a box in the Chinook Centre. It was a simple sheet of paper, not folded, addressed to "detective Crane." No longer did the killer have to rely on the window cleaner's accident for a supply of "Crane"; the stream of articles in the press, not to mention Dummett's article, had taken care of that. The press coverage had also alerted the postal employee to the importance of the message when he saw it lying on top of the other mail. Being on top of the pile meant it had been dropped in the box very close to the five o'clock collection time. He had contacted his office immediately, so the police were able to collect it before it was handled by anyone else.

Chris was already familiar with the note and its hateful contents; he had been on duty yesterday when word of what the postal employee had found came through. It still filled him with disgust as he read it again:

You got Piss poor taste in women Crane.

The "piss" was made up of individual letters.

"That's so sick!" said Gwen.

"He's one sick bastard," agreed Patterson.

"That we know already." Chris frowned. "Now let's concentrate on what else we can learn from this … this …"

"Piece of crap?" suggested Patterson.

"Exactly."

"Excuse me for a minute. I have to make a visit." Chris got up and headed for the washroom, the secure one at the rear of the Homicide section. That gave him a reason to pass by Mason's desk. The burly detective was there, although almost hidden behind his computer. It was easy to see why he was taking refuge there. The man was clearly in the grip of a fierce hangover.

"How goes it, Steve?" asked Chris with forced

cheerfulness. "Don't tell me," he added with a grin when Mason raised bleary eyes to look resentfully up at him. "Out celebrating your collar? With your buddy Gord, I bet. How's he doing?"

"What the hell do you care? He's okay."

"I trust you took a taxi? Like the manual says."

"What's with you, Crane? I can't see you shedding any tears if I got hauled up on a DUI. Yeah, since you're so concerned, we used taxis."

"Good thinking," Chris said over his shoulder as he paused at the washroom door. Mason and Ralston taking taxis instead of driving themselves probably meant nothing more on their part than common sense, although neither of them was noted for that quality. But if Ralston didn't know about Joan swallowing the lens fragment, why should he worry? Because driving around with a broken tail light would increase their chances of being stopped by the police. If nothing else, using taxis could indicate that his car might have a broken tail light. Pure conjecture, but Ralston remained in play. Chris had only seen Ralston's car once, and it was too far away to know whether it was a Toyota or some other Japanese make. The owners list from the motor vehicles branch would tell him that.

He had arranged with Donlevy to have it delivered to the Crime Scenes office, where he could examine it in private. Not completely in private, though. Vital as it was to keep the lid on the broken tail light business, he needed to have Gwen to brainstorm with. No need to worry about her discretion.

The receptionist interrupted Chris on his way back from his unnecessary visit to the washroom to tell him that a parcel had arrived for him at the Crime Scenes office. He thanked her and continued on to the meeting room.

"It seems our colleagues at Crime Scenes need our

expertise," he said to Gwen. "They want us down there ASAP." Turning to Patterson, he added, "I think this note has told us everything it's going to. Unless and until the lab comes up with something."

"Which is highly unlikely. Our boy knows all the tricks," replied Patterson. Fingering the photocopy, he added, "I'll stay here and stare at this for a while. See if anything occurs."

"Good man."

Chris and Gwen donned sunglasses as soon as they stepped outside. "The Stampede does it again!" marvelled Gwen. "Sunshine every day!"

"Except for a year way back in the nineteen-fifties," said Chris, laughing. "When they wanted to start charging the Natives admission. The Sarcees, as the Tsuu T'ina were known then, held a rain dance, and the Stampede was pretty much rained out."

Here, east of Centre Street, there was little to remind them that the Stampede was still in full swing. A Western band playing a lively reel for square dancers in Rope Square could be heard in the distance. "Stampede or not, life and crime go on," Chris murmured, and Gwen nodded solemn agreement.

"Speaking of crime, just what is it that Crime Scenes needs our help on?" Gwen's eyes were hidden behind the tinted glasses, but her eyebrow had a skeptical lift.

"Here's the breaking news." As they walked Chris quickly told her about the plastic fragment found in Joan Cunningham's intestine, how Hit and Run had identified it as coming from a Toyota Corolla manufactured between 1997 and 2000. "TLC will likely know that he has a broken tail light, but I don't think it would ever occur to him that she managed to provide us with this clue."

"What she did is totally awesome!"

"Mind-boggling, isn't it? I've kept it to myself until now. Hoping the serial doesn't have it repaired, or repair it himself, right away. So what's waiting for us is a list of Toyota owners in Southern Alberta. It just occurred to me," mused Chris as they waited for the pedestrian light on MacLeod Trail, "I haven't been back to the Crime Scenes office since I transferred to Homicide."

"It hasn't changed much, just a couple of new faces."

The detective who had been promoted to take Chris's place came out of his office to greet them warmly and then led them to a small conference room. En route, Chris exchanged handshakes and waves with his former teammates.

"It's in here," the sergeant said, unlocking the door. "Have fun."

"Thanks a bunch." Chris grinned, peeling tape from the package then stripping off the heavy wrapping paper to reveal a cardboard box, roughly a square metre in size.

"I knew Toyotas were popular," he said, lifting out the top ring binder. "But not this popular."

"It's going to take forever to go through them," said Gwen, taking the binder from him.

"First, we'll try being a little selective. Let's start with the Rs."

"You're thinking of Gordon Ralston? The ex-cop?"

"He fits the profile. Hates the police, knows how to cover his tracks. *And* he drives a Japanese vehicle. Here he is. It's a Toyota." Chris copied down Ralston's address. "So he falls through the largest opening in the net. Do you know anything about the guy, Gwen?"

"As it happens, I do. A friend of mine often worked

the same shift he did. She didn't like him much. To put it mildly. He lives alone. His wife left him months before the scandal. They had one child, a son. He's in New Zealand, or at least he was. Trying to get as far away from the old man as possible, I guess."

"He could have found another woman since then."

"He could have. That's true. But from what my friend said about him, I doubt that any woman would stick with him for very long."

"So he's free to prowl the night. That makes him even more interesting." Chris opened up another binder. "While we're here, let's take a look at the Gs."

"Irene Gelinas? Ken's friend? Ken has no reason to hate the police."

"I know. But sometimes people like to play games. They have secret fantasies no one knows about. And Irene Gelinas is not what she appears to be. Well, well. What do you know? She drives a Toyota."

"What about that freelance writer? He writes some pretty intriguing stuff. Did you know he's the only Dummett in the phone book?" Responding to Chris's inquiring look, Gwen added, "I like the way he writes. I thought it would be interesting to know more about him."

"He drives a Pontiac. A Solstice."

"Nice," murmured Gwen.

"Very. But it's a two-seater. No room to go carting a body around." Closing the binder, Chris said, "I'll do a drive-by on Ralston. He and Mason were out on the town last night, so maybe he's still at home. There won't be any off-street parking where he lives, so I should be able to spot his vehicle."

The Toyota was there. Parked on the street. Wedged between a fairly new Honda sedan and a Chevy Impala splotched with rust. The houses were small and neglected, on tiny lots with no provision for off-street parking. Nearly all had been optioned by developers and would soon be knocked down to make way for the ever-advancing tide of condos. Turning the corner, Chris drove until he found a space on a side street big enough to take the Durango.

He walked all the way around the block and approached the Toyota from the rear. The licence plate confirmed that it was Ralston's. The ex-cop probably boarded in one of the houses. Both tail lights were intact. More telling, both had a thin coating of dust. It was, of course, possible, Chris told himself as he kept on walking, that a broken lens had been replaced. But there was the dust. It could have been applied deliberately, but that wasn't likely. It was also consistent with the rest of the car, which was badly in need of a good wash.

With Ralston no longer a suspect, and that was what the evidence was telling him, where could he turn next? TLC was out there somewhere, swimming in a sea of anonymous faces with nothing to single him out from the rest of the crowd. Except for what Joan had provided. The killer drove a Toyota. His name was somewhere in that list of registered Toyota owners. A dauntingly lengthy list. With nothing to make the killer's name stand out from the thousands of others. Except of course for Ken Patterson's friend. Irene Gelinas. She was on the list. It was almost lunchtime. He and Gwen could talk over lunch.

Chris shook his head when Gwen made a questioning gesture at a coffee shop frequented by the police. "Let's go to the Hyatt. It's just up the street."

"You won't get any argument from me. So long as you're buying." As a condition of its building permit, the modern hotel incorporated the sandstone façade of a building that dated back to the era when Calgary was known as the Sandstone City and all the important buildings were constructed of sandstone from the Redcliff quarry, near Medicine Hat. In honour of its historic past, the hotel's decor was hard-core Western, with bronze sculptures of cowboys and Indian warriors adorning the spacious reception areas and oil paintings depicting cattle drives, mountain scenery, and Indian chiefs in war bonnets on every wall. The Stampede festivities might be muted over in the vicinity of police headquarters, but here they were in full cry. Throngs of Stampede-goers swarmed the mall, and inside the hotel the lobby was alive with chattering guests decked out in Western attire. Chris loved the hotel's atmosphere. Spotting Chris, the smiling maitre d' led them over to a booth beneath a painting of a mountain goat on a rocky crag.

"I'm kinda glad Gordon Ralston checked out."

"You have a kind heart, Gwen. But I agree with you. Maybe for a different reason, though. It would be a real black eye for the department if the serial turned out to be a former officer. It's possible he could have replaced the tail light, but I doubt it. I think we eliminate Ralston from our list of suspects." He paused, then added with a rueful twist of his lips, "What list?"

Conversation ceased for a moment as a server brought the drinks — Virgin Caesar for Chris and cranberry juice for Gwen — and took their orders — a

Caesar salad for Gwen and a bison burger for him.

"So you're going to check out the Gelinas vehicle as well?" asked Gwen when the server had withdrawn. "I'm willing to bet that will be a non-starter too."

"I'm pretty sure it will. I certainly hope so. At the moment I'm not sure how I'm going to locate it without Ken knowing what we're up to. We know where she lives, but I don't know where she parks during the day."

"I can help you there. According to her licence, her condo is in Kensington. That's within walking distance of Bankers Hall, where she works. It's a lovely day, and parking downtown is the pits during Stampede. Maybe she decided to leave the car at home. The salad is great, by the way," she said appreciatively.

"So is the burger."

For the next few minutes they devoted themselves to the business of eating.

"Who's next? If Gelinas is eliminated." Gwen paused to take a sip of water. "What about Sylvester? The gentleman who goes for red-haired prostitutes. Did the lab turn up anything in his Toyota?"

Chris shook his head. "No. It's clean. If you call two used condoms on the floor of the rear seat clean. We can forget Grant Sylvester."

"And we keep Ken out of the loop? "Gwen asked as Chris signed the credit card slip.

"That's right. Until I check out his gir— friend's vehicle. Which I am going to do right now."

Driving north over the Louise Bridge, Chris saw that Gwen had been right about people walking to and from the downtown area. Pedestrians, most still dressed Western, although a few had reverted to everyday attire now that the Stampede was winding down, walked, singly or in pairs, along the sidewalks paralleling the traffic lanes. Irene Gelinas lived on the seventh floor of an apartment building on Kensington Avenue, three blocks west of one of his favourite restaurants. He turned into a lane behind the building and then drove cautiously down the short incline to the parkade entrance. His luck was in. The door didn't require a code to open. It was activated by a pressure pad lying a few metres out from the threshold. Cutting the head-lights, Chris drove in and parked in the first vacant stall.

The parkade was like its counterparts everywhere: dimly lit, bare concrete walls and floor. Individual stalls, most of them empty at this time of day, were outlined with yellow paint. Chris's eyes narrowed as he spotted a Japanese vehicle. But it was a Honda, not a Toyota. His steps echoing hollowly, he walked over to the concrete stairs leading down to the floor below. Standing on the bottom step, he scanned the parked cars. There were more of them here, and over there, three stalls to his left, was a spotless Toyota sedan. A quick glance showed both tail lights to be intact.

The elimination of two potential suspects, while welcome in both cases, was an appropriate leadoff to a weekend of frustration for Chris. He spent most of it fruitlessly reviewing the details of the case. As it always did, the rou-tine chore of cleaning Nevermore's cage brought a wel-come respite from the endless churning of his thoughts, and the antics of his pet even produced a few smiles.

Sunday was the last day of the Stampede. Chris enjoyed the activities and usually took in an afternoon of the rodeo, followed by the chuckwagon races and the grandstand show. But this year he was in no mood for its attractions. Not with TLC out there somewhere mocking him. But long rides on horseback *did* suit his mood, and he spent the afternoon at Sarah's place, riding both Mango and Linda's thoroughbred, accompanied by an ecstatic Prim.

The fresh air and exercise conferred the added boon of a sound night's sleep.

chapter thirty-two

Now that the Stampede was over, the airlines had laid on extra flights to transport the hordes of departing visitors back home. Chris paused for a moment outside the Andrew Davison Building to gaze up at the orderly procession of passenger jets climbing to their cruising altitude in the eastern sky.

"Good morning, Chris," Patterson, already seated at his desk, called out. "Did you and Gwen solve the case for your Crime Scenes buddies?"

"I think we helped them a bit. They wanted to talk about a case Gwen and I worked three years ago. It had some similarities to one they're dealing with now. Got a minute, Ken? There's something I want you to look at."

"Sure." Preppy features alight with curiosity, Patterson came over to stand beside Chris. Three of the nearest desks were unoccupied, the detectives to whom they were assigned either out on a case or not having reported in yet. It was the nearest approach to privacy the bull pen afforded.

"There's been a new development in the TLC investigation." Speaking in a low voice, Chris began to tell Patterson about the clue Joan Cunningham had left for them, suppressing Patterson's exclamation with a cautionary wave of his hand. In the middle of his explanation of how the plastic fragment could narrow the search, he paused to look expectantly up at the receptionist, who was waiting to speak.

"I hate to interrupt you, Chris, but ground floor reception says you have a visitor who claims it's urgent."

"Who is it?"

"A Mr. Phillip Dummett. He's called on you before."

"I know. Okay, they can send him up. Tell him I'll be with him in a few minutes." The thought of what the journalist would make of the toys in the waiting room provided a brief diversion.

However, when, ten minutes later, he left a pumped-up Patterson and went out to meet his caller, Dummett made no mention of them. He was too excited by his news to take note of his surroundings.

"I've had a call from TLC himself," he announced as soon as Chris closed the door of the interview room behind them. "Well?" he demanded when Chris made no comment. "You don't seem all that impressed?"

"It's interesting, I agree. Very interesting. But I've had too many crank calls over the years to take any of them at face value. What did your caller sound like? Was it a normal speaking voice?"

"No." With a visible effort, the journalist matched Chris's cool professionalism. "It was distorted. Low, growly, like the guy was in the bottom of a barrel. It didn't even sound human."

Chris nodded. "Easy enough to do. First you record the message, then play around with it, changing the speed, lowering the volume, and so on. A technician can restore the speaker's normal voice." Already knowing the answer, he asked, "You didn't tape it, by chance?" If Dummett *had* taped it, he would have produced the tape by now.

"No. There was no time. He hung up as soon as I said something. But I do have caller ID. Here's the number he was calling from."

"Now that's helpful! Very." Chris copied down the number — 290-9878 — from the slip of paper Dummett handed him. "Most likely it's from a pay phone, which we can trace. Who knows? Maybe our guy got careless and forgot to use gloves. We'll dust it for prints. What did the message say? Well, what did it say, Phil?"

"Eh? Sorry." Dummett cleared his throat. "I wrote it down as soon as he hung up." He handed Chris another slip of paper. "He says I don't understand him. Nobody ever has. And you'll see he says he's going to strike again and again. Nobody can stop him. And he promises I'll have plenty to write about."

Reading the words, Chris felt a thrill of recognition. They were similar to the written communications from TLC. Not so much the words themselves, but the tone: brief and challenging. Confident.

"Well, what do you think?" demanded Dummett when Chris finished reading the note and remained silent.

"I think it's probably genuine, and it's telling us that the killer isn't finished yet."

"That's worth knowing, isn't it?"

"Still piling up the credits, Phil? So you can be in on the takedown? There may not be one. TLC could notch up enough kills to satisfy whatever it is that drives him and simply retire. Go underground. Like BTK, the family man who became a pillar of the church and went undetected for years."

"True. But then he began to send messages to the police from a computer he knew could be traced to his church. He wanted recognition for what he had done, and so will TLC when the time comes. I just want to be there when it does."

"No promises," said Chris as he stood up. "Stay in touch."

"Hang on a sec," Dummett protested when they were once more in the narrow hallway and Chris reached out to press the down button for the elevator. "Can I have looksee at the Homicide office? It would really enrich my next article."

Chris shook his head. "No can do. Strictly prohibited. But I'll describe it for you."

Dummett listened avidly as Chris sketched in the details: the open area seating plan, the desks assigned to the officers, the two rows of desks reserved for detective constables when needed.

"Thanks, Chris. That's useful. Let's see what my next article stirs up." Smiling, the freelancer held out his hand.

chapter thirty-three

Although Chris knew that Telus wasn't the only company that operated pay phones in Calgary, he would start with them. Of course, it might not have been a pay phone that was used to call Dummett, but it was hard to imagine the killer would use a phone that could be traced to him. Pay phone or not, the fact that he had the calling number should expedite things. They would also need Dummett's phone number so they could trace the call. The call had come in on his regular phone, not his cell. Flipping the phone book open, Chris saw that Gwen was right about Phil being the only Dummett listed in the directory. As he copied down the number, Chris thought about the name. While never numerous, "Dummett" was reasonably well known back East, as Albertans persisted in calling everything east of the Manitoba border. But it was obviously thin on the ground out here in Calgary. But Dummett had a mother living here. She was a friend of Mrs. Underwood. Ethel, Mrs. Underwood had said her name was. Surely she would have a phone. Probably she had remarried and changed her surname.

To Chris's chagrin, and despite his best arguments, the Telus official took the position that he needed a warrant before they could provide the location of the pay phone. There was nothing for it but to send Gwen off to Provincial Court. Having done that, he had to sign off on a file where the suspect in a fatal domestic stabbing had been convicted of second-degree murder. How he would love to sign off on the TLC file with the arrest and conviction of the perp. Now *he* was using the diminutive. It was mid-afternoon before he thought again of Dummett's mother not being listed in the phone book. Dorothy Underwood would know.

"Oh, Chris, it's so good to hear from you! Dare I hope this means you're going to come by for a little visit?"

Chris hesitated, then, responding to the eagerness in her voice, replied, "There's nothing I would like better. Give me an hour."

With the same air of delighted surprise she always displayed, Dorothy took the bottle of Alvear's Amontillado from Chris and marched off to pour it into a crystal decanter, saying, "My Howard always insisted on decanting red wines before serving them."

There wouldn't be much decanting in the few minutes between his arrival and the first sip. No matter. Chris smiled appreciatively as she returned with a silver tray bearing the decanter and two crystal glasses.

Seating herself on an antique armchair, she smiled fondly as he went through the ritual of pouring the wine and handing her a glass. "That Phil is certainly making a name for himself, I must say. Have you seen him recently, Chris?"

"As recently as this morning. He came around to see me."

"He's so clever, that boy. And so good to his mother."

"That reminds me. Your friend doesn't seem to be listed in the telephone directory. Does she live with her son?"

"Mercy, no. She has a lovely home up in Varsity Acres. But she and Phil adore each other. She remarried after her first husband — Phil's father — died. Her married name is Lewis. She's in the book. Although she's no longer married."

"What happened? Divorce?"

"Not with Ethel. Not ever." Shaking her head, she refilled his glass. "He was killed in an accident. Like Phil's father."

"What happened to Phil's father? How was he killed?"

"He died in a house fire. Phil was only nine at the time. He was quite the hero. He managed to get his mother out, but he couldn't rescue his father. Who was dead drunk and must have weighed over two hundred pounds. Don't ask me what that is in kilograms!"

"What caused the fire? Did they ever find out?"

"They suspected arson. But they never did arrest anybody. Couldn't prove it one way or another, they said. Both of the parents were smokers."

"It sounds like your friend's husband — Phil's father — was also a drinker."

"A drinker and an abuser. He was a wife beater, and I'm sure he did terrible things to young Phil. Ethel never said anything. She wouldn't. But she would show up — when she absolutely couldn't avoid going somewhere — with black eyes and bruises that makeup couldn't hide.

And she looked just sick whenever I saw the three of them together."

"It must have been a relief when her husband died."

"It was. It's a terrible thing to say, but it was. Ethel and Jim Lewis had a good life together. He had just retired and they were going to move to Vancouver Island when he had that accident."

"What sort of accident did he have?"

"He fell down the basement stairs. They were cement — concrete — so he didn't have a chance. Jim liked to drink a bit too, but he wasn't a mean drunk like Ethel's first husband. She still lives in that house, although I don't know how she does it. I certainly couldn't."

"Well." Chris carefully placed his glass back on the tray and stood up. "This has been most pleasant. I'm delighted things are working out so well for you. I must ask you not to mention our conversation to your friend Ethel. I wouldn't want Phil to know we had been talking about him."

"Not a word," she assured him with a conspiratorial smile.

Chris drove west for a few blocks, then parked on a side street. Raising the Crime Scenes sergeant on the mobile, he asked him to check the registry and see if an Ethel Lewis owned a Toyota. Minutes later, the sergeant informed him that Ethel Lewis owned a black 1999 Toyota Corolla. Chris copied down her address: 4569 Viceroy Drive. "That's in Varsity Acres," the sergeant added helpfully. "North on Shaganappi Trail, past Market Mall, then turn right on Valiant Drive."

Varsity Acres was a mature, well-treed subdivision. Chris drove around until he found Viceroy Drive. 4569 was the second house from the end, a small, one-storey stucco bungalow with a single-car attached garage. The garage extended to the edge of the narrow lot and its end wall was windowless. Not that he could go skulking around a citizen's property without a warrant in any case. Although *if* there had been a window …

Tomorrow was Tuesday. The day Ethel Lewis drove her friend, Mrs. Underwood, to the Edgemont Club for an afternoon of bridge.

Gwen was waiting for him when he arrived back at the office. Telus had come up with the information as soon as they were served with the warrant. The pay phone was located in the lobby of the Bank of Montreal Building, and a call to Dummett's number had been made from it.

"Already done," she told him when he said they should have it dusted for fingerprints. "I'm waiting for the report."

"I'll wait with you."

They gazed at each other in silence after the report was telephoned in. The single, wall-mounted phone was clean. No fingerprints. According to the Crime Scenes detective it looked as if it had been recently wiped. He had gone on to say, "It's tucked away in a corner all by itself, so there's not much traffic. It could have been the janitorial staff."

"So I let it slip that we would dust the phone for prints and it turns up clean," Chris finally muttered.

"That slip, as you call it, could turn out to be useful. If Dummett was the one who wiped off the phone, and it almost certainly was done on purpose, it means he placed the call to himself."

"That's the way it looks. He was visibly taken aback when I mentioned dusting the phone for fingerprints."

"His making the call himself is also consistent with trying to win your confidence. Making it seem like he could contribute something. He wouldn't want you to know that, of course."

"That's one explanation, I agree. But we know there's also another one, don't we, Gwen? A much more sinister one."

At one o'clock the following afternoon Chris was parked on 19th Street at the corner of Memorial Drive. He was sitting in a vehicle borrowed from the Strike Force Unit, the squad that carried out undercover surveillance. The Chevy pickup, dark blue, encrusted with dried mud, and with a dented front fender, looked nothing like a police vehicle. Chris was dressed for the part: day-old stubble, jeans, and an open-necked shirt.

A half-hour later he snapped to attention as a black Toyota sedan drove past and pulled into a vacant space a few doors west of Dorothy Underwood's house. The red plastic cover of the right rear tail light was missing. Only an empty cavity where it should have been.

The truck's engine purred with a quiet power at odds with its decrepit appearance as Chris drove back to the Andrew Davison building where Gwen and Patterson were on standby.

"I was on a stakeout," Chris answered his companions' unspoken question.

"Well, you sure look the part. I'll give you that," said an amused Gwen. "How did it go?"

"Productive. Phillip Dummett's mother drives a Toyota with a broken tail light."

"Well, what do you know?" breathed Gwen.

"There's more. Dummett's drunken, abusive father died in a house fire when Dummett was nine. Arson was suspected, but no one was ever charged. And Phil's step-father was killed in a fall down the basement stairs. He had just retired, and he and Phil's mother were going to move out to Vancouver Island."

"So your journalist friend might have killed before?" mused Gwen.

"It's possible. I had the feeling Mrs. Underwood might have been trying to tell me something. But we can't know for sure."

"It fits!" Eyes alive with excitement, Patterson leaned across the table. "Here's a guy who has killed and gotten away with it. You said his father abused him."

"Mavis Ross would find that significant," Gwen interjected. "He's clever and talented. Isn't he, Chris?"

"Very," Chris replied tersely, curious to see where his colleagues would go with the new information.

"He knows he's bright. Much brighter than the other guys. But he's been treated like dirt. A piece of crap. He can never be free of what his father did to him. Something like that can do terrible things to a person." As Patterson said this, Gwen nodded thoughtful agreement.

"He could decide to revenge himself on the world," she said. "A world that he thinks despises him. As he despises himself."

"What about this?" Patterson's fingers drummed on the table. "He turns himself into a serial killer so he can become famous writing about it. That's already beginning to happen."

"And helps the police investigate his own crimes!" An equally excited Gwen chimed in. "Talk about a story!"

"Talk about *chutzpah*!" He looked at Chris. "Okay, you're the boss. What's our next step?"

"Chris will tell us it's all circumstantial," said Gwen with a knowing smile.

"That's what we have. Unfortunately. No hard evidence to connect our suspect to the crimes. We know his mother drives a Toyota with a missing tail light. We *don't* know how long it's been that way and whether our guy ever drove it. We suspect, but don't know, that he may have set the house fire that killed his father ... What is it, Gwen?"

"I was about to say that nine was awfully young to be committing arson, but on second thought, it really isn't."

"And there's his stepfather falling down the basement stairs just before he was going to move to Vancouver Island and take Dummett's mother with him. We think, but can't be sure, that he wiped the pay phone clean of fingerprints. All of which is enough to give us grounds for suspicion but not enough to justify an arrest."

"What about setting a trap for him? With a female undercover cop," suggested Patterson.

Chris shook his head. "Won't work. This guy hunts humans. No set pattern. They're victims of convenience. Except ..."

Gwen winced as she saw the pain flicker across Chris's face. He would always blame himself for that poor woman's death.

"This room will be our command post," Chris declared. "We'll run the operation from here. And the first thing we will do," he said, opening his laptop, "is to prepare a covert operations plan for 24/7 surveillance of Dummett."

"Twenty-four-hour surveillance?" Patterson looked skeptical. "SFU is stretched to the limit."

"They always are. But this trumps everything else." Chris began to tap the keys, rapidly sketching in the background.

"Are you going to ask for electronic surveillance?"

"I'll ask for it. But it's going to be difficult to implement without alerting our suspect. We're not going to serve any warrants on him or his mother. But I will ask for air support, if it becomes necessary.

"HAWC? Those helicopters attract a lot of attention."

"Too much, I agree, Ken. We'll use the airplanes if necessary."

The other two detectives exchanged glances. The fact that the police operated two light aircraft was a well-kept secret. They were much less likely to attract attention than a helicopter clattering overhead.

With Gwen and Patterson standing over his shoulders, offering suggestions from time to time, Chris finished typing the plan. "Now to take it up the chain of command. It won't take long."

He proved to be correct. In less than two hours the plan had been approved by the Homicide Staff Sergeant and the Major Crimes Inspector and been given final approval by the Target Selection Committee.

chapter thirty-four

The covert operation began a little before seven-thirty that evening as a Strike Force operative, wearing faded jeans, a short-sleeved shirt, and scuffed boots, strolled past the low-rise building near the Stampede grounds where Dummett rented a one-bedroom apartment.

The next day Dummett went about what Chris liked to call his "lawful occasions," remaining indoors for the most part, lunching by himself at a Wendy's outlet, and shopping for supplies at a Safeway grocery store.

Things picked up on the second day, Thursday, when he drove to his mother's home and stayed for an hour before driving away in her Toyota, leaving his Solstice parked at the curb. He went directly to Bud's Auto Parts, an automobile bone yard at the intersection of Glenmore and Deerfoot. After checking into the office, he was observed walking through rows of compacted and stacked auto bodies, then returning to the office with what the spotter was able to identify with his binoculars as a plastic tail light cover.

"Ron Donlevy from Hit and Run told me how that works," Chris said to the other two members of his team. "If you want a part, say from a Toyota, you check in with the office, then go out into the yard and help yourself. If you find what you want, you take it back to the office and pay for it. He also said that replacing the cover of a tail light is so simple anybody with a screwdriver can do it."

"Here we go again," sighed Gwen. "He replaces the tail light cover so the car can't be traced to the Cunningham murder — that's too civilized a word for what was done to her — *or* he replaced it as a favour to his mother like a dutiful, loving son would."

"Looks like you're going to have company," the tactical commander radioed in to Chris. "The target parked the Solstice in a lot on Fifth and is walking in your direction."

"What's the breaking news, Phil?" asked Chris when they were seated in an interview room down the hall and around a corner from the temporary command post. Once again Dummett had failed to make any mention of the children's toys, but had cast a beseeching look at the door leading into the Homicide section. "Any word from TLC?"

If Dummett had sent himself a message purporting to be from the killer, surveillance should have spotted him doing it. But Dummett was shaking his head. "Zilch. But I'm doing another piece. The news services are lining up for it. I was hoping," he cleared his throat, "to get a quote that I could use."

Stroking his chin, Chris stared at his visitor. Here was the prime suspect sitting across the table from the lead investigator, calmly asking for help in writing about the heinous crimes he himself was suspected of committing. How cool was that? Maybe he and his team were way off base in suspecting the guy. Mavis Ross had agreed that Dummett could be a possibility when he had run it by her. But still. So many police resources were dedicated to tracking his every movement. What if the real TLC were to strike once again while Dummett was under surveillance?

"You know I can't do that," Chris finally replied, while his internal debate continued unchecked. "Dining with tigers." Where had that come from? Oscar Wilde probably. It sounded like something the sardonic Irish playwright would say. That could be what Dummett was up to. Feeding on the danger and excitement of working in close quarters with the enemy.

"What tack are you going to take in the article?" Chris asked after another pause.

"That TLC is old news. That he's run out his string, and there will be no more killings."

"Jesus, Phil. You can't do that!" This was precisely the tactic that Patterson had suggested — goad the killer into action by stating publicly that the killing spree was over and that TLC had retired from the field, fearing that he was about to be arrested. Chris had vetoed the idea immediately, saying, "We can't invite him to kill again and put some innocent woman's life in jeopardy." Now Phil Dummett was proposing to do precisely that, and Chris couldn't stop him.

"Hell, Chris!" Dummett protested when Chris brought up the risk. "He's going to kill again regardless. We both know that. That way we might flush him out. I'll write something that will get him so mad and upset he could make a mistake that will give him away."

"The target is back in Varsity Acres," the tactical commander reported.

"He'll be going to see his mother again. Maybe take her to lunch." The mention of lunch reminded Chris he should do something about his own. It could turn out to be a long day. Maybe Gwen would go out and get some sandwiches.

"He's still in there," the commander reported an hour later.

"Copy that." Finishing his sandwich, Chris squeezed the wrapping into a ball and dropped it in a wastebasket. "His mother must have given him lunch."

"If you say so." The commander's tone was mildly disapproving, as if chastising Chris for tying up the line of communication with irrelevant domestic detail. But it wasn't irrelevant for Chris, still trying to sort out what made the freelancer tick.

"Attention." The commander's voice was brisk as he alerted his team, a grey Chevy Impala sedan slowly cruising the streets of the subdivision and a Honda SUV idling in a Market Mall parking lot. A five-man tactical team was on standby alert at the Police Centre in the northeast sector of the city. He was also in communication with a police Cessna 182, flying patrol over a known grow-op in the southeast sector. It could be diverted to Chris's operation if required.

"Target has opened the garage door and is backing out a black Toyota Corolla sedan, licence number QRS 814. Now he's driving a Pontiac Solstice, licence number MNE 374, into the garage. Target is waving to older, somewhat overweight, female, probably the mother, standing at the front window, and is now driving off. Unit 5 is to pick up the tail, staying well behind target. Unit 8, take up position and remain one block in front. You are reminded that the safety of the general public has top priority. Repeat. The safety of the general public comes first."

Now the commander's voice came on tight with urgency. "Attention, all units! Target has pulled into the curb and is talking to a young female. Unit 5 reports that they appear to know each other. She is smiling. Female is of ethnic origin. Apparently East Indian. Attractive. Wearing an ankle-length skirt and blouse. Target is out of car and escorting her to passenger side. She appears to be going willingly. Smiling up at target. They have driven off. Do we intercept?"

"Negative intercept. Not at this stage." Grey eyes darkened with apprehension, Chris stared at Gwen, sitting across the table from him. "Activate tactical squad."

"It's the right call, Chris. We don't know anything for sure. It's logical they would know each other. She probably lives in Varsity Acres, and he's around there all the time visiting his mother. He could be just giving a friend a lift, or they could be going for a harmless drive."

"Your journalist friend would love it if we did an intercept and it turned out to be a false alarm. What a story! He would crucify us in print. It would be a lifetime career ticket for him."

"You're right about the crucifixion part, Ken. I can see it now. Jesus."

While Chris and his two partners were having this anxious debate, the tactical squad, clad in camouflage battledress uniforms, climbed into an ordinary-looking Ford Explorer painted a neutral brown colour. The vehicle had been fitted with an extra bench seat, facing backwards. The rear door would spring open at the touch of a button, allowing two of the squad to leap out and confront the target. Bulletproof vests and helmets, and the weapons — Remington 700 rifles for long-range sniping, C-8 CQB assault rifles for short-range, and Glock handguns — were already stowed on board. The overhead door of the police garage opened, and the Explorer drove out.

Back at the downtown headquarters, Chris was trying to reassure himself and the others, mostly himself. "We can always move in at the first sign of trouble."

He had barely finished saying this when the mobile crackled with the terse message: "Contact lost. Repeat. Contact with target lost. Unit 8, circle back to resume contact."

Chris pressed the talk button. "Call in the air unit. Target could have turned off onto a side street."

"Air unit is joining search."

"What happened?" Chris asked when he was sure the commander had finished giving his instructions.

"What else?" the frustrated officer replied. "Construction. A backhoe reversed onto the street right after the flagman stopped traffic. The target was the last car that got through. Our unit was three cars back."

The commander's frustration was easy to understand. Road repairs and construction were the daily norm in the exponentially expanding city.

"I guess Unit 5 couldn't drive around the backhoe?" Chris inquired, already knowing the answer. If it had been possible they would have done it.

"That's right. There's a telephone pole on the sidewalk and the bank drops right off. Unit 8, where are you? Report."

"We're back at the site of the road construction. The backhoe is being loaded onto a flatbed."

"Has contact been established with the target?"

"Negative that."

"The bastard's given them the slip!" Patterson cursed.

"We don't know that. There's nothing to indicate

Dummett knows he's being followed." Chris sounded considerably more confident than he felt.

"They could be heading downtown. Units 5 and 8, turn east on Bowness Road and try to overtake them. Take no further action, just keep them in sight." The commander was once more cool and in control. "Air Unit 2, report your location."

"Passing over Canyon Meadows on a northwest course. Will be on the lookout for a black Toyota sedan on Bowness."

A few tense minutes later the observer in the Cessna reported that they had identified both police vehicles but there was no sign of the target.

"He's on the loose. And he's got that girl! Let's move!" Grabbing the radio, Chris led the way to the elevator and ran out the rear of the building to where a cruiser and uniformed driver waited for them.

The tactical squad reported they were heading west on John Laurie Boulevard. They were not using the siren or lights, so as not to attract attention.

"The air unit should be able to spot them." Chris, sitting in the passenger seat, kept on staring through the windshield as he spoke. "The Cessna is a high-wing monoplane, ideal for this kind of work." Why was he blathering like this? Tension. That's why.

"We may have the target in sight. A black sedan of what appears to be Japanese manufacture is proceeding west on the Old Banff Coach road."

"Ask them to try and make a positive ID," said Chris into the headset mike. "They can fly lower without attracting suspicion. They're getting close to the Springbank Airport, where light aircraft are always taking off and landing." The Cessna's radio was on the same frequency and the crew could hear what he was saying, but protocol demanded that the order come from the commander.

"Subject vehicle has continued on to Springbank Road," the air unit reported. "We are circling north and will fly past the rear of the vehicle in a climbing mode as if we had just taken off. We might be able to make out the plate with the scope."

Minutes later the observer, the engine noise of the climbing airplane loud in the background, said they had a positive ID. The spotter had been able to make out the letters QRS.

"It's a nice day for a drive in the country," Patterson murmured as Chris told the driver to increase speed and they began the awkward process of struggling into bulletproof vests.

"I'll try his cellphone." Chris punched in the number. "Maybe that's all it is. An innocent outing with a pretty girl." A pause. "No answer. He's turned it off. Not good."

"Subject vehicle has passed through the Springbank intersection and is proceeding west toward Highway 22."

"Maybe they're going to Banff," Patterson said, then fell silent as the driver flipped the siren on and off to run the traffic lights at the intersection of Bow and Sarcee trails. The south boundary of Edworthy Park paralleled Bow Trail, stirring a fleeting memory in Chris of the morning when Adrienne Vinney's body had been discovered.

"We're gaining on them," he said, shaking off the too vivid image as they raced along the Old Banff Coach Road and tore past 101st Street.

Patterson leaned forward over the back of the front seat. "FYI, we have just passed the city limits and are now in Rockyview where we have no jurisdiction."

"Hot pursuit," Chris replied cheerfully, buckling a strap of his vest. "A well-known doctrine of international law from rum-running days. You're allowed to follow a suspect into foreign waters if you're in hot pursuit. As we are."

Gwen's only response as Patterson sat back and rolled his eyes was an amused little smile.

"Subject vehicle has crossed Highway 22 and is proceeding west on an unpaved township road."

"Well, they're sure as hell not going to Banff." Chris instructed the constable driver to use both the siren and the flashing lights.

As matters entered what could be the final stage, the commander handed off to Chris. "Copy that," Chris confirmed, then asked the tactical unit to report their position.

"Heading south on Sarcee. Will turn west on Bow."

"Maintain speed," Chris instructed his driver. "We can't wait for them."

The landscape they were racing through consisted mainly of open fields where cattle grazed, dotted here and there with small enclaves of two or three newly constructed houses. A huge transport rig, its cargo destined for Vancouver, ground to a halt to let them cross Highway 22. A cock pheasant stood transfixed on the edge of the ditch as they tore past on the narrow, hard-packed road, its washboard surface devoid of gravel.

"Target is slowing down," the spotter on the Cessna reported. At a gesture from Chris, the driver turned off the siren and flashing lights.

"He's turning off into what looks like an abandoned farm. He's getting out to open the barbed wire gate. He has a handgun. He's pointing it at the passenger. Now he's driving through and hooking the gate back on the post. There's an overgrown track leading to an old barn that looks ready to fall down."

"Can you land on the property?"

"Negative that. It's overgrown with bushes and groves of poplars. What is your location?"

"One and a half kilometres west of 22. You say it's an abandoned farm?"

"Affirmative. The old barn is the only building still standing."

Undoubtedly the farm would be part of a developer's land bank, neglected and in limbo until the time came to turn it into a residential subdivision. Perfect for the evil purposes of a serial killer.

"Now he's making the passenger — a young woman — pull the door open. It's stiff, and she's really tugging at it. Now he's driving in."

"You haven't been made?"

"Negative. To him we are just another airplane. Likely on a training flight. They're both inside now. Do you want us to make a low pass over the barn to let the target know he's got company?"

"Negative. We can't take a chance on what he might do. We must be almost there. Report our location."

"You are approximately one kilometre east of the farm. It's on your left. You can see the barn through the trees. The tactical squad is not far behind and closing fast."

"Roger. We have the barn in sight."

"Give him a blip of the siren," Chris told the driver as they bounced over the track and pulled up some distance from the barn. Weathered and sway-backed, its planks silvered with age, it looked as if the next Chinook would send its timbers tumbling to the ground.

Taking the bullhorn the driver handed him, Chris climbed out and walked closer to the barn. "Phillip Dummett, this is Detective Crane. You are surrounded. Come out peacefully. It's all over."

He could hear something like a shout coming from inside the barn, but there was no way of making out the words. If they were to initiate a two-way conversation with Dummett, they would have to provide him with a bullhorn. The tac team could handle that. Once again, Chris raised the loud-hailer to his mouth. "Everything is cool, Phil. We can resolve this. Nobody needs to get hurt."

Lowering the bullhorn, he saw Gwen pointing back at the Ford Explorer bumping its way along the overgrown track. Guns at the ready, the team jumped out. Chris was pleased to recognize the leader, a tall, fit-looking man with sergeant's stripes on the sleeves of his battle dress. From past experience, Chris knew how Sergeant Floyd would deploy his men. Faced with a stand-alone building, whether a dwelling or a barn, he would station a sniper — they were known as Sierras, for some reason, presumably because of the initial "S" — at each of the four sides of the building. Sierra 1 would be at the front of the building, with the others numbered like a clock, so that Sierra 4 would be on the far side of the barn. They would have to work in close, so each man was armed with a C-8 assault rifle and Glock.

As the snipers reported their positions, an ambulance drew up beside the other vehicles and two paramedics joined the group.

"Sierra 4 says he has some loose boards on his side of the barn," the sergeant told Chris. "He thinks he can pry one of them free, but he needs us to distract the hostage taker while he works on it. Talk to him, Chris."

"You have a lot to live for, Phil." Chris turned up the volume. "You can write a book. Publishers will be clamouring for it. You'll be famous. World famous. Sought after. Biographers and reporters will fight to interview you." Still talking, he glanced at the clip of paper Gwen was holding out with the name of Dummett's captive. "Do not harm Veena, Phil. If you do, all bets are off. Repeat, do not harm Veena."

"He's saying something, but we can't hear it." said Gwen.

"Sierra 4 got the board off," the team leader said. "He's got a clear view of the inside of the barn. The target's holding a gun to the girl's head. The bastard knows what he's doing. He's got his head pressed up against hers. There's no way the sniper can shoot him without hitting her."

"We can't hear you, Phil. What are you saying?" Chris lowered the loud-hailer. Turning to Sergeant Floyd, he said, "The guy is a communicator. That's what he does. He'll be frustrated as hell not being able to make himself heard. I'll tell him we're going to throw in a bullhorn so he can talk to us. If he reaches down for it, it could give the sniper a chance to get off a shot."

The sergeant sent off one of his team with a bullhorn to roll in at Dummett's feet.

"Target appears more and more agitated," reported Sierra 4. "He's jamming the gun hard against the girl's head. He's looking kinda wild. He just hit her! On the side of her head with the butt of his gun."

"Condition Green," the team leader said into his helmet mike in a voice of steel.

Chris could almost feel the sideways look Gwen gave him, but he stared straight ahead. Condition Green meant the sniper was to shoot to kill if he got a clear shot.

"Roger," Sierra 4 acknowledged. "The bullhorn is going in now. Tell him to pick it up."

Chris shook his head. "No. That will only make him suspicious. If I'm right, he won't be able—" He broke off at the sharp crack of a rifle.

"Target down. Hostage standing." The sniper's voice was professionally dispassionate.

The procedure in hostage-taking situations required the tactical team to secure the scene before any further action could be taken. Chris watched the leader and another member of his unit, assault rifles cocked and ready, open the barn door and burst in. A few tense moments later, Sergeant Floyd came out and beckoned the others to join them.

As he entered, and as he had been trained to do, Chris automatically checked to see that the premises were secure. All five members of the squad were now inside the barn, guarding the perimeter. Carrying a stretcher, the two paramedics rushed past him. One knelt beside Dummett's body lying motionless on the dirt floor, while the second tended to the young woman, dazed, holding a hand to her head, silk skirt drenched with blood, but still on her feet.

"No vital signs," the kneeling paramedic pronounced. Indeed, there was no need for him to look for them. An unholy halo of bright red blood, flecked with grey bits of brain matter, fanned out from Dummett's shattered skull. Sierra 4 had executed his assignment perfectly. A single bullet to the non-reactive zone — the area between the upper lip and the eyebrows. A shot in this zone dropped the target instantly, with no chance to pull the trigger or do anything else.

"Veena." The young girl blinked and focused on Chris as he spoke her name. "Are you all right?"

"She'll be okay," the paramedic told him. "She's had a knock on the head, and she's in shock, but she's not hurt bad."

"Thank God. But the blood? She's covered with it."

"That's his. Lie down on the stretcher, dear, and we'll take you out of this awful place."

The Strike Force operative who had said she was attractive had understated the case. Pale and traumatized as she was, she was nonetheless stunning, with the aristocratic features of a young maharani.

"I liked him," she murmured faintly, dark eyes fixed on Chris as she was gently lowered onto the stretcher. "I even had sort of a crush on him." A shudder ran through her slender frame. "He told me all the terrible things he was going to do to me."

"He can't hurt you now, Veena." Chris held the hand she reached up to him. He watched as she was carried out to the ambulance, then rejoined the other detectives gazing down at Dummett's lifeless body.

"Well," he muttered finally, "he always *did* want to be in on the takedown."

Acknowledgments

I am indebted to a number of individuals who have provided information essential to the telling of this story. In alphabetical order, they are:

Dr. Jan Davies, Faculty of Medicine, University of Calgary.

Sergeant Rick Demchuk, Tactical Unit, Calgary Police Services

Detective Paul Malchow, Homicide Unit, Calgary Police Services

Curtis Mayert, stockbroker

Christine Silverberg, former Chief, Calgary Police Service, now a lawyer in private practice

Robin Stoney, Calgary Police Service (Ret'd)

I am also grateful to Mercedes Ballem, daughter and "first cut" editor, Barry Jowett, editor with the "director's cut," and Beverly Slopen, my agent. Special thanks to Erin Dykstra, legal assistant, for coping so well with a succession of drafts.